THE WEDDING GIFT

Also by Alexandra Raife

Drumveyn
The Larach
Grianan
Belonging
Sun on Snow

The Wedding Gift

Alexandra Raife

CORONET BOOKS
Hodder & Stoughton

First published in 2000 by Hodder and Stoughton
A division of Hodder Headline
First published in paperback in 2000 by Hodder and Stoughton
A Coronet Paperback

10 9 8 7 6 5 4 3 2 1

ISBN 0 340 76689 1

Printed and bound in France by
Brodard & Taupin

Hodder and Stoughton
A division of Hodder Headline
338 Euston Road
London NW1 3BH

Part One

Chapter One

The honeymoon was over. Cass, her eyes still seeing the uncompromising mountain shapes and the dazzle of light on the sea-lochs of the west, still exhilarated by the scale and starkness of that exciting landscape, knew as they headed south again that it had been too short, too crammed and racing. Guy's commitments had curtailed it, as they always limited time together, and always would. But it was good that they had managed to get away, even for so short a time – or, she amended with lazy humour, that in view of their prosaic reasons for marrying Guy had agreed to a honeymoon at all.

It was a timely reminder, making her realise that, in spite of herself, she had fallen into the trap of wanting it to be something special. Was she feeling about these whirling three days as she had felt in the end about the wedding, that it should have been more of an occasion, something to stand out warm and glowing in the memory? They had been fun, of course; Guy's crackling energy and capacity to fill every moment had seen to that. Perhaps after the long drive up from London Cass could have done with a little less hurtling round the empty pre-Easter roads of Wester Ross, but the stunning grandeur of the scenery had more than compensated.

You're just tired, she told herself, deliberately relaxing her long limbs in the seat of the Aston Martin as it shook clear of

Inverness and began to eat up the miles of the Drummossie Muir. She would have chosen a more leisurely route, perhaps a loop round Strathglass, coming down the Great Glen to approach Glen Maraich from the west, but Guy had taken one look at the map and tossed it back with a decisive, 'A9.' They were on a section now which cut arbitrarily across the conformation of river, rock and gorge. Like Guy himself. The thought came involuntarily, and Cass caught herself up, once more recognising her tiredness.

She seemed to have been rushing madly for weeks, and occasionally had paused to wonder if there wasn't a message there somewhere – that there simply wasn't room in the close-knit pattern of their lifestyle for extras like weddings.

Carra Castle had been an excellent hotel, in a position on Loch Kishorn sufficiently dramatic to impress even those spoiled souls affluent enough to enjoy its luxurious rooms, its surprisingly sophisticated menu, and the jacuzzi, sauna, pool and fitness centre discreetly tucked away in its 'dungeons'. Cass thought they had more probably been the kitchens. She had wished they could abandon for once the squash and workouts with which Guy liked to burn off surplus energy, and instead walk along the rocky headland from which the castle stared so arrogantly westward, or explore the pale empty beaches with the clean cool wind in her face, watching the clean green waves come curling in.

She had wanted to slow down, put the car away. She had wanted, she supposed, to enjoy the privacy accorded a honeymoon couple, but even on the remote West Coast, even at this stage of the season, Guy had found the colleague of an acquaintance, and they had been drawn inevitably into joining his party for drinks, making up a table for dinner. They were interesting, informed and agreeable people, and Guy was at his best in such a group, but there had never been the time Cass had needed to be alone together, to adjust to the step they had taken.

Getting married had been a practical decision. They had been living together for five years, successfully and satisfyingly but, with the move to the flat in Denham Court, Guy had begun to make noises about the financial sense of pooling their resources. As ever, he had gone into the benefits in exhaustive detail, and as ever in this area Cass, though a business woman in her own right, had trusted to his astuteness and farsightedness. Following his advice on investments had done astonishing things to her own capital in the last few years and she knew he would have sound reasons for the decision.

At least they didn't have to face the whole drive tonight, she thought with relief as they began the sweep over bleak Drumochter. There was one treat still in store, a prospect to which her mind had turned with increasing anticipation during these three days, when something she couldn't quite define had seemed forever tantalisingly out of reach.

What on earth did you expect? she asked herself, with an involuntary movement of impatience. She glanced at Guy to see if he had registered it, then smiled. When Guy was driving he was driving. He loved his car, each car in turn, with an unmatched passion, and the moment he was settled in his seat the road and every other vehicle on it became an absorbing challenge. How attractive he is, she thought, her eye caught by his good looks as it still could most disturbingly be. Clean-cut was the word that always presented itself. Narrow head with smooth dark hair, straight line of nose and brow, square shoulders, all were well-defined, incapable of untidiness. She studied the hollow under the high cheekbone, the set of his mouth as the Aston Martin came up like a wraith behind a muddy, laden estate car and left it contemptuously behind.

There were children behind that dog-guard, Cass noted with a passing amusement she didn't attempt to share with Guy, and was disconcerted by a sudden absurd wish to have smiled at them, to have made contact with that unknown family, not to be hurtled endlessly past things.

'We take a right not too far ahead,' Guy said, as they ran down Glen Garry. 'Can you have a look?'

'Another five miles or so, I should think.' There was little to tell them exactly where they were. With the road atlas open on her lap, Cass looked past Guy to the hills to the south. Somewhere in that tumbled mass, where the peaks and ridges were still crowned with snow, lay waiting – if they liked it, if they agreed – their wedding present to each other. The highlight of their trip. Of their honeymoon, Cass corrected herself hastily, then her choice of the word 'highlight' struck her. Well, be reasonable. After five years together how could a mature couple, she now in her thirties, Guy forty next birthday, expect much in the way of thrills or surprises? It was the honeymoon label itself that was the trouble, indivisible from images and expectations. They should have called it a spring break like the brochures. A less exigent label. Just as they had insisted that the wedding was a party and nothing more.

Had that quite worked, though, her thoughts came round once more. No one at the register office except her sister, plus a boyfriend who to judge from Roey's detached attitude had looked as if he'd be lucky to last the ceremony. Then the gathering at the flat, which she had thought would be the most relaxed form of celebration they could achieve, not allowing for the fact that with such disparate elements introduced as her divorced parents, her much older brother and his wife, Guy's stepmother and one or two friends from the past on each side, it couldn't ever have been a normal, gossipy, roaring party for the group which peopled their everyday lives. Everyone had done their best to make it as low-key as possible, believing that was what she wanted, and inevitably it had ended up as an uneasy hybrid.

With the dual carriageway left behind them, with speed, eye and mind accommodated to the narrowness of the road which led them away into the hills, her spirits rose again at the prospect before them. Though as they climbed out of the wooded river valley above Muirend Guy muttered at the light full in his eyes, she loved the evening brilliance striking crimson from the delicate lacework of birches just coming into bud, and washing steep stone-walled fields above neat patches of spring ploughing. Though the lower reaches of Glen Maraich seemed enclosed and narrow after the bright expanses of the west, once they had passed through the small village of Kirkton she delighted at the larger scale, with the strip of glaciated ground in the gut of the glen dominated by rock-strewn slopes, sparsely clad with last year's faded bracken and heather, climbing into great bare shoulders and soaring ridges. Bridge of Riach, where the road climbed away to the pass by which she had wanted to come, was less than three miles away now, backed spectacularly by a crowding rampart of snow-covered hills.

'Oh, Guy, look! Up there! Could it be, do you think?'

On the hillside to their right a white dot of a cottage, still in sunshine, faced down the glen.

'Christ, I hope not. There's no way in to it, as far as I can see.'

'There must be. Anyway I can see a bigger house above it, with farm buildings, below that plantation.'

'Where are the house particulars? Have a look at the directions again.'

'Do you know, I think it really is the one,' Cass said, after a hasty consultation of the details, finding herself suddenly, ridiculously, breathless with excitement.

'There are a couple more to look at tomorrow, don't forget,' Guy reminded her, scanning the steeply rearing landscape without favour.

Glancing from the folder in her hand to the reality above them, Cass could hardly believe the unimaginativeness of the presentation. In this photograph Corrie Cottage could have been been part of a street, could have had a construction site beside it or a motorway at the door, for all the hint it gave of its glorious setting. On its grassy ledge, with a burn coming down a rough gully behind it and vanishing into sheltering trees at its eastern end, the simple, white-washed, two-storied dwelling with its central porch and two dormer windows perched serenely in the evening light, and Cass wanted it, instantly and totally.

She knew better than to say so. Where a stretch of new road crossed the river by a flat wide bridge, they turned into the looping old one to find the track to the cottage. For a moment Cass thought Guy would refuse to take the Aston Martin up it, but he only remarked, 'Can't say this looks too promising,' as he began to negotiate the rough metalling which had been applied to its most serious craters.

'Access from the public road is along a short stretch of private road—' Cass read out.

'*Road*?'

'—used by Riach estate and adjacent dwelling-house. There is a liability for a share of maintenance according to use.'

'Wonder how they work it out.'

Cass caught the relish for a fight over it already audible in his voice.

The track twisted away behind a grassy bluff, climbing steeply to level out below a high bank thick with the green spears of daffodils. Guy took one look at the loose stones and gouged channels of the entrance which angled up to one side of it and declined.

As she got out of the car, relishing the touch of air on her cheek appreciably keener than the soft air of the west, Cass began to see why a photograph had been taken at close quarters and face on. The clear high call of a peewit from the hill above was repeated in a sweetness that filled her with an intense nostalgia, and she was seized once more by that breathless excitement which she knew could not be communicated to Guy. This might be a pleasure and indulgence they had wanted to give each other, but for him the actual choosing and buying of a weekend cottage was serious stuff.

They went up the steep incline bordered by dark spiky

hawthorns, and came out onto a square of rough grass commanding a view down the length of the glen. A weathered seat stood in the angle of porch and house wall. To sit there on a sunny morning, Cass thought with instant vivid yearning, to look out over those miles of unspoiled beauty ... She could feel the peace and delight of it. The bare tips of small trees, alder and hazel, perhaps rowan, she thought, crowded at the side of the lawn and standing with eyes closed she listened to the voice of the burn they hid, spilling over rocky falls.

Almost she didn't want to go in. She wanted to soak up this sense of openness and height combined with intimate seclusion, the road cut off behind them, the farmhouse higher up the track invisible. She wanted to buy, sight unseen. She didn't want to have to worry about damp, woodworm, dubious wiring or someone else's improvements. 'Tastefully modernised,' the blurb said. It had almost been enough to make them strike Corrie Cottage off the list, and surprisingly it had been Guy who had insisted they should at least come and look.

Did everyone feel this thrill to turn a key in an unfamiliar lock for the first time? Again Cass didn't risk voicing the thought, wanting nothing to spoil the moment.

The inner door of the porch led into a single wide room, where a clumsy wooden staircase twisted away on the opposite wall. The fireplace to the left had been faced with multi-coloured stone, the one to the right crudely blocked in.

'A victim to some fairly arbitrary knocking-through,' Guy commented, his tone reserving judgement. 'I presume they made sure those weren't supporting walls before they took them away.' His eyes assessed and calculated coolly. 'Might do.'

Do for what, exactly? Cass realised sharply that she wasn't sure, any more than she was sure why he had decided on this particular patch of Scotland. As with the wedding, the honeymoon and so much else, there had been no opportunity to discuss it. From time to time in their years together the idea of buying a weekend cottage had cropped up, but Guy had always been firm that Scotland was out of the question. Cass had obediently thought her way round more feasible locations but had always come back to admitting that for her it could be nowhere else. Scotland was where she felt her roots to be; nothing could change that. Not surprisingly, the topic had been shelved.

Now here they were, on this early spring evening with the warmth fading swiftly out of the day, away at the head of Glen Maraich. Because they were married? Because they had a new commitment to each other? Cass put the questions aside. It was happening; they were here; surely that was enough for now.

A door at the back of the long room led to an extension where a sizable kitchen had been added. Its outer door opened onto a concrete 'patio', the nastiness of whose mock crazy-paving, drawn in by a methodical hand, could be forgiven as the last fingers of sunset caught it fair and square. Drinks out here, leisurely suppers, lazy talk . . .

'Did you ever see such a hideous job?' Guy demanded. 'With natural stone on every side.'

'Beautifully sheltered at this time of day though.' With sensuous satisfaction Cass let her eyes travel the dramatic skyline.

'It certainly has possibilities. Let's have a look upstairs.'

Here little had been altered, Cass saw, except that over the kitchen an extra bedroom had been squeezed in beside a minimal bathroom. The two main rooms with their sloping ceilings and deep-silled windows retained their original character.

'We'd need to put in a shower,' Guy said. 'And get rid of these night storage heaters. They must be the first ever made.'

'So you think it's possible?' Cass asked carefully as they clumped down the bare staircase, each in turn lowering their tall heads. Nothing had marred for her the immediate attraction the house had aroused, and its magical setting filled her with such elation that she could hardly manage a casual tone. But Guy was not a man to make a decision of this sort on mere frivolous appeal. Everything had to produce a return. Once more Cass found herself baffled by his sudden decision to buy up here.

'What made you go for this glen in particular?' she asked, swinging round to face him at the foot of the stairs. 'You've never said.'

Guy didn't answer, moving past her to examine a gap below the skirting board where the floor ran ominously away in one corner. 'Hellish road up. No garage. That third bedroom's scarcely more than a box-room. Still, this room's a good size, the kitchen's better than I expected, and even though it's the end of winter there doesn't seem to be any serious damp problem. Worth getting someone to check it out, I'd say. What do you think?'

Cass waited for a second to see if he would turn, come over to her, look into her face to see how she felt. He was investigating the rough-and-ready job that had been made of covering the second fireplace. 'Wonder if the chimney has been closed off too.'

Cass waited for one more moment then went to the porch door which they had left open. Below the ragged lip of the lawn cows grazed a sloping pasture in the chilly dusk, and the gleam of the river threaded the shadowy distances of the the glen.

I want it, she said silently. My present to you; your present to me. To set the seal on our marriage, as wedding and honeymoon have failed to do.

She turned back into the room which now seemed dark after the light outside. 'Oh, I'd certainly think it would be worth having a valuation done,' she agreed in a business-like tone.

Chapter Two

The rain teemed down, fierce gusts of wind driving it every now and then in sluicing sheets down the window where Cass stood, increasingly restless and frustrated. The van bringing the furniture was four hours late and for all that time she had been hanging about in the cleaned, bare cottage, with a most unfamiliar sense of helplessness created by discovering that her mobile phone didn't work here because of the hills.

The telephone in the house wasn't connected yet, though earlier this morning a plumber she'd found in *Yellow Pages* had appeared as arranged to turn on the water. He had flushed the loo, remarked ominously, 'That's no' too clever,' and removed some dirt from a valve. He had checked the taps and, dissatisfied with the mixer in the kitchen, had replaced a washer.

'Does the water always run that slowly?' Cass had asked.

He had given her a little sideways look. 'You'll not expect much better than that,' he had said, adding cryptically, 'There's not many folk up here have a bathroom up the stair.'

He had asked only one question. 'You'll just be up at weekends, likely?'

When Cass had agreed this was all they would manage he had given one damning nod and said no more, gathering up his tools and rattling down the track in his sagging, back-firing, dirty little van.

'Hum,' said Cass aloud, as she turned back into the house. As a first encounter with a local it had not been exactly promising. Still, she now had water, the power was on and the meter read, and she had brought a kettle with her. Work could begin; more importantly she could go to the loo; more importantly still, she could make coffee.

The rain had begun as she took her first sip, building swiftly to this battering downpour. She had had one despairing thought for the furniture, then her usual calm good sense had taken over. It would have to take its chance – if it ever arrived. Most of it would come plastic-wrapped anyway. As was standard form at present, in these hectic days of getting the new offshoot of the agency up and running, she had had to buy everything needed for Corrie Cottage more or less on the wing. Nothing could be spared from the flat, so much bigger than their previous one off the lower end of the Portobello Road. (The thought could still bring a passing pang of nostalgia for that lively place which she had so much enjoyed and Guy so definitely had not.) She would have liked to have had time to hunt down suitable items for the cottage one by one, each appropriate, mellowed by use, lovingly chosen. Instead, seeing that if they were to enjoy their new purchase at all this summer she would have to forget about waiting for Guy to share the choosing and buying, she had dived into John Lewis one hurried lunchtime and ordered the lot, going for the easy, if dull, options of pine, ready-made curtains and rugs that could go straight down without fitting.

And now Guy was absent again, and with this lashing rain, June though it was, moving in promised to be something of a hassle. Aware of rare exasperation, Cass checked. Did this new feeling of resentment that Guy wasn't there to help have anything to do with the word husband? Was he now, automatically and conventionally, in the firing line because he had assumed this role? Because she could legitimately expect him to be here?

She didn't like that much. She had always accepted that the demands of Guy's job were paramount and could take him

away at short notice at any time. As a political risk consultant, advising companies planning to invest abroad, he covered a good deal of the globe from year to year – though Cass had observed that others involved in the same heady game travelled less. He also earned huge amounts of money, his fees supplemented by several other interests. He could never resist the twin drugs of dealing and speculation, was a powerhouse of energy and an unstoppable worker. He was also incapable of discussing these enterprises, partly from a highly developed discretion essential to his primary role, but equally from an inherent instinct to keep things important to him close to his chest. Cass respected all this in him, just as he had respected her need to break away from being employed, however lucratively, and create and build her own business enterprise.

She placed au pairs at the top end of the market, slicing in below those grand establishments which still preferred professionally trained staff, to target the surprisingly large number of well-placed families where being able to saddle the pony was just as important as not drowning the baby in the bath, if not more so. Recently, learning from costly experience that interviews frequently served little purpose, she had launched a new enterprise, directed principally towards country hotels, making staff available at short notice, unseen. Her source of supply was chiefly Australians and New Zealanders, whose travelling style suited instant short-term engagements. She had called it 'Quickwork'. Her staff, led by Diane, her second-in-command, referred to it sardonically as 'Quickfire' or even 'Surefire', but in a surprisingly short time it had proved more successful than Cass had dared to hope.

It had stepped up the tempo to an alarming degree, however. She could really have done without acquiring the cottage in the same year, she thought, glancing at her watch again, starting to turn from the window but at once drawn back because she had nowhere else to go and nothing else she could do.

And could have done without getting married this year? Her

mind snagged on the unwelcome question and she frowned. Why should it surface here? She supposed because in London, locked in the familiar pattern of satisfying work and even more satisfying interludes when she and Guy were able to snatch time together, with a lively circle of friends, domestic demands refined to smooth simplicity, everything necessary for a comfortable and agreeable lifestyle to hand, nothing had changed.

Here other questions presented themselves. Why had Guy suddenly decided to buy something so far from London, in Scotland which he had never much liked, and out of all Scotland in this bare and meagrely populated glen?

'I knew you had this absurd hankering for the land of your fathers,' he had said lightly when she had tried to pin him down on the subject.

'Then we should be up in the Pentland Firth, reclaiming a croft on Stroma, or alternatively somewhere in the Rhinns of Kells,' she had mocked him. Her grandfather had been one of the last men to work on Stroma, one of the hundred or so of its last inhabitants who abandoned it in the thirties, the year before her father was born. She herself had been born in quite a different part of Scotland, in the neat town of Dalry, looking out to the Galloway hills. St John's Town of Dalry. Long after the tear-drenched, despairing departure when she was eight she would roll the name lovingly on her tongue, along with Clatteringshaws Loch, Cairnsmore of Carsphairn, High Moor of Killiemore, the Stewartry ... But not all her incantations had taken them back. London it had been, then and ever since.

To her it would have seemed the natural place to look for a cottage now. Easy to slip off the A74 at Gretna, and a good three hours less than the journey up here.

'Never go back,' Guy had admonished her, in that semi-serious tone which he used to deflect questions he hadn't time for or didn't intend to answer. 'If it's going to be Scotland let it be the Highlands. All or nothing.'

'But why suddenly a weekend cottage at all? What made you decide?' And shouldn't that have been 'us'?

'Perhaps the day's come for relaxing a little. We've both let the pressure build up lately and as long as we're here in London it's hard to slow down. A change of pace and a new scene will do us both good. I've been getting pretty tired – and stale – and in the long run that's counter-productive. And you've been considering setting up a Scottish base for some time. Here's your chance.'

At the time she had laughed at how the promising speech had ended, but now, standing in this chilly and not very attractive room, (must find out where to get logs) in an empty cottage perched on a streaming hillside with only a blur of misty glen visible before her, Cass found it hard to imagine what Guy would find to do in such a place. And there had been, as always when he found himself too closely questioned, a wariness almost amounting to shiftiness in his answer. How he hated being asked to express his feelings, in whatever degree. Cass loved Guy, loved the dovetailed ease of their life together, its pace, the fine balance of independence and need which she had never come close to with anyone else, and during their years together she had come to understand this deep reserve of his. But it could leave a breath of cold on the skin, a shiver of loneliness, which she didn't want to think about now.

She couldn't wait any longer; she must find out somehow what had happened to this wretched delivery van. Had the rain slackened? She persuaded herself that it had. Her coat was among the armful of clothes she had planned to leave up here, flung across the bags in the back of the Volvo. There had been no point in bringing them in till she had somewhere to put them. She would go down to Bridge of Riach and see what resources it offered. There was no shop, she knew that. The house blurb had said the nearest one was at Kirkton. But perhaps there would be a call box, and if not someone who might let her use their phone. It felt weird to be cut off without her own, so weird that she tucked it into her bag on the off-chance that she might find a spot where it would work.

The rain hadn't let up at all. Cass darted across the sodden grass to the car and flung herself in. Her hand was out to turn the key when she paused. She had pulled the big Volvo, after two attempts at the sharp turn and steep incline, up beside the house, out of the way of whatever the delivery men would attempt or manage in the way of parking. Belatedly she registered what she had just seen of the state of the drive, so-called. Opening the door a few inches she surveyed the muddy brown water pouring in a dozen busy channels down to the lane, taking with it earth, gravel and sizable stones. If she got down would she ever get back? And if she stuck somewhere would the van be able to get past? It wasn't worth risking.

'Getting tricky,' she commented cheerfully, her usual stoicism rising to meet the problem. 'I'm going to get very, very wet before this day's out.'

She fished for boots and with cursing contortions managed to get into them, then disentangling her big brown drover's coat from the pile behind her she slithered out into the downpour and dragged it on, tugging her wideawake hat from the pocket. After a second's hesitation common sense overcame habit, and extracting only her purse she threw her bag, phone and all, into the car. Picking her long-legged way down the treacherous slope, gathering in the swinging skirts of her coat and doing up buttons as she went, Cass set off to get some action going.

It was easier walking on the bleached turf than on the streaming track itself, though water oozed round her feet at every step, and there were a couple of treacherous places to negotiate where active little streams, previously invisible, had re-invented themselves. She found herself suddenly light-hearted, perhaps because she had abandoned the frustration of waiting, perhaps because this was new and different, yet harked back to something deep in early experience.

'Atavism? Folk memory? Are you serious?' She could hear

Guy's mocking voice. Yes, probably she did want to believe she had some affinity with this landscape. Not much harm in that, she decided. But how would Guy have dealt with today's problem? He would long ago have leapt into the car and either found a place where his mobile would function or driven to Kirkton, Muirend or Perth if need be, to lash the plan back into shape. He loathed delays, hitches, above all non-communication. Once again the niggling thought that he should have been here reared its head and was once again pushed aside.

As she came out of the track a couple of cars swished by on the straight stretch over the new bridge, disappearing into the veils of rain towards the pass with an indifference Cass fully accepted. She turned right on the old road and saw that in the enclave created between the two a modern house had been built, recently to judge by its raw look. On a large flat lawn, enclosed by a rectangle of wire fence lined by mathematically spaced hedging plants, stood an elaborate bungalow with fancy brickwork, double garage, 'Regency' door complete with carriage lamps, and Venetian blinds at every window which lent a very unwelcoming air. In spite of the rain Cass thought she would look a little further.

In the narrower space left by converging road and river a second house on a less opulent scale squatted in the rain, its garden as overgrown as its neighbour's was barren, a lidless dustbin overturned on its weedy gravel giving a decidedly unoccupied air. Beyond it, in the apex of the triangle, overshadowed by the arch of the old bridge, the rain drummed on picnic tables and beat the dismal detritus round an overflowing litter container deeper into the mud. Opposite, a stone gate lodge guarded a drive which Cass knew from the map led to the big house of Riach, owned by the Mackenzie family with whom there had been negotiations about access and water rights. It too was deserted and unresponsive.

Over the bridge, where the wind caught at her coat with a mad hand, huddled a handful of traditional cottages. On the river bank below two more stood forlorn, their roofs off, the beaten down stalks of willowherb and nettles pale round their crumbling walls. The narrow road that ended at the head of the glen climbed away, shrouded by veils of rain.

That was Bridge of Riach. No call box, no pub, garage, shop or focal point of any sort. Well, start on the cottages. Drawn by what even in these conditions was clearly a well-kept garden, Cass climbed a gravel path to a green front door. No answer. The doors of a shed which obviously did duty as a garage stood open.

At the next cottage a woman in what looked like beach clothes with an anorak on top greeted her with suspicion and a thick Birmingham accent. These were holiday houses, she grudgingly explained, though what anyone was supposed to do with kids on holiday in a place like this, with it chucking it down from morning to night, was beyond her. Behind her, over the quacks of a television, children howled and a man's voice rose in anger.

There was only the ghastly bungalow left to try.

The bell generated mellifluous chimes. No surprise. As Cass cocked her head to listen for approaching sounds the water ran off her hat brim to fall in solid lumps onto her shoulder. Silence.

Silence, yet somehow this didn't feel like an empty house. She rang again, letting the syrupy sounds multiply. This was her last recourse short of taking the car down to Kirkton. The door remained shut. Stepping back into deep wet gravel she walked along the front of the house. The blinds were not fully closed and the room clearly reached from front to back. She thought she caught a movement, and was suddenly as certain as she could be that someone was there. She went back to the bell and tried again, but if she was right then whoever lurked behind that closed door didn't intend to open it. She cast the other way, beginning to feel indignant, trying the yellow up-and-over doors of the garages. Locked.

She shook her fist at the unfriendly place and scrunched resignedly away.

Only as she set off up the lane, more than ever like a fully paid-up stream by this time, did she remember the house higher up the hill. The Mains of Riach. Its occupants too had been involved in the agreements about maintaining the track, or what would be left of it after today's deluge. Surely someone would be there. In all the hours of waiting she had heard no vehicle pass below the cottage. Not that that really told her much, but Cass was a natural optimist. And maybe, even, the furniture van might have come while she was banging on the closed doors of her future neighbours.

With fresh determination, she pulled her hat firmly down over her springy hair and applied herself to the slope, swearing mildly as she rounded the corner and the rain drove into her face. No van. Corrie Cottage looked desolate, its whitewash patched a dismal grey on grey. She ploughed on.

After two or three hundred yards the track swung left and levelled, leading her into a wide cobbled space with a neat dyke along the bottom and a sprawling stone farmhouse above, then vanishing past the end of a barn to continue, as she knew, along the hill to Riach House. To her relief she saw a mud-splashed car in one of the open bays of the barn. Someone was in. She headed for a white door with deep scratch marks below its handle. It wasn't shut properly. There was no bell. She knocked, standing close in to avoid the water sluicing off a rudimentary frill of porch and, in spite of the walk uphill, she shivered, feeling her coat cold against her back. It hadn't been the best of days so far.

Chapter Three

'Come in, come in, don't stand outside, you'll get drowned, whoever you—'

The warm, eager voice calling from somewhere inside the house was drowned in great hysterical woofs which Cass considered a trifle belated. Nevertheless, since she was getting wetter under the concentrated downpour of this silly porch than she had in her entire exploration of dour Bridge of Riach, she pushed the door open.

She found herself in a stone-floored lobby of wild untidiness. Some central piece of furniture, table or chest, was buried under a heap of assorted outdoor clothing. Against the back wall under the stairs an exercise bike was draped with jackets. Sports bags were crumpled in corners, boots and shoes littered the floor, noisome trainers predominating. From one of the open doors came bounding a big, whitish, speckled dog with flying plumes and mad blue eyes. He crossed the hall in two athletic bounces, scattering strewn footwear as he came, but there was no doubting his friendly intentions. Even with his feathery paws against her chest Cass couldn't bring herself to spurn his smiling welcome.

'Don't let Tiree jump up. Be there in a tick, I must just get these out of the oven or – oh, my God, I don't believe it!' A wail of despair turned into helpless laughter and in the doorway from which Tiree had erupted there appeared a girl with a tea towel wrapped round her hand carrying a baking tray covered with golden disks of pastry. She was such an unexpectedly exotic apparition on this mist-shrouded and till now unrewarding day that Cass felt her eyebrows climb, and in spite of all the jostling impressions had time for a second's despair about her own appearance, five-foot-ten (the extra half inch she had suppressed since the horror of reaching that freakish height at fourteen), with mousy hair, spindly limbs, and skin that refused to tan beyond a uniform beige. The woman laughing in the doorway was by contrast vividly, gorgeously colourful, with heavy dark-red hair pulled back into a band from which the velvet ruching was straggling free, a pale skin scattered along cheekbones and nose with just-less-pale freckles, and the most extraordinary wide-set yellow eyes. She was wearing a capacious T-shirt in colours blurring between tan and plum (a blurring intended, or a by-product of the washing machine?) draping loosely over big soft breasts, and an Indian cotton skirt in browns, yellows and purples which dipped to her ankles.

'I can't believe I've done this,' she exclaimed, waving the baking tray at a dangerous tilt and apparently not remembering that she had never set eyes on Cass in her life before. 'I forgot to put the jam in! Not that it matters, jam tarts are incredibly boring, I was only using up the pastry. You know how there's always a bit left over and you never know what to do with it and it seems a pity to throw it away, but honestly, how idiotic can you get? Tiree, get *down!*'

Tiree obeyed by pushing off from Cass with both paws and using the impetus to take him in a whirling leap towards the promising smell of the pastry.

'Oh no you don't!' The girl raised the tray sharply, a tart case fell off and the long jaw snapped, to open again in a howl of pain.

'Oh, poor darling, that must have been sore. Though it serves you right, you know.' Whimpering with the pathos of

an artist the big dog buried his face in her skirt, and she pressed his head against her with her free hand and smiled up at Cass. 'I'm sorry, I don't think we've—?'

Cass stepped forward laughing, her spirits soaring. 'Cass Montgomery. We're moving in at Corrie Cottage – or trying to. Sorry, my hand's wet.'

'How lovely of you to call.' A small hand met Cass's in a warm soft clasp. 'We're so glad it's sold at last. It's been on the market for such ages. So expensive, everyone thought, or is that something one shouldn't say to the buyer? Anyway, I'm Gina Fraser—' The movement of shaking hands caused a further slide on the baking tray. Tiree hastily withdrew his head but regarded this second windfall with more caution, face puckered and soft ears lifted. 'Look, I'd better get rid of this lot before I drop any more. Though what exactly one does with them I don't know. Freeze them, maybe. I put them in the oven to bake blind, because half the time my pastry's soggy, though more for quiches and things, and everyone tells me that's what I'm doing wrong, then I felt, good, that's done, and forgot all about adding the jam. Come in and get warm. Isn't it a truly awful day, especially for moving house, poor you, and this is supposed to be summer . . .'

She led the way into a long low-ceilinged kitchen and swept some ironing (mending, washing?) from a chair and put it on the table, already littered with the aftermath of baking, the day's papers and mail, ripped envelopes included, a heaped fruit bowl where grey fur was visible at the lower levels, and a couple of copies of *The Antique Dealer and Collector's Guide.*

'The thing is, moving in hasn't exactly begun,' Cass explained, dropping thankfully into the rush seat of the ladderback chair, her senses absorbing with gratification a rich medley of colour, warmth and baking smells. This wonderful kitchen, which had kept its traditional air in spite of the discreet addition of modern equipment, and was full of beautiful objects she longed to examine, from the row of serving jugs on the mantelpiece above the Aga to the majolica dessert service on the plate-racks of an oak dresser, must be the handiwork of this startling girl. Certainly the mess had to be down to her. Cass had no doubt of that, even at this stage of their acquaintance, as Gina, pushing the kettle onto the Aga hotplate, turned to listen with eager sympathy to the tale of Cass's woes.

Older than she had first thought, early forties perhaps, Cass decided as she wound up her resigned account with, 'If only my wretched mobile—'

'Oh, hopeless up here,' Gina broke in. 'Laurie goes mad about his, though actually if you stand in the middle of the new bridge they seem to work better there, only there's quite a lot more traffic than there used to be so it's not always convenient. The boys discovered that, that they work there, I mean, only the signal, or the reception, or whatever you call it, isn't brilliant even then, but of course you wouldn't need it unless the real phone was off for some reason, and to be fair it almost never is. But please, help yourself, phone whoever you like. Can I get a number for you or help at all? Where is the furniture coming from? Not that that makes any difference, I suppose. And then I'll make tea – or would you prefer coffee? Oh, but you won't have been able to have lunch, you should have come up ages ago, I'll find something while you phone.'

She hurried off to what was evidently a larder, since Tiree, a look of hope in his eye, pressed hard on her heels.

Cass, after one blank moment when she thought she had left the card with the number on it in her bag, remembered it was tucked into her purse. If she'd had to go down that track again . . . As the number rang she studied a stoneware cow milk jug propping up a sheaf of envelopes marked Inland Revenue, aware of feeling warmed, comforted, amused and safe.

The van had broken down on the Stirling bypass, had been repaired and was on its way. 'We have tried to contact you several times.' A reproof there. 'They should be with you sometime during the next half hour.'

'I should go down to be there for them,' Cass said half-heartedly, eying with a longing almost equal to Tiree's a clove-stuck ham on a blue-and-white platter, and trying not to sniff in too greedily the tang of tomatoes fresh from the greenhouse and the good garlic whiff of Boursin.

'Oh, rubbish. If they don't know the glen road they'll take twice as long as they think. Everyone does,' Gina announced sweepingly. 'Everything's ready and anyway I haven't had lunch myself yet. I've no idea where the day goes.'

Cass, glancing round the turbulent room, thought she could guess.

'What we'll do,' Gina went on, taking the breadknife first to a handsome brown loaf and then to the ham, from which she hacked a ragged slice a quarter of an inch thick, in places at any rate (Cass could see a ham knife on the rack behind her), 'what we'll do – oh, there's nice grainy mustard somewhere, hang on, I'll get it – we'll wolf this down quickly and then I'll come and wait with you. Of course I will, you must have had a horrid time hanging about on your own all morning. And it's miserably cold today and empty houses always feel worse, with that sort of *eating* cold. Then if the furniture still doesn't turn up at least I can come back and phone or something, only the one thing I absolutely mustn't forget, you'll have to remind me, is to fetch Nessa from Kirkton at half past four. She gets so cross if I forget, though you can hardly blame her, it is nearly three miles, and—'

'Nessa?'

'My daughter. Janessa really. She's fifteen and at the High School in Muirend, not that it's ideal but you don't have any choice up here. She comes as far as the village on the school bus and I'm supposed to meet her. And on a day like this I really think I'd better be there on time.' She pulled a face, with a guilty laughing look which suggested how frequently she failed to be. 'Though it's not coming down quite so hard now, what do you think?'

And indeed when they set off after a hurried lunch and some

gaspingly strong coffee, from a Mason's ironstone octagonal mug for Cass, and a garage give-away with a spacecraft on it for Gina, the rain had settled to a gentle if penetrating drizzle. With unexpected good sense Gina left Tiree behind and his wails floated after them, oddly appropriate, Cass felt, to the grey water-logged scene where a couple of hundred yards was the limit of their vision.

'He's such a ham,' Gina commented, doing her best to sound offhand but flinching at the desolate sounds. 'He thinks we're going for a walk.'

Cass thought it a fair assumption since they had ignored the car – 'It would only be in the way' – and Gina had led her straight over the shoulder of the hill, dirty wet sheep with rain-laden fleeces and marginally whiter lambs scattering before them. Didn't that matter? But presumably Gina must know. And Cass was aware of a little childish thrill to think she would do this in future, as a familiar customary thing, run down this steep field after calling at the farmhouse. For the immediate ease between them, the laughter of the very first moments, were signals which couldn't be mistaken. Encountered less frequently as one grew older, impossible to define, but infallibly recognisable.

'I trawled round everywhere else,' she told Gina, as they let themselves into Corrie Cottage, 'before coming up to you. I'd almost forgotten the house existed.'

'No one let you phone?' Gina asked incredulously.

'No one was in. They're mostly holiday houses anyway, aren't they?'

'Well, not all. Though – what day's this? – it's probably one of Nancy's days at the Muirend library. She just does part-time. Nancy Clough, the house with the garden. And no one would be in at the gate lodge. That's Ed Cullane, he's the Riach shepherd and he'd be at work. But surely you got an answer at Sycamore Lodge, the new bungalow?'

'No, but I did have a strange feeling that—'

'What?' Gina hadn't bothered to put on a hat and now

slid the band off her hair to shake the silvery moisture from it, and Cass was momentarily distracted by the glorious heavy mass which slithered free to obliterate her face.

'But Sycamore Lodge – is it really called that?' In this environment the name sounded absurd.

'Oh, there are two sycamores. Though can you imagine anyone actually buying and planting them? They seed themselves everywhere, they're an absolute plague. But go on, what happened?'

Gina's face was alive with expectant amusement as one hand held aside the blinding curtain of hair.

'I don't know, I just had the feeling that someone was there, watching me. I rang and rang and crunched about loudly on the gravel and practically peered in at the windows, though those horrible blinds were down everywhere, and got no response at all. But I thought I saw someone move inside. Probably imagined it. Why would anyone refuse to answer? I don't look that much of a threat, do I?'

Not a threat, Gina thought with pleasure, but different, most promisingly different. 'That would be Beverley,' she said positively. 'She'd have been there, all right. Were both the garage doors down? Yes, she was there, defending her privacy, silly idiot.'

'But why? Who is she? What's her problem?'

Gina perched on the stairs, dragging open the poppers of her cracked yellow oilskin. 'Beverley Scott. She and her husband built that monstrosity and moved in just before Easter. She spends her entire time – oops, you're going to be a neighbour.'

Her face was vivid and amused as she scraped the slippery hair from it and grasped it in a rough fistful to put the band back.

'So what have you decided not to say about her?' Cass enquired lazily, perching on the window sill and stretching her endless legs in faded and unhemmed jeans before her. Her feet were cold again already.

'Oh well.' Gina grinned, 'You'll meet her anyway. And she's not that bad. My chief entertainment here, to be truthful, so I cherish her on that account alone. Only she imagined she was buying a slice of Highland peace and quiet, facing onto the old road which almost no one would use, and not minding about the traffic whizzing by at the back. In fact I think she finds it reassuring. Then the Council decided to make the useless bit of ground by the hump-backed bridge into a picnic area. They stuck up tables and things – you probably saw them – and made a turning place for cars, and even *buses,* so lots of people stop off there and throw things into the river and leave litter, but a good many of them brave a little stroll up and down the road as well, not only going past Syc Lo, as the boys call it, but *looking in at the windows!*'

How many boys were there? 'But the bungalow must be fifteen yards back from the road at least.'

'Of course it is, but up went the blinds, in went the fastest growing hedging material available in Britain, and off went the letters to the Council. As for some completely unknown person knocking at the door, well I mean, that has to be outrageous.'

'But it could have been an emergency.' Gina, I cannot believe I have found you. 'An accident, someone hurt or ill.'

'Nothing to do with Beverley.'

'But what about the husband? Where's he? What does he do?'

Just what I've been wondering about your husband, Gina silently rejoined, and why you're struggling with this move alone. 'Ah, now that's all a bit sad.' Her face was serious now. 'He was very ill for months before they came up here, apparently. A victim to the pressures of the modern world, as Beverley puts it. His business went bust, I think, and he couldn't handle it. Had a nervous breakdown or something. Anyway, no one ever sees him and he never leaves the glen. Well, occasionally Beverley takes him down to some counsellor or other. I'm not sure really because, ready as she normally is to sound off about anything and everything, she never has much to say about Richard. I think his illness was the main reason she chose to come here, so that he could have plenty of quiet. It's not Beverley's sort of scene at all I'd have thought, the glen itself I mean, except that she has some odd idea about breaking into what she calls 'glen society', meaning people like the Mackenzies up at Riach and the Munros at Allt Farr. I don't think they've noticed she's here yet.'

'Perhaps it's the ill husband who's neurotic about people looking in at the windows?' Cass hazarded. 'Perhaps Beverley's protecting him?'

'Wait till you meet her,' was all Gina said to this suggestion.

'So who lives in the—?' Cass was beginning when a labouring grinding sound penetrated the closed windows. 'Yes! At last!'

The delivery men started off by being seriously hostile. Not only had they broken down at Stirling but they had, to their enraged disbelief, been stopped on the glen road by a prowling Customs and Excise van checking for the illegal use of farm fuel. Now they found themselves with the nose of the van pointing skywards on a rudimentary track which offered nowhere to turn, and expected to convey a houseful of furniture – in the rain – up a bank like the side of a cliff and into a cottage with narrow doorways and a staircase with a U-bend designed by some DIY piss-artist.

Never would Cass forget the way in which Gina dealt with a situation already fraught and, with surly mutterings about being out of time and coming back tomorrow, verging on the disastrous. Gina simply poured out warmth and helpfulness in soothing waves which Cass thought would have been nauseating from anyone else.

'What an awful time you've had,' Gina cooed, but with visibly genuine sympathy. 'And what appalling luck to be stopped like that, especially after all you'd been through already. Now, what we'll do—' a comforting phrase already familiar to

Cass – 'we'll all go up to my house, just a few yards further on, just round the corner, where you'll have plenty of room to turn, and you can come in and get warm and have something to eat, then we'll all come down here and whisk everything in in no time.'

Was it the comforting tone or the wide concerned eyes or the shapely breasts emerging from the yellow oilskin which did the trick, Cass wondered in admiration, unaware that the younger and less trenchant of the men was deciding her own legs must be the longest he'd ever seen.

Both men were good-natured at heart, even taking Tiree in their stride when he welcomed the whole party with impartial fervour as though he'd been shut up for a week.

'I owe you one,' Cass murmured to Gina, seeing the reckless slugs of whisky that were going into the coffee mugs, 'but remember we need them on their feet not their backs. And don't forget Nessa.'

'God, thank heavens you reminded me! What's the time? Oh, that's all right, I'll be early for once, then we can both come in and help on the way back.'

'No, Gina, thanks, you've been truly marvellous, but you've done more than enough. I'm sure we can manage now.'

'Try and stop me. This pair may get everything into the house for you, chiefly because they won't want to have to come back in the morning, but that's only the beginning.'

But the hospitality of the Mains and the charm of Gina's smiling cosseting did not wear off so soon. Curse as they might as they struggled up and down the muddy slope, the men were not going to leave Cass with problems she couldn't handle. They did ask once, as with a resigned and infinitesimal communication of the eyebrows they tuned in the television, 'Where's your husband then, love?' (and Cass found herself wondering for a moment whether Guy really had had to go to the Seychelles on this precise day) but they did their best for her. They unrolled carpets, set up beds, removed the supporting struts from the washing machine and attached the hoses, plugged in the fridge-freezer and gave it as their opinion that whoever designed the staircase should be shot. The return of Gina with extra help in the shape of a slim nubile schoolgirl with hair as red as her mother's and smouldering dark eyes added new zest at the critical moment.

Nessa was not particularly forthcoming, indeed she ignored her mother with a completeness which looked extremely ominous, but to Cass she was courteous and definite, when Cass assured her discreetly that they could manage without her, that she wanted to help. Certainly her assistance was more methodical than her slapdash mother's who, flustered by her silent presence, became conciliatory and slightly jolly. When the bulk of the work was done and the others gathered at the new pine table for a final round of coffee, Nessa slipped away without a ripple before Cass had a chance to thank her for all she'd done.

By this stage the incident with the Excise van had become an excellent joke. 'Bloody hell, you're safer on the Al.' The men also felt sufficiently at home to ask curiously, 'Why would anyone want to live in a place like this anyhow?'

Though she couldn't have put it into words, or not into any words they would have understood, Cass knew that, in spite of rain, wind, the mud tracked from end to end of the newly scrubbed house, and all the frustrations of a long day, finding this place had been the most perfect piece of luck.

'It's just for weekends,' she explained sadly.

'Oh, that's not so bad then,' said the men.

But Gina said, as the lorry throbbed away with a final friendly blast on the horn, 'I wish it was to be for all the time.'

Chapter Four

Two weeks later Cass lay stretched out on the rough grass in front of Corrie Cottage in June sunshine under a flawless sky, and thought there could not be a more perfect spot on earth, or a more perfect moment. Heat and quietness and the scent of hawthorn and rowan poured into the sheltered corner. Below her the river curved, its banks white with the mounded blossom of bird cherry, while the brilliant yellow of the broom flaunted on the slopes above. Stretches of rhododendrons were still in flower round the big house with the loch down towards Kirkton; wild roses were out along the lane and the glen road, with the purple of vetch and cranesbill and the starry white of ox-eye daisies below.

Hay-making had begun. I shall walk down later, Cass decided sleepily, and push my face against the still-warm bales and be carried back to childhood and the small hills of Dalry. Except that apart from the pure pleasure of nostalgia there is no need to take that journey. I am here, in an even better reality. Around her, in the shaggy, unfenced garden, lupins and poppies had survived, intermixed with foxgloves and cow parsley. An ancient honeysuckle sagging forward from the house wall was covered in slender sprays of buds. The grass was thick with daisies and self-heal, buttercups and bird's foot trefoil. To her left the peaceful splashing of the burn interwove soporifically with the voices of the bees.

How rare it was to be doing absolutely nothing. Cass closed her eyes and at once was aware of the distant sounds of sheep, mingled birdsong and high and thin a mewing call which must be the buzzard she had seen circling that morning.

The simplicity of walking outside when she had woken at six into the perfect freshness and emptiness of this new world, going out of the little gate in the fence above the house and onto the open hill, still thrilled her. She had followed the grassy corrie of the burn on a neat eight-inch path worn by a thousand narrow hoofs, noting the heavy slabs covering what must be the catchment tank for the cottage and deciding to investigate it soon. As the hollow became shallower and she found herself on the open hill, she had exclaimed in delight to have attained such a view with so little effort. The high cirque of hills shutting in the glen to the north, lost in mist on her last visit, framed a ruined castle she knew must be Allt Farr. To the west the pass notched a soaring ridge she longed to explore. Would they have time this weekend? Certainly there had been no time till now, and there were still curtains to go up and boxes to unpack. She wanted to have the cottage ready before Guy arrived.

As she made a loop above Bridge of Riach, she had examined that predominating need, and been forced to admit that she still didn't have much faith in Guy's commitment to this place. Perhaps after all, she thought as she had thought before, it was just as well he hadn't been available on moving day.

Surveying sleeping Bridge of Riach with new interest, knowing now who lived where, she had thought how attractive it must have looked before the new highway slashed across the traditional picture of winding stone-walled road arching over rocky gorge. A movement in the garden of Sycamore Lodge had caught her eye; a large male figure was going along a gravel path towards the road embankment. The ill husband? Did the unhelpful Beverley let him out alone in the early mornings before anyone was about? What did he do all day, cooped up in that characterless box of a house with its lowered blinds? There had been something slightly disturbing about the sight of that lonely vanishing figure and she deliberately turned her mind away from it.

She was meeting Guy off the London flight at Edinburgh this afternoon. She must leave time to shop on the way, so that they wouldn't have to waste any of their precious weekend on going to town again. She had intended to get more done in Perth yesterday, but for the most unexpected of reasons her meeting with Lindsay had gone way over its planned time. Though work seemed a million miles away, lying here suspended between glen and sky, the sun hot on her back, this new development was so exciting that it scarcely felt intrusive at all.

How swiftly buying Corrie Cottage had influenced her thinking. Realising that made her conscious of the tug-back of Guy's resistance, though there had been no opportunity to discuss this new idea with him yet. She was still not used to needing his agreement. Until they had married neither had considered the backing of the other necessary in any matter involving their work. Nice if there was interest and approval, but their business lives had been essentially separate. Now that they had combined their resources they had a new obligation to each other, and Cass still occasionally found herself resisting it. But this possibility was so promising that she longed to share it anyway.

One of the features which had made the agency a success, had perhaps made the vital difference between failure and survival, was the placing in key areas of what were officially known as contacts. They were mostly married with young families of their own, and worked from home on an ad hoc basis, liaising with clients, visiting newly placed au pairs, sorting out immediate problems like lost luggage and homesickness, and passing up the line such larger crises as girls arriving ill, pregnant or demented. Above all, they were on hand to listen, to both sides, for which reason they were known in the office, succinctly and usefully, as 'ears'. Though Cass still did a lot of driving, liking to be in touch with them directly, their presence at such points as Bath, Oxford, York and Norwich spared her the murderous mileage of the early days.

She had come up to Glen Maraich a day ahead of Guy to have lunch with her 'ear' in Perth, till now a part-time post filled by an ex-colleague from Cass's days in marketing. But its scope had been steadily growing, chiefly during the summer months when shooting lodges on remote islands and windswept moors came briefly to life, and big houses tucked away up quiet glens were bulging with family and friends and needed all the help they could get.

Cass knew that in the last two weeks her thinking about the Scottish side of the business had raced forward perhaps absurdly. But the little cottage behind her, its matchless situation, its atmosphere of peace, even the trials of moving in which had been funny in the end, had hooked and beguiled her, and over and over again her mind had returned to the question of how she could spend more time here.

The answer had struck her a couple of days ago, beautiful in its simplicity. Since the start of the summer season the new splinter enterprise of Quickwork had been running in conjunction with the London office. Cass had been monitoring its success with satisfaction and turning over in her mind where to set up its second branch. Oxford, she had thought, would be the best place, a focus for students and travellers, one of the main centres for employers, and within easy reach during the teething stage. Then the obvious had hit her. Why not Scotland? Where better to mine the endless seam of country house hotels thirsty for seasonal workers, their style ideally suited to friendly willing Australians and enterprising young Continentals anxious to improve their English? And why think immediately of Glasgow or Edinburgh? What was wrong with Perth, closer to the Highlands and within easy reach of the cottage? A slow drive down Glen Maraich, perhaps, but after that a quick whip down the A9. She'd time it today. She hadn't been capable of thinking anything so mundane yesterday, dazzled by the proposal Lindsay had made.

After her marriage six years ago, Lindsay Hume had come back to her home town of Perth where her artist husband owned and ran a small gallery in South Street. Recently he had gone into partnership with a cabinet-maker turned wood-carver, and they had rented larger premises off St John's Place.

'We were half thinking of making the gallery into a sitting-room,' Lindsay had said, 'but in fact we're very conveniently organised as we are, and we're a bit put off by the thought of the windows being right on the pavement. We've discussed renting it out but that could be a lot of hassle. It would have to be the right person, and we've never got round to doing anything about it.'

Over their vegetable lasagne Cass had stared at her in tense query.

'Are you saying what I think you're saying?' As so often when she was excited, she had been actually breathless, a characteristic Guy found childish.

Lindsay, altogether more sober and grounded, had said cautiously, 'Could it be an answer? Would you really want to set up Quickwork here? But you'd want to do the research, get out the—'

'No! No, I wouldn't.' Cass had gazed at her, gripped with determination and certainty. 'Not this time. This sort of chance only gets thrown up once in a blue moon. You have to grab it. No point wasting time totting up the pros and cons. We'll make it work. If you really have the extra time available, that is?'

'Of course I have. That's part of it. I had to be on hand to look after the gallery a lot of the time or Phil could never paint. Now he and Douglas work that out between them.'

'You weren't looking forward to having more time to yourself? Doing less for once?'

'Ambling about at home doing the housework? Would that appeal to you? Come off it, Cass, you know neither of us was cut out for that. In fact, it was another thing that was putting me off the idea of adding the gallery to the house. More space, more objects to fill the space, more cleaning. And all still just for two people.'

'I know what you mean,' Cass had agreed. Stream-lined and sophisticated as the Denham Court flat might be, there was a lot more of it than there had been of the cheerful crammed hovel in Chepstow Terrace.

For the first time it occurred to her that she had not seen the cottage as something which would add to her domestic obligations. How selectively the brain worked. She laughed, pushing herself up, aware as she moved of the damp which had come through the rug and not caring, and observing that far below, past the mauve and pink heads of the lupins which had succeeded the daffodils on the bank, the baler had mopped up three quarters of the hayfield. Was she imagining the faint sweet scent on the light wind? Probably. Today every pore was open to enjoyment.

Guy was in tremendous form. Though Cass sighed privately at the sight of briefcase and lap-top she said nothing, fair-minded enough to recognise that he could no more have left them behind than she would have set off to Scotland without her handbag. Better to forget them, and be pleased that he had had time to change, trim in expensive jeans and cashmere sweater. As always, however brief the interval since they had been together, Cass found herself responding with delight to the sight of him, his lean build, his keen-featured face with the straight dark lashes and clean line of the mouth. And how full of vibrant energy he looked as he came with his quick stride towards her, getting them out to the car and heading north without a second wasted, as though this journey was as vital as any trans-global flight weighty with financial and political implications.

'God, this is good, isn't it?' he said, out on the lawn after an approving prowl of the little house. 'I think we made a good decision. Smell that air.'

He put an arm round her shoulders and Cass leaned her head towards his, filled with pleasure at his pleasure and – more tellingly – relief. Had she been afraid he would be bored with the place now that he had acquired it, scornful of the unoriginal style haste had forced on her to furnish it, the pine, the pale rugs, the cottagey curtains in apple green, apple-blossom pink and cream?

But with her ingrained honesty she knew her relief went deeper than that. Ever since their wedding she had been conscious of a nagging emptiness, its source the fact that nothing in their lives had altered. She knew if she attempted to express this to Guy he would be astounded. Nothing had been meant to change, other than a few practical considerations for which having the same surname helped. Yet she could acknowledge by now that she had hoped for, expected even, without any logical justification, some change in their personal relationship. Reaching this point she would become impatient with herself. Did women have to befog every issue with this sort of emotional need? Then she would find herself protesting, why shouldn't they, it was perfectly natural, and she was a woman.

Now, standing close to Guy in the soft light of the long-drawn-out midsummer evening, almost literally feeling him unwind and slow down, she was aware of a fierce surge of hope that this cottage, this wonderful place, would add the missing dimension she so deeply longed for.

It was a relaxed and contented evening. They sat outside in the sheltered angle at the back of the house and watched the sun slip down far to the north of the Bealach Dubh, the high pass to the west, while the light picked out the new growth of conifers like green gauze laid over the plantations across the glen, and lengthened needle-fine shadows from every blade of grass. With the naïve pleasure of casual observers, they even enjoyed watching the rabbits play on the green-gold slopes.

They ate asparagus and smoked salmon and salad off a packing case, with local new potatoes which had not come sprayed and weighed in plastic bags, and which tasted more like potatoes than any either of them had eaten since childhood. They drank the champagne Cass had picked up in Muirend that afternoon and Guy forbore to say in so many words that it wasn't properly chilled. They walked down the lane and turned into the beckoning spaces of the mown hayfield and wandered and looked and breathed. And afterwards, at ease and receptive to each other, they fell into their new bed and with the window open to the cool night made love with an aware tenderness they had not shared for some time.

Chapter Five

The weekend didn't take quite the form Cass had envisaged.

They woke early from habit, and Guy, prompted perhaps to new ways by the new scene, went down and made tea. Then, as they had not done in the morning for a long time, they made leisurely love again, and afterwards he fell asleep, murmuring luxuriously that it was heaven on earth not be rushing anywhere for once. It was another beautiful day and Cass was itching to be up and out, but it seemed unfriendly to slip away, so she stayed close to his relaxed body, his arm slackly across her hips, and – not without amusement to think how little she would have appreciated Guy mulling over work in post-coital satiety – let the enticing prospects of developing the Perth office revolve enjoyably round her brain.

Last night Guy had been whole-heartedly approving, with the merest formal proviso that they must go into the figures properly. 'It all fits in incredibly well,' he had said, then the familiar cagey look had come over his face, and he had stopped as though the sentence had been incomplete.

'What does?' Cass had asked, though knowing with that look in place that the lightest question was a waste of breath.

'The premises, the demand, and Lindsay wanting the extra work, idiot,' he had said, a touch too pat, lifting the champagne out of the saucepan acting as ice bucket and refilling her glass.

Guy's almost paranoid need to keep things close to his chest whether they mattered or not had its roots in his lonely childhood, and Cass knew it was too deeply ingrained ever to leave him. In their early days together she had innocently thought trust and stability might lessen his need for this fierce reticence, but she knew better now. Guy had grown up in a household where music was all, his father a pianist, his mother an opera singer, the house always full of visiting musicians. His elder sister had effortlessly fulfilled their parents' expectations by not only making her own career in music but by marrying a bassoonist from Bremen, and was even shortly to produce, one assumed, a baby bassoonist.

'Serves her right,' Guy would say with irrational nursery malice if the fact was ever mentioned.

He, however, had had not the slightest interest in music in any form, and his indifference had turned to a violent hatred under unrelenting pressure. His startling level of numeracy, evident at an early age, had been brushed aside as unimportant, his bent for driving a bargain actually deplored. He had been a child coerced away from his natural skills, failing dismally to acquire those required of him, and thereafter disregarded. He had never recovered from this comprehensive rejection, and in spite of Cass's hope for some sign of commitment to her more spontaneous than signing a register of marriage, she knew in her heart that he was unlikely ever to risk emotional dependency. From time to time, when she was feeling dissatisfied with her gawky, mousy appearance, knowing that with his looks (and earning power) Guy could have had anybody he chose, she would convince herself that he had only been attracted to her at all because she was tone deaf. But in the end she would always laugh at her own absurdity. They had been together for more than five years. And he had married her.

Lying beside him, doing her best to quell her eagerness to be up and enjoying the day, Cass reminded herself that this was after all what she had hoped for. Time theirs, letting the hours slip by as they came, soaking up the tranquil mood of this new environment.

They breakfasted with the table pulled close to the sitting-room window, the door open to the sunshine.

'Must get a couple of decent garden tables,' Guy said. 'That corner at the back could be made quite attractive for barbecues and supper out of doors. We could have a look today, order something. And perhaps we'd better put our heads in at the solicitors and arrange for a key to be available there so that things can be delivered.'

'Perhaps Gina wouldn't mind keeping a key for us, the girl who lives in the old farmhouse at the top of the lane. She was very—'

'I don't think that's a good idea,' Guy cut in, frowning. 'We don't want to get involved with the neighbours, do we? One link of that sort and you're stuck with them for ever, and the whole object of having a peaceful retreat is destroyed. We'll see what the solicitors say.'

Cass had been looking forward to seeing Gina and introducing Guy to her as much as anything else about this weekend. She should have taken her chance to go up when she was on her own the first evening. But she knew better than to persist with the subject. Perhaps at least she could subvert the plan to go to Muirend.

'We could phone them,' she suggested. 'Post a key to them, or shove it in their letter-box as we go past tomorrow evening.'

'We've got to go down anyway. I need all kinds of kit, boots, jacket, overtrousers. I'm told there's a decent gunsmith's in Muirend, we could try there.'

I'm told? Who could he have been talking to who knew anything about Muirend? Cass didn't ask.

'It seems a pity to have to leave all this to go shopping,' she tried once more, though even as she spoke she saw the sunlit day by the river or on the hill sliding away from her.

'We can have a look at what's on offer, make a round trip and come back via the glen to the east.'

'Glen Ellig.' Was that so different, really, from what she had planned? The same idea only broad brush; to explore, get the feel of the new locality. Her own hankering to get beneath the skin of Bridge of Riach, speak to the people who belonged here, establish some tiny personal toehold, was too nebulous, and probably too unrealistic, to attempt to put into words to someone like Guy. It could wait.

Flashing down the A1, with Guy taking his turn at the wheel of Cass's Volvo (she was a tall woman and liked a big solid car around her), Cass suppressed reproaches. She had a great capacity for not kicking against the inevitable; it gave her an air of being laid-back and easy-going which could be misleading.

The weekend, their first at Corrie Cottage, which had begun so well, had been curtailed in a way for which she had not been prepared. They had originally planned to start on the return journey late on Sunday afternoon, both content to reach home in the small hours and be up for work next morning. Instead they had left immediately after breakfast, Guy saying he had urgent work waiting which must be dealt with tonight.

'This Dar-es-Salaam project is turning into a bare-knuckle fight. I'll have to go back tomorrow and do some pretty fancy footwork. Every last t has to be crossed and i dotted. Anyway, you should be pleased that I resisted getting down to it here.'

Cass had had to concede that. Guy hadn't touched his PC except for an hour while she had been preparing supper the previous evening, a division of labour which was not normal practice between them and which she had not entirely liked. But the day had been pleasant enough. Guy had even agreed to help with the conversion of a flat-pack into a kitchen cupboard, though he hadn't stayed with it when it became clear that the job was going to take a lot longer than the twenty minutes promised in the instructions. It had taken them that long to get the packaging off.

Cass had philosophically put away the list which began, 'put up shelf bracket bathroom, curtain rail little bedroom, paint splashes windows . . .'

When they set off for Muirend she had driven so that Guy could look about him. He hadn't looked at anything but the next bend; he disliked being driven and disliked narrow roads. Cass had thought it would be agreeable to stop off in Kirkton, buy a few basics at the shop and introduce themselves. She abandoned the idea before they reached the village.

Only once had Guy shown interest, and alert interest at that.

'Slow down here a minute,' he had ordered, as the road began the descent through the woods into Muirend. A drive disappeared on their right into a glooomy tunnel of trees and a brightly painted board announced, 'Sillerton Activity Centre', offering in ornate letters below an impressive list from hang-gliding to hawking, from mountain-biking to golf.

'There's your chance to get some golf in again,' Guy had said. 'My game could do with a bit of brushing up as well.'

Cass had let this pass. Her father had been a scratch player in his day and she and Roey had gone round with him from an early age, and both were naturals though neither took the game seriously. Guy had come to golf much later, seeing it as a useful social asset, and he played with an intense competitiveness which took most of the pleasure out of it for Cass. On her day he couldn't touch her, but there were occasions when she could barely connect and didn't care, and then he beat her with a mixture of gloating and inner chagrin at knowing she was off form which she found very tedious. Now she had wanted to say that hours on the golf course would gobble up huge chunks from all too short weekends, but had checked herself. What was golf if not relaxation? In theory anyway. And how, honestly, did she expect Guy to pass his time when at the cottage?

Business had been swiftly despatched in a Muirend disagreeably thronged with tourists and drifting Saturday shoppers, then in spite of a large late breakfast Guy had headed for a hotel which he had clearly planned to check out all along.

'You'll have read about this place,' he had said, swinging in between ivied pillars. 'They did a big splash on it in *Country Life* last year.'

When did Guy ever read *Country Life*? A great and unreasonable resistance had risen in Cass as they approached a well-kept and un-Scottish-looking mansion set squarely among shaved lawns and clipped evergreens, and Guy had parked among Jaguars, Mercedes and very clean Range Rovers. A slice of Surrey green belt dropped in a broad shining curve of the Tay.

'You might put down a marker for supplying them with staff,' Guy had suggested quite seriously as they were wafted over dense-piled carpets to brocade salon chairs in a bar called the Breadalbane Room. Big sash windows framed lawns sloping to the river, wooded slopes and rugged mountain shapes. Good set, Cass had thought.

'I try to look after my workers.'

'What on earth do you mean?'

'This is so fake.'

'Oh, absolutely not,' Guy had protested, for some reason personally affronted. 'Just look at the panelling and that magnificent plasterwork, all completely in keeping. I can't remember who they got in to do the conversion, but I know they spent a fortune on it. I think it was definitely worth checking out. Anyway, we'll need a local.'

'This? It's miles away.' If you were going to argue with Guy it was essential to produce material objections. 'A local should be a bit handier, surely. And also a place where you meet the locals.' French, American and German voices mingled from the discreetly conversing groups scattered through the big room.

'Well, if the locals are on a par with those morons slouching round Muirend this morning we aren't going to find their company too enlivening,' Guy had retorted, employing the irritating tone which said he knew she was sensible enough to come round to his point of view in the end. Then he had dipped his head into a menu as big as an atlas and the subject had been closed.

Their loop homewards had taken them to Aberfeldy, Kenmore and Fortingall before heading back up narrow Glen Ellig, over the hill and down into Kirkton again. It had been an arrestingly beautiful drive, though for Guy the single-track roads had represented a war zone, and all his attention had been focused on bullying the idling weekend cars into giving way to him.

'Damned tourists.'

We're tourists, Cass had inwardly responded, more depressed than she had any right to be by their own presence among them. And she knew that already, in such a ridiculously brief time, she wanted not to be a tourist, not to belong to that despised class of weekender and holiday cottage owner. She wanted to make sure people – who? – knew that she had an involvement here. That when she was at Corrie Cottage it was not solely to escape the pressures of 'real life'.

So why her sense of disbelieving outrage when, leaving Scotch Corner behind them on the long road south, Guy finally told her why he had chosen to buy a house in Glen Maraich? Particularly when he opened the subject in such a positive manner.

'You know, Cass, I don't think you can go wrong with that Perth venture of yours. Lindsay won't skin you for rental, so I think you should commit whatever you think necessary for office equipment as soon as you can. It's a prime area, and now we have a base up there you can do some of the trawling for clients yourself. You'd enjoy that, rediscovering your calf country perhaps.'

Cass let the teasing that was not quite teasing pass, a minor pinprick. Sharing her business concerns with Guy was still sufficiently unfamiliar for her to feel a definite resentment at being given permission, as it were, to do what she had already decided upon. But then, she reminded herself with her besetting sense of fairness, how much less convenient if Guy, now that technically he had a say in the matter, had disapproved of the project.

'Yes, I'll go for it,' she said. 'Lindsay is the best possible person I could have in charge, short of moving Diane up there.' With the swift progress of plans for her own activity in Scotland, moving Diane was the last thing she wanted to to, even if Diane had been prepared to be uprooted. It seemed likely that a lot more responsibility would devolve on her before long, and Cass felt a rush of heady excitement at the thought.

'It'll work in pretty well,' Guy was continuing, trying to infuse warmth and naturalness into a voice which automatically became offhand as he approached a revelation he knew he must make but instinctively resisted. 'Since I've an interest in the area myself now.'

'An interest?' Cass turned her head sharply, startled by his words, but made much more uneasy by what his tone conveyed.

'I needed to put some money somewhere. You know how it is. The chance occurred to shift it up there.'

'Up where exactly? And into what?' Cass spoke carefully. The new system of combining their interests did not, it appeared, extend to Guy's capital.

'That development. The one we saw yesterday.'

For a moment Cass thought he meant the smug hotel by the river, and she felt resistance instantly harden.

'Near Muirend. The golf course and so on at Sillerton.' Guy clearly found it hard to release the information even now.

'*What?*' Cass's outrage sprang first and foremost from the fact that yesterday morning they had passed the very place; had actually stopped at the entrance on Guy's own request, and he had said nothing. It was incomprehensible, bizarre. Then her mind took in other factors. He had let her discuss the expansion of the Perth agency and still had said nothing. And much further back, even before they were married, he must have planned this, had agreed to the cottage being their wedding present to each other (how exactly had that idea sprung up? She couldn't for the moment recall) pretending the choice of Scotland was to please her, while all the time Glen Maraich had suited his own purposes. They had come to look at Corrie Cottage on the last day of their honeymoon, in the full flush as it were of their new commitment to each other, and he had said nothing.

Cass felt terribly, frighteningly cold, chilled through and through to contemplate the undreamed-of chasms of non-communication which yawned before her.

'Pretty convenient that you'll be involved in a new enterprise of your own just down the road,' Guy was saying, buoyantly now, relieved that he had taken the dreaded hurdle of telling. It was so deeply against his nature, the necessity for it obsessing him for weeks, that it had felt like dragging the long root of a tooth in agony from the clamping socket of the bone. There had been no room to think of Cass's reaction and, since there could be no rational objection, the possibility of her minding on any other level didn't cross his mind.

'But why didn't you tell me? I thought we were telling each other things now.' What infinite care Cass took with that level tone.

'Oh, this deal's been in the pipeline since long before we agreed on that. You couldn't get a scheme on such a scale off the ground in a couple of months.'

The facile prevarication of this, as well as the patronising tone, unintentional as she knew it to be, took Cass's breath away. 'But I thought we went into all our affairs when we – what? – amalgamated seems an appropriate word. What else have you omitted to tell me about? And how could you sit outside the very place yesterday morning and *still* say nothing? It's unbelievable—'

'The files are all there. You can look at anything you like, you know that.'

Guy's voice was defensive now. He could neither explain nor apologise, Cass knew. But he had let her believe he was indulging a special wish of hers in agreeing to buy a house in Scotland, and that hurt. And, now that he was involved in something in the glen, how much time would he commit to it? What did that augur for relaxed weekends, time at last for themselves?

But Cass knew if she threw these angry questions at him he could counter by saying that she was doing just the same thing herself.

It was a silent drive home.

Chapter Six

Cass drove the hired Cavalier at a leisurely pace up the last climbing miles above Kirkton, caught behind a caravan and not minding. It had been a busy week and a touch-and-go scramble to catch her flight, but even coming up the motorway from the airport on a grey evening there had been the special mood of weekend beginning, and she had found herself filled with a sense of expectation and freedom. Part of it was knowing that this time she didn't have to rush back to London after two days. On Monday she and Lindsay were to start organising the new office, planning their marketing strategy and setting up calls on potential clients for Tuesday. And each evening she could escape up here.

There was a different feeling about walking into the cottage knowing she was using it not as a weekend retreat but a working base, and she prowled about finding it hard to believe that matters had rushed so swiftly forward to this point. The sense of liberation was still strong, but there was something else, something she had scarcely hoped for yet, a hint of the inner peace she had vaguely dreamed of but could hardly have defined. The light fresh rooms, the silence, the glen waiting to be explored at her own pace, the absence of demands for two whole days, made a combination of heady promise. She would not think, this weekend, of Guy's startling disclosure that he was involved in the Sillerton development. She had assimilated it now – swallowed it whole without chewing would perhaps be more accurate, she thought wryly – and she could deal with the sense of rebuff she knew he would never understand.

Early July or not, with the silence and peace went a chill she wasn't hardened to yet. The new convector heaters would warm the double room adequately, in spite of the open stairs, but a fire would be lovely. She had never since Dalry lived in a house that even had a fireplace. The chimney was cold, but after a few belches of smoke and some experimenting with windows and doors a purposeful crackling rewarded her. The live presence of the fire made an unbelievable difference to the house, and Cass pulled her chair up close to it to eat a supper of quiche and salad. Tomorrow she would explore the resources of the Kirkton shop.

After supper she pottered about finding places for the last of the kitchen equipment. The phone was still not in – Guy was currently embroiled in a fight about it – and it felt odd not to be able to chat to him, or to call her mother or Roey to share with them her pleasure at being here. They'd love this place. The television picture, except for Channel 4, was adequate – Guy thought it was appalling – but programmes she would have watched without a second thought at home seemed intrusive and irrelevant.

She was drawn out eventually into the cool end of evening, a streaky cloudy sunset evolving in greys and apricots above the ridge, and wandered down through the hillocky stretch between cottage and road to the old bridge beside Riach gate lodge. On the far bank she found a way down the rocky drop and sat for a while on a comfortable stone with her back to the door frame of one of the ruined houses. How many people had sat here in other years, watching the river slip by black and silver in the last of the light? The unearthly light of gloaming. Who had written that? Black silent shapes flickered and arrowed over the water. Swallows? Bats? But whoever had sat here must have had a thicker hide than hers. The midges were eating her alive. Swearing and rubbing her scalp through her densely curly hair Cass abandoned the past and climbed hurriedly to the road.

A woman was standing at the gate of the well-tended terraced garden and Cass paused to speak to her.

'Hello. Cool this evening, isn't it?'

'A wee thing fresh for the time of year.' The woman's voice measured with precision not only the temperature but the warmth she was prepared to accord this stranger with the English voice.

Cass grinned in the dusk. She understood that tone in the finest degree. 'I'm Cass Montgomery,' she said. 'My husband and I have bought Corrie Cottage.'

'Oh, aye, the Corrie,' said the woman, thawing fractionally, giving a quarter nod.

'I think Gina mentioned you the day we moved in. Aren't you the librarian in Muirend? I'm glad we've met.' Cass knew better than to offer her hand.

'Assistant librarian.' But the tone was less chilly. Cass had a friendly voice and easy manner. There was no reciprocal identification, but she hadn't expected it. She knew (remembered, understood?) the deep traditional reluctance to offer one's name, to pronounce it even. Nancy somebody, Gina had said.

'Did you know the people who owned the cottage before us?' she asked. 'Did they use it much?'

'Dundee folk.' Medium damning. 'I never had much to do with them myself.' Definitely presented as a virtue. 'They were forever coming and going at first, couldn't get enough of the place, then you'd not set eyes on them for months together.'

That was loaded. 'We come from London,' Cass said meekly, 'so we may not do much better.'

'London. No, you'll not be managing up very often from there. Especially in the winter months.'

Well, we've got that out of the way, Cass thought as she walked on, hugging to herself the repressive tone of the final phrase. She knew she had been slotted in somewhere on the sliding scale between the holiday people who stayed for a couple of weeks in a letting cottage and were never seen again, and incomers like the inhabitants of Sycamore Lodge who, whatever their shortcomings in glen eyes, at least lived there all the time.

She crossed the new road and went on along the river, remembering seeing a flat unrailed bridge for stock lower down. In the curve between river and road embankment she saw a building she hadn't even realised was there. A rectangle of stone, unlit, it stood close to the water, a few trees grouped round its nearer end. A barn, cut off and made redundant by the new layout? Above it powerful outside lights from the invisible bungalow turned the pale summer darkness beyond their arc to inky blackness. They also threw thick shadows down the river bank, and Cass never saw the quiet watcher who observed her as she paused to look, then went on her way to the wooden bridge.

With a groan Gina heaved the overflowing basket of ironing onto the table and stared at it with loathing. She hardly dared to think what state the layer at the bottom must be in by this time. Probably black with mildew. What would be at the bottom anyway, discarded time after time in the last-ditch domestic triage she was somehow always forced to make no matter how good her intentions? The utility-room curtains, she suspected.

The utility-room curtains? Was that really what her life was reduced to, she thought in sudden outrage. Worrying about bits of coloured material which hung on either side of a glazed aperture and were never drawn from one year's end to the next? Till one day, wishing to perform adequately, to please, she climbed up and took them down and washed them. Then, had she been a good and admirable housewife, she would have smoothed them with a heated metal plate and hung them up again. Only instead she left them where they were from March to July, by which point there was no time for anything.

She had already been to Muirend once today. Nessa was competing in a swimming gala but had refused to go down with Laurie because he had to be at the club early for the Summer Medal. Gina still wasn't sure what that meant, except that no one seemed to win a medal. She knew she should have insisted on Nessa going with Laurie, it was ridiculous to take two cars down the glen within an hour of each other, but she was getting more and more cowardly about confrontations. Not that she seemed able to avoid them; they flared up no matter what she said or did.

Steve should have gone with his father too, but he still wasn't up. Gina knew, though Laurie didn't, that it had been nearly five when he came in. Was it irresponsible of her to say nothing? But at college who knew what he did or when he came in, if at all? And this morning Laurie hadn't asked, tight-lipped and preoccupied about all the things that could go wrong today, angry because the shirt he wanted wasn't ready, though Gina had offered to iron it while he had his breakfast. It was only the cuffs that were damp. He'd roared at Tiree because he'd barked for a sausage just as the weather forecast reached Scotland, and his only goodbye had been a shout from the car window to say he'd told everyone seven thirty for dinner.

Stirring up the ironing with a hopeless reluctance Gina saw that the tail of the shirt in question must have been trailing on the floor. It was imprinted with large black paw marks.

'Oh, Tiree, what a nightmare dog you are!' Even as the tears rose to her eyes, she giggled to think what a drama there would have been if Laurie had accepted her offer to iron the damned thing. But the tears won. She sank down sobbing into the nearest chair.

Tiree couldn't think of anything awful he'd done in the last couple of minutes and bounced forward obligingly. Conversation often led to other things. Pulled into a strangling hug he braced himself as best he could. He wasn't into all this emotion and there was something wet on his head, but it might be worth it.

'You are so incredibly awful,' Gina told him, reaching past him into the laundry basket and dabbing at her eyes with a pillowslip. It didn't work very well. 'But God knows what I'd do without you. You're the only person who listens to me.'

She knew it was her fault that she had let herself become so cut off here. When they had bought the ex-farmhouse on Riach estate just over two years ago, Joanna Mackenzie at the big house had been, in her casual way, helpful and friendly, and through her the way had been open to other friendships, as Gina knew. Yet somehow she had let it all slip away. She seemed to spend her entire time just struggling to keep up – and failing, she reminded herself with fresh tears which made Tiree flick his ears. There never seemed a moment for her own pursuits, and it was a lot harder to make friends after the first warmth of welcome had been squandered. Houses were scattered miles apart; you didn't run into people casually, you had to make a definite arrangement to meet. They were all deep in their own lives anyway. She had found no soul-mates among the Muirend High School mothers, while Laurie's new business associates, or his bosses really, since he was the manager and they all had some financial stake in the scheme, were not the sort of people she found it easy to relate to. In fact they bored her to death, she amended with a giggle, and their wives were worse. Tonight six of them would invade her home, eat her food. Oh God, she'd done nothing whatsoever about dinner, didn't even know what she was going to give them. Groaning, she laid her head on Tiree's silky domed skull, and he got in a couple of swift sideways licks to remind her he wasn't a cushion and had his problems too.

Gina had hoped for more, she knew, of the newcomers at the Corrie. She had so much enjoyed Cass's company on that wet wild moving day. The next time Cass had been at the cottage

Gina had expected her to appear, or had been ready to drop in herself, but the cottage had been deserted for practically the whole weekend. She had learned from Beverley, who missed nothing, that Cass's husband had been with her, but by the time she had got round to inviting them up for drinks before lunch on Sunday they had already left. Now someone was at the cottage again, but with a different car. Perhaps friends borrowing the house. Probably all summer different people would appear, Gina decided, letting depression carry her away, strangers, content with their own company, not looking for contact or friendship.

She heard no sound at the door, but Tiree, for once on top of his job, let loose a shattering fusillade of barks while his head was still under her cheek, then released himself with such violence that her chair nearly overturned.

And when, hastily scrubbing away tear-marks, Gina went to the door, there was Cass, absurdly long-legged in narrow jeans, her blue eyes crinkling to slits as she smiled in the way Gina had liked so much, an outsize red flannel shirt billowing in the wind that scoured the exposed yard.

'Hi. Is this a really bad time? The middle of Saturday morning? Just say if you're busy.'

'Oh, Cass, come in, please come in,' Gina begged, clutching her arm in terror lest she escape. 'I was just thinking about you. Come in and save me from the ironing and deserts of boredom and despair.'

'Sounds heavy.' Cass allowed herself to be towed into the kitchen, impeded by Tiree's welcome. Gina had spoken cheerfully, but Cass had seen the redness of her eyelids and the trace of tears on her freckled cheeks.

'We'll get rid of this lot for a start.'

Gina swung the ironing basket to the floor with the misleading feeling that it had been dealt with, her spirits soaring. 'Coffee, yes? Damn, kettle's empty. Oh, well, I'll use the electric one.'

Without background knowledge of the war Laurie waged against this needless extravagance, Cass had no clue to the reckless defiance in her voice.

The dishwasher yawned open, waiting to be emptied. Breakfast dishes were piled on the worktop above it. A blackened frying pan with a fish-slice balanced on it, burn marks on its handle showing where it had been propped there a hundred times before, was on the Aga, both lids of which were up.

'I can't tell you how pleased I am to see you,' Gina confessed, as she put a carton of milk and a beautifully decorated earthenware biscuit jar on the table.

'Is something wrong?'

'Nothing special.' Gina beamed over her shoulder as she took mugs from the dishwasher. 'Just my life.'

'That all? Let's talk about something else then.'

Gina laughed. 'You know, I've wondered once or twice in the last few weeks whether I'd imagined it. I hadn't, had I?'

'You hadn't.' Cass didn't need any explanation. As she came up the lane she too had wondered if the instant ease would still be there, conscious for one thing that she knew little of Gina's timetable and might have chosen an inconvenient time. Now, seeing Gina again, in a yellow shirt and another drooping skirt, this time of scuffed cinnamon velvet, and hideous slipsox with squashed-sideways soles, reassured by a welcome whose warmth could not be mistaken, she knew they had found something good.

'So anything in particular about life?' she enquired casually. Colourful outgoing people like Gina should not be found weeping in empty kitchens.

'Infuriating young, a disgusted husband, perpetual domestic crises brought on by my own ineptitude, and a dinner party for eight tonight. Laurie wants four courses and everything smart, and it's all for the most ghastly people you ever met in your life, half of whom I don't even know.' Gina rattled this off tragically, but a little downturn of her mouth and a sparkle in the yellow eyes told she could see the funny side of it.

'I'm not sure about the logic of the last bit,' Cass remarked, 'but the rest sounds a bit dire. Who are the young, besides Nessa?' There had been a couple of references to 'the boys'.

'Laurie's two sons, Steve and Andy.'

'How old are they?'

'Steve's twenty-one, one year to go doing business management at Strathclyde. Andy leaves school any minute now and has two aims in life, to make money and spend money. Any interval spent getting hints about the means to the first is regarded as a waste of time.'

'And Nessa is your daughter and Laurie's?'

'No, we've only been married for four years. Nessa's the product of my first marriage.' Gina began to laugh. 'Wretched creature. On the way to Muirend this morning she took time off from informing me that every single girl in her year wears a skirt shorter and tighter than hers, to point out my incredible thoughtlessness in giving her a name with two s's in it when there's already an s in her surname. Which is Pascoe, by the way.'

Cass laughed. 'I blamed my mother because I'm six feet tall and have this madly curly hair, though neither applies to her.'

'Not really six feet?' Gina exclaimed, diverted.

'It sometimes feels like it. But what were you doing going down to Muirend so early?'

'Nessa's swimming. I'll have to go and get her soon. Steve should have come with us, having missed a lift with his father, because he'd promised to caddie today, but he's still in bed. That was what annoyed Laurie. Among other things,' she amended fairly. 'Oh, I don't care,' she wound up, dumping herself into a chair with an air of settling in and picking a piece of shortbread from among the duller biscuits. 'It's all too tedious for words. Tell me how you're getting on at the Corrie instead. I know Ed left logs for you during the week. Is everything else all right?'

Cass looked at her with amusement. Ahead lay a marathon of cooking, cleaning (possibly) and driving, yet here Gina was, prepared to go into the minutiae of Cass's affairs with the friendliest interest. And how much nicer, she noted in passing, 'the Corrie' sounded than 'Corrie Cottage'. Nancy whoever-she-was had called it that too.

She got to her feet. 'Look, why don't I get stuck into the ironing while we chat? It would get that much out of the way for you.'

'Goodness, would you? Oh but no, I can't let you, you can't iron other people's clothes.'

'Why not? They're clean, aren't they? They *are* clean, aren't they?'

Gina giggled. 'Mostly. Except for this.' She pulled free the paw-patterned shirt. 'That's what I was crying about.'

'No it wasn't.' Cass pressed a testing hand on the ironing board which had a knock-kneed look she didn't much trust. 'Do you want to tell me?'

Gina looked at her calm face, concentrating on laying a shirt sleeve along the board and pulling it straight. She knew she could say, 'Not yet,' and it would be accepted. Or she could allow herself, tentatively, to put into words some of her oppressive sense of her own inadequacy, her feeling of entrapped frustration which could sometimes surge up to boiling point. The almost forgotten comfort of being understood spread through her like the reviving warmth of a hot drink on a cold day.

Chapter Seven

Cass was having a quiet lunch tucked into the porch out of the wind. There was unquestionably a feeling of luxury in being peaceful and alone after the charged emotional atmosphere generated by Gina. Gina herself had gone to fetch Nessa. What an endless chore that must be in a place like this. Contentedly Cass reviewed her own day.

The shop in Kirkton had been an agreeable surprise. Once the damning, 'You'll just be here at weekends, though?' ('weekends' with the stress firmly on the second syllable, which took her back a bit) was out of the way, she had been received in a cordial manner, and looking round at what was on offer had realised her expectations had been seriously out of date. With the glen road widened and improved a lot more traffic nowadays took the tourist route over the pass and this had had its effect on the village. She had bought baguettes and peppered mackerel, wine, cheese, fruit and salad stuff, delighted not to have to go to Muirend.

After that she had spent a couple of hours exploring, tackling the steep face above the Mains, perching on a boss of rock halfway to the ridge to study the glen spread out below her – and to recover her breath, for even the busiest London life didn't produce the kind of fitness required here. She had looked down on the big square house of Riach set on a wide level space unadorned by gardens. Beyond it a grassy track led invitingly to the head of the glen and the other imposing building of Allt Farr. Did anyone mind where one walked? Gina would know.

But would she? Cass wondered now, grinning. What a glorious lunatic she was. If she could ever spare the odd moment from domestic chaos what rewarding company she promised to be.

A car came fast and noisily up the track. Gina herself, rushing home to start cooking? No, the vehicle had jerked to a stop below the bank and was now, with much over-revving, backing into the Corrie driveway. The racket cut off. Cass got to her feet and went to look. The filthy Subaru she had seen at Mains of Riach was sitting askew with its rear against the bank and its nose pointing downhill. Gina was getting out. The car moved slightly and she hurriedly got in again. There was a bounce as she pulled on the handbrake. Cass hoped, picking her way down the uneven steps smothered in alpine lady's mantle, that she had also left it in gear this time.

'Don't tell me you've got to go down the glen again. What have you forgotten? Not Nessa?' For only Tiree was in the car, nearly buried under seas of shopping, most of which he appeared to have already investigated.

'Nothing I've thought of yet, though there's bound to be something. No, listen, I've had the most brilliant idea.' Gina's face was beaming and vividly alive, as though this morning's tears had never been.

Tiree, clawing his way back to the seat after being tipped sharply floorwards with a great many other objects into a space too small for him, relieved his feelings by barking at Cass.

'Shut up, Tiree!' Gina yelled, banging her fist on the car roof. It did little to soothe him.

'What's happening?' Cass asked.

'Tiree, I'll brain you if you don't cut it out. You know perfectly well who Cass is. Hang on a sec,' Gina told Cass, diving into the car again to scrabble for something on the passenger side. Cass waited peaceably. She had all day.

Tiree, attracted by the sound of wrappings, stopped barking and began to climb into the front seat via the direct route over its head rest. Cass turned her face up to a blink of sunshine, awaiting developments, reflecting that in terms of forward planning there was little to choose between dog and owner.

'There.' Gina emerged breathless and triumphant. 'The first of the season. Blairgowrie ones, the very best. I couldn't resist them, though they're still madly expensive. Oh, well, you know what I mean. I got some for us as well. They'll be marvellous for the summer pudding tonight.'

'Doesn't summer pudding have to sit in the fridge for hours?' Cass asked, gratefully accepting a punnet of raspberries, the top layer flattened into oozing cubes, and feeling an amused affection for this generous careless girl.

'Plenty of time for that,' Gina said airily.

'Really? And where's Nessa? I thought the chief object was to fetch her.' Though by the look of the car dinner party pickings would have been thin without this trip for afterthoughts.

'Oh, *unbearable* child,' Gina exclaimed, her face crumpling in a look of hurt exasperation. 'She'd decided to stay overnight with a friend. Yesterday evening they were never going to speak to each other again in their lives. Nessa vowed she'd tried to phone and I'd like to believe her but she had the most shifty look in her eye and quite honestly I don't. Isn't that awful, not to trust your own daughter? On a less moral level, I'd hoped she'd give me a hand this afternoon. Still, when I discovered I was going to be on my own, I did allow myself a few cheating things like frozen pastry and frozen vegetables, because the only thing in the garden at the moment seems to be everlasting spinach and I didn't think it would go with carbonnade of beef.'

Cass, trying to remember how long that took, didn't think either purchase sounded much like cheating.

'Then there was smoked cod's roe on offer,' Gina rushed

on, 'and I just snatched it up, though I'm not sure what I can do with it now I've got it and I didn't dare look at the sell-by date. Anyway, that's all boring stuff, nothing to do with why I stopped. As I said, I've had this marvellous idea. Get in, and I'll tell you on the way. Oh, will you be able to get in?'

On the way to where? Did it matter? 'Perhaps if you pulled forward a little?'

'Don't take that resigned tone with me.' By the sound of Gina's giggle as she reached for the key she was feeling as light-hearted as Cass was. Cass looked at the punnet in her hands; brilliant juice stained her fingers. She put the raspberries in the grass by the steps and caught up with the Subaru, which had leapt out into the lane. With her knees up to her ears, still searching for somewhere to put her feet among the shopping, Cass rocked sideways as Gina took off. Judging by a bitten-off yelp behind her Tiree was also in difficulties. Presumably he was used to it.

'It suddenly struck me,' Gina shouted, taking the first corner at a speed which assumed no one else would ever appear on the track, 'that this would be the ideal opportunity for you to—'

'Do you need the choke out? You've just driven about forty miles.'

'Good thinking.' The engine calmed down gratefully.

'So what were you saying?'

'When I was in the chemist's they asked if I'd bring up some stuff Beverley had ordered. She gets pills and medicines by the crateload, though they may be for Richard of course, but she spends a fortune besides on all kinds of junk, lotions and creams to rejuvenate the eyelid, reshape the jawline, re-something all the bits of her the rest of us have given up worrying about. Not that you have to worry much. Ow, what fell over then?'

'Don't panic, I shouldn't think there's anything left to smash if you've driven like this all the way from Muirend.' Cass held on to the dash as they spurted aside the tidy gravel of Sycamore Lodge.

'Anyway,' Gina said, crunching to a halt, 'I thought it would be a good chance for you to meet. We all live so near each other, and Beverley's really the only person I ever see here. She's had a rough time, and it must get lonely sometimes.'

It seemed vain having reached this point to enquire whether, with a dinner party to prepare for, and a husband who wanted a four-course meal, a demand which still made Cass's hackles rise when she thought of it, Gina really wanted to spend time introducing her to the neighbours. Though Cass was conscious of a certain interest of her own in meeting someone capable of hovering behind drawn blinds, while a stranger stood on the doorstep in the sluicing rain seeking help.

The woman who opened the panelled door, which had been stained to a strange purplish 'mahogany', made Cass feel that this entire slab of bungalow and garden should be lifted on a giant shovel and put back where it belonged, in some socially striving, neighbourhood-watch-stickered, tidy, stressed-out English suburb.

Beverley Scott was short and dapper, groomed to the last millimetre with pain, care and anxiety. Her small body, naturally tending to roundness, was held in, held up, pampered and penanced with unremitting attention. Her beige linen-look skirt, cream silk shirt and gold jewellery proclaimed her terror of bad taste, the threat of which had dogged her with dread and uncertainty all her life. Her yellow hair, whose obsessively concealed threads of white gave her actual nightmares, fell in a neat bell shape, drawn back from a thin-nosed, sharp-eyed face by a black velvet band.

'Oh, Gina, it's you,' she said dismissively, her small colourless eyes fixing on Cass with the kind of inborn suspicion which did not accord with black velvet hairbands. 'You never know who'll come knocking at the door these days, there are people everywhere.'

She nodded towards the road where a straggle of white-haired coach passengers tottered aimlessly past, eyes blank, minds on the state of their feet and the miles between them and the next cup of tea and the next loo. Beverley drew in her breath in a hiss as they paused to point out to each other with sudden animation the gaily painted wheelbarrow planted with pansies and lobelia just inside her gate.

'I've brought the things you'd ordered from the chemist,' Gina was saying in her friendly way. 'And I thought you'd like to meet Cass, who's moved into the Corrie. Cass – oh, lord, I've forgotten your other name, what an idiot I am.'

'Montgomery.' Cass was about to offer her hand when Beverley snatched the package from Gina as though embarrassed by it, snapping ungratefully, 'You really needn't have bothered, I was going down on Monday anyway for my massage. I'm very tense at present, though I suppose it's hardly surprising with all I have to cope with, and Yvonne is going to try a new blend of oils which she's prepared exclusively for me as she knows I have special needs. Though of course it's still based on my favourite fractionated coconut and jojoba.' She peeped into the bag and closed it again quickly.

Cass, fascinated by this welcome, studied Beverley's eyelids and decided they looked no younger than anyone else's of forty or so. Unless of course the wonder cures were doing their job and Beverley was actually ninety. With delight Cass recognised a rich vein of absurdity, there for the quarrying.

'How do you do?' she said courteously.

'Yes. Well. Hello.' Beverley had never been able to bring herself to say 'How do you do?' in return; it didn't make sense. She failed to produce a smile but tendered a painted and beringed paw which spent most of its day in a Marigold glove.

'Aren't you going to ask us in?' Gina asked in her cheerful direct way.

'I didn't know how much of a hurry you were in,' Beverley said quickly, not concealing her annoyance.

She didn't add 'Come in if you must', but the words quivered on the air as she led the way in with crisp steps.

Though Sycamore Lodge, behind its barricades of swiftly growing *Leylandii Rheingold* and neat rabbit netting, bore little relation to the landscape around it, Cass thought the height of Beverley's heels remarkable for anywhere. Oh, Gina, you star, she exulted, as they followed her resentful back into a sitting-room of monstrous affectation and eye-battering colour.

'I suppose this is the wrong time of day to offer you anything,' Beverley said, perfunctorily waving them to a gleaming sofa tightly covered in kingfisher mock-velvet (washable). 'Just after lunch and too early for afternoon tea.'

From the gossip Beverley so assiduously gleaned she knew that Corrie Cottage had been bought as a weekend cottage, and she shared whole-heartedly local resentment of such purchasers, indignant at any encroachment on the privacy for which she had paid so steep a price. Her ambition was to be received on friendly terms by the families whose big houses dotted the glen, the Mackenzies of Riach, the Munros at Allt Farr, the Forsyths lower down at Alltmore. The acquaintance with Gina had developed more by proximity and default than anything else, and sometimes Beverley regretted it, wondering even if it might stand in the way of her acceptance into more desirable circles. The Frasers had only lived here for about two years, and were definitely borderline with Laurie's job in leisure management, but holiday home owners were a notch down even from them.

'Coffee would be lovely, though,' Gina was saying comfortably. 'It was such a rush in Muirend that I didn't have time for lunch. How about you, Cass?'

'Yes, I'd love coffee. Thank you,' Cass said warmly to Beverley as though it had been her suggestion.

'Well, it will have to be instant,' Beverley said crossly. 'I haven't time to get the percolator out at present.' She disappeared through an archway, her heels clacking in indignation as she hit some uncarpeted surface, and though Gina made hasty signs to warn Cass that they could be heard, she dissolved in laughter herself as Cass's eyebrows climbed exaggeratedly at this disobliging reception. In desperation she picked up the nearest cushion and pressed it to her face. Discovering painfully that it was thick with beadwork she collapsed completely.

'Is my face all pocked?' she gasped out, recovering slightly, then finding the word hilarious let out a low moan and got up hastily to walk to the window.

What could Beverley be busy with in a house like this, Cass wondered, hoping that concentrating on her surroundings would steady her. What was left to do? The coloured glass ornaments, the brass warming pan and hot-water cans which had never been called upon to perform their function, the winking fire-irons and vase of dyed bulrushes and honesty on the polished hearth, the carved magazine rack and occasional tables, had been scourged of the smallest speck of dust. The 'Persian' carpet looked as though it had been laid yesterday. No traces were visible of any human activity other than sitting face to face with the twenty-four-inch television screen.

Surely she must notice we're both red-faced and damp-eyed, Cass thought with shame as Beverley rapped down on a glass-topped table a tray decorated with a highly fanciful map, giving the distribution of the Highland clans from Otterburn to Unst.

Beverley only said, 'You should try these biscuits, Gina, they use Q-negative-factor flour-substitute and ninety-eight per cent cholesterol-free fat, and they're specially aimed at breaking down unwanted tissue round the hips. I could get some for you if you like, you won't find them in the shops. I get them through Madame Elise – my beautician,' she added to Cass with what could only be called a simper, handing her a flower-painted bone-china cup of coffee to which she had added milk without asking. To judge by the watery-looking surface layer and the odd colour, the milk too came from some cholesterol-free (and udder-free) source.

'No thanks,' Gina managed briefly in a strangled voice. Cass caught the faint rattle of her cup in the saucer and hastily called her facial muscles to order.

'I gather you won't be here very often,' Beverley said, putting a plate with a knife holding down a triangle of paper napkin in front of Cass, and offering her the wan biscuits with an air of little hope that she would have the intelligence to appreciate them. No alternative was available.

Beverley was making polite conversation, according to her lights, but Cass was taken aback for a moment. Where had Beverley 'gathered' this?

'We haven't done too badly so far,' she remarked, her voice even, reviewing the long journeys.

'You moved in a month ago, isn't that right?' But Beverley's attention was elsewhere. Her plan for the afternoon had been to watch and tape *On Moonlight Bay*, and when the doorbell had so infuriatingly rung she had thrust under the sofa the box of chocolates she intended to indulge in at the same time. Now she caught sight of its corner poking out from the pleats of the valance and was terrified Cass might spot it. Gina was too vague to make anything of it, but this uncomfortable beanpole of a female with the observant blue eyes which always seemed to be laughing at something would think it a big joke.

'Yes. I called here the day we moved in, as a matter of fact,' Cass was replying, on a lazy impulse to see what Beverley would say. 'I rang several times. Didn't you hear me?'

'Oh, I'd have been out,' Beverley said too promptly. 'If I'd been here I'd have come to the door at once.'

'I'm sure you would. Especially as it was pouring.' Cass observed with interest a pink which didn't match the tawny-peach blusher rise in Beverley's diet-hollowed cheeks. Her suspicions were confirmed as Beverley turned swiftly to a safer topic.

'You really should have come to the aromatherapy session, Gina. I did send you a card. It would have been most beneficial, especially the section on soothing and calming. You're always so het up about everything.'

Cass thought that for a woman facing a dinner party for

eight in something under five hours, with a house in the state Mains of Riach was in, Gina was remarkably laid-back.

'There are some marvellous new blends. I took the opportunity to go into it thoroughly during the consultation period.' Cass wondered how long the queue behind her had been. 'Mentha Citrata and Neroli are key ingredients. Not for myself, I'm a very together person as you know, but I do have a responsibility to explore all the avenues.' She said this with a brave sigh. Cass wondered what she was talking about.

But Gina had been given the cue before. 'How is Richard?' she asked, and in spite of her giggles over Beverley's behaviour a few minutes ago, the question was put with genuine concern.

'Well, of course, it's not easy for me,' Beverley responded, with a little wriggle of her hips as though settling herself for a familiar exposition. Unappealing as Cass was with her unnatural height and elongated hands and feet and careless clothes, she was a new audience. Really, though, by this time of day she might at least have got round to doing her make-up, she was as bad as Gina. But this reminded Beverley of her film and she darted a quick look at her willow-pattern plate clock. She would tell Cass about her problems another day. Taking Gina's cup and putting it down with finality on the Macleans of Newtown St Boswells, she gabbled off briskly, 'I do sometimes feel that with all I've had to contend with in my life there isn't much justice in the world, but I have to do the best I can, that's really all any of us can do, isn't it, and now if you'll excuse me I know it's Saturday afternoon for some people, but I have so much to get on with . . .'

'Is it really serious about the husband?' Cass asked as she and Gina went to the car, the door already shut behind them and Beverley flying for the on button.

'I think it must be. Certainly he's rarely visible. He has a workshop down by the river and has started doing upholstery and furniture renovation, probably as a form of therapy. That could be very useful if he's any good. Oh, dear, was I dreadfully unkind, laughing about poor old Beverley? She really isn't so bad at heart.'

'Hm,' said Cass.

Gina laughed. 'I can't help feeling fond of her in a way, in spite of all you're not saying.'

'I think I'll reserve judgement. Now listen, about this dinner party – how are you going to manage with no Nessa to give you a hand?' And half the afternoon gone in social dissipation.

'Actually if she's in the wrong mood Nessa can be more hindrance than help,' her mother admitted.

'How about me then? I'm no cook but I can peel a spud or chop an onion. And are you remembering carbonnade needs all that French bread and mustard rigmarole at the end? Is it the best choice?'

'It's Laurie's favourite. Would you really help?' Gina asked yearningly, slowing below the Corrie as though satisfying her conscience by offering Cass the chance to escape. 'Wouldn't it be a desperate bore, especially when you have so little time here?'

'Just think of me as one of those people for whom it's Saturday afternoon.'

Though the mess in Gina's kitchen was mind-blowing, though Tiree drove her mad with his ceaseless mooching, and laying the dining-room table involved first shifting bits of mountain bike and an oily rag, then removing those traces of both which had penetrated to the wood, Cass enjoyed the rushing, chatting, laughing afternoon. She felt very contented as, lifting her squashed raspberries from their grassy niche by the steps, she heard what she presumed was Laurie's car coming up the lane.

Gina was as ready as outside assistance could make her; any cock-ups now were of her own devising.

Chapter Eight

As she drove out to Heathrow, Cass was conscious not only of a keen longing to see Guy again, but of a need for him. This was Thursday, only ten days since they had been together, nothing unusual in their lives, but she had an odd feeling of having been apart from him, mentally and emotionally, for a long time. Examining this with a stir of concern, she realised that at the Corrie she had hardly thought of him. More, when she had it had been almost with a sense of being pulled in a different direction, as though the idea of him was out of sympathy with the mood of the place. Now that she had brought the feeling into the open it worried her. It seemed based on so little; one visit when their ideas had differed about what they should do. That was all.

No, that wasn't all. There had been a sense of freedom in being there alone, and she didn't want it to be like that. Being apart because of the demands of work had never produced that insidious and even guilty feeling. It had simply been part of their lives, and the anticipation and pleasure of being together again had made it acceptable. At the cottage this weekend Guy had dropped with startling completeness from her mind.

Perhaps it was because there had been so much to do, and the extra days tacked on to the weekend had made the time seem longer than it was. With the greatest ease her mind slipped back there.

Hearing the cars threading up to the Mains on Saturday evening, it had amused her to know exactly what – given some activity on Gina's part in the interval – their occupants would presently be eating; to know that the cushion of one of the spindle-back chairs in the clean dining-room had been turned over to hide some nasty oil marks, and that of another had come from Tiree's basket; and to know there was every chance that the summer pudding would be more like a bowl of fruit and cream. Above all though, it had been luxury not to be the person who had to dress, make up her face, despair of her hair, ask tedious questions of tedious strangers to which she didn't want to know the answers, and consume large amounts of food and drink because they were there.

The next morning had vanished at startling speed. She had slept later than she had meant to, waking to deep silence which as she listened became threaded with the calls of birds, the thin ceaseless background sound of sheep, the clatter of a tractor. On overtime, the business-like part of her brain recorded. It had been good to go down, still in her sleeping-T which left a mile of leg exposed, and out, stepping heron-like into the bright morning, secure in the privacy of her high sunlit ledge.

Later, she had intended to make a start on tidying the garden, but wandering along the hill fence had decided she could scarcely improve on the natural grouping of foxglove and cow-parsley, pink campion and vetch, yarrow and willowherb. It seemed pointless because they were designated weeds to howk them out, with a good deal of effort, and replace them with other plants which would then need looking after. She had cleared strangling grass from around a few hardy potentillas, though they were blooming happily without the attention, and had had a look at the big sagging honeysuckle. Almost drowning in its scent and getting a faceful of tiny black flies, she had decided to cut it back in the autumn and train it up the wall. She had gone down into the cool mossy cavern of the burn, delighted to find it thick with wild mimulus, and out into the stony heat of the lane to survey the bank above, vivid with yellow bedstraw, clover and ox-eye daisies. How could she improve on that, except by removing the grey-green furry seed-heads of the lupins to encourage a second flowering?

She had been temporarily distracted by a young oyster-catcher, fluffy in grey plumage, with pale legs and pale bill, hurrying across the track. Was it lost, was it all right? But anxious though its expression had been, it probably had a better idea of where it should go than she had. Then a violent chack-chacking had arrested her, and she had seen a small flat brown face peering at her from a chink near the bottom of the dyke, a half-eaten bird nearby. The face voiced some serious indignation before withdrawing and reappearing a yard away and higher up, this time examining Cass aggressively. She caught a glimpse of a slim body with white chest and underbelly, then a second head had shot out briefly, and as Cass stood motionless the two appeared from different crannies for several minutes, defiant and vocal.

Eventually she had started on the lawn. It had clearly been pointless to try the Flymo, though as she had raked and sheared the flattened mess of last year's grass clogging the new growth she had imagined Guy's mocking comment, 'Pretty primitive, don't you think?' But to have that small patch cut was really all the garden needed; the rest she would tidy with a light hand, preserving its sleepy beauty.

It was a long job and she hadn't hurried, allowing herself to be drawn to other things as they caught her attention, digging a few dandelions from the path, screwing the bolt more firmly onto the shed door, distributing the spoil of molehills round needy plants, allowing herself a reading lunch but dozing off over a Margaret Atwood she'd been enjoying in London but which had been all wrong at the Corrie.

The best part of the weekend had been that afternoon. Gina had come down the field with Tiree, full of the highs and lows of the previous evening, wearing a huge straw hat with a piece chewed out of the brim, and a lime-green, loose-knit cotton sweater whose stitches Cass thought had not originally been intended to stretch so far. She had brought generous leftovers.

'I had to hide some of the smoked roe tartlets you made, they were so popular. You can try them for lunch. I brought some of the summer pudding too. You were quite right, it needed far longer in the fridge, but it's perfect today, I promise you.'

'That's really kind, Gina. I suppose it would be ungrateful to point out that it's after three?'

'Honestly? As late as that?' Gina had tried to look surprised but her dimples always gave her away. 'I suppose I'll just have to miss lunch altogether then.'

'Idiot. I'll get some wine. Red or white?'

'It seems odd that you don't know,' Gina had observed. 'It feels as though we've known each other for ever.'

'Corny line, but I know what you mean. I still need to know the answer though.'

Gina had laughed, collapsing on the roughly hacked grass. 'White please, though after last night I'm not sure either's a good idea.'

'That good?'

'I don't think that's quite the—' She had broken off as Tiree, with a low-pitched howl, threw himself down the bank, smashing through the lupins as he went. 'What happened – did something sting him?'

'There are weasles in the dyke.'

'Oh, good – that should keep him away from the food. Unless of course he brings the whole dyke down,' Gina had added peacefully, closing her eyes.

As Cass took the wine out of the fridge it had struck her that she had said 'dyke' not 'wall', as though the language of childhood came naturally here.

'So did the rest of the food work out all right?' she had asked as she tried a tartlet, making no comment on the fact that the only part left to Gina, the garnish of hard-boiled egg, had not materialised.

In the shadow of her big hat Gina's face had filled with laughter. 'Oh, those appalling people, they came absolutely on the dot, all of them at once. Don't you hate punctual people?'

'No.'

'I'd luckily done all that business with the carbonnade, only I'd burned my fingers. You know where it says, "push the bread well down into the gravy"—'

'You are allowed to use an implement, you know.'

'I did of course, but I burned my fingers anyway. So I'd just hared upstairs—'

Could Gina hare anywhere? Cass had wondered idly, deciding the wine from Kirkton shop was quite adequate for the garden.

'—and leapt into the shower when I heard them arriving. I hadn't put out nibbles or anything – what a ghastly word nibbles is – so I leapt out again and threw on one of those sixties' dresses with a little quilted bit over the boobs and the rest all loose.'

'And nothing?'

'No time for anything else, just banged a brush at my hair . . .'

Cass turned her face up to the sun, eyes closed. What a pleasing image, Gina serenely welcoming her guests damp and knickerless, while her correct and fussy husband . . . What had he been doing anyway, while she was racing round? Cass had formed a most unfair picture of Laurie as one of those men who take for granted the domestic services of a wife. The image was based on little more than finding Gina in tears over the ironing, though not forgetting the damning phrase, 'a four-course meal'.

After lunch they had made a brief unhurried circuit of the fields below the lane (Gina did not strike Cass as a walker), ending up at the Mains where Gina had shown Cass over the untidy house, beautifully furnished with the cottage antiques for which she had such an excellent eye, and decorated in the rich warm colours she was naturally drawn to.

'And here's the source of most of my problems,' she had said ruefully, reaching out with a swift, almost secret, touch to the grand piano taking up too much space in the sitting-room, its top severely empty, a notable exception in that household. 'I ration myself to half an hour and suddenly the morning's gone, or I'm late for Nessa, or there's no food and the shop's shut. I can't even play now, that's the worst part.'

Her smiling lively face had looked suddenly sad, and Cass had been for the first time conscious of the gap in their ages. Here was a mature woman, talented, Cass suspected, certainly creative and original, caught up in a life which trammelled her, condemned by marriage and motherhood to swimming perpetually against the stream. Why did it have to be like that? But it had not been the moment for serious probings into woman's lot.

'Did you play professionally?' she had asked instead.

'For a while.' But for once Gina had not been disposed to talk, her hand laid on the closed lid of the piano as though in finality.

After a pause full of unspoken questions, Cass had turned to other things. 'Where's Nessa today? Where's everyone, in fact, on a Sunday afternoon?'

'Thank heavens you reminded me,' Gina had cried, looking at her watch. 'Nessa decided to stay another night at Kim's and go to school from there, so now she has to do her homework tonight and wants me to take her books down, and her uniform, I mustn't forget that. As for the others, Sunday's one of Laurie's busiest days of course, and Steve actually got up in time to go with him this morning, inspired no doubt by yesterday's loot.'

'They couldn't have taken Nessa's things?' Cass asked, not because at this stage it was a useful suggestion but because already she felt protective towards Gina.

But Gina knew she brought most of her problems on herself.

She had grinned at Cass across the tea tray set between them on the old wooden seat facing down the walled garden. (Its iron arms were beautifully cast in the form of twined serpents, and she still hadn't confessed to Laurie what it had cost.) 'Come off it, I'm not the sort of person who thinks of things like that at eight o'clock on the morning after a party. And if I thought of it, I'm not the sort of mother who has the shirts ready ironed. No, alas, it's another trundle down to Muirend for me – and I mustn't leave it too late because of being here when Laurie gets back. He's always in a foul mood after the weekend at the club, so I try to do reasonable grub.'

Cass had decided she liked Laurie less and less. 'What is this club?' she had asked, without much interest in the answer.

'It's part of the leisure centre just outside Muirend, on an estate that used to belong to people called Hay. They'd owned it for years, but when old Lady Hay died none of the family wanted to take it on, or death duties did for them, or something. Anyway, it's been developed for sporting activities, with plans for lots more, and Laurie runs it. What? Why are you looking at me like that?'

'Are you talking about Sillerton?'

'Yes? Have you been there?'

'Guy's a shareholder. It's one of the reasons we bought a cottage here.' For a second she had been tempted to tell Gina how much she had minded Guy concealing the fact, but her sense of betrayal was not something she was ready to examine yet.

'Not the missing shareholder from my party? The mysterious man from London? You can't be serious? Your husband, and you've bought the Corrie?'

With similar reservations forming in their minds, though differently weighted, they had gazed at each other with unspoken misgiving.

Laurie resents all the directors, Gina had thought in trepidation. He regards them as high-handed and arrogant, and thinks they believe a mere cash involvement gives them the right to interfere, while he struggles at ground level to make things work.

Guy will feel his privacy threatened, Cass had instantly foreseen. With his fanatical need to keep all dealings close to his chest, he'll bitterly resent someone he'll see as the foreman living just up the lane.

'Could this be a bad thing?' she had suggested cautiously.

'It's pretty weird at the very least. Are you thinking what I'm thinking, that your husband won't like it one little bit?'

'Yes, and bother them both. Let them find out for themselves.'

Thank goodness we can say this to each other, Cass had thought, trying to quell her dismay. Guy was quite capable of selling the Corrie without a second thought if this didn't suit him, and she had found herself filled with a great determination to hang on to it no matter what.

The time spent with Lindsay had been fruitful. Cass, turning south for the airport, knew she was deliberately turning to more positive thoughts before meeting Guy. Or was she just ready to see in a favourable light everything connected with the Scottish end of her new enterprise? No, the two days had been full of sound promise.

They had also been hard work. Lindsay was a reliable and conscientious person, supremely capable, but she was single-track in her approach and even between calls there had not been much light relief. But the whip round the relatively populated area had filled Cass with mouth-watering anticipation for the long miles of the north-west and the even more alluring prospect nearer home.

It had been Gina, dismissing potential male aggro as too boring to contemplate, full of enthusiasm for Cass's new undertaking and openly delighted that it would bring her to the Corrie more often, who had pointed out that there might be clients on the doorstep.

'All the big houses here take on extra people in the summer, just as you describe. At Riach itself there's lots more coming and going than there used to be. James Mackenzie lost his first wife, about five years ago I think, and had been living rather a hermit's existence, in spite of having small twin girls, but a year or so ago he married one of the Munros from Allt Farr, who already had a daughter almost in her teens. Now Joanna's expecting a baby, Ed said so the other day when he came to tell me to keep Tiree in because he was shifting sheep. Then at Allt Farr they let holiday cottages, and always take on student help in the summer, though I expect they're probably already there by now.'

'Probably, but the idea of Quickwork is to fill the gaps when plans fall through, when staff are ill or bored or decide they need a holiday before term starts – or realise they haven't touched their vac work.'

'I do know what you mean,' Gina had sighed. 'You couldn't employ any of my lot, could you, preferably in residential jobs so far away that they'd have to do their own washing?'

No use suggesting Gina could be a bit tougher with them at home. 'Any other ideas for local clients?'

'You might try Penny Forsyth at Alltmore. Or over in Glen Ellig there's Drumveyn with a biggish family. Or better still, there's Grianan, a small family-run hotel, very friendly and pleasant. There are lots of places, now I think about it. Let's go in and make a list.' Gina had got up eagerly, Nessa forgotten.

'We could have a jaunt round together perhaps,' Cass had suggested.

'Oh, how I'd love it. A day of not thinking about cooking or ironing or this wretched garden. Well, I love it really, but it does overwhelm me at times. We could have lunch ...'

'Steady on.'

But the prospect had enticed her as much as it had Gina, and she had tucked it away as a treat to be enjoyed when the hard graft had been put in with Lindsay.

Perhaps therein lay the seeds of guilt in her feelings for the cottage and the glen. She had plans that did not include Guy, and she intended to let Guy find out for himself that Gina's husband was his employee. And something else nagged at her, now that she was back in 'real life'. On Monday the telephone had been connected at the Corrie and she had not attempted to contact Guy; had felt a real reluctance to do so, as though to talk to him would be to let outside things intrude.

Outside things. Guy. That was appalling. Approaching the terminal she was seized with an almost panicky longing for him, for time together just as it had always been, with their own special, light, undemanding but satisfying touch. She was glad that for the next month commitments of various kinds would keep them both in London, in their shared familiar world, where they depended on each other yet maintained with the ease of long habit the delicate balance of their separate obligations and needs.

Chapter Nine

During those few weeks of hectic happy normality there threaded a feeling of relief which Cass did her best to ignore. She liked the life she and Guy shared. It wouldn't suit everyone, she knew. She wouldn't suit everyone. On a physical level it could still surprise her, alarm her almost, that Guy had chosen her, with her rangy height which matched his own. It had always seemed odd for a deeply competitive male. She knew what his previous girlfriends had been like, small, slight, sleek and chic. Reminders of them could rock her even now, and her self-confidence as far as her appearance was concerned remained paper-thin.

Guy, for his part, had seen too many of his friends marry lively, attractive girls, good company, competent at their jobs, who became very heavy in hand as wives and mothers, making confident claims on the time and attention of husbands, wanting to know when they would appear and the reason why when they didn't. That, if nothing else, Guy could not have endured.

As Cass and he ordered things, domestic matters hardly impinged. They were both organised and tidy, and the ultra-functional flat was cleaned twice a week by a semi-efficient and costly ghost. In the early days, soon after they moved into Chepstow Terrace, Cass had keenly ironed a couple of Guy's shirts. He had reverted without delay to the shirt service. As to food, they ate out or picked up something on the way home.

Breakfast didn't figure and they rarely had lunch in. The only trap was that when they entertained, which they enjoyed doing but with their separate schedules rarely managed, they were apt to discover basic ingredients missing or defunct.

Cass still hankered occasionally for the visual pleasure, the smells, the colour and the feeling of being closer to the natural origins of the food, which she had enjoyed in the mix of ethnic shops round the corner from the old flat.

'Well, now we're round the corner from Harrods,' Guy would point out.

Throughout this time, though in close touch with Lindsay and pleased by the response their initial marketing was producing, Cass refused to think about the Corrie. Sometimes, in spite of her good intentions, she would be caught unawares by simple longing for its peace, for sweet air, for the glen still tantalisingly unexplored, but she pushed the images aside as though they were some kind of temptation.

She had to spend a lot of time in the office as Diane was spending a couple of weeks with her brother in New Zealand, plus the usual 'exotic' stopovers en route. I pay her too much, Cass would think glumly, finding the day-to-day grind a lot less stimulating than it had been when she was starting up the agency four years ago.

Socially, she and Guy were busier than they had been for months, both enjoying the time spent together which in turn reflected on their sex life, returning it to an ardent level which, ironically, it had never reached since they were married.

In the middle of July they spent the traditional long weekend with Cass's family for her mother's birthday. Cass's brother Thomas and his wife ran a clinic for herbal medicine called Havenhill, near Stroud, and last year their mother had, to everyone's surprise, agreed to move into a flat in the main building. Cass had never believed either of her parents would leave London, though she had begged passionately throughout her childhood for a move back to Scotland, but when they retired within a few weeks of each other, after more than twenty shared busy years as GPs in the Finchley practice, the marriage had swiftly disintegrated. Her father had married again and was now living in Sweden, and her mother seemed happy in the Cotswolds, occupied with gardening and village affairs and reading in great indiscriminate draughts.

As the Aston Martin whispered westwards loaded with champagne and presents, an unsettling thought came to Cass. Her parents' marriage, which had always appeared to her so unshakeable and strong, had succeeded only when its foundation had been equal, interdependent work. There was an inference there she wasn't ready to examine, but it persisted on the edge of her consciousness all through the weekend, a vague discomfort which every so often would make her pause to check what was worrying her.

Roey was there, in excellent form since no dim hanger-on was taking up her energies, and various friends and family members turned up for the party in the still-beautiful drawing-room of the dignified house. Guy had never been entirely at ease at Havenhill, finding the family pace too slow and Thomas irritatingly bound up in his own tiny world. Cass sympathised on the latter point, for she and her bother, divided by a six-year age gap, had never been close, but she had naïvely hoped that with his new status as son-in-law, brother-in-law, Guy might on this occasion feel more relaxed. The opposite seemed true, she found sadly, as though it was only now dawning on him that he was formally connected with the family, committed to it. He didn't last till Monday as planned, but pleaded for release on Sunday evening, and Cass didn't make an issue of it.

The following weekend there was an elaborate garden party in Godalming, the golden wedding of friends of Guy's, who had been best man to their son.

The Saturday after that there was a much livelier wedding party on a barge on Marston Lock, and at lunch on the terrace of an Abingdon pub the next day two other friends announced their engagement. It was at this point, though she and Guy both enjoyed such parties, and it was good to have him home for so many of them, that Cass found herself too conscious of the wedding theme. It came as a shock to remember she was married herself. Somehow, still, it seemed she and Guy were marking time, that even in their present relaxed mood she, at least, was waiting for something to begin. Was she envious? She was horrified to find the word presenting itself. Certainly they had married for unromantic reasons. Sensible reasons. Sensible? More like cold-blooded, she thought, with an obscure feeling of having been defrauded as she saw the way the newly engaged couple were looking at each other. She threw bread into the water for a swan. At a swan, she realised with some shame.

But suddenly, with Diane back in the office, though wondering too often and too loudly why anyone ever came back to England at all, and with the crowded month almost over, Cass felt she could allow herself to look forward to being at the Corrie again. And once she had let the images in she couldn't wait to get there.

Then problems swam up on every side. Some dormant bug picked up in Bangkok or Hong Kong, or wherever Diane had felt obliged to support the tourist economy, now struck her down; the Norwich ear took a full-time job at no notice and phoned to say she was no longer available; and an au pair near Kidlington broke her leg. As she was a professional ski instructor at home in Norway during the winter this was more serious than at first appeared, and faced with hospital visits, an over-protective father and complicated insurance tangles, Cass saw her longed-for weekend at the Corrie slipping away.

To her surprise, Guy said he'd go alone. 'I really ought to show my face at Sillerton again.'

When had he shown it before? A totally new resentment swept Cass.

'There are several new plans and work has to be started the moment things quieten down in the autumn,' Guy went on. 'And there are things to be done at the cottage as well – putting in more power points for one.'

Cass buried instant possessiveness by trying to be pleased that he was interested enough to organise it, and promised herself a visit very soon. All the same, it was strange to see him off on his own, and she was forced to recognise that she regarded the Corrie very much as hers. Was that, as Guy teased her, because she felt her roots were there? Well, deep down she knew she did. There was something in the whole mood and feel of the place to which she responded.

Much as she had longed to be back, she was surprised by the excitement which gripped her as she left Muirend behind at last. Two months since she had been here. The garish sign at Sillerton briefly stirred an uncomfortable memory, but it was overtaken by speculation as to whether Guy and Laurie Fraser had discovered they were neighbours yet, and this led much more agreeably to the prospect of being with Gina again.

Cass hadn't seen Guy since he was here three weeks ago. He had stayed longer than she had expected and when he came home she had been in Kidlington, thankfully seeing off a tamed but discursive Norwegian father who owned a bookshop in Stavanger and was seizing his chance to air some peculiarly precious English. By the time Cass got back to London Guy was halfway to Oman and, to judge from the spew of panicky faxes which went on pleading for him till he arrived, looked likely to be there for some time.

Cass turned eagerly into the lane, noticing at the bend below the Corrie that the surface seemed rougher than she'd remembered it, as though heavier traffic than normal had used it recently. Then she was round the corner and before her there opened a scene of totally unexpected and brutal ravagement. A great bite was gouged out of the bank where the steep entrance had turned in. On its nearer side the line of hawthorns had been ripped out; on the other a third of the lawn had been eaten away. Concrete hard standing had been laid, from which concrete steps led up in a rigid curve. For a moment's floundering disorientation Cass thought she had somehow come up the wrong track. Shaking, dumbfounded, without even the wits to park in the new place, she got herself out of the car. A robust barricade of what she thought, dredging up the term as though a fact, any fact, would reduce her bewilderment, was called ranch fencing, ran round the remainder of the lawn. As she went clumsily up the new steps, distress and outrage filling her, her eyes not on her feet but on what new horrors she might find at the top, she saw that her clipped rough grass had been lifted wholesale and new turf unrolled in its place like a carpet.

'Fucking Surbiton,' she said aloud, in blind choking rage. 'He's turned it into fucking Surbiton.'

No more could you sprawl on the lawn and look through the bright spires of the lupins to the long fall of fields and river, the narrow gut of the glen spreading outwards as the hills smoothed into rolling moors above Muirend. I suddenly see what Muirend means, she thought, with a hysterical need to clutch at something, anything, except the devastation Guy had wrought on this drowsy little place, which had fitted as aptly into the landscape as the tumbling burn itself.

He hadn't turned that into some winsome grotto? Scarcely daring to look Cass crossed towards it, and saw that the rowans had been lopped to make room for the new fence; next year their blossom would no longer form a scented canopy above the speedwells and buttercups.

'Yes, well, don't get too poetic,' Cass said savagely aloud, forcing herself with bitter determination to subdue her rage.

Even so, she could hardly steady her hand to put the key into the lock. At the right of the long room, obliterating the covered fireplace with finality, a long (teak) built-in desk housed fax machine and answerphone, computer and printer.

He had to have those; you expected that. We always have

those. They will be a huge boon, for me too if I'm going to work up here sometimes. They are part of our lives; it would be absurd to object to them.

But I don't think I'd have put them there, a small voice wailed. I might have turned the little bedroom into a study, so that a door could be shut on all this.

Then you should have said so. Anyway, that could still be done. So let this one go, let it go.

In the kitchen she didn't at once see any changes. Outside its door the concrete paving had gone and stone slabs had been laid. Now that is better; you've got to admit that's better.

But all the time, in raw protest, unable to take it in, her mind kept turning back to the crude and disfiguring excavation below the house.

There was now a stone-built barbecue. Too much cement, perhaps, had been used to point it, but it was an excellent addition, no question of that. The rickety weathered gate to the hill had been replaced with a new one. It would weather in its turn. Then Cass saw something which, out of all the rest, for some inexplicable reason destroyed her resolve to be pragmatic. Between two rough leaning posts a sagging washing line had run. Cass had enjoyed seeing her shirts blowing there, had liked the softness of her towels and the smell of duvet cover and pillowcases after a day in the sun and wind, had been reminded of the top of the garden in Dalry where she used to help her mother to fold the sheets, pretending to flap each other away on the wind, before dropping them into the big wicker basket.

Posts and line had gone.

Going back into the kitchen, stony-faced, she saw that the washing machine she had bought had been replaced by a washer/dryer. What had Guy done with the original one? Chucked it away, she supposed. Given it to the plumber maybe. She went upstairs, into each room in turn. There was a television with video recorder in their room, a telephone by the bed. All right, no harm in any of that. In the bathroom a shower had been installed. Well, she preferred a shower herself. But the bathroom window looked out over the back garden; from here she could see the rough places in the grass where the washing line posts had been yanked out.

Tears oozed from her eyes, then spilled over. She leaned her forehead against the centre upright of the window and cried and cried.

You're crying about a washing line, she told herself in helpless incredulity. But she knew she wasn't. Something she had loved here had been uprooted with a ruthless hand; by the man she had married, by the man who was completely confident that she would view all these 'improvements' in the same light as he did, who had thought they would be a wonderful surprise for her when she arrived. Or had such an idea crossed his mind? Was this not just Guy shaping life to his own needs as he always did? Had he thought of her at all?

Hollow with disillusionment, she turned to splash cold water over her face. No water came from the tap.

Chapter Ten

No water came from any cold tap in the house. Running the hot ones would presumably only empty the tank so Cass didn't dare switch on the immersion heater. Or was there some sort of safety device which prevented that happening? She didn't know. Damn, what on earth could be wrong? Get a plumber. Cass tried vainly to remember the name of the one who had come to turn the water on when she had moved in.

Then with *Yellow Pages* in hand she checked. Was this really her only recourse, summoning help from Muirend, which would appear God knew when – it was Friday afternoon – without even attempting to work out the problem for herself? She applied her mind to more basic questions than she was accustomed to having to think about. Had the supply dried up? But the burn was still running, she knew that. Was it running into the tank on the hill, though, or bypassing it for some reason?

Abandoning *Yellow Pages,* she loped upstairs to change into jeans and sweatshirt. At least she knew where the tank was. Well, it wouldn't have taken much working out if she hadn't, she conceded, as she went out through the new gate in the fence and headed for the burn. Unless Guy has had this moved somewhere else too, a slightly hysterical voice suggested, and pushing down panicky thoughts, rare for her, about what she would do if no water was coming in, she realised how shaken she was by what he had done to this perfect little place. And how particularly she minded after what had seemed the greater closeness between them which she had found so good. Reaching the lip of the deep-carved corrie which gave the cottage its name, she leapt and slid carelessly down its bank of eroded turf, earth and loose stones.

As far as her uninformed investigations could tell her, all seemed well. The burn was low, but a steady flow was coming into the intake, which she checked was clear. Her ear to the sun-warmed slab, rough with dried lichen, which formed the lid of the tank and which she couldn't shift, she could hear the clear resonant tinkle of water falling into water, while below the tank the outlet ran briskly. So where did the pipe go after that? Not up the bank, clearly. Going down the burn, it was not difficult to work out the only line the water could take to reach the house. No ominous wet patches were visible as she followed it.

What next? The immersion heater filled from the main tank in the loft; did that have anything in it? She recognised that she was keeping her mind focused on this single immediate problem with a dull stubborn anger, deliberately holding at bay the deeper significance of the devastation Guy had created.

The cold tank in the loft – which wasn't floored and which presented some tricky problems in the cobwebby gloom, with its low rafters and random junk balanced on the joists – was full. Dirty, hot, annoyed with herself for not having a torch or any form of emergency lighting in the place, Cass let herself down the loft ladder and at last came to the obvious conclusion. The water had been shut off. While the shower was being put in, she supposed, and no one had turned it back on. With shame, she realised she should have thought of this first. All right, so she'd worked it out in the end, but where and how did she get the damned water running again?

To her grateful surprise two images clicked into place with ready clarity: a small, square, cast-iron lid with long grass round it, which she and Roey had been strictly forbidden to touch after they had posted several treasures down the dark mysterious hole below; and an implement among the tools in the garden shed at Dalry, seen a hundred times, a narrow iron bar with a spanner at the bottom and a crosspiece at the top. How extraordinary to remember them, but the big garden and outhouses had been her childhood world, familiar in all its minutiae, the element she had grieved most passionately to lose.

How useful though. Greatly cheered, Cass began to prowl round the Corrie then, disgusted at her stupidity, realised she only need look between burn and house. She was glad no one was there to watch her plod through these obvious steps.

She located the toby easily, since not surprisingly the nettles around it had already been flattened, but there was no sign of the water key anywhere. Doggedly she searched again, looking through the long grass behind the shed and along walls in case it had been tossed down somewhere. But it would be visible even so; it had been used in the last couple of weeks. Unless the Corrie didn't possess such an item and the plumber had used his own. Oh, damn him, and damn Guy.

No one answered the phone at the Mains. Cass let it ring and ring, sure Gina must be there, determined Gina should be there. She'd have to fetch Nessa soon. But Nessa wouldn't be back at school yet. Nor would the boys; so where were they? Too idle to pick up the phone? Or perhaps the whole family were away on holiday. No, surely Laurie couldn't get time off from Sillerton in the middle of the season? A waste of time to speculate anyway. She could still go up and see if a key was visible. No one would mind her borrowing it if she could find it.

There were several possible hiding places around the old steading. Seeing the vital object clearly in her mind Cass began her hunt with enthusiasm, but search as she might she was concentrating at ground level and never saw the key on its pegs on the back wall of the barn, neatly suspended in Laurie's orderly fashion beside the ladders slung below the eaves. The sunny stone-walled farmyard mocked her in sleepy afternoon quiet; she'd have even welcomed Tiree barking.

It would have to be Beverley, though whether the refined lifestyle of Sycamore Lodge would yield such a basic piece of equipment seemed questionable.

Cass took the straight line down the hill, remembering as she went that her car was still parked in the lane. Plenty of room now for anyone to get round her, she thought bitterly, not pausing.

At the bungalow the door of one empty garage was up, the neat garden shed padlocked, the house shut and screened from inquisitive eyes. Cass's heart sank at the prospect of another trawl round a dead Bridge of Riach. The alternative was to take the car and go up to Riach itself, or the farm further up the glen towards Allt Farr.

Then another possibility struck her. All she wanted was the essential key; armed with that surely she could manage the rest. Would Beverley's husband be out with her, or down in the workshop by the river which Gina had mentioned? But he was ill; would it be all right to disturb him? And how ill? Would he know what she was talking about, or would it merely land her in more delays and problems to ask him for help? But hadn't Gina said he restored furniture or did upholstery or something? So he couldn't be entirely helpless. And probably all he'd have to do was produce a key to the garden shed.

Making up her mind, Cass headed for the underpass created to save Riach stock crossing the new road, and went through its dark, sheep-smelling tunnel into the brilliant sunlight which filled the grassy curve in the loop of the river. Sheltered by a couple of big firs, rowan berries already bright against its grey walls, the old barn looked so quiet and lifeless that even as she walked towards it Cass decided she should have cut her losses and gone straight up to Riach. And was the water after all so urgent? She could have waited till Laurie Fraser or one of his sons came home. Even Gina might know what a water key looked like.

But she kept going across the uneven grass, thick with wildflowers, noting that down here the sound of the summer traffic was blanketed by the line of birches and hazels below the embankment, and overtaken in any case as she neared the water by the rumble of the river shouldering its way though the gorge beneath the old bridge. As she followed grassed-over ruts round the end of the building, she saw that its big doors were standing open to the river and the summer air, revealing a busy workbench along the back wall and on one side a toppling collection of abused furniture – legless tables, chairs with ancient coverings decayed to fragile ribbons, overturned sofas with innards spilling out like soldiers on some appalling battlefield.

In a broad bar of dust-dancing light in the central space, a man was bending to run a hand over the saddle seat of a hoop-back Windsor chair, an almost listening look of concentration on his face. As Cass watched he straightened up as though satisfied, nodding. He was a big, big man, perhaps in his early forties, barrel-chested and broad-shouldered, giving an impression of strength rather than excess weight. He was wearing heavy workman's jeans and a shepherd's-plaid shirt, both pale-furred with sawdust, which also whitened the front of his curly short-cropped hair. But what struck Cass most was his air of calm, his quiet movements, giving even in that swift second an impression of contained contentment. His skin looked brown and healthy, the skin of an outdoor man, and he clearly wasn't the person she was looking for. This man was no convalescent, belonging to quite a different world from that of Beverley's strained gentility. An assistant her husband – what was his name? Richard – employed? Or perhaps he owned the barn and let Richard Scott help him, as therapy? There certainly seemed to be plenty of work on hand. But whoever he was, and whether or not he had access to the Sycamore Lodge shed, this competent-looking character would produce some answer to her problem, Cass was sure.

She moved forward. The man had turned away to his workbench and had his back to her. I'd jump a mile if someone walked in on me down here on a quiet afternoon, Cass thought. Beverley would shriek her head off.

'Excuse me. Hello.'

The man turned quietly. Perhaps if you were that big you didn't find much to alarm you in any encounter. A square face, eyes crinkled up against the light, surveyed Cass calmly.

'Good afternoon,' he responded. 'Not many customers find their way this far. What can I do for you?'

Courteously said, but was there a hint there that customers weren't meant to appear uninvited? Voice and manner didn't suggest a local tradesman. Intrigued, and deciding no matter who he was he was very attractive, Cass said hastily, 'I was actually looking for Richard Scott. I'm a neighbour, from the Corrie, the cottage up the hill, and I was hoping to borrow a key to turn my water on.'

The big man regarded her silently for a moment, as though weighing the validity of this request. Then turning to put down the soft cloth he had picked up, he said, 'I think we could do something about that.'

'Do you have access to—?'

But now that she was closer to it Cass's eye was caught by the beauty of the chair he had been working on. 'Have you just stripped this down? Are you going to stain it next?'

'I made it.' His voice was deep, and slow like all his movements.

'Made it? It looks at least two hundred years old to me.'

'Good. And that dates the style pretty accurately.' He was evidently amused.

'Totally uneducated guess,' Cass assured him. 'I haven't a clue about this sort of thing.' How Gina would love to be let loose in here. 'It's very handsome, but those rails underneath are a bit unusual, aren't they?' she added, stepping back to have a better look.

He tipped the chair back. 'Stretchers,' he said. 'Cow's horn, these are known as.'

'What a perfect description.'

'Most of the old terms are satisfyingly simple.' Cass saw him give the chair a tiny pat as he set it on its feet again. 'Ladder-back, comb-back, spoon-back, all everyday objects.'

Perhaps his unhurried calm had infected her, but Cass felt she could happily spend hours in this peaceful place, patterned with blocks of sunlight, cut off from all outside sounds except the voice of the river.

'And how about this emergency of yours?' The deep voice was mildly amused.

'Oh, yes, my emergency. You wouldn't happen to know if the Scotts have a water key, would you? Or where it might be kept? Oh, God, though, do they all fit, or will it be a different size? I hadn't thought of that.'

He said nothing, just walked down the barn with measured stride and in silence went back with her through the underpass, and led her into the garden of the bungalow via a gate Cass hadn't noticed. There, without hesitating or altering his pace in the slightest degree, he crossed the gravel to the shed, taking a set of keys out of his pocket as he went.

He must be Richard Scott. He couldn't be anyone else. But this man wasn't ill. Or was his silence, his failure to introduce himself, a sign of something not quite normal? Watching as he undid the padlock Cass found she couldn't drum up any apprehension of any kind. It didn't take him long to find what he was looking for.

'Oh, thank goodness,' Cass exclaimed.

He appeared not to see her outstretched hand and, still without speaking, started towards the road.

'I'll be able to manage, I'm sure,' Cass said, discovering as she followed him that, long as her legs were, his even stride took some keeping up with, a rare experience and not a disagreeable one. 'Please don't bother to come all the way up. I don't want to take you away from your work.' It occurred to her, though not apparently to him, that he had not only left the shed open, but the workshop too.

But he went steadily on, obviously seeing no need for discussion, with an air, which Cass couldn't seriously object to, of unstoppably doing whatever he intended to do, at whatever pace he chose to do it. There seemed little point in arguing. If anyone could sort out practical difficulties, this giant of a man patently could.

'It's not the usual time of year to have the water turned off,' he remarked as they came to the bend below the Corrie.

Back with a rush came a vision of the horrors waiting ahead. 'My husband – we – have had some work done.' Cass could hear her voice rough with emotions that couldn't be released, anger, distress and resentment churning again, while deeper still lurked more frightening implications she didn't dare think about yet. If the man at her side registered any of this he gave no sign.

Nor did he react at seeing the raw, clawed-out space in the bank, the mangled remnants of the hawthorn hedge, the new ribbed concrete, other than to say without emphasis, 'That will give you more room to turn.'

'I hate it!' Cass burst out in spite of herself. 'It's hideous, it's all wrong. And it wasn't even necessary.'

He paused, turning to look at her, frowning slightly, taking his time to study her face. 'You hadn't agreed on it?'

'I didn't even know it was being done! I arrived today, this afternoon, and discovered it, and lots of other things besides. Oh, I know it was all done with the best of intentions. I *know* that,' she insisted, ashamed of having given Guy away to a stranger, 'and most of it's very sensible and a great improvement . . .'

He nodded, as though understanding it would be better to ask no more for the present, and led the way up the concrete steps and round the corner of the house.

'Perhaps I should see how it works,' Cass said, as he lifted off the iron lid.

He handed her the key and stepped back. It was tricky to fit it over the tap, but eventually she located the spot. Then she found it impossible to budge the key, not even sure after a couple of moments of struggle which way it ought to go. Panting and scarlet-cheeked, she did her best. She despised dainty little females who wouldn't put a bit of beef into things. Also it seemed important to establish that she could have done this for herself if the necessary tool had been to hand.

Without the slightest movement of masculine readiness to brush her attempts aside and take over, her friendly rescuer watched patiently.

'No good,' she admitted at last. 'Can't shift it.'

She relinquished the key, wrists aching, palms red and pitted with rust flecks. Two gigantic hands descended where hers had been and without any visible output of effort the key sweetly turned one quarter turn.

'I hate you,' Cass said, her eyes disappearing to blue slits of amusement as they met the carefully bland darker eyes to which, in such a novel and agreeable way, she had to look up.

'I had a bit of a struggle myself,' he said politely and Cass laughed, something which an hour ago would have seemed very far away indeed.

'Oh yes? Look, I can't tell you how grateful I am. Now that we've got water again, how about a cup of tea? I was longing for one when I arrived, and by now that feels as if it was hours ago. And I'm sorry, I haven't introduced myself. Cass Montgomery.'

She held out her hand, conscious as she did so that she was glad he wasn't going at once.

Propping the key against the porch the man took it in a big warm clasp. 'Rick Scott,' he said.

Chapter Eleven

Cass had guessed who he was, but felt momentarily confused just the same. It was difficult to reconcile this relaxed, unhurried man with her image of Beverley's mysterious husband, who needed occupational therapy and had to be cared for and protected, and worse, kept out of sight. This was one of the sanest, most together people she had ever met. His whole aura was one not only of immense calm, but of immense competence. Coming up the lane just now she had felt quite certain that whatever needed to be done he could and would do it. His very size and strength made nonsense of the picture she had formed of him. Also, she was conscious of an inner protest. This man and the little, tripping, empty-headed Beverley, with her petulant mouth and measuring eyes, didn't match up. Physically, it was impossible to visualise them together, the bear-like bulk and the dapper figure with its daffodil hair and silly jewellery and carefully held-in stomach.

I don't like this, Cass decided, then, disconcerted by the discovery, hastily pulled herself together. But not quickly enough. The square, composed face watching hers became expressionless. 'Don't worry, I'm harmless enough,' he said with an irony he managed to keep free of bitterness. 'But if you'd rather I didn't come in . . .'

Cass's cheeks flamed. 'I'm sorry. I was just startled. I hadn't realised you were Beverley's husband. I'd heard you were ill. I mean, you didn't seem—'

'Or mad?' His eyes would not let hers evade his, and his sardonic tone gave her a glimpse of a world of feelings she could hardly guess at. Her own embarrassment didn't matter. Meeting his eyes, Cass mentally took a deep breath.

'Please,' she said quietly, 'won't you come in?'

His features relaxed and a faint smile appeared. 'You're right,' he said. 'Let's start again. I've got a bit out of the habit of social niceties lately. My own fault. Solitude has become too attractive, and once you go down that route it's hard to return.'

But Rick had his own reasons for not wanting to go yet. He had been appalled to see what had been done at the Corrie, always hating the havoc unsympathetic hands could wreak in an environment whose beauty was being eroded at fearful speed. But he had also recognised Cass's distress, and her reference to other changes made him want to save her from going in alone to face them.

'Perhaps we should at least make sure the water's on,' he said easily, following her into the kitchen.

'Success.' Cass beamed at him over her shoulder as she ran the tap. 'A new shower has appeared over the bath so I suppose the plumber had to shut the water off while he was doing the work.'

'Bob Henderson.' Rick looked around him. The kitchen had been smartened up. Beverley had dragged him up to look over the house when it was for sale. Sheer curiosity, of course; she would never have dreamt of living in such a simple place.

'How do you know that's who it was?' Cass asked.

He smiled. 'I saw his van. You can't imagine the glen not knowing which plumber you employ?'

'Well, it's more than I do,' Cass said, and Rick liked the unfussed tone, though he observed that her voice became carefully casual as she added, 'Guy organised all this.'

'Henderson's not the man I'd have recommended, I must say. I hope he made sure you've enough head of water for a shower. And knowing him he'd probably lost his own water key somewhere along the line, so helped himself to yours.'

'He must have taken it by accident, surely?' Do I want everyone here to be nice guys, Cass mocked herself.

'Accident or not, he forgot to open the cock again before he took the key out. I think we'd better make sure you get it back. I'll give him a ring for you.'

Cass stood by the boiling kettle testing a feeling of uncomplicated pleasure. But Guy had thought he was looking after her too. It was essential, and only fair, to keep that clear in her mind. In fact, before she saw him again, she must do some serious work on preparing a positive reaction to what he'd done.

'He'll send it back on tomorrow's mail van,' Rick reported. 'Said he was going to anyway. Hmm. He didn't have a lot to say for himself when I asked how he thought you were going to manage tonight.'

'Richard, thanks for helping so much. It was good of you to do that.'

'Rick. Now, what else has been done to the house? Are you going to show me?'

'I suppose it's not really much to get upset about, compared to the outside,' Cass was able to say by now. Following Rick as he carried the tray into the sitting-room she could hardly remember what she'd minded about so much. She certainly wasn't going to confess to this equable man that she had wept over the disappearance of a clothesline.

'I suppose it was a bit of a shock to find the hardware installed,' she temporised. 'It looks so incongruous in here, particularly with that cat's-cradle of leads all over the floor. But it will be as useful for me as for Guy. I was just being silly.'

'You'll work from home? What is it that you do?'

There seemed a lot to tell him and Cass hardly noticed when he led her back to the subject of the torn garden, knowing that mattered to her most, and listened with scarcely a word as she released at last some of her distress at the sight of it.

But Cass learned little about him. He didn't want to talk about his illness, or about moving to Glen Maraich.

'It suited our needs at the time,' he said briefly, and Cass asked no more, though she still found it hard to imagine him with Beverley. Not only did it seem an unlikely partnership in physical terms, but it was hard to imagine him in such a setting as Sycamore Lodge. Yet it was his home; it must be what he and Beverley had chosen and liked.

Rick parried her interest in his present way of life with quiet non-answers. 'The barn's an ideal workshop ... Yes, there's always plenty to do ...'

Yet when the imperative blowing of a horn out in the lane broke across their talk Cass knew she had found it completely satisfying.

'Gina or somebody wanting to get by, I expect,' she said. 'Don't go. I've only got to move the car.' Gina could have got round it in fact – though perhaps that wouldn't have been such a good idea.

'I've taken up too much of your time.' Rick was on his feet.

How good it felt to be topped by inches. 'You've applied excellent therapy,' Cass told him gratefully. 'I shouldn't have let it get to me so badly when I saw the garden, it will all grow over in time. It was only because I loved the place so much as it was.'

He nodded, but his relaxed mood had vanished. 'I'll let myself out by the back way,' he said, and the questions about his state of mind and his reclusiveness swarmed back. But he wasn't a man on whom you tried to impose your will. As Cass stood at the kitchen door, sorry to see him go, Gina passed the window of the long room.

'How lovely that you're back,' she exclaimed, tumbling in smiling, hair everywhere. She scraped a handful of it from her face and threw it over her shoulder as though she thought it was unattached and would be gone for good. Heavy and unmanageable, it slithered straight back again. 'I could probably squeeze past, but it was too good an excuse to come in and say hello. How long are you up for?'

'Only till Monday, I'm afraid, but we hope to be back for a week or so later in the month.' In spite of regretting that Gina's arrival had driven Richard – Rick – away, Cass felt a big answering smile spread over her face at the sight of her.

'Oh, good. That'll be—'

'And don't even think of squeezing past,' Cass went on firmly. 'I'll move the car. I think I've learned that much. Have you got time for tea?'

'Not really, but I'll have some anyway.'

'No family abandoned in the car?'

'Family, what's that? No, only Tiree.'

'Well, we're not having him in.'

'I think we'll have to, or there'll be nothing to eat for the weekend.'

It was fun – simple, immediate and natural – to be with Gina again. It was even a pleasure to be exuberantly greeted by Tiree, though Cass didn't have much faith in his powers of memory and suspected he was just glad to be out of the car.

'You've decided to make a garden then?' Gina enquired as they went in.

A deliberately non-negative question, Cass knew, and felt affection for her deepen. 'Not as far as I'm concerned,' she confessed ruefully. 'It's a complete nightmare.' But now she could laugh about it, wail about it, be as wrathful and outspoken as she liked.

As Rick had done (and Cass, careful to preserve his privacy as she knew he would have wished, didn't mention his visit), Gina asked with a frown. 'A shower? Upstairs? Have you got the pressure?'

Cass put down the teapot she had refilled. 'Perhaps we'd better find out.'

The shower produced a spatter of reluctant drops which after a minute or so coalesced to a trickle.

Cass and Gina stared at it and at each other and began to laugh.

'Who on earth did you get in to do that?' Gina demanded, vainly twiddling the controls.

'Someone called Henderson.' About to say, 'And the fool went off with the water key as well,' Cass checked. The episode of the afternoon was private and special, not to be shared even with Gina.

'Bob Henderson?' Gina squawked. 'Oh, he's hopeless. He was probably drunk. He's had to start up on his own because no one will employ him. He did a job down at the Cluny Arms in Kirkton and only connected the hot water or something and scalded all the guests. No, Wally Petrie's the man. I'll give you his number. He personally knows every inch of every pipe in the entire glen. He'll have to put in a pump. Your poor bathroom's going to end up in a bit of a mess.'

Guy, what have you done to me?

Though she did her best to be matter-of-fact about them, the depredations to the little house she already loved made for a restless night, and by five thirty Cass gave up trying to sleep. She got up, made tea and went back to bed, but the frustrated, almost betrayed, thoughts persisted. She couldn't read, couldn't relax. Well, she wanted to explore, didn't she? What better time to begin?

She was startled to find the smooth new turf of the lawn white with ground frost, though it was only early September, and she could smell autumn in the air as she crossed the lane and went down the field below, an undefined but firm impulse making her avoid the sight of Sycamore Lodge.

As she reached the field of still-ripening barley by the river a movement caught her eye. A pair of roe, alert heads raised from the bearded ears, had spotted her. One gave a harsh bark and as they began to move off in staccato leaps she saw another, two-thirds their size, bound to join them. This year's calf, she supposed, watching as they bounced through the golden expanse towards the hill dyke, their coats a rich red-brown after the weeks of summer feeding. They vanished behind a group of stunted birches where odd branches were already yellow. Cass felt a lump in her throat from sheer delight at being alone in this empty world to see such a sight. She longed to share it, and without surprise found Rick Scott in her mind, and knew she had found with him the same instant, certain rapport she had been so sure of with Gina. Smiling, she walked on.

A mile or so below the Corrie she left the river and turned up into the dazzle of morning sunshine on the flank of the hill. She was warm enough as she reached the watershed an hour later. This was higher than she had been yet, and the view was spectacular. To her left, the great hills of the west had swung into view, mile upon mile of them; to her right, she could look down into narrow Glen Ellig. She felt an absurd desire to get inside this landscape, to belong to it, be absorbed into it.

Setting off along the ridge, she felt she could float through the miles. September sunshine was warm under a pale sky dredged with cirrus which feathered to nothing as the morning passed. The colours didn't spell autumn yet, more end-of-summer, the first fronds of bracken turning, heather still purple. Cass felt consumed by a longing not to miss any of it, not a day or an hour, but to see every gradation of colour and change. It would be impossible, of course, but perhaps in time she would come to know the glen in all its moods.

With interest, she noticed how often and naturally the thought of Rick surfaced as she went. He had intrigued her, there was no question of that, but not merely because he was so different from the image she had formed of him, or so different from the way Beverley, via Gina it must be said, had represented him. In spite of his reticence there had been a sense of peace in being with him, of time slowing, of unimportant things taking on a truer perspective. There had been comfort from a stranger, and it had not seemed odd at the time, any more than thoughts of that same stranger seemed out of keeping with her delight in these sunny heights.

It was mid-morning by the time the Mains of Riach lay below her, the sight of the Corrie further down the hill rekindling a spark of rebellion she couldn't avoid. Would Gina be busy? But she had urged Cass to look in whenever she liked.

How truly perfect, she thought as she crossed the deserted, sun-baked yard, glimpsing through the gate of the walled garden bright masses of Michaelmas daisies, asters and montbretia. Perfect to walk out of the cottage as the impulse took her, free to go where she liked in this breath-taking beauty, not meeting a soul in all those miles, and then to come to this friendly house, confident of her welcome. And of being given sustenance, she supplemented hopefully.

As she let the knocker fall she heard the piano. Music meant little to Cass, tone-deaf as she was, but this torrent of sound seemed to her brilliant and amazing, and something more – disturbed and seeking in some way that made her wish, frowning, that she hadn't knocked at all.

But Tiree, who liked music even less than she did, had been covering his ears in the hall, hard against the door which he considered should never have been shut in the first place, and the bang of the knocker came as glorious deliverance. He bayed with uninhibited relief and the sound of playing broke off abruptly.

Chapter Twelve

Cass had never seen Gina when she had just spent time at the piano. There was a drugged look in her eyes and about her movements, and though she made a tremendous effort to be welcoming, indeed seemed almost grateful that Cass had come, her responses to what was said were sluggish and disconnected.

'Look, are you sure you want to be interrupted?' Cass asked, guilty for having dropped in, her hopes for a late breakfast fading as Gina asked three times in succession whether she wanted tea or coffee, then turned with the coffee jar in her hand having evidently forgotten the answer yet again. 'I can look in later, or you could come down to the Corrie when you—'

'No. *No!*' Gina interrupted violently, then said quickly, with a jerky brushing movement of her hand as though to obliterate that, 'I'm sorry, Cass, I didn't mean to snap at you. I'm delighted you've come, truly. Just give me a minute or two. I'm always like this when I've been playing. I just sat down to – oh, no, that can't possibly be the time. It can't be!'

She looked so distressed that Cass asked in concern, 'Were you supposed to be somewhere? Don't let me keep you if—'

'I'm not going anywhere,' Gina cut across her words again. 'Not doing anything. No meals to cook even, if you can believe that.' She made an attempt to sound cheerful, but the result was disturbingly hollow.

'Gina, what's wrong?' Cass took the coffee jar from her unresisting hand, spooned granules into the mugs, then put her palm to the Aga kettle Gina had been about to use. Lukewarm. Cass filled the electric kettle and switched it on, while Gina stood acquiescent, taking no notice of what she was doing.

'Do you mind if I scrounge a biscuit? I've been walking. It's such a glorious day.' Cass turned to the likeliest looking cupboard.

Gina woke up at this. 'Cass, I'm sorry, I'm sorry. I'm hopeless when I've been playing, I can never come out of it straightaway. Wait a minute, there's cake, or would you like some toast – or how about a bacon roll if you're really hungry?'

'Now you're talking.' Cass thought a little practical activity might do Gina no harm. 'How about you, have you eaten?'

'I don't think I have,' Gina replied vaguely, shaking her head as though to clear it and sending a big tortoiseshell comb clattering against the fridge. 'Damn, where did that go?' she demanded in a more ordinary tone, blinded.

'That hair of yours has a life of its own.' Cass retrieved the comb before Tiree could get to it.

'It only stays out of the way if I put a really heavy band on it, but then it drags my scalp half off and is so tidy I don't feel like me any more,' Gina lamented, sounding to Cass's relief much more relaxed.

'Well, it would be a crime to cut if off, which is the only alternative,' Cass said, putting mugs on the table. 'Wow, that bacon smells good.'

'Nessa won't come home,' Gina said, sweeping her hair back with her forearm and ramming in the comb with ferocity.

'But where is she?' Cass asked after a blank fraction of a second, pausing with her bacon roll a couple of inches from her mouth. This sounded so final and dramatic.

'At her father's, in Lancaster. She was supposed to come back two weeks ago, to get ready for term starting.' Cass remembered that Scottish schools went back earlier than English ones. 'I phoned this morning, to check her train time, but Clifford's not sending her back. He says a few days off can't do her any harm. But it's so bad for her, not only missing school, but knowing we're arguing about it and that her father's overriding what I say.'

'But he can't do that, can he?' Cass wasn't sure. Nessa's relationship with her father, the state of play between Gina and her ex-husband, were areas they had never touched on. She wanted to help but dreaded intruding.

'Well, I suppose technically he can. I mean, I never insisted on any rules about custody or anything.'

Cass could imagine it. 'But no parent can keep a child out of school,' she said.

'But don't you see,' said Gina, lifting tear-filled eyes, her chin trembling, 'it's not that he's keeping her, it's that she doesn't want to come home.'

'Oh, Gina.' Cass was moved by her harrowed look. 'How can you know that? Surely Nessa wouldn't—'

'She hates everything here,' Gina broke out passionately. 'She hates the place and being miles away from everything, and she says I'm always doing things for the boys that I don't do for her. And she fights with Laurie all the time, and she despises and loathes me, I know she does. She can't bear the way I'm always late and disorganised, and the way the house looks. She's so tidy herself, just like her father, and I simply don't know what to do about any of it. I've tried and tried and everything I do just makes things worse ...' And Gina laid her head down on the table, the comb fell into her plate and a swathe of hair spread round it with the inexorable weight of water poured from a bucket. 'Oh, Gina, you poor darling.' Cass pulled a stool close and put an arm round the shaking shoulders. 'Come on, tell me what brought this on. What's been happening?'

'I shouldn't dump all this on you,' Gina protested, sitting up but looking weary and defeated.

'I've got all day. In fact, I've got till about half past eight on Monday morning. Unless there's anything you have to be doing?'

Gina managed a watery half smile but when she answered, 'There's no one here,' fresh tears spilled out. 'I was expecting Nessa to be back, and the boys both said they'd be home this weekend, and Steve was going to bring two friends with him, so I've got in masses of stuff, the biggest leg of pork you ever saw because that's their favourite, and now none of them are coming. And Laurie has a prize-giving and dinner at the clubhouse and I wouldn't go because of its being Nessa's first night back and he was furious because it's important. But when I phoned to say that I could go now he said the table's all made up, and though of course that's rather a blessing because it's the last thing in the world I feel like doing, I do feel terribly guilty about it. And then all that food ... Oh, God, what am I talking about food for? What on earth does food matter? Tiree can have the lot for all I care. But I'd so looked forward to seeing Nessa. I've missed her so much ...'

'Oh, Gina.' Cass had tears in her own eyes as she hugged the well-covered shoulders and let Gina talk out her raw disappointment and hurt.

'But how selfish I'm being. You were starving, and I haven't even given you the chance to eat your roll. It must be cold by now – shall I do another?'

'No, no, it's fine.' Cass couldn't face the whole process beginning again. 'But look, I've had an idea. Why don't we take off for the day, just the two of us? Have a pub lunch somewhere?' She recalled Gina's enthusiasm at the suggestion once before, as though for her such a piece of mundane routine would be an unaccustomed treat.

'You're just having breakfast,' Gina pointed out, but already sounding ready to be persuaded.

'Won't make any difference to me,' Cass said, disposing of her roll with a despatch Tiree himself might have been proud of. 'Come on, you think of somewhere where as a first priority we can sit outside, and where as a second the food's edible.'

'And we can take Tiree,' Gina added, cheering up with astonishing speed.

'Oh, God, must we?'

Gina giggled. 'Leave all this stuff. It would be marvellous to go out. I never have the chance just to buzz off on a whim.'

It did cross Cass's mind to wonder what kept Gina pinned to the house day in and day out, but it wasn't the moment to ask.

'But are you sure you don't want to be at the cottage?' Gina remembered to enquire as she rattled plates and mugs together and shifted them a couple of yards to the worktop and left them there.

'Plenty of time for that.' Cass recognised with a pang that she was glad of the chance to put off for still longer the necessity of facing the ugliness of its new scars. But she was careful not to let the conversation swing away from Gina. She guessed that Gina had a lot more unburdening to do.

'Everywhere will be busy,' Gina remembered as they went out to the car. 'It's Saturday.'

'We'll just make them busier then,' said Cass, who hadn't yet acquired the local dislike, resentment even, of busy pubs crammed with strangers enjoying themselves.

Sitting in the unkempt garden of the Cluny Arms on the hillside above Kirkton, where there were more seedheads than flowers in the borders and a couple of greedy ponies hung over the fence being fed haddock and chips and Mars Bars, Cass gently drew Gina out to tell her what had caused that storm of tears.

'You must think I'm hopeless,' Gina said, taking a solacing gulp of wine. Cass reconciled herself to driving the Subaru home. 'Every time you come to the house I'm in floods of tears.'

'It had occurred to me.'

'But I'm not really a crier,' Gina assured her rather wildly. 'I promise you I'm not. At least I never was.'

'It's about Nessa, isn't it? She's at the root of it all?'

'I sometimes think she'll never forgive me for breaking up the family. That's how she sees it.'

'But did you? Was it you?'

'I suppose in the sense that I didn't make Clifford happy and he looked elsewhere.'

'He looked elsewhere? Then why isn't Nessa blaming him?'

'Oh, she could see how unsatisfactory I was, unsatisfactory in her father's eyes, I mean. He likes everything to be so meticulous, just as she does, despising muddles and scrambles and disasters.'

Which husband are we talking about here? Cass wondered, somewhat surprised to think Gina might have made the same mistake twice, for she had heard her say all these things about Laurie. But Cass held her peace. Around them tables emptied, shouting children were dragged from the lop-sided swing, a few more ketchup-stained paper napkins blew into the snowberry bushes, glasses and coffee cups were left unheeded, and Gina in an incoherent but grateful tide poured out her woes.

The tone of her tale was far from criticism or complaint. The day-to-day rub seemed to be that in an effort to please Laurie Gina tried to do all she could to look after Steve and Andy, and that when she turned to Nessa for the help a teenage daughter could be expected to give there were explosions of resentment about unfairness. Underlying this Gina was quite capable of seeing her lack of self-confidence with the boys, who, not at an age where a new stepmother was particularly relevant in their lives, never bothered to meet her halfway. She openly admitted her inability to steer an even-handed course through these stormy waters, but listening to her willingness to accept the blame, all Cass could see was blatant abuse on the part of all three males. Why didn't that husband of hers put his foot down? But he sounded worse than his sons. And the first husband had apparently treated her in the same way. Why had these two efficiency-mad men, as Gina represented them, chosen a casual, artistic, untidy woman with no sense of time, with whom, as far as Cass could see, neither had shared any interests at all? Then Cass looked at the soft curves of Gina's generous body, the wonderful texture of the pale skin, the amazing hair and the sweetness of her smile, and knew the question was ridiculous.

They pieced together a good deal of the background of their lives that afternoon, Gina drinking a lot of white wine in the process, the September sunshine soft and yellow, the ponies drifting away as the lunch supply dried up and drifting back for shortbread and digestive biscuits as teas began. Tiree dug a hole under a plum tree then disappeared for some time. When he came back he was very hot and had a guilty air. Both Cass and Gina hoped earnestly they would never find out where he had been.

But though Cass learned about Gina's childhood in Haddington, a period in Exeter where her father lectured on the history of art, the years in Lancaster when she was married to Clifford, and how after their divorce she had lived with her mother in Auchterarder and met Laurie when he was working at Gleneagles, Cass told in return only about Dalry. To talk about London brought Guy too close. She had not even begun to sort out her reactions to what he had done at the Corrie, or, more vitally, what those reactions had revealed.

She did her best the next morning to examine the question honestly. She and Gina had whiled away several hours at the Cluny Arms, till the sun had disappeared and abruptly they had been shivering, with no jackets or even sweaters to put on, bundling hastily into the car and racing for home. As Cass had been driving it had been natural to go in when they reached the Mains, and almost without a pause in the conversation they had lit a fire in the sitting-room and gone on talking and drinking wine. After a time, though not able to do much with a leg of pork, they had broached the supplies Gina had laid in and had rather a splendid supper.

Now Cass made herself explore, inch by inch, the changed character of the Corrie garden, studying with pinched face the raw, new-turned, stony earth along the fence which Guy obviously intended to be borders. We should have talked about this, Cass protested. That's what hurts. It wasn't discussed or shared. And there, no longer to be dodged, was the fundamental question. Could Guy share anything, properly and openly? Did they truly share anything? It was a bleak moment, as though their whole busy, smoothly flowing life together, which Cass had believed so contented, so suited to their individual temperaments, was suddenly in doubt.

When the phone rang she thought it would be Guy and felt jolted and unready to talk to him, further from him than she could ever remember being. But it was Gina, groaning about the state of her head but otherwise in good form once more.

'I've been lifting potatoes and they're absolute beauties. Could you use some? I'm going to take some to Nancy and Beverley. Do you want to come with me?'

Cass would not have confessed to anyone her sensation of being rescued. Introspection was an unprofitable game, she decided, going down to lean on the dyke and wait for Gina. Cass liked things to be peaceful and uncomplicated, people to be easy-going and accommodating and kind to each other. She enjoyed exactly the sort of simple pleasure to be found in walking down the lane with Gina, leaving a bulging carrier bag against Beverley's fence meanwhile, pausing as they passed Riach Gate Lodge to speak to Ed Cullane, on his back under a piece of junk in car shape which looked as though it hadn't passed an MOT for the last ten years, then going over the bridge to be shown round Nancy Clough's garden and given terrible coffee and still-warm gingerbread in her compost-smelling, plant-ramping back porch.

As Gina activated the irritating door chimes at Sycamore Lodge, Cass wondered if they would see Rick, noting with objective interest how much she hoped to. Would he be in his workshop, or would Beverley exact the Sunday morning rites of car washing and lawn mowing?

With an anxious afterthought Gina peered into the bag of potaotes. 'I hope I gave Nancy the right ones.'

'What's the difference?'

'Beverley's have to be washed. If you take her earthy ones she says they're nicer in Tesco's.'

'Why bother then?' Cass very reasonably asked.

'Oh, that silly thing of not wanting to waste stuff I've grown, I suppose.'

And wanting to share good things with other people, Cass mentally added, smiling at her affectionately as the door opened.

'I've just done the living-room, you'd better come into the kitchen,' Beverley greeted them, her glance raking Cass's man-sized sweater and well-worn jeans, and settling with special disfavour on her boots, which still bore traces of garden inspections. Gina Beverley ignored, snatching the potatoes from her almost indignantly.

Did she regard them as an insulting handout? Cass wondered, then forgot the question in awed delight at the sight of the kitchen. It was almost enough to make her forget the hope of glimpsing Rick. From wrought-iron vegetable racks to British racing green kickstep, from electric copper kettle to the hob covers discreetly concealing the prosaic function of the cooker rings, this was the kingdom of the absurd.

'I was just about to have my little break,' Beverley admitted grudgingly, bundling Gina's offering out of sight so that its uncouthness should not mar the streamlined perfection of her citadel. 'It's covered by my RDA,' she added defensively.

'Your RDA?' Gina's voice already sounded wavery.

'Oh, really, Gina, my recommended daily allowance. You'd better move the plants aside if that's where you've decided to sit. I was trying out my new leafshine wipes and I think they've improved my aphelandra no end, don't you? Oh and, though I know you don't worry about such things nearly as much as you should, I've bought you a little present.'

Trotting briskly in the happy conviction of performing a worthy act, she disappeared briefly, returning with a varnished wooden object in the form of a curved arm sticking up from a round base, which she put proudly on the table in front of Gina.

'Thanks, Beverley.' Gina turned it round cautiously to see if another angle would offer a clue. 'What is it?' she mouthed at Cass, as with satisfied dabbing movements Beverley smoothed a cloth over the tray she proposed to carry five feet to the table.

'Search me,' Cass mouthed back, her blue eyes sparkling in a manner which made Gina look hastily away.

'It's very kind of you, Beverley,' she said earnestly, as Beverley poured out pale pink herbal tea from a silver-plated teapot. 'But I'm not *exactly* sure what it is.'

'Oh, honestly, Gina, you're so out of touch,' Beverley cried with unconcealed triumph, offering Cass rice-cakes with a gesture so restrained that Cass felt discharged of the obligation to take one. 'It's a banana tree, of course. If you put bananas in your fruit basket the ethylene gas they emit makes the other fruit ripen too quickly. I thought everyone knew that.'

'Did you see the tartan microwave plate warmers?'

'And the Ingenious Nifty Lifter?'

'The last time I was there she was making an embroidered bread roll holder with pockets.'

Gina and Cass went reeling up the lane.

'We shouldn't laugh about her.'

'No, you're quite right, we shouldn't.'

Pause.

'She probably has a personalised pastry crisper.'

'No, a personalised spring action potato masher.'

'We're being horrible.'

'We are, but goodness, doesn't she do one good?'

'Why do her Marigold gloves always look brand new?'

'Why does she always say Law-rie?'

'Lorry sounds common.'

But under the laughter Cass found herself wondering with real bewilderment how Rick (who had not appeared and not been mentioned), Rick with his air of good sense and down-to-earth integrity, could choose or tolerate a woman not only of such silliness as Beverley, but of such meanness of spirit.

Chapter Thirteen

Back in Denham Court, Cass found it oddly difficult to confront Guy about what had been done at the Corrie, partly because in this urban and elegant setting it seemed too trivial to fight about, but also because several things had by this time intervened to take the edge off her first disbelieving rage.

There had been two rewarding days with Lindsay, starting with the busy Stirling area, making a loop through Callander and the Trossachs, then heading west to Oban and Inveraray. They had looked in on mostly settled and contented au pairs (and one who was vocally set on flight in spite of all they could say), and visited several hoteliers interested in the instant supply of short-term staff. Cass had seen the calls principally as putting down a marker for next year, but had found this was precisely the time when hotels became desperate for help, with the season holding on into November, and students vanishing from early September onwards.

Guy had been in Funchal when she got back to London but the demands of ordinary life had at once engulfed her and the Corrie felt far away. It had seemed unreasonable to attack Guy the moment he appeared and Cass had put off the thorny question for another day or two. She deeply disliked quarrelling and it had never figured in their relationship. Also, now that she was with Guy again, she could see so clearly how he would view the work he'd had done. He would be astonished to find she wasn't pleased about it, and hurt too, but that he would hide behind a practised dismissiveness.

Yet the Corrie was precious to Cass. It would serve no purpose to protest about what had already been altered or destroyed, but surely it would be worth trying to establish an agreed approach as to what was done next.

'Are we sure we want to make a garden, for instance?' she asked, having been as positive as she could about anything there was to be positive about.

'Of course we want to,' Guy said flatly. For him this was done, settled, of no interest at this moment and in this place. 'Houses that have stood empty always have a bleak look. I hate it. When I was there on my own the whole place depressed me, to be honest.'

'I rather liked it the way it was.' Cass said carefully. She had to be realistic. Guy had not agreed to buy the Corrie because it attracted him as it did her, and it was useless to mind that. All the same she knew she felt defensive, almost protective, about it, and must make an effort to rationalise these feelings.

'A civilising hand is what it needs,' Guy stated before she could go on. 'Some order and colour to banish that dreary air of neglect.'

His words. Simplicity and drowsy peace. Her words. Guy was already turning back to the report he had been reading and Cass recognised with a chill of apprehension how opposed were not only their aims for the Corrie, but their responses to it. She had tried to be altogether too fair, she saw, too temperate, conveying to him none of her true outrage and distress. She must make him understand them before they went any further, and before all this began to matter too much.

But without creating an emotional scene it was difficult to break through Guy's cool preoccupation with what he had been doing before she interrupted him. Cass hardly knew how to begin. The cornerstone of their successful relationship had been a genuine acceptance of each other's needs and ways. Cass had watched the sparring and frustration of other couples in their circle with amazement. Why stay together? What sort of basis was that for living? She often thought about Gina with that same bafflement, finding it hard to comprehend why two unhappy people insisted on clinging together when there was a world full of other options outside the door. For Guy and herself the only point of conflict had been her family, Guy always exasperated by the gentle unwordly atmosphere of Havenhill, but even over that they had compromised. And though Cass might think Guy's estrangement from his own family could perhaps have been repaired in adult life, she never said so. In day-to-day matters their compatibility was real and effortless, but now Cass saw that an element had entered their lives about which they felt entirely differently. She could see, now that she stood back from it, how much that was her fault. She had been swept up in euphoria about the Corrie and Bridge of Riach and the glen, getting carried away about her Scottish heritage in a way which must have been very tedious for Guy.

She studied his smooth head, his absorbed face. Why did his shirts never look like chewed rags after a flight like everyone else's? He never loosened his tie when he came in, never seemed to feel the need to get into slippers, literally or metaphorically. As always, however objective she tried to be, she was conscious of his attraction and, inescapably, still, the accompanying surprise that he could ever have been drawn to her. What would it take to eradicate that deep-rooted self-doubt? Would it ever fade? She had imagined marriage would drive it away for good.

Her face unhappy, as it so rarely was, Cass turned away, filled with an unease which she didn't want to recognise as loneliness. Their marriage had been exactly what Guy had intended it to be – a step that made sense. If confidence in his feeling for her was ever going to come it would not grow out of signing a contract.

* * *

Every surface in the small kitchen of the Corrie was stacked and piled. There was nowhere to put anything, nowhere to work. Growling with frustration, Cass knelt to reposition the oven racks, wondering if the odd smell wafting into her face would affect the food. Just newness, she told herself optimistically. She hadn't used the oven yet but she couldn't possibly deal with all this stuff in the microwave.

From the long room came laughter and the sound of voices hearty with that special plumminess induced by pre-dinner gin and tonic. An oven shelf jammed at an angle, and Cass made it stick tighter by yanking at it. Where the hell was Guy?

Hang on, she admonished herself, slightly surprised at her own anger, Guy is where he should be, looking after the guests. Or where one of us should be. Guy was very good about taking his turn in the kitchen. But not, she grasped for the first time, cooking. When Lester and Dorothea – well, Dorothea more probably; Dorothea was always at the bottom of things – had decided it was too cold to eat outside, though the barbecue was going well and starters, silver, plates, glasses, drinks and wine were already set out on the new table, there had been no real question as to who would salvage the plot and get dinner going indoors. What Cass couldn't be quite so laid-back about was that idiot Gerard saying cheerfully, 'We won't need this then,' and emptying an ice bucket over the glowing coals. Apart from the choking fumes which had rolled round them, and which were still forcing her to keep the kitchen door and window shut, it would have been a lot less trouble to cook the steaks and chops and devilled turkey out there than to struggle with this damned oven.

But Cass knew her exasperation went far beyond being left to cope on her own in an unfamiliar and limited kitchen. It was only dinner for five, for God's sake; she could surely manage that. No, this was the culmination of a long day when she had felt like an animal with its fur being continually brushed backwards.

Nothing about the day had been actively unpleasant, but she had felt restless, trapped, out of step.

When Guy had said, casually, as though the plan was already in place, that the Pykes would now be coming on Friday not Saturday, adding in passing, 'Oh, and Gerard's flying up with them. He's been tempted by the Sillerton project for some time so it might be an opportunity to lure him in,' she had been thunderstruck. The Pykes were American associates of Guy's based in London whom she barely knew, and Gerard Norman, a waspish solitary who for some reason had clung on to Guy since Cambridge days, was someone with whom she never felt at ease.

She had envisaged, based on nothing at all as she could now see, certainly not on previous experience, spending the precious week at the Corrie alone with Guy. She had looked forward to finally having time to get to know the place together, and perhaps reconciling Guy to its mood, persuading him of its beauty. She had planned to introduce him to Gina and, wanting all to go smoothly, to find a tactful way of telling him that Gina's husband was his own manager. It was no surprise that Guy hadn't found it out for himself; he considered the private lives of his employees their own affair. Or more accurately, would have been bored to death to have to hear about them.

Why had she pictured it like this? When, even on their brief honeymoon, had she and Guy ever spent a holiday alone? The pattern had always been the same – a group taking a villa or apartment, friends coming and going, business colleagues appearing for a couple of days and vanishing again. It was part of their lives, completely accepted. And in the relaxed setting of well-serviced accommodation, with long cold drinks and hot sun to add a gloss of goodwill to the deals clinched on terrace or poolside, with a choice of restaurants in which to feed their guests, it had been perfectly painless. Today it had seemed as if Guy had been trying to coerce this quite different environment into fitting the well-tried pattern, and she had found herself resisting all the way. She had also had to work quite hard.

The morning had begun with a long-drawn-out breakfast during which she had been on her feet for most of the time, doing her best to meet a succession of requests which the Corrie was ill-equipped to meet. Freshly squeezed orange juice, decaffeinated coffee, skimmed milk, porridge and kippers were not to hand, and the substitutes she provided were received without favour. It had taken forever to get everyone out of the house, the single bathroom and the length of time it took the loo cistern to refill giving rise to jokes which became less and less jovial.

The plan had been for Guy to show them what had been done at Sillerton, then have a round of golf followed by lunch in the clubhouse. To Cass, however, it had been clear that her morning would be unavoidably spent in supplementing not only rations but household equipment, from linen, towels, feather-free pillows, larger pans and extra utensils to a case of Kleenex.

She had been promising herself some golf at Sillerton for weeks but had never found the time. As they had gone down the glen in the Range Rover Guy had hired, the prospect of Saturday shopping had looked very uninviting indeed, and Dorothea's complaints about being dragged in to make up a four had not helped. But after one mouth-watering glimpse of a beautifully laid-out course making the most of river and woodland scenery, Cass had been quite relieved to slip away. Guy hadn't troubled himself to phone ahead but instead had set about abusing his position to oblige a boot-faced starter to fit them in where no tee time existed.

It had been an unfortunate way to meet Laurie Fraser, summoned to arbitrate, and though Cass knew she was, without much justification, prejudiced against him on Gina's behalf, she had not taken to a narrow red face under sandy hair, thin compressed lips, a choleric eye and a clipped voice.

When Cass had got back to Sillerton, the four had been barely on its way in again. The starter, by now even more hostile after a morning of dealing with disgruntled golfers, had disgustedly pointed them out to her on the eleventh and she had winced to see the gap in front of them. Disliking the too-bright bar, the too-light new woodwork and tartan carpets which sat uneasily with the solid old house, Cass also avoided the pro's shop in the stables, the stone outbuildings being knocked about to house bowling alley, squash courts and other 'indoor leisure facilites', and instead had explored the gardens now reduced to grass and evergreens, especially liking an extravaganza of fuzzy ex-topiary filled with silence and green gloom.

The disgrace she had found herself in over lunch still rankled slightly. She was not the only one who hadn't thought of ordering. The hungry golfers, a bitter silence almost total between them after the pleasures of their eighteeen holes, had hardly been able to believe lunch was over and the kitchen closed. No amount of angry pressure from Guy had helped this time. No one on duty had been capable of producing food of any description, and no one had intended to try. Laurie Fraser had been 'somewhere about the course' but hadn't for some reason had his radio on.

Guy had taken the flamboyant way out. He had gone where money would talk. He had phoned the country house hotel where he had previously taken Cass and had summoned out of nowhere lunch for five at three thirty in the afternoon. This achievement had put him in an excellent humour, as though beating the system gave him a genuine kick, and he had behaved, as they were seated by an unforthcoming waiter, as though he owned the establishment. Perhaps he did, Cass had thought with a humour edged with a bleakness she had not intended.

'How's it going?' Guy asked, bustling in with a hands-rubbing manner which meant not that he wanted to help but that he wanted his dinner.

That is a perfectly normal enquiry, Cass told herself carefully.

'Slowly,' she said. Good – uncontroversial and light. 'A bit strapped for space, though.'

'Christ, this thing hasn't even begun to make more ice. Dorothea isn't going to be too pleased. I'd better stick some extra trays in the freezer.'

'Put those in if you want to hurry them up. There aren't any more.'

'You're telling me there are only these two? In the whole house?'

I don't keep spares in the bedroom. But Cass didn't say it. ''Fraid so.' She prodded a potato without much hope. Although she had part-cooked them ready for putting in the barbecue she couldn't see them catching up with the chops. So the chops would have to come out. These oven gloves were attractive but pathetically, if not dangerously, thin.

'We'll have to get an icemaker,' Guy said. 'Can you put it on the list?'

He's serious, Cass thought blankly, her face aflame, trying not to bump into him as she got to her feet, and letting the burning hot roasting tin bang down on the cooker top with relief. 'Can we think about that some other time?' she asked.

'Not sure where we'd find room for it though. Here by the sink do you think? I say, aren't those chops a bit overdone? These are Americans we're feeding, remember. They'll want to see blood. How's your glass doing? I'll get you a refill.'

Cass stripped off the useless gloves and flipped her burning fingers, then stood very still in a deliberate effort to calm down. Hot woman in kitchen, struggling to rescue meal designed to be cooked quite differently, debarred from laughter and conversation; give her two fingers of gin and she'll be all right. Well, two fingers to you, Guy. Cass found herself wishing

Gina was there to laugh with her. But she could laugh on her own. What did any of it matter anyway, she could hear Gina asking.

She smiled her thanks as Guy handed her her recharged glass, and emptied it at a draught. That should improve the cooking, she thought, giving her head a shake to banish a momentary dizziness. It didn't help much but she felt a lot less worried about dinner.

It was to this that she later attributed the start of her decline from forbearance. This and the claret Guy had been bothered about opening so soon after its journey. Then there was Gerard's request for mineral water, Lester's booming cautionary tale, lasting through two courses, about a friend who had gone offshore at the wrong moment and as far as Cass could gather sunk there without trace, and Dorothea's audible whimper at the sight of her chop. But it was when the conversation turned to the imbroglio of the morning and Gerard said bitchily, 'I wasn't too impressed with that touchy little character you've got running the place, Guy. I'd advise you to keep an eye on him,' that Cass, perched on a kitchen stool which made her tower over the complaining group like an unsteady ostrich, had thrown good resolutions to the winds.

'Did you realise that Laurie Fraser lives just up the lane, Guy?' she broke in. 'He's Gina's husband, the girl I told you about. We must have them down for drinks or dinner. Or,' turning to Dorothea, 'perhaps we could go up and call tomorrow morning.'

'You're not serious?' Guy demanded after a charged pause, his face darkening.

'I'm not altogether clear on tomorrow's schedule,' Dorothea hedged hastily, aware of undercurrents but unable to interpret them. 'I have our itinerary all written down but it's up in our room. Lester honey, do you remember what we had planned for Sunday?'

How deeply rude of them, Cass thought detachedly. I thought I was the hostess.

'I've no intention of getting involved with Fraser socially,' Guy rapped, his eyes meeting Cass's with a definite warning.

'Gina's great fun,' Cass went on conversationally, still addressing Dorothea. It had been a horrible day. 'You'll love her.'

'I don't think we much loved her husband,' Gerard put in, and the moment slid by in general laughter.

But Cass could feel Guy's anger, and regretted the impulse which had made her provoke it. It would hardly reconcile him to this place, and she had a depressing glimpse of how completely outside it he would wish to remain, no matter how often they used the cottage.

Chapter Fourteen

During their entire visit Cass saw nothing of Gina. Nor, which she didn't mind a bit, did she see Beverley, though her mind turned surprisingly often to Beverley's friendly if enigmatic husband. She felt hopelessly out of contact with her surroundings, as though, like her visitors, she was using the Corrie as a less than comfortable lodging place, situated at an inconvenient distance from anywhere anyone would want to be.

'I would find it a serious negative consideration to be situated in such a remote location and obliged to travel that same stretch of road every time I had to be some place else,' as Lester put it.

And that was really the trouble. They didn't want to be perched on an empty hillside looking out over miles of hill and glen bright with the varied shades of early autumn. They found no appeal in such surroundings, and after the mandatory photographs to record the visit had been taken they never looked about them again, certainly never walked anywhere. And as the days passed, crowded with too-ambitious plans, they became more and more resentful of the shortcomings of their accommodation.

'Well, Guy, I guess I wouldn't lose much time installing a few amenities round here – or necessities even,' Lester joked heavily when he had tried yet again to have a bath too soon after someone else and found the water lukewarm. Cass was convinced he did it out of a subconscious desire to impose his will, not accustomed to being thwarted.

He didn't make jokes on the morning when the water supply failed altogether. It was Cass who went up the burn to see what was happening, fantasising wistfully as she went about someone imperturable and muscular like Rick Scott materialising over the skyline to help her.

'The water's still coming in,' she reported when she came back, 'but terribly slowly. We've just run it off with all the baths and the dishwasher, so hopefully it will fill up again while we're out.'

'Never thought of getting onto the mains?' Lester asked, as to a pair of incompetent children.

'From where?' Cass enquired. What did he actually see when he looked out of a window? 'The burn's low, that's all.'

'Well, tap into another one,' Lester said half-teasingly, half in exasperation.

'It's the end of summer,' Cass said with restraint. 'There hasn't been much rain lately. We're making heavy demands.' Excessive and unnatural were the words she would have liked to have used. She wondered whether the extra demand from the Corrie was affecting anyone else's supply lower down, a consideration which clearly had not occurred to anyone else. Perhaps Beverley would appear on the warpath; the possibility rather cheered her.

The poor television reception was another source of acid complaint. Lester and Gerard pretended they wanted to watch because they had to keep in touch with the markets, maddened out of all proportion when, having shouldered each other aside to adjust and readjust the tuning, they only made the picture worse.

'I should think it's the problem we have with the mobiles.' Cass did her best not to sound sarcastic, but did wonder in passing why she was the one doing the placating. 'Hills, you know.'

'But you should get someone up, get a booster ...'

'There is a booster.'

'Get Sky.'

'It's all in hand,' Guy assured them, and Cass longed to follow that up but was wary of another clash. What was happening to them?

Private conversation was impossible anyway during the days packed with touring, sight-seeing and shopping, after the slow quarrelsome starts which frustrated her so much. After three days they put Gerard, to the general relief, on a flight from Edinburgh, and that led to a long day trawling Princes Street, visiting the castle and Holyrood, with some sentimental drooling at Greyfriars which Cass could have done without. Guy dodged it by vanishing to a meeting which he hadn't mentioned till they were crossing the Forth bridge.

There were expeditions to Blair Castle, Glamis, Ballater and Braemar, the latter enlivened for Cass by Dorothea's disbelief when she was shown the famous Games field. Everywhere they went the Pykes bought wool, whisky, tweed, curling stones, Celtic jewellery, heather honey, tablet, haggis, tartan, claymores and targes. They also had vital calls to make at chemists' wherever they went, and pursued an untiring hunt for food items which Cass, Kirkton and Muirend failed to provide. The cottage lost its charm under sliding piles of expensive carrier bags, the pressures of overcrowding and deepening tensions.

For Cass breaking point nearly came when, having waved off the Pykes in their turn, this time at Glasgow airport, after a morning of dramas spent arranging for the despatch of their possessions, Guy announced on the way back that more guests, not even vaguely known to Cass, were already on their way.

'How about fitting in a game of golf before they get here?' he suggested as they ran into Muirend, apparently unconscious of the explosive quality of what he'd just said. 'We've hardly seen each other during the last few days, and when Roderick's here we'll have to spend a lot of time on the Funchal project, which will leave you to look after Phyllis. We should have time for nine holes. Fraser can make himself useful and find us some clubs.' There had been no further talk of inviting Laurie or Gina to the Corrie.

Cass was swept by rare anger. 'Guy, look, pull up, will you. Here, anywhere. Just pull up.'

'What's wrong?' Looking startled, Guy swung without argument into a drive entrance. 'Are you feeling ill?'

The question was not unreasonable. Cass was leaning back rigidly in her seat, taking deep breaths.

'What on earth's the matter? Cass, tell me. Are you all right?'

With a huge effort Cass ordered her anger, her face, her voice. 'You hadn't said anyone else was coming.'

'Oh, surely—? Well, no, maybe I didn't. But it doesn't matter, does it? We generally have someone around. And the room's there, it's no trouble.'

'I'm sorry to be tedious about this, but though the room is there it isn't ready. It and the bathroom are both tips after Dorothea's occupancy. There are no clean sheets because there hasn't been time to wash any, and there is nothing whatsoever in the house to eat.'

'It's not like you to get so worked up over domestic trivia,' Guy began in genuine surprise, then took another look at her face. 'Well, all right, I can see it all has to be done, but how long will you need—?'

'We. How long will we need.' Cass spoke very levelly indeed.

They faced each other with a new crackling hostility. But what lies beneath all this? Cass wondered in sudden fear.

They didn't come to open battle. Cass was too level-headed, not prepared to inflict on the new arrivals the sort of atmosphere it would create. They didn't play golf, though. They shopped, they transferred the Pyke mountain to the small bedroom Gerard had used, to await the carrier, they left five bulging bin bags at the end of the lane hoping that they would disappear in due course, they made beds and they cleaned. But Guy's too-calm manner showed that he thought Cass was being unreasonable and he magnanimous, and the mood was not amicable.

Nor did they attempt to deal with the constraint between them during the remainder of their stay, when with the utmost reluctance Cass found herself treading once more the circuit followed with the Pykes, this time lumbered with a fat apathetic female who could only talk about her daughter, her daughter's understandably absent husband and some deeply boring grandchildren.

Once back in London, it was tempting to bury the memory of that appalled moment when an outright fight had come so near. Cass could see from this distance that Guy had done nothing which wasn't entirely normal for him; it was her reaction which had changed – and the assumption that she would do all the chores in a cottage totally unsuited to the use Guy had put it to, she would add grimly, then would feel petty for minding.

Her reluctance to tackle him about something over and done with was reinforced by Guy unexpectedly suggesting another weekend at the Corrie and promising that, apart from one essential site meeting at Sillerton, they would be entirely on their own.

It was good to be going back so soon, and Cass was in exuberant spirits as she locked the garage on the Volvo on Thursday evening and let herself into the flat. She had spent the previous day in York, and today in Norwich, then an unforeseen call in Saffron Walden on the way back had delayed her. Guy had been home all day, however, so there would be no waiting for him, the more usual state of affairs.

He was impatient to get away so, not wishing to cloud the mood of the weekend by making him hang about, she snatched up the few extra things she would need and without even bothering to change headed straight out again. At least the traffic wasn't quite so bad as it would have been tomorrow, and before too long they were arrowing northwards, catching up on each other's news then falling comfortably silent, letting the pressures of the week ebb away.

We've only had one weekend like this, Cass thought, as Guy turned into the lane just before four. Six months since we bought the Corrie and this is only the second time we've come here on our own. That's awful. And for both of us it's become tied up with work, which wasn't how it was meant to be. This weekend we must try to relax and give the place a chance to work its magic.

For the first time there was a damp smell as they went in. There had been no time to tidy anything as they had left, late and harried, with Roderick and Phyllis, and the rooms looked unwelcoming. There were spiders in the bath and earwigs in the kitchen sink. Cass wrinkled her nose at the whiff of unwashed tea towels she had forgotten to take away with her, and raised her eyebrows at the army of empty bottles formed up by the fridge. Had they really drunk that much?

'Bloody cold,' Guy said, rubbing his hands together and hunching up his shoulders in his cashmere sweater. He disliked bulky clothes. 'We should have left some background heating on. It would have made the place a bit more welcoming to walk into.'

'We'll have to think about protecting the pipes from frost anyway,' Cass agreed.

'Oh, surely not yet, it's barely October.'

'It can get pretty cold up here in October.'

'Up here. You know no more about conditions "up here" than I do,' he mocked. 'Don't trot out your fey Highland second-sight stuff this weekend, I beg you.'

When have I done that? Cass wondered, startled. Or when has he perceived me to be doing that? His tone had not been quite joking, the dig a little cheap for him.

'Right,' Guy went on briskly, having dealt with that. 'I'm ravenous. What have you brought in the way of food?'

It was a moment of private flashpoint for Cass, and though she recognised that what Guy had said a moment ago made her ready to overreact, she also knew the root cause of her anger went far deeper. Summoning control, she asked courteously, 'What food have you brought?'

Guy missed the signal. To be fair to him, Cass was an extremely equable person to live with, the last person in the world to take issue over trifles.

'Well, nothing of course,' he said, turning on the tap to flush the earwigs down the plughole. 'Isn't that your department?'

'My department?' Cass found her breath failing to produce her voice efficiently. 'Since when has it been my department?'

'Well, I don't know. Here, I mean. You always organise everything here.' Guy looked round with a shrug at the blank faces of the cupboards.

'Guy, you've been at home all day. I spent about six minutes in the flat all told.'

'You've always brought stuff before.' Guy knew he'd made a serious error. Of course Cass had expected him to get something together, or if not at least to warn her that he hadn't. That was routine between them. But his reason for doing neither, that in his mind this cottage really did seem her department, had been so instinctive, and so clearly didn't bear examination, that he took refuge in aggression.

'Don't make such a big deal of it. There must be something in the freezer.'

After feeding that pack of gannets, Cass longed to explode. But still habit and good sense held her back. Also she was aware of a terrible foreboding that any quarrel, however negligible in itself, would carry them to places neither was ready to approach yet. And four o'clock in the morning after a long journey, shivering and hungry in this messy kitchen, was not a good time to start discussing where their relationship was heading.

When they did talk it must be without accusations. Certainly not accusations about who forgot the food, Cass amended, her sense of proportion reasserting itself as it usually did.

'All right, let's see what we've got,' she said, though for her part she would have been content to write the day off and fall into bed, going down to Kirkton to stock up when they woke. They made an unappetising meal of frozen peas, instant potato and tuna, and hungry though Guy was he too began to wish they hadn't bothered as conversation floundered in the minimally heated room.

The sound of an engine woke them, reversing loudly into the new parking place.

'Can that be Gina?' Cass asked muzzily, coming out of a heavy sleep and wishing she hadn't so recently succumbed to the spurious comfort of red wine.

'Surprise for you,' Guy said, together and alert as he always was the moment he woke. 'Come and see.'

Why should his bright tone seem so ominous?

'Guy, not guests after all? You promised,' Cass wailed, hauling herself out of bed and going unsteadily to join him at the window. Below stood a white van on which, in a border of leaves and tendrils, green lettering said, 'Muirend Nurseries.'

This isn't right, this isn't what I wanted. The unhappy voice would not be silenced as, smiling and cooperative, Cass contributed to the discussion about where to plant the viburnum tinus, the garraya, the variegated holly, the photinia. What in God's name is a photinia, she asked herself in cold despair, agreeing that it would do well in this corner against the clumsy raw wood of the new fence. But she didn't ask, leaving it to Guy to discuss heights and dimensions, which he did as cold-bloodedly as if he were furnishing an office. She begged only that nothing large should be planted at the foot of the lawn. One day it might be possible to remove the barrier which now cut so arbitrarily across the view she loved.

The nurserymen departed at last, leaving spaces of bare earth raked smooth round neat bushes with neat labels.

'That's going to make a big difference to the place,' Guy said with satisfaction.

'It certainly is.' It was clear to Cass that making an issue over this would serve no purpose. Nothing would bring their attitudes closer, and nothing would return to this garden the unkempt charm she had loved.

She was not prepared to be so tolerant on another subject where their viewpoints differed.

'I suppose we've said goodbye to breakfast,' Guy said, 'but food of some kind is becoming an urgent matter. I'll shoot down to the village.'

'It would be quicker to go up to the Mains and borrow eggs or something,' Cass suggested.

'No!' Guy's voice was sharp. When Cass looked at him in surprise he added hastily in a more reasonable tone, 'It's almost as quick to go to the shop and there must be several things we need.'

Cass wasn't ready to let him get away with it. 'But why did you bite my head off like that?'

He turned away frowning. 'Oh, come on.'

'Guy.' She blocked him, facing him squarely, and a tiny part of her brain registered that, as sometimes happened, she felt taller than him and didn't like it.

'All right then,' Guy responded, annoyed at being forced into this. 'I don't like you running up and down to the neighbours all the time to borrow things. I don't want that kind of involvement.'

All the time? 'But I want to be involved.'

'Yes, well maybe that suits you, and I can't prevent you doing whatever you like, but it's not what we're here for, and just now I'd like to eat, if you don't mind. I've got a meeting to get to this afternoon, in case you've forgotten.'

Not what we're here for. Cass had an unpleasant feeling

that to ask what he meant by that could lead them into a discussion which could take them through the whole weekend and far beyond. Was she ready to embark on it? She knew she wasn't.

Chapter Fifteen

Cass pushed herself up the ladder among the resistant branches towards the highest and best of the apples, and the blustery wind, cut off by the stone walls below, tugged at her, faintly damp, smelling of autumn. The borders edging the sheltered garden were bright with ramping nasturtiums, mallow, cranesbill, the tall seedheads of fennel, roses and autumn crocus. She was feeling much better after a blowy and invigorating circuit of the hill, and calling at the Mains had found Gina about to make green tomato chutney, three recipe books open before her and a collection of ingredients or roughly approximate substitutes ready assembled. Cheek by jowl with these on the table, within the danger zone Cass would have said, various pieces of fabric were spread out, one of which, she assumed, was destined to cover the tattered seat of a spindle-back nursing chair waiting nearby.

'Oh, good, I can stop and do nothing,' Gina exclaimed at the sight of her, bending back with both hands a cookery book which wouldn't stay open, then turning it face down on the table in a way which made Cass wince.

'No, don't stop,' and, 'Oh no, you can't,' came in unison from Cass and an indignant Nessa who, having been given a lift home by Nancy had decided as she was so early for once she would treat herself to a face-pack, then had been asked to pick apples. She wanted the boring job over and done with; her mother was quite capable of letting her start the pack and then trying to drag her away in the middle. With her capacity to be two entirely different people at once, however, she gave Cass a friendly smile as she flounced about finding suitable baskets and emptying mixed dross out of them, muttering just audibly at what she found.

As Cass smiled back she wished there had been more opportunities to get to know Nessa. And she had never even met Gina's stepsons. After the brush with Guy before lunch she was more than ever conscious of how completely she had remained the holiday cottage dweller, even after all these months.

'I can't believe Nessa can be so charming,' Gina remarked when they had staggered in with full baskets and Nessa had removed herself with a swiftness which said, 'Pick apples, yes, if you poor old things can't get yourselves up trees, but sit and peel them listening to you gabbing and giggling, oh, please . . .'

'She's very pretty, though her hair isn't as dramatic as yours.'

'Colour or behaviour? Hers is a lot more inclined to do what it's told, lucky girl.' Gina had tied her head in a scarf in a Slavic peasant manner suited to apple picking, and Cass had privately admired the shape of her skull and her strong cheekbones. Now the scarf was slithering down and her hair was once more on the point of escape.

'Nessa's pretty enough when she smiles, I suppose,' Gina conceded, with a mother's constrained praise. 'Only she never smiles at me.'

'Wait a year or two.'

'I always hope when the boys are away and she's getting all the attention that things will improve, but she seems so *angry* with me all the time.'

'Resenting you leaving her father? Does she still want to be with him?'

Gina brightened up unexpectedly. 'Oh, that was quite funny. On her last visit she actually came back a day early, because Ruth had found her condoms and made the most almighty uproar about them.'

'You don't mind her having them?'

'I'm relieved she's got that much sense. I'm not sure I had at that age. Anyway, they're more a status symbol, aren't they? Essential equipment. Like our mothers' generation passionately wanting bras whether they needed them or not, and our generation throwing our underwear away altogether.'

'God, Gina, I don't know what kind of circles you moved in,' Cass said prissily, enjoying the warmth of shared nonsense and laughter which even more effectively than her walk was soothing away the tension and nagging anxiety left by the events of the morning.

Guy's meeting had been scheduled for three, but he had gone down early to have a private policy-defining chat with the architect beforehand. He had confirmed the time with him before leaving and had been told a 'get-together' was being organised in the clubhouse to follow the main meeting.

'Just drinks, apparently. No mention of dinner,' he had told Cass. 'You'll come down for it, won't you? You could meet one or two of the wives.'

Cass hoped her inward shudder at the phrase had not been reflected in her face. 'Now that is something I seriously, seriously, would not want to be drawn into,' she had said as lightly as she could.

'Can't say I blame you, meetings always run over and it's irritating when time constraints are imposed by knowing people are waiting.'

That wasn't quite what she had meant. 'I don't really want—'

'You haven't got a car, though. I was forgetting how hamstrung one can be in this damned place. There wouldn't be time to come back for you. You could get a taxi, I suppose.'

'No, I won't come, thanks.' But the tone in which he made the suggestion had told Cass that this complication made the whole thing too tedious and he had already lost interest in the idea. 'I'll go up and see Gina.'

'Fine,' Guy had answered, his mind locked onto his own concerns once more.

In the kitchen at the Mains, with Tiree in his basket surrounded by apple fragments he had tried and failed to like, and Gina with drawn-down brows studying her cookery books, Cass smiled a little wryly. Her feeling that she should tell Guy she was coming here, and his indifference in spite of what he had said earlier, said so much about them both.

'Vinegar, got that, not the cider kind but it won't matter. Onions, got a million. Cayenne pepper, not sure but chilli'll do if we're careful – or is it the same thing anyway? This one says sultanas but the others don't, let's put some in anyway. Ground cloves? I'm not grinding up cloves, how about nutmeg? Three large apples . . .'

'Three large apples? Gina!'

'What?'

Cass waved at the heaped baskets. 'For three apples we hardly needed Nessa or the ladder or even anything to carry them in.'

'Oh, well, I hadn't read all this then. We only need a pound and a half of tomatoes, would you believe? We've got ten times that amount. We'll have to mutiply up.'

'Don't say that as though it's the only reasonable course. How much chutney were you originally planning to make?'

'Not sure. Only Laurie likes it really.'

'Oh, Gina.' Cass found she was suddenly happy again. What, after all, had happened with Guy? Nothing. No real quarrel.

'I can give some to Beverley, in fact I might offload some of the apples onto her. You can have lots of course, though I don't think it would be much use offering any to Nancy. It's as bad as trying to give away rhubarb, everyone's swamped with the stuff at the same time. The extra jars will always come in useful for bring and buy sales. We'll make double the quantity, that should do, and then the sums will be easy.'

'Give me the book.'

'No, wait, this one sounds best. All you have to do is put the tomatoes in salted water and leave them overnight. I always like recipes where you leave things overnight, it feels as though most of the work's been done. Let's go for that one, then there's nothing to worry about till tomorrow and we can talk properly.'

How like Gina, Cass thought with affection, rapidly skimming the recipes. 'It says you have to skin the tomatoes first. Did you miss that bit?'

'Oh, that's easy, you just dip them in boiling water for a couple of seconds.'

For green tomatoes the seconds turned into minutes and even then the skins had to be scraped and peeled. Cass prevented Gina from going on obliviously with the whole ten pounds, and suggested putting the rest in a drawer to ripen.

'Oh, yes, good idea,' Gina readily agreed. 'I sort of know these clever tricks but generally forget about them till it's too late, or remember them at the wrong time of year. Now, an empty drawer ...'

Cass saw that might be a problem.

'And then if we're not bothering with the chutney—' the 'we' had been in place since the moment Cass arrived, which she had found not disagreeable '—we could take the apples down to Beverley and give Tiree a run at the same time. She might even give us tea.'

'Do we want her to? Anyway, she won't let us in if we've got Tiree with us. Why don't we have tea at the Corrie, and ask her to join us, then she can carry her own apples home?'

'She'll come like a shot. She's been dying to get her nose into the Corrie ever since you moved in, and her comments are bound to be rewarding.'

As they set off, Nessa declining in a muffled voice from

above an invitation to join them, Cass belatedly reviewed what she had to offer. But Guy had made a comprehensive trawl at the Kirkton shop. With her four-in-the-morning comments in mind? She felt ashamed to remember them now. She had made far too much of what had really not been much of a problem in the end.

'Don't let me stay too long, will you?' Gina begged as they went up the steps. 'Gosh, you have got on with your garden.' She sounded too warmly approving, obviously taken aback, but Cass knew it wasn't something she could talk about yet.

'Though goodness knows what time either of our husbands will appear from this wretched meeting,' Gina chattered on, and the moment passed.

'You're not going down for the drinks?' Perhaps I could have had a lift after all, Guy, coming down with your manager's wife, surely the most natural arrangement there could be?

'Oh, no, I never go near the golf club if I can help it. I hate all that sort of thing,' Gina said with a shudder.

Beverley made the expedition up the lane in a Jaeger coat, a pheasant-patterned scarf artfully tied, spotless green gumboots and gloves, and laser-beamed her way round the Corrie with open *schadenfreude*.

'The deer will have every plant in the garden,' she cried pityingly, 'not to speak of the rabbits. You'll need much, much higher fencing and it will all have to be covered with netting as well. And I'm sorry to tell you, but you're going to find that end wall above the stream terribly damp. That's the worst of moving into places in the spring, you simply don't know what horrors you're going to find later. And then in a spot like this you've no protection from the north, have you? You'll find the house dreadfully exposed when winter comes, but then most of the time you won't be able to get up the track anyway so I suppose you won't notice . . .'

'We can't both escape in here,' Cass hissed, as a scarlet-faced Gina precipitated herself into the kitchen to help with the tea.

'Isn't she marvellous? A dose of Beverley is worth all those stimulants she tips down her throat. She doesn't know what she's missing.'

'Keep your voice down. And take this lot in, she'll wonder what we're doing.'

'Not she, she's going through your desk, probably microfilming everything.'

Since meeting Rick, Cass found herself looking at Beverley in a new light, unable to believe that two such improbable people could form any kind of relationship. Perhaps memory had exaggerated her impression of being so much at ease with Rick, her pleasure in his calm good sense and quiet humour. It seemed that it had when Gina asked, as she always kindly did, how he was and Beverley replied, lowering her voice for dramatic effect, 'I'm afraid I'm having a very difficult time at the moment.'

She was having a difficult time? Didn't she mean Rick was? But she sounded more complacent than concerned, Cass thought with distaste, as though a decline in her husband's condition produced a corresponding rise in her own sense of worth in caring for him.

'He's deeply withdrawn,' Beverley went on. 'He's a long way from being out of the woods yet.'

I'd withdraw if I had to live with Beverley. And what condition? No one had ever said precisely. Depression? It was a term Cass found hard to relate to someone who had seemed so relaxed and in control as Rick. Or had she met him on an upswing, at the positive pole, or however it was expressed? Was he now at the opposite point?

They had just persuaded Beverley that she really wanted several pounds of cooking apples, and that she could easily carry them home without assistance, when Guy phoned. The drinks were now to be followed by dinner. It had all been laid on and Cass was invited. Her soul shrivelled at the bare idea. Guy didn't sound much surprised when she refused, she noted.

Nor, it was clear, did he share her slight disappointment that they weren't going to spend the evening together. Well, why should he? It was the hallmark of their way of life that they pursued separate interests with complete freedom. But this was meant to be a weekend for them to share.

'That means Laurie will be stuck too,' Gina was saying, taking the chance, while Beverley was rewrapping herself for the journey home, to turn over the top apples so that some black speckles didn't show.

Cass wondered whether Laurie had been included, knowing how Guy felt about him, but she only said, 'If he is, how about staying for supper?'

'I've got Nessa to feed,' Gina reminded her. 'Why not come to us instead?'

'I wish I could join you,' said Beverley, looking round for a mirror and annoyed not to find one, 'but as you know I'm tied hand and foot. With commitments like mine I'm not free to do whatever I like on a selfish whim as you two are.'

'No, Beverley,' they said humbly.

Nessa, still invisible, reported that Laurie had phoned to say he wouldn't be back for dinner, adding that you weren't supposed to speak *at all* or the whole thing was pointless, she'd have thought anyone would have realised that. There had been, it seemed, no mention of Gina being bidden to dinner but she didn't appear to notice the omission.

She embarked on a chicken bake because there were some leeks she wanted to use up, which Cass guessed was about the usual sum of her menu planning, not deterred by having to cook the chicken first. Cass supposed they should be glad it wasn't a frozen one. When Nessa was eventually called she came stalking in with a thunderous expression and things looked briefly unpromising. However, Cass thought her skin was looking marvellous (possibly owing more to the texture she had inherited from her mother than to her recent ministrations) and said so, and though Nessa stayed strictly for the duration of eating, she was perfectly friendly towards Cass while she was there, talking readily about her decision to do A Levels rather than Highers, and her chosen subjects. Then her mother asked if she'd like icecream as there wasn't any pudding and her face closed in scowling disdain and she leaped up, knocked her knife and fork to the floor and banged out leaving them where they were. Cass saw Gina, looking miserable and guilty, decide against calling her back.

'It can't be easy,' she said sympathetically. 'But she's all right, you know. She's articulate and intelligent and interested in things. Would it be irritating of me to say it could be a lot worse?'

'You're right, I know,' Gina admitted. 'And I'm as bad as she is, circling round the problem the whole time, letting her see how much I mind when she gets impatient with me. We're just so different. She's so efficient, everything done way ahead of time, nothing forgotten. I drive her mad, but I can't seem to change. Come on, let's open another bottle of wine. It'll have to be something different though, I can't think where it all goes to . . .'

It was late when Cass walked home, not greatly aided by a torch lent by Gina, designed for little more than assisting one to put a key in a lock, and dying into the bargain. In spite of the hazards of the track, there was a strange sense of simplicity to be out in the windy darkness, mellow with wine and good food and cheerful company, with no need to drive or be driven. And though there was a momentary check to see that the Aston Martin wasn't back, it was at once followed by philosophical acceptance, almost relief that the relaxed mood would not be impinged on. She did not use the word spoiled. All she had to do was go upstairs and fall into bed, with the window open so that she could hear the owls calling, and the river far below, running high after the rain.

On Saturday they slept late and had a silent breakfast, not unusual in itself, though there was a quality in their silence neither was quite comfortable about, and Guy's brain kept jibbing against the absence of newsprint. Before he got as far as a second cup of coffee he disappeared to the village, coming back disgustedly with a Dundee *Courier*.

'I suppose I should be thankful it's today's,' he grumbled, eviscerating it with a look of disbelief. But he soon recovered and, faithful to his word, let nothing encroach on the day together. They set up a working system to suit them both (Cass not passing on Beverley's prognostications about the wall against which the new desk had been built), brought in a stack of logs, agreed on how the bathroom was to be decorated, and even discussed knocking through the end wall of the kitchen and taking in the outside store, though Cass wasn't sure about the hidden agenda of needing a larger kitchen.

The freezer had to be restocked. Guy gave a longing glance at his notes from yesterday's meeting but when Cass offered to go alone, said they could combine the chore with finding somewhere for lunch, so Muirend, jostled by wet shoppers on a day of pelting showers and lowering skies, it was once more.

It rained even harder on Sunday and the weekend died on them.

I don't understand this, Cass thought helplessly, turning back yet again from the window, depressed by the sight of the rain sluicing earth off newly mounded borders and exposing the stones which were their real substance. I should be perfectly contented at Denham Court to have Guy tapping away at the computer, leaving me free to – what did she do? For a moment she could hardly think. Well, at home there are always things to do. Now she realised she was waiting; a female with no resources of her own waiting for a man to stop working and give her his attention. That was appalling, the very antithesis of how she and Guy functioned. And if he switched off the computer and said, 'Right, what do you want to do?' what could she suggest?

They had planned to play golf, but Guy had taken one look at the weather and refused to move.

'We'd better phone and cancel then.'

'Why? No one else is going to want to go out on a day like this.'

'Scottish golfers don't worry about the weather.' It had been the most general of remarks, not related to herself, but Guy had leaped on it with real anger.

'You're not a Scottish golfer, for Christ's sake.'

Why did London weekends always seem so full? They centred, she realised for the first time, on the gossipy bar-lunch sessions which usually lasted well into the afternoon. There were dozens of things she and Guy enjoyed doing together, even fun shopping, not to be compared to trudging round Tesco's in Muirend.

She made a special effort over lunch, which they had in front of a leaping fire, and after it Cass would have liked to go to bed. But Guy never liked making love in the daytime. In the end, leaving him peaceful and engrossed, she went out and walked, standing for a long time on her way back on the hump-backed bridge, misty drizzle driving into her face. She began to play the childhood game of focusing her eyes a few feet away on the thundering brown water patterned with creamy foam, and presently achieved the sensation of being free, sailing faster and faster, so giddily that in the end she almost felt sick.

A curious form of entertainment, she mocked herself as she turned away, but she knew she wasn't happy. She had seen no one, spoken to no one, the whole time she had been out, and felt as alien as she had on her first day here, searching for a phone.

It was a surprise when Guy asked, wresting himself away from the screen long enough to have tea, 'How vital is it for you to be back tomorrow?'

'Why?' Cass's spirits rose.

'I'm not happy about Phase II of the Sillerton plans, the part supposed to start in the spring.'

Ah.

'I don't feel all the options have been gone into, so I've arranged to meet the architect again tomorrow.'

'You've arranged it already?'

'I can put you on a flight tomorrow morning, or this evening if you need to get back.'

A flight this evening, if she could get onto one, would mean leaving now. The weekend she had so looked forward to, expected too much from, had slipped away.

Calmly she reviewed her diary. 'No, no appointments tomorrow. I can phone Diane. Going down on Tuesday will be fine.' Then why do I feel so ruffled?

'You could come down with me and see what's going on, if you like. It's your club too.'

Cass had heard more pressing invitations.

'I can use the time for the agency, thanks,' she said, then was struck by a very appealing idea indeed. 'There are one or two calls I could make.'

'You've no car,' Guy reminded her. 'Do you want me to run you down to Perth and collect you later?'

Or do you want me to drop you off at Sillerton and collect you later? Cass didn't make the point.

'I'll organise something,' she told him. These calls she could walk to. Guy enquired no further.

Chapter Sixteen

Monday was a very different day.

After the rain and gloom of the weekend it seemed to Cass that she had woken in another place. The wind had dropped the previous evening and the temperature had fallen sharply. Now, having left the cottage in the chilly greyness of first light, she felt almost too stirred by the beauty before her to deal with her response, as she looked with delight down into the bowl of the glen russet under early sun, bracken vivid against the silver of rimed grass and the white mist wreathing along the river. Far down at Alltmore a patch of gold backed by dark plantations showed that the poplars had clung to their leaves in spite of yesterday's battering. Below her the big chestnut by Riach Gate Lodge was a parti-coloured mound of green and yellow, though Beverley's younger sycamores had fully turned. The *leylandii* rectangle enclosing the bungalow struck an intrusive note, unnatural and crude. How long before it shut out the view entirely?

Cass knew where that thought had come from, her eye travelling to the other rectangle divided from the first by the new road, a stone rectangle completely congruous in its setting. It often came into her thoughts, and so did the quiet man she had found working there. They had become almost symbols of what this place meant to her.

Because she felt the need for such a focus? Frowning, knowing it was time to get to grips with the question, for it had been nudging at the back of her mind for weeks, she pushed herself up from the damp rock, turned to choose her line to the ridge, and saw Rick himself not twenty yards away.

There was the initial shock of seeing anyone so close in a world which, in this empty hour with the sun just up, had seemed her own; there was the clash of her thoughts about this man and the reality of his presence; and there was a flurry of uncertainty, because Beverley had referred to having 'a difficult time' and Cass didn't know what that meant, what form his illness took or how serious his condition was. Then these questions vanished in the simple pleasure of seeing him there, walking towards her at the unhurried pace she remembered.

'There seemed no way of not startling you,' he said as he came up, smiling in his easy friendly way – smiling *down* at her. What a lot of him there was.

Had he seen and interpreted her surprise and apprehension? But even as embarrassment rose Cass knew with certainty that he wouldn't mind. With him once more, his tolerance and good sense could not be for a moment in doubt.

'How nice to see you!' she exclaimed spontaneously. 'Isn't this the most fabulous morning you ever saw?'

He laughed, not taking his eyes off her, as though he had absorbed every detail of the morning so thoroughly he had no need to look again. 'Where are you off to?'

'Up,' Cass told him, with a large reckless gesture of her arm.

'Then let's go "up" together.' His tone teased her exuberance, his eyes approved it.

'But should you? I mean, is that all right?' Between Beverley's dark hints and her own ignorant preconceptions she hardly knew what to ask.

'I spend half my time on the hill,' Rick assured her.

As they started up the slope he found to his pleasure that

he hardly had to adjust his stride to hers. She had the longest legs he'd ever seen on a woman. And the warmest smile. He hadn't been able to believe his luck when he realised who it was perched on that rock, the long brown skirts of her coat sweeping the grass, gazing out across the glen under the big brim of that dashing hat. A figure slightly eccentric, but looking very good against these colours and in this setting.

'Do you really?' Cass still sounded unsure, and he turned to smile at her.

'I can't turn chair legs all the time.'

He had a way of making things simple and Cass laughed too, gripped by happiness. It was marvellous to have someone there to share the morning, the warmth coming into the sun as the mist thinned along the river and plumed in wisps tenuous as smoke from the stands of conifers on Riach, while their own footprints, at first deeper white on the frosty grass, became green as the rime thawed. The faint mew of a buzzard sounded above them and as they rounded an outcrop Rick's hand caught her arm and they stood motionless to watch a swift lithe shape, its thick tail very noticeable, streak for the cover of a dark slit in the rocks fifty yards away.

'Wildcat?' Cass asked, thrilled. 'I've never seen one.'

'Feral probably, his coat was very dark. But with that tail there'd be wildcat somewhere.'

Then there was no breath for talking, for Cass at any rate, as they applied themselves to the sharp pull before them. And no need to talk. Cass was aware of an absence of need for questions or explanations. They were there; the brilliant morning was there; the hill was there. She climbed on. Breasting the ridge, the frost gone now except for a white line here or there in shadow on west-facing slopes, she exclaimed in pleasure at the view before them, miles and miles of tawny ridges defined against misty hollows, turquoise sky without a cloud.

'I had no idea you could see so much from here,' she said,

unashamedly out of breath after keeping up with Rick's smooth and deceptively easy pace.

'Remember we start at about a thousand feet at Bridge of Riach.' Rick was looking at her with an expression she couldn't interpret. Approval she thought, because she wanted it to be there, amusement at her lack of breath and scarlet face, and something else oddly like satisfaction. There was no time to pin down the impression. Rick was turning to name the peaks for her, from Ben Vrackie's pointed tip beyond Glen Ellig, Schiehallion's symmetry and the rugged masses of Ben Lawers, to Ben More and the giants of the west.

'It's stupendous,' Cass said reverently, 'and so near in terms of time and effort. Yet it would be easy to enjoy the glen from below and never see this at all.'

'That's why the Bealach Dubh,' Rick nodded towards the dip in the ridge below them, 'is so popular with the tourists now the glen road's been improved.'

'But it's not the same as coming up on your own two feet, is it?' Cass said dreamily, still gazing.

Rick, smiling, said 'No, it's not the same.' She had taken off her hat to fan herself with it, and he took in with pleasure the strong planes of her face, the even tone of her skin, the soft, densely curly hair that blended with it so well. He liked the blue eyes, not so far off the colour of this morning's sky.

'You seem at home in this landscape,' he suggested, when having drunk her fill of the view she came to join him on a broad rock slab dried by the sun. He couldn't have said anything to please her more, particularly after the edgy atmosphere of the last two days. And it was an invitation to talk, if she wanted to. Cass recognised the moment in a new encounter when discovery begins, and welcomed it.

'I'm one of those Scots who feel they've never gone away. I've spent the last three-quarters of my life in England and it still seems temporary.' It was so easy, here, with Rick, to confess to it. Then Cass realised it was Guy's attitude which made the word appropriate.

'I know what you mean,' Rick agreed. 'I'm an even worse case. Only holidays as a child with my Scottish grandparents, yet this is my country.'

'Where did your grandparents live?'

'A good step north of here.' He pointed across his chest, up past Allt Farr.

'How far north?' Where would that line reach? Kingussie? Inverness? Dornoch? Or would you be in the Dornoch Firth by then?

'Ever heard of the Dava Moor? The River Findhorn? My grandfather worked all his life on a big estate there, dry-stane dyking and fencing.' Rick checked and his face became sombre in a way Cass hadn't seen before, reminding her with a small jolt that this man was supposed to be 'disturbed'. 'Anyway,' he went on, dismissing whatever had produced that look, 'it was a marvellous place, looking over the moor to Lochindorb, miles of nothing, a boy's paradise. I spent every moment I could there.'

'And where was home?'

A small huff of dismissal. 'Liverpool.'

'Liverpool?' She couldn't see him in a city.

'Well, it wasn't that bad,' he protested, half laughing at her tone, half conceding that it had been.

'No, of course, I – it just doesn't strike me as your sort of environment.'

'You're right, it wasn't.' He sounded grim, falling silent to gaze across the glen to the big house of Riach randomly set down on its bare acre of grass.

What pressures there had caused his illness; what memories had she carelessly stirred? 'So you returned to your roots?' Cass asked, so lightly it was hardly a question. 'Though a touch south of the Dava Moor.'

'And you came back to yours,' he parried. 'Where were they?'

The subject of Liverpool was closed. But how easy it was to tell him about Dalry, and as a natural progression express something of her feeling of being at home here in Glen Maraich. All the things she could never say to Guy, a bleak inner voice reminded her, but she didn't want to listen to it in this place, at this moment.

They moved at last, going down by a different route, talking absorbedly. The Corrie, the new office in Perth, Lindsay and the other 'ears', Quickwork and her plans for it in Scotland – Rick knew a good deal about all of them by the time they came out above the bypass.

'And today I'm going to try to make some contacts closer to home,' Cass told him, pausing to lean over the parapet of the old bridge, a compelling ritual Rick also seemed to find it natural to observe. 'I'm going to phone and see if I can call at Riach and Allt Farr.'

'Go for it,' Rick said, turning to nod at her approvingly. 'They're great people, you'll enjoy meeting them. And it's all part of this.' He raised his broad hands, fingers interlaced. 'The mesh of ordinary life. Glen life.'

The gesture conveyed so aptly what Cass had been groping towards that she was momentarily disconcerted.

'Do you see much of them, the Mackenzies and – the Munros, isn't it?' she asked, taking refuge in the ordinary. As she spoke she remembered Gina telling her that Beverley was always trying to get her foot in at the door of the 'big houses', without success.

'When I'm out and about on their ground I do,' Rick said. 'There can't be many lairds with a more hands-on approach than Max Munro. He gets into every corner of Allt Farr and we have a blether when we come across each other on the hill. His brother-in-law, James Mackenzie, isn't quite so active on Riach, I have to say, though his family make up for it.' The thought seemed to amuse him and Cass's interest in meeting both families increased.

They went on towards Sycamore Lodge and she wondered fleetingly whether their returning together would present any problem. It appeared not. Rick continued past the gate with her, talking easily, his leisurely stride never altering.

'Aren't you going in?' she asked. It was as though once more in this environment – Beverley's environment – doubts surfaced again. Had Rick forgotten where he was or what he was doing? Oh, don't be so absurd, she caught herself up angrily. Could anyone in the world be more relaxed and 'normal' than he was?

'Go in there?' Rick turned to look at the bungalow as though viewing it for the first time. 'No thanks.'

What was there to say to that?

They paused at the foot of the lane.

'Thanks for coming with me, Rick.' Cass said. 'A morning like this needs to be shared.'

'I know.' Rick nodded, but his voice was abstracted, his eyes on hers in a way that was for the first time vaguely disturbing. Then as he turned to head for the tunnel leading to the barn he said something so entirely unexpected that through all the events of a busy and enjoyable day Cass couldn't get it out of her mind.

It felt odd to be walking across the open space towards the building she had seen in doll's-house scale from the ridge this morning. The day had fulfilled its promise and was very still, hazy with mellow warmth. Someone was sitting on the front door steps, a girl with floating amber hair, wearing a lovat green sweater which, Cass saw as she came nearer, was not only snagged and felted, but had both elbows out. She was engaged in grooming a red setter. A few yards away across the gravel a second setter lay, chin down, front paws splayed, yellow eyes watchful, ready to take off the moment anyone suggested it was his turn. Cass now saw that the rigid stillness of the dog receiving attention was not down to impeccable training but to the fact that he was tied to a mammoth cast-iron bootscraper. Puffs of red hair floated buoyantly as thistledown to catch in the rabbit netting protecting what looked like recently planted climbers against the flaking white wall.

The dog in the queue took his mind off the horrors to come long enough to register the arrival of a stranger, and let loose a wild volley of barks on which Tiree himself couldn't have improved. His captive friend did the same, exploding in corkscrew twists and plunges.

The girl held up a brush densely clogged with dog hair to shield her eyes against the sun. 'Hello. Cass, isn't it? How nice of you to come. Shut up, you idiots! Go on, then, I'll let you off for today – if you'll just stop pulling for one second so that I can unfasten you.'

Released, the setter fled, the whites of its eyes showing, to tear with its friend in mad circles round a lawn which, though separated from it by iron railings, was indistinguishable from the mole-hill adorned and sheep-mown grass outside them.

'Shall we chat out here? At this time of year I always want to snatch every blink of sun, don't you, and the weekend was so ghastly. I'll get you a cushion.'

Standing on the steps in the sunlight, watching the dogs rolling and snarling in mock battle, their coats a vibrant colour against the grass, discovering the new view of the glen which a couple of hundred extra feet and a different angle gave, Cass felt contentment seep through her. Joanna Mackenzie's smiling welcome had been very like Gina's. Preliminaries unnecessary; conversation could begin.

'Mind you, the shape I am at present it would probably be easier to bring a chair out,' Joanna remarked, sinking down awkwardly on the steps again.

'When's the baby due?'

'Beginning of December. And it won't be a moment too soon, believe me. Oh, good, here's Laura. Half-term. The little girls – James's twins – were full of indignation at having to go to school today. It had conveniently slipped their minds that they had a fortnight for their own half-term from the glen school.'

'Tattie picking,' Cass said.

'Exactly.' Joanna beamed as though Cass had unexpectedly used some code word. 'It's still clung to, the children dragged back to school in August while everything's still going on. I don't suppose it will ever change. Laura, come and say hello.'

Cass watched with pleasure a slim teenager, hard hat faded to grey-green rammed down over straight fair hair, inflexibly bring a flighty-looking pony to the exact spot she chose and make it stand there.

'Darling, this is Mrs Montgomery. My daughter Laura.'

'Oh, Cass, please.'

Laura leaned to offer her hand. 'You live at the Corrie, don't you?'

'Whenever I can manage it.'

'Your new garden will be very nice.'

That's a piece of kindly good manners if ever I heard one, Cass thought, amused but grateful. 'Have you seen it today?' she asked.

'No, why?'

'We had visitors in the night.'

'Deer?' Joanna asked. 'Oh no, they really are a total pest. Did they get much?'

'The lot.'

She had come back from her walk to find Guy white-lipped and fuming, striding from one leafless stump to the next. 'You must have seen this when you went out,' he had said angrily.

'It was barely light.' Cass thought she couldn't have done much if she had seen it, but recognising Guy's need to accuse someone had held her tongue.

'What a shame,' Joanna said in sincere commiseration. 'But you have to make your mind up to it, I'm afraid. If you want a garden you have to fence, and nothing under five feet six is the slightest use.'

Cass thought of the prison compound look of Sycamore Lodge and her soul rose in revolt.

'As you see,' Joanna went on, 'we've chosen the alternative.' She nodded at the barren expanse before them, and she and Laura exchanged a smile. 'I used to garden more or less for a living before I married James. Now I'm liberated.'

'I was actually quite happy with what was there before,' Cass admitted, and then felt disloyal to Guy.

'It's probably the best way, especially if you can't spend much time here. A few things survive even the rabbits, and the more mature they get the less vulnerable they are. But scratch up some fresh earth and you're invaded at once.'

I feel at home here, Cass thought, without surprise. There was an atmosphere of time not mattering, rules not mattering; sun beat back warm from stone, the hills slumbered in the still air.

'So are you going to produce some nice friendly nannies for us?' Joanna enquired. 'My sister-in-law Kate is pregnant too, though only just, and we think it's perfect to have a nannie-provider on the doorstep. I thought I could take you up to Allt Farr to see her and that would save you saying everything twice. Unless you were very keen to walk? I don't want to spoil your plans and you couldn't have a better day.'

'It would be very kind of you to take me. I must admit that grassy track along the hill had been tempting me, but it can wait. Is it all right to walk that way?'

'Of course it is, any time you like.'

'What about the stalking?' The voices of the stags roaring in the frosty night had been the last sound she had heard as she fell asleep.

'Well, meantime it probably would be best to check. James and Max are both out today. Just look in any time you like, there's always someone around. I have two stalwarts with heavy hands and big hearts who rarely stir from the teapot and the telly. Laura, are you coming with us?'

'Yes, I need to see Doddie about something. Don't go without me.' Laura sent the pony off in a standing leap. Yelling, the dogs tore after it.

'That wasn't entirely necessary,' Joanna remarked, surveying the gouges in the gravel without emotion. 'Doddie's my brother's gamekeeper. I daren't think what business Laura has on hand with him.'

Cass didn't think she sounded unduly worried.

At Allt Farr, a light and sunny house constructed in part of the castle burned down two years ago, whose ancient walls provided an impressive setting, she was welcomed by Kate Munro, gentle, softly spoken and unexpectedly young. It appeared she was expecting Cass to stay for lunch. Guy hadn't said how long his meeting would last. But Cass knew the thought was perfunctory. Whenever he returned, this would not turn into a day to be spent together.

Lunch was carried out to a sunny paved corner halfway down the lawn, where in spite of a recent hip replacement Joanna's mother limped to join them, an old lady with a tart tongue redeemed by humour. They were all very enthusiastic about Cass's project, ready to supply the names of half their friends as possible clients.

'Everyone gets snowed under with guests in the summer,' Joanna said, 'and the estate people are too busy to help much, with work at its peak and their families descending on them just as ours do.'

'On Allt Farr we need help for the whole season because we let our cottages. Could you supply people for those too?' Kate asked, adding shyly, 'I may not be able to do very much by next summer.'

'Max will see to it that you don't,' her mother-in-law told her crisply, but Cass caught the smile that went with the words.

'Are you going over to Glen Ellig to see Pauly Napier at

Drumveyn?' Joanna asked. 'She's always up to her eyes. I can give her a ring if you like. And the Danahers at Grianan run a hotel which gets busier all the time.'

There was a sense of being accepted, of being looked after even, which had been totally unlooked for, and as Cass went down the burn to the Corrie she felt the elation of the morning surge up once more. With it returned Rick's enigmatic parting words, which had hovered intriguingly somewhere in her mind all day, in spite of new meetings, new scenes.

She saw again his intent look, demanding her attention and credulity as he said, 'I'm not ill, you know.'

He had read her doubt – wouldn't it be part of the condition to deny it? – and had stepped closer, his height and bulk lending emphasis to what he said.

'There's been nothing wrong with me for months. It's important to me that you know that.'

Part Two

Chapter Seventeen

'Road Closed Ahead.' The laconic message of the Council sign used to raise a flurry of panicky questions for Cass. Where was it closed? How far ahead? Was it sensible to go on or should she turn back and find somewhere to stay in Muirend? Now, though clearly there had been a recent and quite heavy new fall, she could be fairly sure that unless the board were more specific the snowplough would have got as far as Bridge of Riach. It would be the Bealach Dubh that was closed. And possibly the last stretch of the glen road.

She grinned as she took the swings up through the leafless woods, passing the Sillerton entrance without a glance or a thought. She knew all about the running warfare Max Munro had been conducting with the Council about clearing the three steep and narrow miles which climbed to Allt Farr. The new loop created at Bridge of Riach had created far too tempting a turning place and whenever the men on the plough could reasonably pretend that conditions were too bad to go to the head of the glen they swung round there, throwing up a bank of snow across the road below Nancy's as they did so, stopped for a lengthy tea break now having plenty of time in hand, then roared home again. Max had worked out that they were five times less likely to reach his gates than before the road had been altered, and battle continued.

For Cass, knowing about it, having heard Max on the subject when she met him bringing his own plough down from Allt Farr the last time she was here, was part of the pleasure of becoming involved in glen life. She still only appeared at weekends, was still the holiday cottage owner, but irrespective of driving conditions, the hazards of weather or the demands of work, she spent every second that she could here, and to her that made all the difference. Imperceptibly through the winter months the Corrie had become the primary focus of life. The corollary, that the flat had become a mere necessary London base, she was not so ready to acknowledge, for that brought too sharply into focus the widening rift between Guy and herself.

As the road climbed towards Kirkton, the hills an unearthly blue-white in the last light of a dusky afternoon, the road black at this height though bordered by snow, she deliberately turned her mind to the positive aspects of being here. One of them was the car she was driving, a Volvo again, but now an all-wheel-drive estate which had been a delight to handle on the run up from the south. Often, to save time, she flew to Edinburgh, but even then the cars she rented, tough little jeeps usually, reflected not only the changing season but her own changing attitudes. Now she was here for a whole week, and part of the treat was the new car.

Guy thought she was mad. 'What on earth will you do up there for a week in this weather?' he had demanded. 'You're miles from any decent skiing. And you've said yourself that only a fraction of the hotels stay open at this time of year so you can't pretend to be working.'

'This is exactly when they have the chance to organise staff for the new season,' she had retorted. 'And nannies are hardly a seasonal requirement.'

'Well, if half the roads are blocked you won't be able to get anywhere anyway.'

She had let that go. Though what she had said was true enough, and she and Lindsay had one or two plans in place for the coming week, it was not the reason she so deeply wanted to be here.

There were a dozen threads to the mesh – Rick's word – which beckoned her so enticingly, but with a skill perfected by practice she kept her mind on the most superficial of them. With an enjoyment Guy would have found ludicrous, she recited the names of farms and cottages as she passed them, relishing the sparseness of the lights brightening against the violet evening. She stopped for supplies in Kirkton, her regular habit now, and liked being greeted by the other customers chatting in the crammed little shop. Since the Hallowe'en ceilidh in the village hall most faces in the glen were familiar and many she could put names to. It had been a lively evening. The Mackenzie and Munro clan had appeared in full force, plus Forsyths of Alltmore and a big party of Napiers from Drumveyn in the next glen. She had gone with the Frasers; Guy had been in Nassau.

Ed Cullane came in for cigarettes as she was filling her basket and called, 'You'll get up no bother, Cass. I was round with the blade on the tractor this forenoon. Gina's no' long ahead of you, though whether she gets up or no won't be altogether to do wi' the state of the track.'

There was a laugh from another customer. 'That one'd no' be sure of getting home even though it was a tank she was driving.'

A general laugh this time, the amusement without malice of a small community where no one's mistakes or disasters escaped ironic observation. Cass went out to the car feeling absurdly warmed by it. The three street lamps were on but the evening light was holding its own in a way that proclaimed spring was near; the very smell in the air was exhilarating.

Driving on, however, she was reminded that winter was still very much in control, finding the banks of snow dramatically higher on either side as the road climbed. Always, coming up with that ominous warning sign in mind, no matter how used she had become to conditions which would formerly have daunted her, the question hovered as to whether or not she would make it up the final twists of the lane. Though, by an arrangement long ago established, she could leave the car at Sycamore Lodge if she had to – the anticipation underlying all her thoughts nearly distracted her here – and carry up what she needed, after an exhausting week and a long journey how nice it would be to get right to the door. But Ed had cleared the track, this car was supposed to be as good as any off-road vehicle, and she was certainly going to have a crack at it. Even if she came to grief plenty of people were on hand to dig or push, willingly, without question. And comforted by this reassuring thought, Cass was swept up in the delicious, almost uncontainable excitement that Guy found so exaggerated and irritating.

Thinking of the joke in the shop at Gina's expense she laughed again. Gina – what chaos and drama always surrounded her. She had been pulled out of snowdrifts three times this winter already to Cass's knowledge, though the last time she had merely run out of petrol and had thought she ought to pull off the road out of the way. A sensible and public-spirited idea, but she had put herself in the process into a three-foot ditch, providing much local entertainment.

These crises could be laughed at, but the emotional upheavals over Nessa, and less explicitly but more seriously over Laurie, were another matter, though as she had got to know Gina better even these Cass had learned to view more objectively. For a long time she had been blindly partisan, seeing Gina doing her best to please everyone, appreciated by no one, and receiving little support from a husband who wanted to be looked after in the old-fashioned way and was callously unsympathetic to her creative needs. Laurie Fraser had had on the whole a bad press, between Gina's tearful wails and Guy's castigation of his working methods, and for far too long Cass had accepted him at their evaluation. Till one November day, as she set out on an early morning walk, she had realised where she was heading and what she was hoping for, and angry with herself had turned back, determined to remove herself from temptation. She had barely used her membership at Sillerton, and the image of the sweeping course beside the river, with the wooded bluffs above it still in autumn colours, was attractive enough to reinforce the impulse.

She had just got her card and was diving into the pocket of her golf-bag for her gloves when Laurie had come out of the starter's office.

'Good morning, Cass,' he had greeted her in the clipped voice that always made him sound as though he had no time to spare. 'I hear you're going round on your own. I was about to snatch nine holes myself before a day at the desk. Would you like a game, or were you looking forward to a peaceful solo?'

Cass had hesitated, not sure she wanted to spend an hour and half with Gina's irascible husband, who so often left Gina in tears over the breakfast dishes. And there had been a lure in the empty course, the dark full-flowing river, the fairways lined by yellow birches still dredged with mist. Besides, what was Laurie's handicap? Cass hadn't played for ages; would she hold him up? But the image of them solemnly playing round one after the other had been too silly. She barely knew the course; who better to show it to her than Laurie? And he was out for fresh air and relaxation, not a needle match. They were neighbours after all, and she had never made any effort to get to know him. These thoughts had passed through her brain more or less simultaneously, most of them transparently clear to Laurie, then she had smiled at him, her blue eyes crinkling in the way she never realised was so engaging, replying cheerfully, 'Good idea, though I ought to warn you I'm pretty rusty.'

'Don't worry about that,' Laurie had said, with a nod of satisfaction. 'I shall be glad of the company.'

Watching him rather fussily getting ready Cass had begun to regret her decision. What were they going to find to talk about? Or, which was more probable, was he the kind of golfer who wouldn't want to talk at all? Gloomily she had followed him along the pitted path to the first tee.

Laurie had surprised her. Though at first their conversation was confined to the game, an undemanding tone had quickly been established, and before long it had seemed natural to chat of other things as they strode down the fairways – or in far too many cases Laurie helped to hunt for Cass's ball in the rough. He had been unruffled by the vagaries of her game.

'The basics are there,' he said in his crisp way. 'You just need to get your eye in again.'

After watching her for several holes he had suggested a different grip. Cass had resisted a bit then tried it. A sweetly struck drive down the middle of the fairway had spoken for itself.

'Can't argue with that,' Laurie had commented mildly, and they had laughed as they went on. It had been the easy exchange of friends, and Cass had found herself enjoying his quiet affability, his unexpected dry humour, his open pleasure in the scene around them in spite of this being his daily place of work.

The encounter had been a turning point in her perspective of domestic life at the Mains. After it she had begun to concede that some of Gina's woes might be self-inflicted. Previously, finding Gina crumpled in despair after yet another outburst from Laurie, she had wondered what Gina found to cling to in such a marriage. She had rarely seen them together, but on the few occasions Laurie had been at home when she called at the Mains he had remained a repressive background figure, and a slightly too-punctilious host, as though wishing, whether consciously or not, to compensate for Gina's slapdash approach. There was always a frown between his eyes, a rigidity in his manner. But remembering the easy companion of the golf course, Cass had begun to see there might be some justification for his exasperation. Though she herself had grown steadily fonder of Gina as the months went by, she couldn't deny that the endless chaos she created around her must be a trial to someone of Laurie's efficiency and love of order. And Gina shared none of his interests, never supported him in his job, and only kept him fed and clothed by the skin of her teeth.

Theirs was not the only improbable marriage – but Cass pushed the reminder away, keeping her thoughts firmly on the Frasers' relationship. Not only the difference in their personalities was against them. Gina had by this time got herself into an untenable position with all three offspring. She treated Steve and Andy with an anxious indulgence which they didn't particularly seek but casually abused. Why not if it was there? Gina had come into their lives at an age when they didn't need a mother figure and had no interest in any new partner of their father's. He was so old it was embarrassing anyway. They didn't dislike Gina, but she bored them, and they made it clear they blamed her for landing them in this inconvenient and pointless place. Nessa was much more vocal on the subject than they were, missing no opportunity to complain about the remoteness of the Mains, the unfairness of never being able to 'do anything' with her friends, and just about everything, as far as Cass could see, that her mother did or offered. Gina met these tirades with an erratic mixture of conciliatory tears and short-lived bursts of discipline which never went near the root of the problem.

Then Cass forgot the whole family and their problems as she neared the fork into the old road. There was one brief glimpse of the barn, a dark shape on the semicircle of snow bordered by black river and shadowy trees, but it gave no hint of whether anyone was there or not. The curtains were already drawn at Sycamore Lodge. Beverley always closed them the moment dusk came on, hating the idea of anyone being able to see in.

Although she took the turn into the lane with care, Cass felt the back end of the Volvo swing. She relaxed her hands and was relieved when it came out of the skid smoothly, taking the hill with ease. Once it crabbed sideways into soft snow, but pulled away again and Cass was very pleased as she turned into the parking space Ed had kindly cleared for her.

It was so good to be here – *so* good. With her arms full she felt a way up the half-buried steps. They were certainly safer than the old tilted ones would have been. Then she laughed at herself; how conscientious and fair she was being. And she knew exactly why.

The house for a moment felt odd, not immediately hers. Roey had used it last with some friends, and though they had faithfully left it tidy there was a lingering air of other occupation. Then as she began the routine of waking it to life its familiar welcome emerged, bringing the pleasure that never failed. Warmth was part of it.

Guy had objected, was still objecting, to leaving the heating on all the time. He had wanted to shut the house down completely. 'We'll get the water turned off and forget the place till the spring. The cost of keeping the heating on would be exorbitant.'

It was the nearest they had come to a fight on the subject of the Corrie.

'I intend to go up whenever I can,' Cass had said quietly.

'Then you'll go on your own.'

'Then I'll go on my own,' she had agreed.

Guy had stared at her, cold-eyed, but after a crackling moment of challenge had turned away to open the nearest file on his desk and start reading it.

Cass had found it hard to deflate her anger, yet she had known she was as little prepared as he to make an issue of this. The whole basis of their life together was one of unilateral choice, unilateral action. The factor which remained disturbingly in her mind was not so much that they disagreed about using the cottage, but that Guy had used cost as the basis of his argument.

Though Guy had all the comfortably affluent man's dislike of being forced to part with his money – paying his taxes actually hurt, and he could be immovably mean about free-loading acquaintances or demands he saw as opportunistic – he was ready to spend freely on himself and Cass. And he used to spend freely on travelling and holidays together, Cass reminded herself. She had been responsible for changing that. Though the decision to buy the Corrie had been a joint one their desire to spend time there had been seriously out of step, and Cass realised that she had never properly considered what that had meant to Guy in terms of reducing time shared in doing other things.

She turned up the heating, took paper and kindling from the box Roey had with surprising forethought left by the radiator – or had she found a lover with brains for once? – laid and lit the fire, fetched more stuff from the car, put away food, then went up to take bedding from its damp-proof binbags. She checked the taps, found the water running safely and switched on the immersion. She removed three corpses from the mousetraps and reset them. In the still chilly bedroom she hurriedly changed into wear-softened brown suede trousers, Shetland wool polo, a padded overshirt bought at the Kirkton garage, thick socks. The weekend had begun.

Going out by the front door – she had seen from the kitchen window that the hill gate was nearly invisible under a drift, and she could imagine how much snow would have blown into the hollow of the burn – she started up the lane, revelling in the smell of snow on the air, the fainter tang of resin and wet trees, the darkness which paled to grey snow light as she went on without using her torch. It was such luxury to know the journey was behind her, the little house below warming up and well stocked with all she needed, hers and hers alone for nine whole days.

And ahead was Gina's hug and Tiree's dotty welcome, and the agreeable prospect of settling down at the table in the warm bright kitchen with a glass of wine – in desperation Laurie had taken over the cellar so that could now be guaranteed – and letting herself slow to the different tempo of her other world.

The lights of the Mains streamed out across the tracked snow of the yard, the icy remote shapes of the hills climbing behind them. Someone's music – Nessa's? All pop music sounded exactly the same to Cass but it was certainly loud enough for hers – streamed out with them.

She was here, and tomorrow waited with its promise of the pleasure she had looked forward to every day of the time she had been away.

Chapter Eighteen

Cass was awake before dawn. She went down to make tea and brought it back to bed, then, unable to concentrate on a book, she switched the light off again and, propped against the pillows with her warm overshirt round her, she listened to the silence and waited for wan winter daylight to come fingering round the curtains.

She waited peacefully, feeling happiness as sure and comforting as the duvet over her and the soft shirt wrapped round her shoulders. Soon, when the morning came, she would be able to dress and go out, down the snowy lane, across the road, through the tunnel to where the river ran between its broad white frills of ice . . .

Cass had talked to no one, not even to Gina, about Rick, though she knew the truth now.

Beverley, entirely focused on her own needs and ambitions, which Cass had come to believe were so overriding that they had created almost a fantasy world beyond which she could no longer see, still held to the dogma that Rick hadn't fully recovered. Though her references to his condition were elliptical and mysterious, and she passed over them hurriedly as though they would not stand up to investigation, in general terms she continued to speak of him in much the same way as she had when Cass had first met her, martyred about the burden of caring for him, using it as both weapon and defence, and sticking to her version of events to the point of blind obsession.

After that October sunrise when Cass had climbed with Rick to the ridge above the Bealach Dubh, she had been eager to see him again, wanting to learn the facts behind his parting words. But though she had walked early again the following morning, feeling self-consciously visible in the empty landscape, knowing she should be getting ready to start south, ashamed to be there on the off chance of meeting someone who had given her no indication that he wanted her to do any such thing, there had been no sign of Rick. Angry with herself, she had made herself review the bald facts. He was a married man living more or less at her gate. And he was married to Beverley, a choice which could hardly state more clearly that he could have little in common with Cass. Her brain had accepted the reasoning; her feet had carried her along a route from which barn and bungalow were always in sight. Whatever common sense could say, there had been something about Rick's company, his air of unrufflable serenity, which had powerfully appealed to her.

But the glen had lain empty and quiet, except for a hedgehog in the lane which paused with lifted snout to check her presence, birdsong she barely registered because it was meaningless to her, and the single harsh bark of a roe startled from the rough patch of alder and hazel beside the river.

Suddenly embarrassed to think watching eyes might have interpreted her movements accurately, she had gone quickly up the lane again, and become very busy about making breakfast for Guy and packing the car. She had hated leaving.

On her next visit to the Corrie, though not concealing from herself how much she had hoped to see him, there had been no sign of Rick. That had been the weekend of the combined Hallowe 'en and Bonfire Night ceilidh in Kirkton. Remembering his assertion that he was not ill, Cass had convinced herself he might appear, but though every other soul in both glens seemed to be present, including Beverley, who spent most of the evening trying to attach herself to the Munros and Mackenzies and their friends, and being gently and with great courtesy prevented from doing so, Rick had been absent.

It was two weeks later, at the cottage on her own again, that Cass had gone out to walk on a soft moist November day and, in order to preserve some self-respect, had headed away from Sycamore Lodge and the barn, deciding to explore at last the grassy track above Riach which led to the head of the glen. There, three miles from the Corrie, she had met Rick.

He had been sitting peacefully just above the track, looking towards Allt Farr with its ruined tower, the big hills crowding behind it. Cass had checked at the sight of him, then had been conscious of trying to walk naturally as she went on. This was a meeting she need have no guilt about having contrived, though the phrase 'appointment in Samarra' did go through her mind.

Rick had turned his head and smiled as she came up, and she had been certain he'd known she was there, had probably spotted her coming a mile away. And waited? The possibility had filled her with a pleasure which had startled her.

'You're finding your way around,' Rick had commented, his smile deepening, as he moved to make room for her beside him on a comfortably shaped rock. As before, their talk had been effortless, rising naturally from what was around them.

As Rick was telling her this was the old road the caterans used to use, coming over from Glen Ellig to raid for cattle, a small party of walkers had passed, pounding grimly along, eyes on the ground, hands gripping the straps of coloured rucksacks which bobbed up and down on their blue, green and purple backs. All wore woolly hats. The women walked behind the men, trudging resentfully as though they hadn't been given any choice about the pace. The whole group avoided eye contact as they went by, though one man produced an indistinguishable mutter in response to Rick's greeting.

Rick had shaken his head in mild amusement as they hammered on out of earshot. 'Not very relaxed. Quite sad, really. No one tries to stop them using this route, except asking them to respect shooting and stalking seasons, but they get all uptight and aggressive if they meet anyone remotely likely to belong to the estate.'

'We're not tattered enough to be lairds, surely?' Cass had commented, surveying Rick's worn-in, heavy-duty jeans and capacious waxed jacket, and liking the way he looked.

He had laughed. 'You've met the Mackenzies then? Oh, yes, I remember, you were going to call on Joanna. How did you get on with your sales pitch that day? And did you go up to Allt Farr to talk to Kate Munro as well?'

Cass, oddly pleased that he remembered so much of their conversation, had been reminded of the unexpected way it had ended. The inconsistency between what Rick had told her and Beverley's version of events had nagged at her in the intervening weeks, and not pausing to consider how odd the leap might seem, she had asked frowning, 'What did you mean that day, that you aren't ill? Are you really better now?'

Rick's silence had made her aware that the question had been intrusive and her manner of asking it crass. She had coloured hotly as she apologised. 'Rick, I'm sorry, it's none of my business. I had no right to ask that. Do forgive me.'

'It's all right,' he had said sharply, and even in her discomfiture Cass had thought the tone not one she would have expected from him. 'I brought the subject up myself on that occasion, if you remember.'

He hadn't continued, however, and Cass had waited uncomfortably, wishing she had kept her mouth shut but discovering as the silence stretched just how much she wanted the mystery cleared up. It mattered to her to know. Then, without knowing how, she had been sure Rick was going to explain, was merely taking time to order what he wished to say. This strange certainty, which calmed her annoyance with herself for having been so tactless, had given her a glimpse of a new level of perception about someone else's feelings. She had had a vivid sense of Rick mustering his resources, satisfying himself that he was ready to speak. After a few moments he had turned to face her. They had been close to each other and, seated, Rick's extra inches even more noticeable. Cass had found herself acutely conscious of his nearness, and the solidity of his muscular frame.

'It was time I tried to talk to someone. I had to make myself open the door a crack, commit myself in some way.' Rick had spoken brusquely, as though it was hard even now to embark on this. 'Perhaps I knew you'd be the one person not to let it pass, to come swinging back at me with that forthright, "So what the hell were you talking about?" approach.'

'I didn't quite—' Cass had protested, but a big hand on her arm had stopped her.

'No, I know, but hang on a minute, will you? Let me try to get this off my chest.'

She had nodded and felt the grip on her arm briefly tighten in thanks before he released it.

'I'm not proud of any of this,' he had warned, gazing away down the bracken-covered slope falling steeply to the river below, his voice quieter, almost deliberately detached, as though he had wished to forestall uninformed and meaningless sympathy.

'I was ill, seriously ill, for a long time. Nearly a year. Diagnosed as having ME, or chronic fatigue syndrome, or whatever you like to call it. I went completely to pieces, couldn't get myself out of bed in the morning, couldn't be bothered to dress, couldn't concentrate on anything, sometimes couldn't even lift my limbs. I abandoned my business, cut myself off from everyone and everything, totally lost interest. Beverley was marvellous.' His voice had subtly altered on those three words, refuting argument before it was offered. 'She looked after everything, looked after me, even struggled with the business single-handed for a time. Security fencing, alarm systems,' he had added tersely, as though recognising Cass might need the information but knowing if he got side-tracked he would not be able to go on. 'Then when it became obvious I wasn't going to be able to get myself together she sold up, built the bungalow, and moved here so that I could live in stress-free surroundings, with no reminders of anything that would upset me – and never again in my life have to lift a finger to do anything useful.'

His voice hadn't become bitter. Rather Cass felt the bitterness he had refused to allow it to reveal.

'But you said you were better?' she had asked, puzzled but careful to make the question as unprobing as possible. Though from everything she had seen of him she could not imagine there could be any doubt of it.

Rick had turned to her again, with a quiet deliberate movement, to examine her concerned face. Then he had smiled.

'The doctor here didn't believe I had ME at all, and she was right. She eventually established that I'd developed a sugar allergy. Simple, wasn't it?'

Cass had stared at him, not sure she had fully understood. 'You'd lost your business, your home, your entire way of life, all because of a mistaken diagnosis? But why—'

The multiplicity of the 'why's' she wanted to ask had overwhelmed her. The anomalies that had nagged at her all along swarmed bafflingly in her brain – the gulf between the vulgarity of Sycamore Lodge and the beauty of the objects Rick made and restored in the barn; the choice of Glen Maraich in the first place, so incongruous an environment for Beverley; Beverley herself, and the impression she cultivated that Rick was incapable of normal social interaction, and indeed Rick's own reclusiveness. It added up to something bizarre, and what Rick had told her only made it less comprehensible.

'Why indeed?' he had repeated softly, once more falling silent, and Cass had divined that what he had said so far was not, for him, the important part; that what was to come would be far harder for him to tell. She had waited, filled not with curiosity now but with an acute compassion for someone else's torment which she could not remember ever having felt before.

'As soon as the sugar levels were adjusted I recovered at miraculous speed,' Rick had resumed, briskly, as though the clinical facts were the easiest to deal with. 'It was like walking out of a fog and finding all the small things of life still in place, bright, ordinary, in their familiar order. It will sound absurd, I know, but it was magic to have everyday actions like cleaning your teeth or tying your shoelaces, which had been a colossal and tedious effort, suddenly normal again, back in perspective, so that you never noticed them. Yet at the other end of the scale my larger world had vanished; what I did, what I was, all that had been wiped out. I was in a new place, with no purpose or function, and billed as a sick man.'

'But Beverley – I mean, you still have to go for counselling?' Cass was conscious of grasping at any immediate fact, floundering among the implications of this new picture.

'Counselling? I have to have my sugar levels checked regularly.'

'But – Rick, this is truly awful.' Seeing the grimness of his face she had cast around for something to be positive about. 'But you liked the place where you found yourself?' she had asked, with a gesture to take in their surroundings.

'The glen? I could hardly believe my luck,' Rick had replied with reassuring vigour. 'But the bungalow? I just wanted someone to tell me it wasn't happening.'

Cass had laughed, not bothering to analyse why that cheered her so much. 'But why do you stay in it? And why do you let people go on thinking—?' But that had seemed dangerous ground and she had let the sentence hang.

'Ah. Crunch question.' Rick had kept his eyes on the patch of blue sky reflected in the curve of river below Allt Farr. 'By a curious chance, an almost unbelievable chance, I had found myself in exactly the kind of place where I wanted to be. I'd been handed the sort of freedom I'd been afraid I could never hope to achieve. Personal freedom.' His voice had become so quiet Cass had known he was talking more to himself than to her. 'At first, while I was recovering, I needed time to adjust. Then – well, I just let things slide, am still letting things slide.'

Cass had understood this was the crux for him, but with her new perception of what he was feeling she had also sensed that he wasn't ready to discuss it and she had turned to another aspect, almost more baffling.

'I don't understand why – only please say if this is something you'd rather not talk about – but this place seems so improbable for Beverley, so remote from all the things she seems to enjoy and want. How will she like the winter here, for one thing?'

'She'll survive as long as she can get up and down the road,' Rick had said curtly, and Cass thought ruefully that she should have known better than to ask a man she barely knew such a question about his wife.

Then he had added abruptly, 'I'm not sure I can make you understand, but for Beverley it fulfilled a dream to move somewhere like this – a small rural community where she thought she could acquire ready-made social status by building a posh house, driving about in a big car, and shedding the past. That was always her goal, but she'd thought she'd have to wait till I retired to realise it. For different reasons the plan suited me. How I longed to get out of the city! Not that I'd ever dreamed Beverley would consider Scotland, but when I was ill and she had to make the decision alone she chose that for me. She knew I had always hankered to come back.'

Cass thought Beverley had probably had some private agenda of her own, though what it might have been she was unable to imagine.

'No links.' Again Rick had sounded as though he was addressing himself. Nevertheless Cass had found the courage to ask, for everything she could learn about him was important to her, 'Why did that matter?'

'Ah, well, Beverley has spent a lot of her life trying to forget the past. She had a rough childhood, poor girl. She'd adored her father, and he was killed in Korea. Then she was taken from her mother who was convicted of neglect, and brought up by various foster parents who maltreated her in one way or another. She really has had the lot. Then to find that her husband had more or less fallen to pieces in her hands ... What better place to hide him away than at the top of Glen Maraich?'

This time the bitterness had been there, raw and unmistakable, and Cass had found herself wanting to fight it, refuse it on his behalf.

'Hiding from what?' she had asked quietly.

'Oh, associations. The neighbours, if you like.' Whatever had produced that bleak tone, he was not going to enlarge on it. 'Beverley wanted a fresh start, and who can blame her? She's had a lot to contend with and she's coped marvellously.'

That word again. A 'so be it' which had struck Cass as a formula he had grown accustomed to employing.

When by unspoken agreement they had made a move and started back towards Riach, her mind had turned over the story with dissatisfaction. Too many questions had been left unanswered. Why did Beverley cling to the myth that Rick was still convalescing? What purpose did that serve? And if Rick was no longer ill, why did he continue to lead his secluded existence? Why didn't he take hold of his life again? He knew he should; that was the real source of his bitterness. His words as he began the story had come back to her. 'I'm not proud of any of this ...'

Above all, why should a man of his type, strong and, Cass would have thought, not easily deflected from any course he chose, let selfish, silly Beverley make the choices for them both? Perhaps the clue had lain in the tone of protective sympathy in which he had related the circumstances of her early life, and remembering it Cass had been stabbed by a pang of unexpected envy. There was more to this story, she was convinced, and she had found herself hoping that one day she would be allowed to learn the rest.

Chapter Nineteen

Coming out of the sliding, formless half thoughts, half memories, Cass opened her eyes to find the light round the curtains had strengthened to the grey-white of winter dawn. At last she could allow herself to get up, dress and go out.

Months had passed since that conversation with Rick, which they had continued at every opportunity since. By now he was an essential part of her life, or of her life in Glen Maraich, where so many responses and feelings were stirred which were not only dormant in her London world, but which she had begun to see with some anxiety had never existed there.

She had wanted to be at the Corrie for Christmas, but over the years Guy had become resigned to spending the holiday at Havenhill and it would have been difficult to justify tossing the arrangement suddenly aside, quite apart from disappointing the family. She had consoled herself with a short-lived plan for snatching New Year at the cottage, but in the end had not even suggested it to Guy. After the festivities at Havenhill they had both needed a little space and quietness, and Cass had not been able to convince herself that Hogmanay in Glen Maraich would provide either.

She had come up shortly afterwards, visiting some of the hotels theoretically in the swing of their skiing season but in fact waiting, empty and with mounting overheads, for snow. It had not been the best time to talk about staffing, so in business terms she had not achieved very much. She had flown up for a long weekend at the end of the month; Guy had been in Dubai.

On each occasion she had seen Rick, but formally as it were, which had been a new development. The first time had been on the afternoon when Gina called at the Corrie announcing that she was on her way to his workshop with a chair to be mended. Cass had been surprised to find Gina on these terms with him, then amused to realise that for a second the discovery hadn't been particularly palatable. The chair had turned out to be a collection of fragments which Gina had shown Cass with great excitement. Cass said she'd have used them to light the fire.

'That's just the trouble,' Gina protested with indignation. 'That's how all these treasures are lost. This chair is beautiful, and it's probably been in constant use since about the middle of the eighteenth century.'

'But not too recently by the look of it.'

'Don't be so callous and philistine. Actually, I'm not a hundred per cent sure of the date because of the legs, but Rick will know.'

Cass had found herself unable to ask the obvious questions – why was Gina so sure of that, when and how had she got onto such terms with Rick, and how was he? But listening and watching as he'd turned over the bits of chair with loving hands, and he and Gina exchanged brisk knowledgeable comments about pierced splats and diagonal struts and early leg shaping, arriving at an almost definite date of 1770, she had had to accept that this was not the first find of Gina's to arrive at the barn for resuscitation, and she had felt a pang of exile as envious and sharp as any she had suffered when uprooted as a child from Dalry.

At least, she had comforted herself, she had now met Rick officially and could openly refer to him, for a deep reticence had prevented her from speaking of their earlier encounters. She hadn't been sure the reasons for this reluctance would have stood close examination, but it had been deep and definite.

On her next visit she had met Rick at Sycamore Lodge. That had been the day of the expedition to Muirend with Beverley. Cass laughed to remember it as she pulled on her boots in the porch and let herself out into the waiting morning, where nothing moved on chill windless air.

Needing one or two items beyond the scope of the Kirkton shop, she had found she couldn't get her hired car to start, and Gina had come to the rescue, confessing that she hadn't shopped for the weekend herself yet because she'd forgotten what day it was, and roping in Ed Cullane to have a look at the car.

Ed, who had been led astray the night before, not for the first time, by Doddie Menzies the keeper from Allt Farr, disposing of his entire week's wages in the bar of the Cluny Arms in the process, had been only too glad to put some cash in his pocket, and they had left him at the Corrie with his head under the bonnet doing his best to keep his eyes open till they'd gone. When Cass saw the state of him she hadn't been sure she should let him touch a car that wasn't even hers, and a swift vision of how Guy would have dealt with the problem had increased her doubt – the peremptory call to the hire company, the firm placing of the ball in their court. Anywhere else, wouldn't she have done exactly the same? But that wasn't the way of things here.

Gina, with her usual kindness calling at Sycamore Lodge to see if anything was needed from Muirend, a habit Cass had come to think would have been more useful if practised the other way round, had explained this to Beverley.

'Oh, I can certainly give you a lift to Muirend if that's what you want, Cass,' Beverley had said, not listening properly, her tone disapproving, as though Cass must have brought her problems on herself. 'You only have to ask, you know. After all, we are neighbours.' It had not escaped her notice that whereas Gina seemed content to remain immersed in a world of her own, Cass had by some means achieved an enviable level of familiarity with the households of Riach and Allt Farr and therefore, however annoying she was, might have her uses. The sugary smile that went with the words had made Cass's eyelids quiver.

'No, Beverley, Cass isn't looking for a lift. I was just explaining why she's coming with me,' Gina had persisted, but she might as well have saved her breath.

'I was thinking of going anyway, so it's no trouble to me, I assure you,' Beverley had replied with the illogical obliviousness Cass found so rewarding. 'I need to exchange my videos. My *Beauty Through Movement* videos,' she had added quickly, in case there should be any silly misconceptions. 'I do firmly believe that our level of fitness, and therefore of emotional vitality, lies in our own hands, don't you? Tone the muscle and your whole aura will be enhanced, as Yvonne says. I'm afraid I can't offer you a lift too Gina, if you have that dreadful dog with you. I refuse to have him in my car.'

'Then you could come with us,' Cass had said innocently. 'Or we can exchange your videos for you if you tell us what you want.'

'I have every intention of taking the Mercedes,' Beverley had said more sharply, going pink.

'It's all right, Tiree's not—' Gina had begun, when Cass had cut across her saying, 'Then we'll come with you, thanks, Beverley.'

'We could just have taken both cars. You might end up regretting this,' Gina had warned, as they ran round at Beverley's bidding turning off lights, locking doors, moving the Subaru to the furthest corner of the gravel 'to be out of the way', and meekly accepting a reprimand for having left the gate open when they arrived.

'I couldn't resist the prospect. She's such an idiot.'

'Yes, a dangerous idiot.'

It was not that Beverley couldn't drive the big car, in fact she handled it surprisingly well, it was just that she regarded everyone else on the road as beneath contempt, if not deliberately conspiring against her by being there in the first place. As cars, vans and farm pick-ups found themselves with their nearside wheels off the road, and tractors, seeing they were being offered no quarter, climbed banks and lurched into ditches, Cass, turning to watch them scrambling back on course in the Mercedes' wake, had felt the wild giggles only Beverley could provoke rise in a threatening tide.

Gina, sitting in front, had evidently decided her only recourse was to gaze straight ahead and see nothing, and her air of brave martyrdom hadn't helped.

But in the end Cass had been unable to suppress a protest as Beverley kept a hapless van behind her for miles by pursuing an immutable system of cruising slowly through the bends and sweeping majestically away on every straight.

'Have you noticed there's someone behind you?' Cass had felt compelled to ask at last.

'Or course I have,' Beverley had replied crossly. 'I'm very conscientious about using my rear mirror. It's the hallmark of the good driver.'

'Then haven't you realised the poor man has been trying to get past you for the last five miles?'

'I don't think he can expect to overtake a Mercedes,' Beverley had said pityingly.

'But you're holding him up. He knows the road better than you do.'

'I don't know why you should think that,' Beverley had snapped, ruffled. 'But he can't keep up on the open stretches. I should have thought if you notice so much you'd have realised that for yourself.'

'You could let him by,' Cass had suggested, and the quiver of Gina's shoulders had told her that her voice wasn't as strictly under control as she had supposed.

'Oh, really Cass, what would be the point of that?' Beverley protested, quite roused by this time. 'I'd lose my place. You'd never get anywhere doing that.'

Away she had surged once more and the joiner in the rattling van behind, who had taken far longer doing a homer for a chum than the couple of hours he had sworn to his wife he would be away before taking her shopping, had fallen back with fluent curses.

'But we're not in a hurry,' Cass had objected, though having serious trouble with her voice this time. 'And he looks as though he is.'

'Then he should have set out earlier,' Beverley had responded obdurately. Cass had half expected her to say, 'Then he should have bought a Mercedes.'

Once in Muirend Cass and Gina had been told where and when to report back, the appointed time taking more account of Beverley's shopping list than theirs.

'Now, they have some very good sock-drawer organisers in the craft shop on the square. I checked and they're no more expensive than the ones in my *Home of Your Dreams* catalogue, and getting them here will save the postage as well. Perhaps you should buy some too, Gina, I should think you'd find they'd come in very handy in your house. After that I have to call at my florist's. Now please don't be late back. Having to bring you down has made a considerable hole in my day, as I'm sure you appreciate.' Beverley had been kind enough to soften this with a gay little laugh as she hurried off.

'Don't start laughing yet,' Cass had pleaded as she caught sight of Gina's face. 'But I think we've earned coffee after that. Or have you got masses to do?'

'Masses. But we're bound to be late anyway, so ten minutes more won't make any difference.'

'What a philosophy, but I have to say I'm all for it this time.'

'I think we should have gone with Beverley to the video shop. Did you notice she was carefully keeping the vids under wraps. What do you bet they really were?'

Speculating enjoyably on this, they had recklessly squandered precious minutes on cappuccinos and succulent wedges of carrot cake.

In spite of being late, and offending Beverley by the uncouth nature of the household shopping they expected to put in her car, she had recovered her good humour by her own means – first by remarking as they passed Sillerton that she had heard work was being held up so badly that they couldn't possibly hope to open the new facilities in the spring; then by gathering a long tail of infuriated Saturday shopping cars behind her; and finally by delivering an unwanted dissertation on the relaxing, toning or invigorating properties of shower gels. All this so refreshed her that she had actually invited Gina and Cass to come in when they reached Sycamore Lodge.

And, quite unexpectedly, Rick had been there, and for Cass there had been a floundering moment when private images met reality, and eye and mind had resisted seeing him in these surroundings of affectation and absurdity. Her reaction of protest, of outrage almost, had been calmed by Rick's easy smile and friendly welcome, though he had had little to say. Cass decided that if Beverley always wittered on as she was doing now he had probably long ago settled on that as his wisest course. But he had not for a moment been at a loss, and Cass had received the clear impression that demand and throw orders about as she might, Beverley did not ultimately have the upper hand. The conviction had been oddly satisfying.

Rick's calm had not deserted him even when Beverley had taken a hand in the conversation he was having with Gina about the current round of the debate about art treasures leaving the country.

'Half the news was taken up with that last night,' Beverley had cut in disdainfully, as though they had been guilty of trying to show off some specialist knowledge. As she spoke she had pointedly slipped a coaster of Grace Darling rowing through waves higher than the lighthouse under Cass's cup and saucer.

'It's just a waste of viewers' licence fees. Quite enough lottery money goes on art as it is. Take that fuss about 'The Vanished Tankard' – it all came to nothing in the end. I think they should concentrate on people's real needs, like cutting prescription charges or doing something about that road to Muirend. It's a disgrace . . .'

The crown of it, where you spend your time, is fine, Cass had wanted to say, while her brain chased down the reference to 'The Vanished Tankard'. She had seen Gina work it out just as she did, and realised from Rick's expressionless face that he was already there. It had been a good moment. He really was as she had seen him, incongruous in this awful house and, no matter what else their relationship might be based on, he moved in a different mental world from Beverley's.

The biggest surprise had come as she and Gina were leaving, privately promising themselves some decent tea at the Corrie. Rick had turned to Cass and said in a normal voice, making no attempt at concealment, 'Do look in at the barn any time you feel like it. It would be good to talk some more.'

'I'd love to,' Cass had said without hesitation, though in her surprise she had been unable to check an involuntary glance at Beverley. But Beverley had been recommending some special worktop savers to a patient Gina – 'though in your case, if you don't mind me saying so, Gina, it's probably too late' – and had had no attention to spare for anyone else.

The naturalness with which Rick had spoken had been very pleasing, and Cass had felt happy as she extracted her shopping from the heap in the back of the Subaru. (Beverley had not volunteered to take the Mercedes up the lane to save transferring it.) There had been nothing clandestine about his invitation, and Cass liked that. Though she decided only a woman so blind to everything outside herself as Beverley could have missed such an exchange, however innocent, between her husband and another woman.

* * *

Leisurely talks in the barn, pulled up close to the stove Rick had installed, in a couple of fire-damaged Allt Farr chairs designed in the days when furniture took account of the human frame, drinking the strong tea which never appeared at Sycamore Lodge . . . Walks into the snowy empty hinterland beyond Riach, up to the high corries where the burns spilled so boisterously down at this time of year . . . Quiet time spent by the fire at the Corrie on their way down from a windblown walk along the spine of the ridge above the Mains . . .

During these precious hours Cass had learned more of the background to Rick's strange situation, recognising his need to talk to someone who was not fully part of this place, where by a bizarre chain of events he had found himself. She knew this was all it was for him, and on that level found deep satisfaction in their developing friendship. An honest examination of what it meant to her she had so far resisted, knowing there was more to the question than her feelings for this kind and quiet man, so strangely trapped by conscience and circumstances.

As Cass knew, the original link between Beverley and Rick had been her loneliness and need after a deprived and harsh childhood and adolescence, and his compassion and instinct to help. A familiar story, and though as Cass heard more of it she could not deny that Beverley had had an appalling time, she still felt Rick had allowed himself to be manipulated. But for his part, Rick believed he owed a great deal to Beverley too.

He had been enmeshed by more than marriage. When he came down from university – he had read geography at Durham – he had faced pressure to go into the family business, at that time rapidly expanding in response to the growing demand for security fencing and protection. He had agreed to stay for five years, with vague plans to move out of Liverpool after that and either set up some rural branch of the company, or start an independent business.

'It doesn't take a psychologist to work out what I was really hankering for,' he had admitted to Cass. 'I saw myself doing what my grandfather had done – spending solitary hours on windswept hillsides mending dry-stane dykes or putting up deer fencing. How I loathed the city.'

'But why did you stay?' Cass could not see him, in spite of what he had told her, as a man who would allow circumstances to push him where he didn't want to go.

'Both my brothers had settled in New Zealand, my father was asthmatic and my mother died soon after Beverley and I were married.' He had believed at the time that there had been only one course open to him; he still saw it that way. 'Beverley was amazing. She learned the whole business from top to bottom and ran the office side of it for years.'

She had been greedy and ambitious, and he had been obliged to fight a hundred battles over her summary methods, particularly with struggling debtors, but at the same time he had understood how much financial success had mattered to her.

'Did you still see your grandparents?' Cass knew as she spoke that the question was not solely prompted by wanting to move on from the topic of Beverley. Rick's need and love for Scotland was a link with *her*.

'Not in the cottage above Lochindorb, I'm afraid,' he had answered with regret. 'My grandfather died a couple of years ago and my grandmother moved to a council flat in Nairn.'

There had been a finality and sense of loss in that which had left Cass nothing to say.

On another occasion, with sleet pelting against the skylights of the barn, and Beverley on her way down the slushy road to Muirend to see her beautician, having to her hysterical dismay found a hair on her chin, Rick had told Cass more. He had been engaged in the boring job of sewing in the springs of a chesterfield, and very glad to be interrupted. This was the day when he had tried to put into words, for himself as well as for Cass, his fears when he had first become ill, and the vast, oppressive sense of personal failure, as the debilitating lassitude grew and he and everyone around him had been sure he was suffering a nervous breakdown.

'I was never a natural businessman, and the pressures these days are unbelievable. One major customer defaulting is enough to tip the balance, and the bank's like a panther waiting to spring – well, why am I telling you this, you know all about it.'

As Cass had looked at his open kindly face, grim at present with these memories, she could imagine how unsuited he must have been to the cut-throat battleground which so stimulated Guy.

'And I woke up again,' Rick had resumed, self-mockery in his voice, 'to find that against all the odds I had been given precisely what I wanted. Business gone, city life a bad dream behind me, living in one of the most beautiful glens in Perthshire, with nothing expected or demanded of me.'

But still trapped in his marriage. More than ever trapped, because Beverley had not only looked after him while he was ill and dealt so competently with their joint affairs, but had sacrificed her own preferences to bring him to Scotland.

'But don't you mind Beverley telling people you haven't recovered properly yet?' Cass knew as she asked that she was the one who minded it for him, and also, as Rick didn't say anything, his face shuttered, that she should never have put such a question.

But he had answered her. 'She can say it if it suits her. Why not? It explains me, doesn't it? Explains my not plunging back into the arena; not, as Beverley would say, getting a proper job. And that gives me an odd kind of freedom,' he had continued slowly, not looking at Cass, picking up the first thing that came to hand, the tool he used for straining webbing, and concentrating all his attention on it, pressing its sharp end idly against the ball of his thumb. 'It's a useful cover story which allows me to do more or less as I please, and it keeps me clear of the social rigmarole Beverley's so keen on. I've ended up where I wanted to be, and by the greatest good luck I've found I can turn an enjoyable hobby into a full-time occupation. Who am I to complain?'

His tone had been deliberately light, rounding off the subject, but Cass had felt there was much more that he wasn't saying, divining that for him this situation mirrored in some important respects his previous one – the choices had not been his, and his sense of obligation was more binding than ever.

Chapter Twenty

It was impossible to tell from the tracks across the snowy space by the river if Rick had already come down to the barn this morning, and Cass felt doubt and hope churning as she went towards it. No light, no sounds.

I shouldn't let it be this important, she warned herself, but the caution was swamped by expectancy. This was the core moment of each visit to the Corrie – the moment of seeing Rick.

Rounding the corner of the building she saw a line of light between the big doors. Trying to quell her bounding relief, she took hold of one of the handles, feeling the iron cold through her glove, and rolled the heavy door a few inches aside to slip sideways through the gap, trundling it shut behind her with a slight thud which bounced it off its other half again.

The main part of the barn was cold and dim, but at the further end light spread from the doorway of the small section Rick had partitioned off round his workbench, to enable him to work comfortably during the winter. He had already raked out the stove and stirred it to life, and was in the act of flipping out a match after lighting the gas ring. He turned to look at her over his shoulder, and smiled. Cass felt stifling joy rise up again and nearly choke her then, overtaking and calming that unsettling tide of delight which she could never quite control, a warm simple sense of arrival.

Rick watched her walk towards him into the light. He was still smiling and Cass wanted to keep going, straight up to him and into his arms. But he had never touched her; they had never touched each other. It would have been unthinkable in the kind of relationship which had developed between them, yet in another way utterly natural.

'Timing's good.' Rick gestured at the two mugs beside the kettle, a spoonful of coffee in each. Neither he nor Cass took milk or the sugar Rick had once used so freely and which had broken his life apart.

'Marvellous. Just what I was needing.'

'The stove won't take long to warm up.' Rick pulled the door in the partition to and Cass relished the instant, unfailing magic of their seclusion in this little enclave, smelling of woodsmoke and sawdust and turpentine, overlaid with the whiff of Gold Blend as she raised her steaming mug to sip cautiously.

There was a straightforward acceptance that they would spend this first empty hour of the day together. Cass had no wish to probe the quality or extent of Rick's freedom, or venture on the treacherous ground of what Beverley might know or think. Nor, still, had she made herself look at this friendship in the context of her own life, though she couldn't evade it much longer.

'How did the new car perform?' Rick enquired, turning off the gas with a pop as the kettle began a whispery shriek, apt voice for the early hour, the pallid dawn light struggling against the glow of unshaded bulbs and, outside the thick stone walls, the white hills crowding.

'Sailed up,' Cass boasted. He was so good, always remembering what was going on in her life, always interested. It was an unaccustomed luxury. 'It's going to be the perfect car for here.'

'It's a lot of motor certainly, but I still think you should have gone for something that would be a bit more solid around you.'

'A Volvo's solid,' Cass said peaceably.

'Well, we'll see how you get on,' Rick said, and Cass liked not only the inference of time stretching ahead, but the sensation of being looked after. But I'm not the sort of female who likes being looked after, or wants to be told what kind of car she should drive. She smiled into her coffee mug.

'In fact, we'll probably see quite soon,' Rick was saying. 'Have you heard the forecast for the next few days?'

'No. What does it say?'

'It says snow.'

'My chance to get blocked in at last, do you think?'

Rick laughed at the yearning tone. 'Has Ed been round past you with the plough?'

'Yes, and he cleared a space for me to turn as well, which was really good of him.'

'Gina's been having fun and games getting up and down, I gather.'

'So they were saying in the shop last night.'

'She shouldn't have any trouble in the Subaru. It's ideal for the job. Max says he's thinking of getting one for Kate.'

'How is Kate?'

'Very well, according to her mother-in-law, who made Doddie bring her down the other day in the Hilux with a few more charred remnants she's instructed me to resurrect. God knows where she's been stashing them. But far be it from me to argue. She took the chance to have a good ferret round while she was here. Lit on that chair of Gina's with a 'Hah!' of acquisitiveness that made my blood curdle. Doddie kept muttering things like, "Man, you're in it up to your neck now, I'm telling you," as he tramped in and out with more and more disaster victims.'

'Will you be able to do anything with them?'

'Keep the stove going maybe,' Rick grumbled, but his smile belied the tone, and Cass knew how much satisfaction he derived from restoring these damaged objects to their former beauty.

Glen gossip; home gossip. Trivial and unimportant. As satisfying as the hot coffee and the warmth from the red mouth of the wood-burning stove, where the small logs Rick had fed in were taking hold. Satisfying not only because Cass enjoyed the links she herself was forging with this place, but also because Rick, though he still enjoyed working quietly here in solitude or going for the long walks which took him over every inch of the glen, had established his own contacts with this community. And had done so with an ease which had eluded Beverley.

'Will you be going to the television meeting on Tuesday?' the thought prompted Cass to ask.

'I shall be represented,' Rick said drily.

'I wasn't sure why we were invited as we have Sky. And you do too of, course.' Beverley's had been the first satellite dish in the glen.

'I think they're keen to keep the scheme going for those who don't want to change over yet.' Rick didn't add that Beverley was more likely to attend through a determination not to be left out than from altruism.

A private transmitter, essential to provide even the poor quality picture that had so disgusted Guy, had long ago been installed, and meetings on the passionately debated subject of its funding were a feature of glen life. This one was being held at Riach, and Cass went up the lane on a night of bright starlight, icy enough to make it sensible to leave the car at home, to walk along the hillside with the Frasers.

Gina, however, a scuffed velour jump-suit in bright coral straining round her increasingly generous curves, had her head wrapped in a towel and said she couldn't be bothered to dry her hair and dress again.

'I hardly ever watch the wretched telly anyway. I can't think what everyone gets so agitated about.'

'If we don't go on contributing there'll be no television at all for the people who really need it.'

Cass surmised from Laurie's tone that this was not the first time he had made the point.

'Well, I think we'd all be a lot better off without it,' Gina retorted in the defiant tone of someone who knows they are talking rubbish. 'Music, books, art, self-expression – what happened to those?'

'I imagine the boys would rather watch the rugby than express themselves,' Laurie said tartly, tying a woollen scarf neatly round his neck. 'No, Tiree, this is not a walk, though you could be forgiven for thinking so.'

Tiree gave a ringing bark of protest. He knew boots when he saw them.

'They should play rugby, not watch it.' Gina was clearly arguing for the sake of it now. 'Anyway, they spend more time on computer games than anything else, they're completely addicted. And if they want sport we can get Sky, then it doesn't matter what the reception's like. Or does it?' she added, abandoning aggression for doubt.

'Come anyway, Gina,' Cass urged, then wondered why she was trying to persuade her. During recent visits she had observed the mood between Gina and Laurie growing openly more spiky, and though she hated Gina being made miserable by it she had been forced to accept that Laurie had plenty of justification for his sharpness. She had only to look around her. The kitchen this evening was in an even worse state than usual, dishes from lunch still in the sink, two chair seats on the table with rusty tacks, rotting webbing and some disagreeably smelly horsehair scattered round them, a slew of fabric pieces on the floor being stepped over by humans and lain on by Tiree. Pounding music from above registered Nessa's protest. There was no sign of preparations for dinner.

The meeting, as Joanna had explained when she invited Cass, had been timed to suit those who had high tea after work.

'If once we let them escape to the pub they'll never turn up. We have to forget about dinner till it's over and believe me it can grind on for hours.'

Welcoming Laurie and Cass now, not commenting on Gina's absence – and it struck Cass not for the first time how little contact

Gina had troubled to make in her years at the Mains – Joanna led them through the bare and freezing house.

'We're in the old servants' hall,' she explained. 'I wanted to have the meeting in the dining-room so that everybody could sit round the table but James said people would be struck dumb if they couldn't sit at the back, and of course he's right. It was just that I thought the dining-room might be marginally warmer.'

It wouldn't have been difficult, Cass thought, as they went into a gaunt high-ceilinged room where a table at the far end faced a couple of rows of assorted chairs, still mostly empty. Two gas radiators purred on either side and a convector heater had been drawn as close as an extension lead would allow from a solitary socket at the other end of the room. Cass wondered why the chairs hadn't been put there but, quivering in the gale which whirled in every time the door was opened, she soon saw why.

Nancy Clough, token lipstick applied for the occasion and spectacles on a chain round her neck, was already in the secretary's chair, busily arranging papers. Beverley, dressed as for a day at Perth races and hoping to be photographed there for *Scottish Field*, was warming her bottom at one of the heaters, wearing a fixed smile to show how relaxed she was.

Keeping her options open about where to sit, Cass concluded, and was not entirely delighted when, in the absence of any more satisfactory alternative, she came to join Cass and Laurie in the front row.

'Did you drive up?' Cass asked. Even walking conditions had been highly treacherous.

'Certainly not,' said Beverley, acknowledging Laurie with a queenly inclination of the head. 'I wouldn't dream of risking the car on a night like this. That drive has scarcely been touched.'

'You walked?' Cass felt momentarily guilty. She should have found out if Beverley needed company.

'Of course I didn't walk,' Beverley said, astonished at such an idea. 'I came with Nancy.'

Whose car was clearly expendable.

The back row was furtively filling with men with scrubbed red hands wearing fat wadded jackets in navy or pale grey, and women in brighter anoraks who greeted each other less inhibitedly. One or two had put on pleated skirts of dim colours, worn over woollen tights and gumboots, and Cass speculated on where their journeys this evening had begun, crossing muddy steading yards to pick-ups or Land Rovers, opening gates on high snowy tracks. Everyone kept their coats on. Most sniffed.

Considering that the gathering consisted strictly of Bridge of Riach inhabitants – Kirkton had its own separate reception problems – a surprising number had turned out, including the owner of the weekend cottage next to Sycamore Lodge and his wife, who felt having television available for their occasional visits sufficiently important to bring them all the way from Dundee on a winter's night.

Contentment filled Cass to be part of it, to have walked here with Laurie along the hill in the vast, white, cold and starlit landscape. She mentally shared the feeling with Rick, as had become inescapable habit.

With a surge of noise and briskness the contingent from Allt Farr came in, Max and Kate bringing with them old Mrs Munro, who at once shattered the quiet gossiping with her usual peremptory meddling.

'Lexy, what are you doing here? You should have stayed at home with Robson and let Colleen come. She would have had more valuable comments to contribute, I imagine, than any you will bring yourself to make. Though perhaps the lure of the Cluny bar afterwards was the decisive factor? Good evening, Nancy, I see that daphne of yours by the porch has hardly a flower on it. Had its day, do you think? Good heavens, Joanna, what time did you put the heaters on in here? Ah, Ed, just the man I want—'

A laugh arose as Ed flattened himself back in his chair, his eyes rolling like a cornered stirk's.

'Rather him than me,' muttered an anonymous voice, which might have come from Doddie Menzies, and the laughter increased. In fact with Mrs Munro's sweeping entrance the whole atmosphere altered, and laughter and talk could almost have been said to break out.

'I'm not sitting there,' Mrs Munro declared, disdaining the empty chairs left in the front row, and greeting its occupants with one raking look and firm nod. 'I need to be *much* closer to a source of heat. Present day luxi-living at Allt Farr has sapped my once hardy spirit. Yes, thank you, Doddie, that's much better.'

'We'd best burn down Riach as well then,' Doddie commented, drawing a second chair closer to the gas radiator for Kate and giving her a little wink. Cass didn't understand why this produced quite the delighted laugh it did.

James Mackenzie, theoretically the host, slipped in last, giving people shy nods as he tramped with heavy booted tread to the sanctuary of a seat beside Joanna, his gloomy heavy-jowled face suggesting this was an interruption to his life he could have done without.

'That the lot?' Max Munro asked, taking the chair. The brisk authority of his tone, and the habitually grim expression of his lean face and dark eyes gathered in his audience without effort. 'Not a bad turnout for a February night. Thanks for coming, all of you. Now, you know what this is about – cash, not to put too fine a point on it.'

Cass was aware of a ripple of movement behind her, almost of breath drawn audibly in. Mrs Munro laughed.

Before Max could continue, or his audience settle themselves again, the door opened and in burst two lolloping females in dingy sweatshirts and tight jeans, followed by the two red setters, the latter astounded to find so many people in their house, having failed to notice the arrival of several unknown vehicles.

'Out!' roared Max.

Of the trusting quartet none seemed in doubt as to whom this applied. The setters fled and the two girls embarked on a raucous round of greetings.

'Bridie and Dot, if you want to stay, though I can't imagine you'll have anything to offer that Joanna can't equally well say on your behalf, then sit down and shut up. The meeting has already started.'

'Aye, and if we'd been sitting here ready and waiting there'd be some folk looking for their dinners later on,' the livelier of the two riposted, dragging a chair to where she wanted it by screeching its feet along the floor, and grinning round to share her relish in her own wit.

'You've been watching *Home and Away* with the twins, not doing anything about dinner,' Joanna said calmly. 'Go on, Max.'

'Yes, well, so long as the twins don't decide to join us as well.'

'Becky's got them battened down.' Joanna smiled at Cass. Becky was the Australian nanny Cass had found for her last December, and she had been a great success.

'Right,' said Max. 'Back to business. You know what we're here to discuss. Now that there are different options available, we have to vote on whether the scheme is worth preserving. No, hang on, you can all have your say in a moment. Though we'd hoped to get by without doing any more work on the transmitter it does need repairs at present – you'll have noticed the blank blue screen when we get a lot of rain—' groans, 'so we have to agree on whether we want to go ahead with those. To help us decide, Nancy will give the current financial position.'

Nancy made the most of her chance, reciting with relish the causes of damage to the transmitter over the past year, including gales, the attentions of sheep and cattle, and wasps building their nest in the transformer and shorting the circuit. (Here several stories about wasps' bykes in strange places were cut short by Max.)

However, as Nancy began to itemise invoices and make pointed comments about outstanding contributions, torpor descended on the gathering while a smell of muddy overalls, rubberised over-trousers, mildew and dry rot wafted ceilingwards with the heat. Cass thought she detected a whiff of gas as well, but no one else seemed to notice it. Those who longed to smoke decided not to risk it. It might not be her house, but Mrs Munro had a tongue on her just the same.

Interest rekindled when Max, after a summary of the options, said he'd canvass views. Everyone rushed in.

'I'm no keen on having one o' they ugly great dishes stuck on the side of ma house, I can tell you that.'

'Ach, they're half the size they were nowadays. Where've you been keeping yourself, man?'

'But you're no' able to get Scottish, even supposing you go on to satellite or digital or whatever it is. We'd need to keep the transmitter for that, would we no'?'

Max confirmed this, knowing since it was the case the outcome could probably be taken for granted.

'Well, it wouldn't be right just to have English programmes.'

'The picture's terrible on Scottish though, especially if the wind's from the east. There's always another channel coming through at the back of it.'

'My brother gets that, he says it's handy for the results.'

'And he doesna' even pay his licence.'

Laughter.

'It's all very well talking about digital and Sky and the rest of them,' an aggrieved voice arose, 'but you've to pay for those over and above the licence fee. We've to pay for the scheme and a licence for it.'

'Aye, yon lads from London,' a phrase Cass savoured, 'don't do badly for themselves. They admit they can't give us decent reception and then they take extra money off us. They should give us a reduction instead—'

'Yes, OK,' Max cut in. 'We've gone into all that. We know it's a fact of life. What we have to decide is, do we keep the scheme going for those who want to continue with the present channels, and for those who may make other arrangements but want to have Scottish as well.'

'I don't mind going on the way we are, but that big beech across the drive is no' much help, and it takes away the light from my windows too,' Ed Cullane took the chance to complain.

'No one's going to cut down a tree that's taken several people's lifetimes to mature, just to improve the football for you, Ed,' Mrs Munro told him crisply.

'As it's a Riach tree I think we might take a look at it.' James Mackenzie made his first input in a mild tone which set elbows digging gleefully into ribs.

'I don't see the importance of keeping the local channel,' Beverley butted in, perhaps feeling that the lower orders had had sufficient attention. 'No one could call the majority of the programmes exactly cultural.'

A faint mutter, formless as the wind passing through a larch plantation, swelled behind her, but she bowled obliviously on. 'Before we had Sky the only programme it was possible to watch was Channel 4 but that's mostly rubbish too, as I'm sure you would agree.'

She addressed this in a bright tone to Mrs Munro, confident of support from such a quarter.

'Channel 4 has the racing,' Mrs Munro said with finality.

Apart from enjoying the cameo roles Cass was impressed by the way Max kept the meeting moving, quelling arguments about the date of the last storm and anecdotes about who had been obliged to watch the Three Tenors without the sound and who had followed Wimbledon for three years without being able to see the ball.

With a vote finally taken, inevitably opting to maintain the status quo, and with dutiful nods all round when warned that contribution requests would be sent out, though it was obvious where the bulk of the money would come from, the meeting broke up into now animated groups. Dot and Bridie thumped in and out with tea and slightly blackened sausage rolls and James gave the men drams, though when it was clear that glasses would not be refilled a drift towards the door soon began.

As Nancy was still deep in official consultations with Max, Beverley took her chance to air a few more opinions on what the intelligent viewer really wanted, this time to gentle Kate Munro who was too polite to get rid of her. Cass saw James move in protectively.

Joanna came across as she saw Cass and Laurie preparing to

leave. 'It was good of you to come,' she said. 'How's Gina? We were sorry not to see her.'

It was a courtesy, as Laurie's answer was courteous. Joanna had been welcoming when the Frasers came to the Mains, taking instantly to Gina, but she had soon seen that any friendship would be a one-way business.

She turned to Cass to add, 'It's so nice to see you during the week. How long are you up for this time?'

'A whole nine days,' Cass told her luxuriously.

'You must come up and see Jamie, or if admiring babies doesn't appeal come and see the rest of us. You might like a chat with Becky, as you haven't seen her this evening. Though I have to warn you it's half term, for the twins as well as Laura, which might be a deterrent.'

'I'd love to come.'

Cass suspected that if she hadn't been with Laurie she would have been invited to stay for dinner which would have been fun, especially with the Munros there. There was an ease about the household at Riach which attracted her, the sort of readiness for laughter which had first drawn her to Gina.

As she and Laurie started along the hill, packed-down snow squeaking under their boots, Cass deliberately kept her thoughts on that, because she would so much have liked it to be Rick walking beside her in the starry half light, not the pleasant but colourless Laurie. She had become adept at turning her mind away from such longings, which formed an undercurrent to everything nowadays.

Perhaps this week would provide the chance to spend time with Gina and talk without a dozen other things going on at the same time. Though no one but Gina and Laurie could resolve the deadlock they appeared to have reached, it might help to be able to talk about it. It was a shame Gina wasn't interested in the friendly glen contacts Cass so much enjoyed. Anything that took her out of her self-imposed isolation would surely help.

Would dinner be ready when they reached the Mains? Grinning, Cass decided that was a silly question.

Chapter Twenty-one

For the first time the flat refused to accept her, holding on to that air of unfamiliarity which places can have on a return from holiday. It looked bare rather than tidy (Cass decided she'd had too much of Riach and the Mains), its sophisticated colours lacking warmth. And it seemed dark, which she had never noticed before. Or was it merely the contrast with the dazzling sunlight off snow which had poured into the Corrie, or the effect of days spent in the glen where after the last fall the dykes had been obliterated, and only plantations and the narrowed line of the river had stood out against its white bowl?

For a day the road had been closed and nothing had moved but a couple of tractors up at Allt Farr, and Ed Cullane grinding about with the Riach plough moving large quantities of snow, though not entirely profitably as by now there was nowhere to move them to. An agreeable sociability had sprung up, those able to reach each other's houses on foot dropping in freely, first to make sure all was well, then to swap bragging stories about snowdrifts to the eaves blacking out downstairs rooms, buried logpiles, huge branches torn down by snow, sheep being dug out and deer browsing six feet above ground level. The power had been off for several hours and Cass had been amused at the matter-of-factness with which emergency systems had kicked in. She had decided that paying their dues to the television fund would be a good excuse to drag Gina out to call on Nancy, ('And that's a wee bit sharper than last year's, Gina, if you don't mind me saying so. I was whistling for that for long enough.') and had considered the conditions created by the power cut a positive treat.

The kettle was boiled on the calor gas cooker, they made toast of Nancy's home-made bread at the fire, ate it with Allt Farr Jersey butter and Nancy's Victoria plum jam, and followed it with one of the least substantial layer cakes Cass had ever eaten. The paint-flecked, crumb-clogged sixties' wireless, which ran on batteries anyway, interspersed its mainly Scottish music with a homely patter of bulletins, not about motorway pile-ups, derailed trains or snowbound airports, but about an injured shepherd being air-lifted to hospital and curlers taking joyfully to the ice.

Nancy's industry had been unchecked throughout their visit. 'I've been meaning to get at this sweater for long enough,' she said, needles flying. 'But what with one thing and another ... Now I've no excuse.'

Even deeper than the pleasure to the senses had been the rare feeling of personal responsibility being removed. They were stuck; there was nothing anyone could do about it; it was marvellous.

Coming out of Nancy's warm cottage into the brilliance of the keen air, they had seen far above them at Riach a little group of figures, and two sledges hurtling down towards the river gorge.

'I expect Laura's thankful she's home for half term and not missing this,' Gina had remarked wistfully. 'My lot can only groan because they're cut off from their mates and with no electricity there's Nothing to Do.'

'Are they all there?' There was no recognisable pattern in the comings and goings of the boys.

'Even Steve. He can't believe this has happened to him and now he's stuck.'

Gina had sounded tired and depressed. Relations in the Fraser family were clearly not improving.

'Are we brave enough to call in and see how Beverley's faring?' Cass asked.

But of course it had been inevitable. Not to see if she was all right in practical terms, there was no one more capable than Rick of seeing to that, but because the mutual support system could not be ignored, improbable as the three were as friends.

At Sycamore Lodge there had been none of the cheerful adapting to circumstances, or the downright comfort, of Nancy's cottage. Unplug her appliances and you unplugged Beverley. Until the phone went off as well she had spent the afternoon haranguing the emergency line. Somebody had to be to blame; she paid for a service and it should be provided. Without even this recourse, without television or videos (or husband to badger, for Cass saw with no surprise that Rick was not there, and with sharp longing pictured him occupied in solitary peace in the barn), a truly frightening chasm of time yawned before her.

'It just isn't good enough!' Beverley greeted them. 'I can't do my exercise routine, I can't get any washing or ironing or cleaning done, I can't cook, I can't telephone anyone, I can't listen to music, I can't clean my teeth or wash my hair. You've got no idea what it's like.'

'The water's probably still hot enough to wash your hair,' Gina suggested helpfully. 'Then you could dry it by the fire. I often do that anyway.'

The dried flowers were gone. Someone, presumably Rick, had built a huge fire in the unsullied grate.

'Well, that may be all very well for you, Gina—' that often-heard cry '—but it would do my hair no good at all, and having the fire on will make everything filthy as it is, and who's going to have to clean the house afterwards, that's what I want to know.'

No wonder Rick had vanished. 'You could boil water on it,' Cass had suggested.

'Ruin one of my precious copper-bottomed pans with all that smoke and grime! I'll do no such thing,' Beverley had squawked in horror.

The Corrie had hardly been better prepared, her big torch and the fire being all the resources Cass had been able to muster, somewhat to her shame.

'Don't worry about it, you're coming to us. Of course you are,' Gina had told her as they went up the lane. 'No one sits on their own during power cuts.'

'That's nice of you, Gina. But don't forget I'm far better off than Beverley. I haven't been deprived of the means to clean my teeth.'

'No, please don't make me laugh, I'll never struggle through these ruts if you do.'

'I'd better stop off to make up the fire and collect my torch.'

'Stay the night, don't be silly.'

'We'll see. Thanks for the invitation, but the power may be back on by then. I'll do the fire anyway. Mustn't risk the pipes freezing.'

Though she didn't attempt to explain it to Gina, Cass had been eager to spend the night in the Corrie, to cope on her own, however badly equipped she might be.

She was glad Gina had waited for her in the lane, taking the chance to get her breath back, when she discovered a note on the kitchen table. 'Anything at all that you need, don't hesitate to ask, R.'

He had been here. The kindness, the sense of being looked after, was nearly as good as having seen him. And when she went to see to the fire she found it had been built up as efficiently as the one at the bungalow.

At the Mains, where lamplit windows welcomed them through the blue dusk, Laurie already had a double ring set up from one gas cylinder, a heater from another, and CANDLES writ large on the kitchen memo board.

Even Nessa had been drawn down from her fiercely defended retreat, and as they all helped to prepare supper and settled down after only minimal argument to play Monopoly (Gina relinquished without a word the idea of an evening at the piano in firelight and lamplight) there had developed a creditable appearance of family accord which had prompted the question in more than one mind, 'Why can't it be like this more often?'

Nothing could be less like that mellow, cluttered scene, the 'scratch' meal which had turned into a feast, the hospitable friendliness and the special level of warm security lent by being cut off, than this London interior with its cool colours and simplicity of line. Stark, Cass thought, with a shiver of apprehension, as though the contrast frightened her.

She made a big effort to adjust. London was looking its best, full of spring sunshine and crocuses. It was hard to believe it was in the same country as Glen Maraich, with only a few hours' driving between them. No major crises had arisen in the au pair world in her absence, and for once she and Diane managed a long lunch together to catch up on news. Guy would be home in four days and this weekend there was the joint anniversary party for three couples in their immediate circle. There had been some discussion about she and Guy including their anniversary – the first, when everyone exclaims, 'A year already! I can't believe it!' – but it had been decided that leaving it till its proper date in six weeks' time would provide the excuse for another party.

But the word anniversary was in the air, with phone calls all week about plans, trying to decide on a present for Guy, and turning over ideas for their own celebration. It should have been fun but, fatally alone for those few days, and with too many solitary evenings in which to think, Cass had to face at last the truths this milestone forced upon her.

She was further away from Guy than she had ever been. Their existence together in the flat could not in any specific point be faulted, indeed it must have seemed to most of their acquaintance highly enviable, yet it was a failure. They seemed to have left behind in Chepstow Terrace – what? – warmth, laughter, fun, their pleasure in each other. Or were they merely getting older? Briefly Cass let herself believe that. Thinking around their friends, she convinced herself that there wasn't much zest and sparkle in the majority of the partnerships. Then she wondered what an objective observer would see, adding her own marriage to that list, and winced. But as she tried to focus on externals, reminding herself how busy Guy had been over the past year, how busy she herself had been, starting up Quickwork, expanding in Scotland, a terrible inner honesty waited its turn.

The evening before Guy returned, refusing to admit doubts about whether she was looking forward to seeing him, giving the flat an extra furbish which she recognised as propitiatory, filling it with wildly expensive spring flowers, listing Guy's messages on the answerphone for him, reducing his faxes to order, cold reality had come crashing in as she was trying on the dress she had bought for Saturday's party.

She didn't want Guy to come home. She dreaded the weekend, when she foresaw a chilling reckoning could not be avoided. Perhaps it's the dress, she thought, in a last-ditch effort to stave off the truth. It looks awful in this light, draining me. Perhaps I should have my colours done as Beverley's always tactlessly suggesting. But Gina's never had hers done and look at the fabulous things she wears, perfect for her hair and skin.

Stop dodging, the tall figure in the mirror ordered coldly, and she stared back at it in defeated honesty. All her despair at her height, her mousy hair which could only be cut close or it looked like a gorse bush, her long limbs whose thoroughbred stalking grace she could never see, flooded back as destructively as in her teens. How could a man like Guy . . . ? She used to answer that briskly with, 'Well, he did. You're here, aren't you?' But that no longer worked. Why had he married her? She knew, with sick certainty, that he too must ask that, had been asking it all year. Since the wedding they had been on diverging tracks and where were those tracks leading? She had never dared wonder. For where could they lead?

Very still, face set, Cass gazed into the mirror, finding no comfort there. The silence between them could not continue. In any relationship it was impossible for one half to feel like this in isolation. Another truism she had been too cowardly to admit.

The very difficulty of finding the moment to talk underlined the problem. Impossible on Guy's first night at home, when they hadn't seen each other for nearly three weeks. And indeed the irritation which almost every message he had received in the interval produced, and the prolonged phoning and e-mailing they generated, consumed most of the evening. Then on Saturday it seemed hardly appropriate to insist on an in-depth exploration of where their relationship had gone wrong, while others were demonstrating with the conventional rites of the tribe the success of theirs. Success one assumed. But Cass sheered away from the cynicism. To let a universal doubt creep in was too unnerving.

So she put her own concerns aside, comforting herself with the reflection that at least she wasn't one of those women who hound a man at ludicrous moments, like crouching to complain, peering past his legs while he's struggling with some tricky job under the car, 'You never want to talk about US.' Cheered up by this image, she put the issue out of her mind, enjoyed the party and the new club they went on to, and was relieved to wake with a controllable hangover.

But then came Sunday afternoon and returning with Guy, after a late lunch in the wine bar with a few party survivors, to a flat strangely alien and dead. What would they normally have done? Cass was shaken by the way in which her own emotional turmoil had so radically altered the mood of these familiar rooms. The time till dinner stretched emptily ahead, Monday looming with its power to claw Sunday evening into the week to come.

But Cass knew these thoughts were peripheral to the core of fear at what she might uncover by insisting on the truth. She stood in the kitchen, coffee made, the tray ready to pick up, and found herself taking in details of the objects around her, their texture, the way the light fell on them. Ominous.

But all her forebodings had not prepared her for the revelations which came.

Guy did his best to avoid them, knowing better than she where any admission of unhappiness or failure would carry them. He protested that he had to work, that after being away so long he had a mountain of things to catch up on, but such considerations could not deflect her now.

'We could go on and on for ever not talking,' she insisted doggedly. 'We're always busy, always rushing, always flying off in different directions.'

'Well, neither of us is likely to change our jobs,' Guy pointed out, still trying to stall.

'But we never have time for each other. We never have fun together as we used to.' I sound like the petulant woman sticking her head under the car after all, Cass realised despairingly. She tried again. 'I wondered if you felt that too, that we were drifting apart?'

'We're fine.' A hollow cheefulness there did nothing to reassure her. 'Let's leave it, shall we? I do have a hell of a lot to get through before morning.'

'Half an hour,' Cass said, hating what she was doing but knowing she couldn't give up now. 'You can leave it for half an hour.'

'There's nothing to talk about.' Still fending off a serious note, Guy picked up his cup and turned away.

Cass, shaking, put hers down and stood up. She hated scenes; above all else, she had not wanted a scene, only a reaching back to find something again that once, surely, they had shared.

'I'm not happy,' she said, her voice quiet and thin. 'Are you?'

Guy turned to her, slowly, containedly. His narrow face was startlingly drained of colour except for a mottling of red along his cheekbones, which suddenly were starkly prominent. 'Don't lift the lid off this,' he warned her, his voice tight.

'But are you happy?' A tremble Cass could not control.

For one moment more he looked at her. 'No,' he said.

After the first tense moment once this was said, as Cass, staring into the cold eyes level with her own, saw nothing there but implacable blankness, an obdurate refusal to reveal himself to her, things seemed to move forward in one appalling unstoppable wave, which rose and rose and towered above her, and finally thundered down upon her head.

Yet all this awfulness, this distress, seemed hers alone. Guy remained rational, chillingly prosaic.

'I knew it was a mistake the moment we were married,' he said, as though it was something he had come to terms with so long ago it could have no impact now. 'Commitment. It baffles me that we didn't see how fatal that would be for us. We'd seen it clearly enough for five years, for God's sake. Why did we have to change something that worked? Oh, I know it was my idea, and there were plenty of sound reasons for it, you don't have to remind me, but neither of us thought through the personal implications, did we?'

The personal implications. Loving and belonging. Shaken, floundering, Cass couldn't speak.

'I should have known I'd be no good at that sort of relationship,' Guy went on with an inward-looking bitterness which took no account of Cass's grief. 'That' not 'this', as though he already saw it objectively. 'I never have been, and it was absurd to think any profound changes were going to occur because of a few words on a piece of paper.'

Was that how he had seen the vows which had meant so much to her? 'But we hadn't intended to change anything,' Cass managed to say, and wasn't even sure which side of the argument that fell on.

'That sense of possession. Loss of freedom,' Guy went on, still more to himself than to her. 'Another person's expectations. Well, I did my best.'

'How did you? I mean,' Cass eliminated challenge from her voice, making it a simple question, 'how do you see yourself as doing your best?'

'That damned cottage,' Guy retorted, downing his coffee in one angry draught as though the conversation was over.

I knew, somehow, that that would come, Cass thought. The Corrie is at the heart of this, and always has been. 'What do you mean?' she asked quietly.

'It was madness to get something so far away.'

'But you chose it.' She could hear her voice wavering, and knew this subject more than any other would pose a threat to her self-control.

'We needed somewhere. I thought you'd be pleased. But I also thought it might get the Scottish whimsy out of your system if we started with one up there. I hoped you'd decide the idea was fine but a quarter of the driving would be better. Then you began to get excited about your Perth branch, which wasn't quite what I'd planned.'

'But you're a director at Sillerton. You were before we found the Corrie. You wanted to be nearby.'

'Oh, well, that was then. I've sold my interest in Sillerton now.'

Cass found her legs would no longer hold her up; the region of her knees seemed to consist of a space. She sank down on the sofa with her eyes fixed in disbelief on Guy's face. He wouldn't look at her.

'You've sold your shares?'

'The set-up's a shambles. The accountant was given a free hand and that never works. They refused to call in an independent adviser. The whole place will go down the chute before long and it was high time to get out.'

Laurie. Gina.

'But you didn't tell me—'

'Christ, Cass, can't you see that's the whole point?' Bitterly angry now, Guy rounded on her. 'I can't stand being answerable to you, or to anyone, ever. Right or wrong, unnatural, some hang-up I can't deal with, whatever, but that's how I feel. I can't endure having to explain or justify what I do.'

'But I've surely never made you feel—'

'Don't you see, it's far, far more than that?' He was shouting now, his anger rising uncontrollably. 'When I look ahead to years like this, of being tied, trapped, I shrivel inside. I want to concentrate on my own affairs, without any drag away. It's a lack, a flaw, you don't have to tell me that, but I can't eradicate it. To know you're always here, waiting for me, is a nightmare.'

'But I don't wait,' Cass pleaded, her voice breaking, knowing what she said was absurd because Guy was talking about something that went far deeper than this single point, but fixing on it as though its cruel unfairness could be logically refuted.

The naked hurt in her voice caught at Guy's conscience, pulling him out of his anger.

'Oh, Cass,' he said remorsefully, putting a hand on her shoulder but not leaving it there, as though there was no room in his mind at the moment for the distraction of contact. 'I know, I know. This is about my failings, not yours. No one could have had a lighter touch, or been more generous and easy to live with. It's just that it's grown into more and more of a sham. And lately I've begun to feel you're more interested in that damned glen than in life here. Buying the cottage to disillusion you about Scotland can hardly be said to have worked, can it?'

'Did you always hate it?'

'Oh, you know me. Temporary enthusiasms. It did seem for a while it would fit in with the Sillerton enterprise. And, in spite of what I said just now, I did want our marriage to work. I know we went into it for the wrong reasons, but for a while I really did hope . . .'

He had hoped, Cass saw with a desperately-held calm, that

he would be able to sustain a 'normal' human relationship. That was all it had been.

'So – where do we go from here?' How had this unimaginable question rushed upon them in a single conversation? But for Guy marriage had merely been a project which had failed; it could be aborted in the same clinical manner as it had been conceived.

'We can take our time over a decision,' he suggested, more comfortable now that everything was to be resolved in a civilised manner. For a moment Cass wished she had not held onto control, had not made this easy for him. 'I suppose nothing much need change. That feeling of being tied which did the damage has gone already, merely by being dragged into the light. But for the moment I really must get this lot sorted out . . .'

I think I'll laugh about that, Cass decided as he turned to his desk. Crying would upset me very much, and would certainly baffle Guy.

Chapter Twenty-two

Dark times followed. The early promise of spring was forgotten in the drab weeks of March, as days of lowering cloud and squally showers followed each other in soul-destroying monotony. Studying the weather map morning and evening with what she knew was childishly intense interest, Cass saw that the raindrops over England and Wales were snowflakes over Scotland and longed to be there, part of it, as ardently as she had ever longed for anything in her life.

But she was ridden by the feeling that to flee there would be cowardly, unforgivable. Her marriage might have come apart in her hands, but some effort should surely be made to repair and preserve it if that could be done. Yet there was Guy forging on busily with his life as though he scarcely remembered the shattering fact which had been acknowledged between them.

Well, that was not entirely true. Once or twice, with painful constraint, they re-opened the subject, more because Cass needed urgently to know where they were heading, and because intellectually Guy recognised that this had to be established, than because either of them wished to uncover any more agonising truths.

Once Guy did try to describe his fundamental sense of inadequacy, putting his present failure into the context of home and childhood, telling Cass more of that emotionally barren environment than he had ever brought himself to reveal before. But the details and events he made himself dredge up, bringing back a sense of isolation and rejection which seemed as he talked as real today as it had been then, caused him such evident distress that Cass gently silenced him. She understood what he was attempting, and she was grateful, but nothing could be achieved by tormenting himself in this way.

But what concerned her most, and woke in her a new and frightening loneliness, was the realisation that Guy seemed ready to go on as before; to accept the mechanics of co-habitation, including sharing a bed, while accepting with relief that they were now somehow, by admitting mutual reservations, independent of each other once more. He appeared to have shut all other aspects of their situation out of his mind, ready to plunge back into the all-absorbing enterprises which he no longer had to remember to share with Cass.

'But we can't go on as though nothing's happened,' she protested finally, wrung out with inner arguments, driven to unendurable frustration by Guy's tacit assumption that everything had somehow been resolved.

'No, there's still the business of being married to sort out, I suppose,' he agreed, with exactly the suppressed exasperation he would use when asked to deal with some minor matter like an unpaid account or a tedious social commitment. 'What we could do is get a divorce, then see if it suits us to go on living together. It worked well before and this flat's so perfect it seems a pity to pull the whole set-up apart if we don't have to.'

Winded, Cass tried to gather her wits. Then, as ever, humour came to her aid. Could anything, on the face of it, be more logical? The previous arrangement had been successful; this one wasn't. Then revert, remove the element that had done the damage. It was she who was obscuring the issue by wanting to bring feelings and hurt and need into the equation.

Those weeks of gloomy weather, busy but finding work for once an unwelcome demand on her attention, appeared in retrospect a shadowland of floundering helplessness, with no pointers of experience or even clear objectives to guide her out of it. An instinct she suspected of being not sensible but cowardly tempted her to cling to the status quo; lift no more lids, do no more harm. But a deeper integrity knew that was impossible, dishonest even, now that so much had been said.

With a painful irony, but inescapably because it was part of that joint existence still formally in place, the question of their anniversary began to dog her, pitching her from the extreme of deciding it couldn't be mentioned let alone celebrated, to a shrugging, 'Oh, let's have a party anyway, everyone's expecting it. And what difference will it make?'

But the difference it would make was that the very thought of it twisted a knife in her heart. One year ago. Hope and happy confidence.

She did her best not to regard the Corrie as a retreat where in some simplistic fashion all wounds would be healed. Places didn't work like that; wherever you went you carried your baggage of disillusionment and anxieties with you. But still the little house beckoned with its simplicity and peace, and still, inextricably tied up with it, longing ran always behind her thoughts to be with Rick in the friendly haven of the barn, or on the hill in the pristine freshness of dawn, able to talk out all this misery.

It was an image, she knew, as idealised as her picture of the Corrie. Most of her present pain could never be put into words to anyone; there would be no short cuts in coming to terms with it. Yet the comforting visions refused to be banished, and her mind turned to them continually like a drug.

Her determination not to bolt to the glen, knowing such a flight would widen the rift with Guy, was helped by the fact that Roey and some friends were borrowing the Corrie again for a couple of weeks.

That will save a few battles with my conscience, Cass told herself philosophically, the evening Roey phoned to say they had arrived safely but that since her last visit she had forgotten how to work the shower. In fact knowing she was cut off from the Corrie had the opposite effect, making her long for it with a blind and jealous single-mindedness which startled her, so remote was it from her usual laid-back calm.

In the end, angry because she had taken so long to accept it, the impossibility of holding any kind of party for her and Guy's anniversary became obvious. How could she have contemplated it for a second? Embarrassed, guilty, though a forlorn inner voice protested this wasn't all her fault, she unpicked arrangements already half in place, releasing an avalanche of questions and protests and, she was sure, speculation and gossip. Guy took the decision with the familiar thinning of the mouth and lift of a shoulder with which he met a *fait accompli* he didn't care about much one way or the other. He did, however, reveal a rather surprising comprehension of what doing this had cost Cass.

'That will set the tongues wagging,' he said, speaking lightly but looking at her carefully. 'It doesn't matter in itself, let everyone think whatever they see fit, but would it help to disappear from the scene about then? A few days in the sun perhaps? We haven't had a holiday all year.'

It was no odder than most of his suggestions, Cass supposed with brief amusement. Gratitude for it, and for the unexpected sensitivity which had prompted it, was shot through with the rueful realisation that no visit to the Corrie had represented a holiday to Guy. For a second she was tempted. No one could think it odd to scrap the plan for a party if she and Guy were off in Lanzarote or the Seychelles. But her basic truthfulness rejected the prevarication at once. Also a vision arose of being with Guy, on holiday somewhere traditionally considered to offer all the ingredients for a romantic interlude, memories of a year ago inescapable, and faced by contrast with the crippled pretence their marriage had become. And to conjecture on the difference between those memories, the disparity of their hopes and intentions at the time of their wedding, would hurt even more.

A sham. Even as the word stung there came into Cass's mind another sham, the strange pretence that was Rick's marriage. Rick allowing the story of his illness to be perpetuated, agreeing to live in that appalling house, tolerating Beverley's ridiculous pretensions . . . Suddenly Cass found herself furious with him, and blinking back the tears she hadn't even known were near, faced the fact that she had been wanting far more deeply than she had let herself acknowledge the sanity and reassurance of his company. Anger at the way he condoned his odd situation was really anger at the falseness of her own position.

Though Guy and she were living in outward respects much as before – he perhaps even more buried in his work, she setting herself a taxing programme of calling on all her ears before the season began – one vital element was missing. They never made love.

For Guy, sex had never been high on the agenda, and it was very much part of the pattern of their lives that, when he returned from some demanding trip, unwinding and slowing down did not include wanting Cass physically. That belonged more to leisurely awakenings after ten hours of unconsciousness had restored some energy – belonged to nights when he hadn't something more interesting on his mind, Cass could add with rueful frankness. Certainly it had not been an overriding need for him, and she had long ago accepted that.

Now, unexpectedly and unreasonably, she minded it. Minded it very much. To her in these uncertain hurting days physical closeness would have given comfort and reassurance, telling her that something remained between them which was worth preserving, worth working for. But she made the mistake of letting Guy set the pace, even now not understanding his chronic vulnerability and a need for reassurance far deeper than her own. She waited and he waited, and they sailed irrevocably away from each other on a sea of tentativeness, respect for each other's privacy, and self-doubt.

With their anniversary having achieved the status of a taboo subject, though neither could quite have said how that had come about, the next arbitrary milestone to present itself was Easter.

How helplessly we are caught in patterns, Cass thought with frustration, realising some decision would have to be made, some plan formulated which would probably highlight the gulf between them. She didn't mention the Corrie, knowing that much as she yearned to be there it was not the place to spend time with Guy in their present state of unresolved truce, with all its reserves and uncertainties.

It was Guy who, to her surprise, asked if she would like them to spend the weekend at Havenhill. Easter had never been one of their ritual visiting times there; had instead been a holiday kept for themselves. For a moment the proposal tempted her. The wider context of family interchange, a tension in this quarter, a confidence there, the usual pleas for Cass to approach her mother with some suggestion the others had failed with, might spread a useful safety net. Perhaps she and Guy would find they didn't need to tread round each other as cautiously as they had of late.

At once, in the alarming way in which at present she could swing from one certainty to its opposite, so unlike her usual detached good sense, Cass saw that this too was cowardly. If she and Guy were to re-establish a workable way of living together, it would not be done by hiding away in surroundings where private conversation was impossible.

'It's nice of you to suggest it, Guy, and I do appreciate it, but I think I'd find it hard to be there with the family, pretending everything's all right when there's still so much we haven't sorted out.'

'What do you suggest then?' Guy's tone was carefully expressionless, his manner that of being prepared to listen to another point of view while knowing already it would be valueless.

'Could we just be here?' Cass said, her confidence in the idea undermined by his tone. 'In our own space, I mean. Not rushing about doing lots of things or seeing lots of people. Just by ourselves, with time to be peaceful and talk.'

'Certainly, if you think that would serve any purpose.' Discussion over; decision, whatever he thought of it, made.

At the time Cass saw it as the biggest misjudgement she had ever made. Later she came to regard it as a swift, clean and probably essential piece of surgery. But during the edgy, endless weekend she saw only her own idiocy in inflicting this misery on them, and even believing it would achieve anything.

Never had the flat seemed so barren, so hostile to their presence. There seemed a crackling charge of electricity in its very fabric, like that produced by walking on synthetic carpet on a frosty day and taking hold of a metal stair rail. Their tension and helplessness to communicate bounced off the very walls. They filled in the time, circling in orbits which were careful not to touch. Guy spent most of the time at his desk. Cass tried to read, tried to watch programmes she had taped and had never had time to look at, and even embarked on some ambitious cooking till she realised what she was doing, stunned to find that under stress she could resort so haplessly to this stock female ruse of conciliation and appeal. Like me, like me.

They failed to talk. Cass had hoped some admission of how each felt would emerge from this time together, feeling even a confrontation would do more good than harm, but as the time crawled by, padded out by lunchtime visits to a local thronged by foreign tourists, and solitary walks in the park for Cass, she knew she had never before felt such a sense of entrapment.

Later, she saw that nothing could have been resolved that weekend because Guy would have felt himself coerced into any discussion she tried to initiate. It was not his chosen time or place; not, she would amend with pain, his choice of weapons.

It was two weeks later, arriving with no signals, no cathartic row, no further revelations, that the final blow was dealt. Just Guy's unemotional voice, as courteous as ever, saying, 'Look, Cass, I think we've got to face the fact that this hasn't worked out. We made a mistake, so how about cutting our losses? What do you feel?'

What do I feel? I feel a pit opening at my feet. I feel breathless, appalled, shaken to pieces.

'D-do you mean—?' Cass found she was stammering and made a huge effort to pin down the central question which seemed to be fragmenting into a thousand splinters of protest and doubt. 'Do you mean you want us to separate? Not live together, even if we divorce?'

In spite of her anguish at what was rushing upon them the objective part of her mind could still find bleak amusement in the oddity of the question.

Her voice tailed away at the sight of Guy's face. There was something ungiving and brittle in it which told her he would not be able to make this easier for either of them. Her heart suddenly made itself felt, bumping and hurrying.

'Guy?' She wasn't sure the attenuated thread of a sound would reach him.

'I've done my best,' he said, speaking rapidly, as though from a list of prepared facts. 'I suggested spending time away together, to give us a chance to recapture what we'd had before.' (But you hardly put it in those terms.) 'I was even prepared to spend Easter with your family, thinking it might give us the chance to get back to some sort of rapport together, but you wouldn't meet me halfway. I don't blame you, I'm not saying that, but it showed me how far apart we've grown. I'm not what you want or need.'

With a chill Cass saw that he needed to believe this, needed to be able to say – to whom, when? – that he had tried to salvage the relationship. With these two limping, almost contrived instances.

'Oh, Guy.' Cass felt terribly alone. What words could penetrate that shell of emotional self-protection? She read his terror of tears and accusations and regret, and gazed at him in stricken silence.

'Yes, well, look—' his well-known way of turning from some unrewarding exchange – 'there's something I wanted to talk to you about, only there's no urgency to decide anything. A new possibility has come up.'

A business opportunity, involving a long absence abroad? Cass was aware that she was choosing some bearable option, while knowing at a more primitive level that the dread which had hovered all though these weeks was finally taking shape, coming close.

'I was wondering if you'd feel happier on your own,' Guy went on, still in that tone of tamped-down practicality, which even in her distress Cass knew was the only way he could handle this. 'It's all become very strained, don't you think? I imagine we'd both agree we've reached the end of the road. I was talking to George Medmenham and he's very keen to come in.' Even now Cass thought he was referring to some business deal. 'Money's no object with him, as you know, so he'd buy you out at an excellent price. The flat's too big for me on my own, but I don't want to part with it at present. George is in no hurry, and naturally I'm not anxious to push you out or anything of the sort.'

The ordinary phrase, one Guy might have used to any friend or acquaintance, to any flatmate, in fact, with whom a sharing arrangement had not worked out, put the whole matter into perspective for Cass, and even enabled her to achieve a similar tone, in spite of the turmoil of loss and shock milling inside her. She noted detachedly that Guy's thinking had progressed a good deal further than his approach to this dialogue had suggested. Did that matter? Hardly. Perhaps it was as well to have overleapt a painful thrashing out of details, and with it the recriminations it might have been difficult to avoid. Perhaps, even, it was best to ignore, as Guy seemed determined to do, any admission that they were no longer lovers.

Yet to abandon that without a word seemed a very desolate thing to Cass, diminishing something she had held dear.

Chapter Twenty-three

Cass crossed the lane, stiff and creaky after the long drive, and leaned on the field gate with a mixture of weariness and still-disbelieving thankfulness to be here. She had not let herself take it in yet, as though even now there would be barriers and obstacles, things to be attended to and finalised. During these last harried weeks, struggling to come to terms with what Guy had done, felt and chosen, she had only got through all that had had to be done by keeping this longed-for place as far as possible out of her mind, not allowing images of it to influence or distract her, and half feeling that if she dreamed of it too self-indulgently she might risk it in some way.

Now she could mock that superstitious caution, let realisation seep in. She looked down the field, dotted with quietly grazing ewes whose lambs were bucketing about in the bottom corner where trodden earth round a rocky outcrop showed their favoured playground. Last year's lambs had played there too. A year. The waft of hawthorn reached her faintly from beyond the burn. When they had bought the Corrie that scent had been thick and heavy from their own bushes by the driveway, the bushes ripped out by the JCB.

Cass folded her arms along the top of the gate and rested her head on them, her weight on one hip to accommodate her height. The thought triggered so many associations she could hardly deal with – nostalgia for the hopes and happiness of that first visit, residual anger at Guy's tangled motives for coming here and the changes he had so carelessly made, and deeper yet, still hard to come to terms with, the completeness of his final rejection. But through the pain a dazzling relief threaded, that the dark, numb period of unravelling and jettisoning was over.

Down by the river a cuckoo called. The clear note slicing through all background sound woke as it always did reminders of childhood, in this moment almost too acute to bear, and actually brought tears to Cass's eyes. I'm tired, she told herself, I pressed on too hard, I should have stopped more often on the way. But in truth tears had been close all the time during the past couple of days. Guy had not been there to help with the final disbandment; he had been in Malta. It had seemed to Cass an unnecessary ramming home of the point that their lives had remained, in spite of marriage, good intentions and sensible planning, ultimately separate.

Don't think of that; it's over. She straightened and turned her back to the gate, looking across the lane and up the bank. A few random daffodils had survived the upheaval of Guy's landscaping and dipped their heads in a light breeze where last year the bank had been yellow with them. The solid boards of the ranch fencing above were clumsy and intrusive. Could the untouched look she had so loved ever be recreated? Or was that a contradiction in terms? Would the house have to be shut up and abandoned again for that sequestered air to return?

Well, it wasn't going to be abandoned. With a sniff and a grimace to hold back more tears Cass turned and went up the lane, not going as far as the Mains, but turning right above the hill dyke. She wasn't ready to meet Gina yet – or anyone.

Be honest, it's Rick you're not ready to meet. This wasn't a time of day when he was likely to be out walking. Beverley might talk about dinner but all her habits and instincts drew her to a much earlier meal, and her timetable had all the rigidity of the truly selfish person. And this grassy track, the continuation of the caterans' road below Riach, was not somewhere Rick often came.

But why am I saying that, she demanded in sudden impatience. At this moment she felt she knew nothing about Rick. She had kept him out of her mind so resolutely for the last two months that he had almost become a stranger, and any assumption she made about him, however trivial, was an impertinence.

But she was the stranger, the incomer. Her thoughts ran loose, unable to fix on anything. How long would it take her to relax? It had seemed to take for ever to sort everything out, yet the end had rushed upon her with frightening speed and now she felt vulnerable, hustled and unprepared.

A rabbit thumped and vanished into the dyke, and the hollow sound startled her nearly as much as she had startled the rabbit. Brown shapes stretched out in flight, leaping for their burrows. She hadn't noticed them till they moved. She stood still, consciously trying to slow down, make herself see, hear, smell, feel. She had come back at the most magical time of the year and the glen looked almost too lovely to take in. But it was no use; as soon as she moved on her mind began its circling again. It was impossible to tear apart one way of life and step calmly into the next. Nothing was that easy. In its own time her mind would swing to here, to now, to what she had done. Time was all she needed and time she had.

Flat hunting for herself, when she didn't want a flat and didn't want to be alone, had been a grim business. And not something Guy, in the nature of things, could help with, even if he had had the time to do so. She had thought of passing the word round to see if anyone in their circle was on the move or wanted to share, then a fierce reluctance to announce private disaster so openly had made her discard the idea. Also, though Guy insisted George was in no hurry to move in, there had been a growing feeling that both he and Guy were eager to have the new arrangement in place. Cass couldn't have said quite how this was made clear. George had appeared at the flat more often, but open references to his living there were avoided. Nothing crass was done like starting to move in his belongings. Yet when he and Guy were together there was an ease between them, as though something had already been settled. Well, it had been settled, Cass would remind herself.

It had been more than that. There was an impression of anticipation, of some satisfactory *modus vivendi* having already been worked out. What did that imply? A relationship? Nothing physical, of that Cass was sure, but a sort of certainty which had been absent between her and Guy even before they were married. Perhaps that was what Guy needed, sharing without ties. Perhaps? Of course that was what he needed. But that he should find the ideal situation with another man was still vaguely disquieting, increasing her sense of inadequacy. Lack of desirability, you mean, she would add in more unforgivingly abrasive moments.

It had not been hard to decide what to do about the Corrie. Cass had bought Guy out.

'I'd thought you might sell and find somewhere nearer, more accessible,' he had said, as though he still saw this as the obvious solution, and Cass had stared at him, baffled. Had he wanted that so much? Did he feel it had been an issue that had affected the outcome?

'I wouldn't want a cottage anywhere else,' she had answered, trying to speak without emphasis.

'Ah yes, Scotland.' Guy had turned away. 'Always bloody Scotland.' The bitter tone had made Cass realise how little trouble she had taken to understand the deep-rooted insecurity which made him so jealous of what he saw as an unrealistic obsession. But Scotland, in the shape of the Corrie, had been the one sure and good thing to hold on to, once the process of dissolution had been carried to its conclusion.

Coming with tired step down the lane again, wishing she hadn't walked so far, the sight of the laden car, unlocked, her bag lying on the seat, seemed to sum up the safety and simplicity of this place, in sharp contrast to the automatic precautions of the city. She had stepped back into glen ways without a thought. In her present mood such a tiny thing had unreasonable significance, and she almost could have cried again.

She slung the bag on her shoulder and went up the concrete steps. They'd probably have to stay; she could disguise them with plants, something the rabbits would leave alone. She knew she was stalling. The familiar thrill she could so successfully conceal under her casual manner gripped her as she walked along the now tidy path. The porch door stuck after the wet weeks of a long cold spring and she put her shoulder to it. Would the long room feel different? But why should it? How could four stone walls reflect human emotions?

But they did, unquestionably. The room was at once familiar and welcoming, yet exciting and different in its new guise of home. Shakily, hardly breathing, Cass walked to the fireplace and spread a hand on the smoke-hazed wall above it to steady herself. No tears now, just a consuming sense of fitness, of sanctuary and joy.

How could she have been so blind, so hidebound, as to have ignored this answer for so long? It was as though she had been unable to see beyond the solutions other people presented to her, too devastated by the catastrophe which had rushed upon her to be capable of evaluating her own needs. Move out of the flat. That had been the one objective when she realised Guy no longer wanted her there. Divorce, the unwinding of their affairs, would follow as soon as they could be put in train. Sole ownership of the Corrie was part of that. (But we gave it to each other. The pleading voice had been ruthlessly silenced. Nothing had revealed more blatantly the gulf between them than acting on that sentimental impulse.)

Cass could pinpoint the exact moment when the obvious had hit her. She had been looking at the eleventh flat. She was running late and the house agent had been barely civil. It had been yet another of those rainy days which would be associated in her mind for ever with the disintegration of her life with Guy. The flat had been well appointed, well decorated, disgracefully expensive and oppressively dim. Dark green silk shrouded an entire wall and when Cass drew it back she found full length curtains of heavy net obscuring windows which looked across an alley to a blank wall. The lighting was subtle, or poor, depending on how you looked at it. The only way to live in such a place would be never to look out. It would provide a high degree of comfort, efficiency and convenience, and it would be a prison of gloom and muffled sound to which to return each evening alone.

Why am I doing this? Simplest of questions, forgotten for surprisingly long periods by conditioned, stressed and over-committed people. There had been no turning back once it had been asked.

No one had approved, not even Diane, now a partner and in charge of the whole operation of the agency in England and Wales.

'But are you sure it will be *enough*?' she kept asking.

'Enough income? There's the whole of Scotland just waiting to be tapped into,' Cass had teased her, hoping to keep the tone strictly practical.

'No, but enough for you. Challenge, interest, all of that.' Diane, still dazed by the thrilling development in her own life, had found it hard to believe Cass would be satisfied to limit hers to one small operation.

'I'll have more than enough to do, don't worry,' Cass had assured her. But in fact she had done no serious weighing of the prospects. She had barely envisaged the pattern of her days, let alone worried about her long-term future. Whatever that turned out to be it would be spent in Scotland. And in Scotland she had a place to live so perfect that it shook her to think of it.

Guy had shrugged. 'If trying to earn a living stuck away up there doesn't destroy the fantasy nothing will. I shudder to think what the winter will be like. Half the time you won't even be able to get to the office.'

Cass grinned, remembering, and turned to look behind her. How fortunate after all that Guy had equipped them with everything she would need to work from home. And now she could do what she had once thought of before, turn the little bedroom into a study for herself. All this would be part of her own life. She walked the length of the room and laid a finger on the cover of the printer. She had not made much effort to understand Guy's needs. She must not be so blind in this new beginning. It was all very well to rush up here crying, 'I've arrived, I'm here! I'm not a holiday cottage person any more.' There were other views to be taken into account.

No one here knew what had happened. When she was away from Glen Maraich she was in contact with no one, not even Gina. Though in her mind it had become the focal point of her life, to everyone else she was just someone who appeared occasionally and vanished again to her real world. Appeared very occasionally. She didn't care to work out how few days she had spent at the Corrie during the past year. Would people think, as Diane and Guy and her brother and indeed most of her friends had done, that what she had decided on was extravagant and ill-thought-out? She was conscious of a sudden unexpected shyness, of confidence falling away, as though she hardly knew how to face Bridge of Riach and the glen on this new footing.

But as she began to unload the car, get the house into working order and think about food, she knew where the root cause of that uncertainty lay. However far her thoughts about Rick had gone, however strong his attraction was for her, those thoughts had no substance outside her own mind.

Reality was this. Rick lived, by his own choice, with Beverley, at Sycamore Lodge. That was his life. He had found a means of existing which, outwardly at least, satisfied him. Living here, she could not allow herself the indulgence of thinking about him in the same terms as she had when cut off from all contact in London. Here she must keep the true position clearly before her.

She had made herself do some thorough soul-searching once the idea of leaving London had seized her. Was she using the Corrie, the glen, the convenient existence of the Perth office, to conceal her real reason for wanting to be here? She honestly thought she wasn't. She had always known Rick was not free, and from the beginning had understood how strongly he felt committed to Beverley. To him, breaking up his marriage would be unthinkable.

And there were absolutely no grounds for believing he had ever for a second regarded her as a reason for doing so. The very thought of him supposing her move here had anything to do with him made her blush with shame.

That was clear enough. The question remained, would she be able to see him and be with him in the same way as before? It seemed unlikely. The meetings on the hill, the shared walks, the quiet early morning conversations in the barn, though she had been greedy for them and they had always seemed too infrequent and brief to her, had really been rather remarkable in the context of Rick's life. She hadn't let herself worry about it; he was a man who always seemed to know very much what he was doing. She had been able to leave that to him, enjoying whatever time they could share, and disappearing again for weeks or months. For Rick these would have been brief interludes cutting across normal life from time to time. How different it was going to be now that she was here permanently. (Permanently. What a word to savour.) One thing she knew. She must not show, ever, in any way, how she felt. She had made very sure she believed she could handle that before deciding to come.

There would be so many other marvellous things, though. Her spirits lifted at the prospect. There would be time to spend with Gina, to listen, perhaps even to help stabilise a situation which had looked increasingly fragile this winter. And apart from Gina there was the promise of other friendships, with Kate Munro and Joanna especially. Becky, the nannie she had found to look after Jamie Mackenzie, had seemed outgoing and lively in the brief glimpses she had had of her, and it would be good to get to know her better. Then Kate's nannie, hand-picked by Cass herself, would be arriving soon, and hopefully would be as much of a success as Becky had been.

Now there was time for all of it. Cass drew a deep breath, feeling as though the bubble of happiness to be here would have to burst or she would explode. How exaggerated and preposterous – and how comfortable to think there was no one to say so.

Chapter Twenty-four

Cass had not expected to sleep. Indeed she had felt afraid of trying to, dreading the moment when the light went out and she was left alone with her restless brain. She had gone on unpacking and sorting, not very effectually, reminding herself that the objects she was putting away now had no other place to live, there would be no more packing and unpacking the car, no more journeys, but she had been dismayed to find that happiness refused to take over. She had paused to watch an apricot and blue sunset fade slowly over the Bealach, sure it would work some infallible charm, but still had felt frighteningly removed from her surroundings. Going to bed, she had thought she was glad to be able to open the window wide to the cool scented air without arguments, but this time the thought had brought only a searing sense of loss. It was not so much missing Guy as the knowledge that their parting had affected him so little which hurt. That was something it was going to take a long time to put behind her.

Yet once in bed, in spite of her fears, there had barely been time to register an owl call from the hill before she was out, gone, oblivious, the harried weeks of stripping away one life and shaping a new one wiped out. She slept for hours, and her instant reaction on waking was simple – she felt safe.

Her next thought was that, for this morning at least, she

needn't go through hoops about whether or not she would see Rick. It was after nine, well past their quiet private morning hour for meeting. In any case, she reminded herself firmly, the new regime had begun.

Rick waited, not working, not doing anything, the big doors rolled back on the clear-cut rhomboid morning shadow thrown by the barn across the dewy grass. He had seen the car at the Corrie last night. It had been a long silence, a long wait.

For one blank moment, as the reality of the changed situation hit her, in spite of the self-discipline she believed she had in place to meet it, a void opened before Cass. No contact would be possible with Rick beyond the chance meetings one might expect to have with a neighbour – a neighbour who was married and lived virtually next door. All right, that was understood. But quite apart from that forbidden pleasure, in terms of ordinary everyday living, what had she looked forward to so much? She saw that everyone had been right. There was nothing to do here. The things she had promised herself she would do at last, things she had never found time for in the rushed weekends or even during her longer visits, suddenly looked trivial, to be polished off in an hour or two, quite incapable of filling the oceans of time now stretching emptily before her.

What had they been anyway? The garden? Walks? What else? For a scary second she couldn't think of anything. What had she done to her life? It was the classic piece of self-deception to fall in love with a dream holiday place and then believe you could live there. It never worked. It was one of the worst moments since she and Guy had decided to part. Then a furious resistance drove Cass out of bed and up. How utterly feeble. Whatever she made of this new beginning was in her own hands. There was no need to think beyond today. Do one thing, then the next.

There was surely enough immediate delight on every hand to make that easy.

She opened the doors onto a bright blowy morning. Cushions of white cumulus bowled across a blue sky; it was hard to believe the emerald of the grass clothed the same fields she had last seen buried in snow. She made herself listen to the faint windborne sounds, always lambs' cries at this time of year behind the rest, letting them draw her into the moment, and, taking her time, traced the descending lines of the hills towards Muirend. She consciously savoured drinking ice-cold orange juice as the sun warmed her skin; closed her eyes to inhale the sweet morning air laced with the smell of percolating coffee from the house. She had been alone here before, had done all this before, but now, inch by inch, she must find her way into the scene.

Dogged by a feeling that she ought to get through the final uprooting and the move alone, she hadn't told even Lindsay when she was arriving. Next week they must have a meeting and discuss the implications of Cass being here full-time. Now that the Perth office was to be her working base Lindsay might be feeling side-lined and unsure of her future, and Cass wanted to scotch any such fears at the outset. She intended to work as much as was feasible from home and foresaw no changes in Lindsay's role. Hopefully, their market would expand and there would be plenty for both of them to do.

Meanwhile, there was Gina. There was a very special pleasure in setting off for the Mains now, as the impulse came, on a sunny weekday summer morning, and to know this was the pattern of the future. It produced the most stimulating sense of freedom. As she crossed the burn and started up the field another bonus occurred to Cass – it would be agreeable to talk free of the smouldering aura of Nessa, which could fluster her mother even when Nessa was in her room at the other end of the house. Also, during the week Gina only had to worry about ferrying her to and fro from Kirkton, as opposed to the ceaseless weekend chore of getting her to Muirend to pursue her social life. Not that

Nessa was entirely to be blamed for her moods and selfishness, Cass conceded as she let herself out of the field gate. Gina could be pretty exasperating.

Across the windy yard thundered and rippled cascades of notes, unintelligible to Cass but impressive just the same. A lot of drama there, she thought, pausing to listen in simple admiration that human fingers could move so fast. It seemed a shame to interrupt, particularly if this was therapy after some marital upheaval. But Tiree, who had been sniffing his way along the last part of his regular morning circuit now appeared from behind the barn and yelled his head off at the sight of an intruder.

The music stopped. Well, if there had been strife, on past form it would probably only have been about running out of tea-bags or something, Cass decided, giving up trying to fend off Tiree who had finally discovered who she was, and running for the door with him leaping joyfully beside her.

She was shocked at the sight of Gina. She had always been the untannable white of a certain kind of redhead, but now the rich creamy skin was pasty. There was a puffiness about her eyes and jawline which had not been there before, and her hippy, well-covered body, instead of looking sturdy and robust, looked slack and over-indulged. Her yellow T-shirt had a coffee stain down the front and her splendid hair, straggling out of a purple band, needed washing. But all that was forgotten in the delight of her welcome.

'Cass! It's been such *ages!* God, I've missed you. Come in and settle down for a huge gossip. Have you got time? How long are you staying? And what are you doing appearing on a Wednesday? Clear off, Tiree, she's had quite enough of you for the time being.'

Bursting to tell the great news that she was here for good, Cass was swept into the kitchen on a wave of mutual pleasure, but as they shot disjointed questions and answers at each other while Gina filled the kettle and rinsed a couple of mugs, Cass saw with concern that all was far from being as it should. Where previously there had been an engaging mess silting up the room with a swirl of colour and creativity, now a squalor prevailed which Cass could not pretend was attractive. There was a smell of scummy water from the sink, of unwashed dog from Tiree's beanbag, of rotting fruit from the bowl on the table. The usual clutter of laundry basket, half-finished ironing, sewing begun and not finished, washing-up abandoned, seemed against this background less acceptable. Cass thought of Laurie. Poor man, so immaculate and fastidious, how could he endure it?

Opening the fridge to look for milk, she noticed a black mildewy rim down the door seal. Three opened cartons confronted her.

'Got a jug?' she asked.

'I don't think there's one clean,' Gina said vaguely. 'We don't need one, do we?'

Cass sniffed at the carton she'd picked up and realised how sour her face must look. She watched Gina bring the mugs to the table and flop down with an exhausted and defeated sigh of which she was clearly quite unconscious.

'Gina, what's wrong?' Cass asked, her own affairs forgotten.

'Don't ask, I'll only get upset,' Gina warned in a strangled gasp, splashing milk clumsily into her coffee so that more reached the table than the mug.

'OK, cry if you must, but tell me what's going on.'

Gina giggled, the giggle cut off by a gulp as tears welled. 'How I've needed your sensitive caring touch.'

'You look awful,' Cass told her, the concern in her voice making the blunt words acceptable.

'I know,' Gina said, sniffing and looking round for something to mop her eyes.

'Most people use a tissue,' Cass commented, watching her choose a piece of unbleached calico.

Gina giggled again, her shoulders visibly relaxing as tension loosened its hold. 'There aren't any.'

'God, Gina, how many times have I come up here and found you in tears?' Cass demanded. 'You can't go on like this. It's no way for anyone to live. Can't you talk to Laurie, or Nessa, or whoever it is that's reduced you to this state?'

'It's true, I don't think I can go on,' Gina confessed. 'You've no idea what it's like.'

And we haven't even got as far as our coffee, Cass thought philosophically, though not without compassion, as she went round the table to put her arms round the shaking shoulders, so much fleshier than she remembered. Gina seemed no more in control of her own existence than Tiree himself. Or maybe less, Cass amended, waiting for the sobs to subside. Tiree after all had his priorities unshakably in order.

'It was Easter that started it,' Gina was able to explain eventually. 'Nessa went to her father's, though I knew really she should have stayed at home and revised, but she absolutely refused and it seemed such a bad time to make a fight of it, with exams coming up. And then she wouldn't come back, it was just like last summer all over again, only this time I decided to go to Lancaster to fetch her and it was all so humiliating, you can't imagine.'

'You didn't let them know you were coming?'

'That's what Laurie said,' Gina admitted, looking guilty. 'I just rushed off without thinking. Ruth was terribly hostessy and correct, once she'd pulled herself together, and though she treated me like someone out on parole she insisted that I stayed. You should have seen the nightie she lent me, one of those hideous two-layer things, I didn't know they still existed. It was so tight it cut into me round the armholes. I suppose as you get older that's the sort of place you put on weight—'

But this attempt at a prosaic lightness wavered into silence and the tears overflowed.

Cass did her best to comfort her, and understanding her need to unload all the misery, coaxed her back to the core of the subject.

'Clifford was so angry with me. For turning up, of course, but for everything else as well. He'd believed everything Nessa had told him, and when I tried to explain he got so impatient. He says I'm the most muddled thinker it's ever been his misfortune to meet. But it isn't true that I do everything for Andy and Steve and nothing for Nessa and he should have realised that.'

'I'm sure he knows really,' Cass consoled her. Gina's problem was that she did far too much for Nessa, and Nessa, while trading on it shamelessly, probably wouldn't have minded having a few boundaries imposed to help out her not very powerful conscience.

'And though Nessa thinks I run around after the boys they're never satisfied either,' Gina wailed, returning helplessly to the well-worn groove. 'I was so determined to be a good stepmother, and to please Laurie, but everything I do seems to go wrong.'

'Where's Nessa now?'

'She's at school,' Gina said, sounding surprised. 'Oh, I see what you mean. She's back, Laurie went down to fetch her.'

'Laurie did?' Cass had never imagined he would intervene between Gina and Nessa, though she had long suspected that in his quiet way he circumvented a lot more hassle from the boys than Gina ever guessed.

'He didn't even tell me he was going. He just phoned Clifford and drove down and Nessa came home without any fuss at all. I was so hurt, Cass. I mean, glad she was back, but dreadfully hurt that she wouldn't come for me. And now she says she won't stay on at school, no matter how well she does this year. She's given up all idea of university and as soon as her exams are over she's going to get a job, any job, so long as it's not in Glen Maraich . . .'

'Oh, poor Gina,' Cass said softly, hugging her. 'But there'll be plenty of time to sort that out. The main thing is she's back. And if Laurie was able to persuade her to come home he may be able to help you talk to her about the next step.'

'Oh, I know, I know. It's just that sometimes I feel

everything's beyond my control. And now there's this business of Sillerton.'

Cass had known this must come. Often during the last couple of months she had thought she should talk to Gina about it, and warn her that something was happening. Or if she already knew then find out whether Laurie's job would be affected. But the impossibility of involving herself in such a way in any concern of Guy's had always prevented her. And how could she offer sympathy when the blame lay at Guy's door, and so, indivisibly to other eyes, at hers? Guy had refused to discuss what his bowing out would mean for the enterprise he had been so enthusiastic about a year ago. Indeed he had made it clear that he didn't know or care.

'Someone bought me out. Ask him,' he had said tersely. What could it matter?

'Yes, what's happening about Sillerton?' Cass asked Gina awkwardly. 'You'll know Guy has sold his interest, I expect. Is the work still going forward?'

'I'm never quite sure,' Gina said distractedly. 'Laurie gives away so little. There seems to be endless in-fighting about where funds should be allocated. The architect is taking the company to court because he hasn't been paid for Phase I, but the directors are saying he didn't do an adequate job. The accountant's been sacked, I think. Laurie won't talk about it any more. He just goes down day after day, and if I ask he says, "I've still got a job to go to," and that's it.'

'What other job could he find here?' Cass asked, dull anger rising against Guy for his indifference.

'Here? Oh, he wouldn't want to look for anything here,' Gina exclaimed. 'He gets very frustrated at having to trail up and down all the time. He wanted to live in Muirend when he originally got the Sillerton job. Well, everybody did to be honest, though now the boys are both away at college they don't mind so much. No, we live here because of me. This was my dream house. This and the walled garden and the views and the remoteness.'

As she said this she fell into a yearning tone as though she was still describing the dream, not the reality. She sounded as though even now she didn't see anything selfish about making her family live miles from where any of them wanted to be, for what seemed to Cass a whim as arbitrary as Beverley's choice of a site to build her fearful bungalow.

This was a new angle on Gina, and one Cass needed to examine. But whatever conclusions she might come to she was thankful that she would be on hand. Gina's warmth and generosity had meant a great deal to her when she had needed them, and it was good to be available to offer support in her turn.

This looked like the moment to break her news. One thing was clear, however. Gina needed not only help but someone to talk some sense into her.

Chapter Twenty-five

Rick came to the Corrie that evening. Came without self-consciousness or embarrassment, as though calling to say hello when Cass arrived was the most natural thing in the world to do. She was sitting outside by the kitchen door on Guy's 'patio' – not an improvement she intended to do away with – and wondering whether adding a few tubs would be asking for trouble and if the alternative of hanging baskets would be a bit Syc Lo, that useful phrase of Steve and Andy's, when Rick came quietly round the corner of the house, startling her into speechlessness.

But what a rush of pleasure seized her as she came to her feet. He had been in her mind all day, the hope of seeing him before too long always there, beneath worries about Gina and the mental adjustments Cass was making about her own situation. Putting the latter into words as though explaining them to Rick had been a good way to deal with them, though she hadn't done it for that reason.

Now here he was, smiling and calm, twitching a heavy garden chair round to face the last of the sun and putting it down near hers, his big hand making it look like a matchstick toy. The eye-filling size of him delighted her, as it always did, and she found herself laughing, swept into happiness.

'How did you know I was back?' It didn't matter what she said.

He gave her a look of mock reproof. 'Oh, here now. In Glen Maraich?'

'Rick, I'm so pleased to see you.' Her happiness would not be contained and she took his arm, solid as a branch, in both her hands.

About to sit down, he checked, turning to face her. The gesture had been a new one between them, but its underlying warmth was not new. He put his hand over hers and for a moment they looked into each other's eyes, not smiling, not speaking. Then Rick nodded, giving her hand a little pat as though some message had been exchanged and understood between them, and easily and naturally they sat down and began to talk, no formalities such as offering a drink or asking after Beverley intervening. It did cross Cass's mind to wonder whether Beverley knew he was here, but the thought had no impact, dismissed as irrelevant even as it occurred to her.

'You've been away too long,' Rick said, his eyes still examining her.

What would he see? Cass wondered. Everything, was probably the answer to that, and she found it didn't matter. She said simply, 'I'm here for good.'

The words stunned Rick. They seemed immense, life-altering, and for one hurtling moment he thought, 'No more waiting,' and thankfulness flared up. But in the same instant the blaze of feeling sank again, quenched by the unchanged and unchangeable reality. None of this was revealed by his expression, except that the line of his square jaw became more rigid, and his intent examination of Cass's face more concentrated.

'Yes?' he said. And then devastatingly, his deep voice very gentle, 'You've been going through the mill, haven't you? Do you want to tell me about it?'

With violent determination Cass checked the tears this instant and simple understanding brought. Gina, deep in her own problems, and accustomed in any case to Cass being at the Corrie on her own, had seen this new development as changing Cass's life, providing her with much of what she had always wanted, allowing her to be permanently where Gina most wanted and needed her, on the doorstep, but she had barely looked beyond this to wonder what the break-up of her marriage had truly meant to Cass. She had made the conventional noises about it, of course, and been loving and comforting, but she had perceived nothing of the agony.

Now Cass knew that if she wanted to she could pour out the pain. At this moment or later, when she was ready. This tolerant, down-to-earth man would be capable of understanding, she felt certain, the shock of the abrupt ending, the self-doubts and sense of failure that gnawed at her, yet her acceptance that what had happened had been inevitable.

With Rick she didn't have to organise it into an orderly narrative. Although, clinically added up, the hours they had spent together had not been many, they had talked about so much of their lives to each other that explanations and details could be overleapt. With the break with Guy behind her, public, raw and final, Cass could refer openly to things glanced upon with discretion in the past. Putting it into words for Rick she felt as though only now was she realising how much Guy had hated being at the cottage, how critical and restless he had been there, how profoundly out of harmony with his surroundings.

'I was so naïve,' she said blankly, 'so bound up in my own picture of what marriage meant that I completely ignored the facts. Guy didn't mislead me or pretend anything. I created the whole thing in my mind.'

Rick wanted to say, filled with protective wrath and compassion for her, that she had merely expected from marriage what everyone in the world was entitled to expect from it, and that Guy's interpretation had been not only bizarre but criminally cruel. But he didn't want to check the flow, knowing very well that this release of hesitant, almost exploratory, words had been urgently needed.

Only once did he interrupt in involuntary protest. Cass had

been, with unforced fairness, ascribing Guy's chronic reserve to his loveless upbringing, and had added, with a small laugh that showed how well the therapy of confession was working, 'He probably liked me because I'm tone-deaf. Music doesn't exist for me. What a relief for him, after all the demands and competing in his family. And another thing occurred to me recently. He must have felt even safer because I wasn't his type, as far as looks were concerned, I mean. He was never going to have to worry about responding to overwhelming physical attraction. He could feel quite unthreatened because I was a great gawky lump of a female—'

'Gawky? You're lovely!' Rick exclaimed, with a sharp movement of anger rare for him.

'Me?' Cass stared at him in surprise. 'Rick, don't be so—'

'Don't tell me what to think,' he said brusquely, leaning towards her with an authority that was quite daunting for a moment. 'And don't put yourself down, I hate it when you do that. You move like no other woman I've ever seen. Those endless limbs would catch every male eye no matter who else was around. No, listen to me—' as Cass, embarrassed and startled, began to protest '—you've made half references to this in the past, and I can see it's something that's ingrained in you, this feeling of unattractiveness. And that selfish bastard you married let you go on believing it, probably never took time to realise that you do believe it. But take a good look at yourself in the mirror when you go to bed tonight, Cass. Look at the even colour of your skin—'

'Beige,' Cass protested. 'It won't even tan.'

'Shut up for a minute. Look at the clean-cut planes of your face, the line of your jaw. Look at your eyes. Where have you seen that colour before? In an autumn morning sky, that's where. It's the exact same blue. Only what you'll miss is the way they crinkle up when you laugh. And something else you won't see in your mirror,' he was smiling now, 'is the extraordinary sight the rest of us enjoy, of this weird stick insect stalking about the hill in tall boots and big hat, with its coat-tails swirling behind it. *That's* the picture I treasure.'

Cass was laughing, able to accept an image painted in such terms. 'But I hate my hair,' she offered meekly.

'God, women! But yes, I suppose we have a disaster there. Thick and soft and curly, who cares? It's undeniably mouse, and now that you've left London no one will be able to cut it so that it balances that long jaw. Yes, the hair's a problem, no denying it.'

'Now that I've left London,' Cass repeated, leaning back luxuriously in her chair. 'Oh, Rick, can you believe it? I've spent all day trying to take it in and it's still unreal.'

'There's a lot involved in it.' His voice was serious again. 'It's going to take time to adjust. But what better place in the world to get through the adjusting than here?' He nodded towards the sharp-etched skyline before them, and as they looked the sun slid behind a grey dolphin-shaped cloud, rimming it with gold. They shivered, suddenly cold.

'Time to make a move,' Rick said, stretching.

'You're not going?' Unguarded, sharp, the words were out before Cass could reflect on them.

'I'm not going anywhere.' He had this ability to make things comfortable and ordinary, overlaid with no special inferences. 'Do you want these chairs put under cover somewhere?'

Was that Beverley's training? But this was no time to think of Beverley. 'They're supposed to survive, thanks.'

'Are you going to make coffee?' Again the question was easy and straightforward.

'Rick, I'm so sorry, I've just realised I haven't offered you anything. Would you prefer a drink?' Cass couldn't even make a guess at how long they had been sitting talking there.

'I don't drink. Coffee will be fine, thanks.'

Did he not drink because of the allergy problems he had had? It seemed extraordinary that she didn't know that about him. She felt as though she had known him for ever.

'Would you like something to eat?' If Beverley was a high-tea person by nurture and a dinner person by aspiration which would win? 'Pitta bread, soup, pizza? Or there's ham, cheese—'

'Pitta bread and everything. Do you want me to light the fire?'

It seemed the most urgent and essential thing. All heat had vanished at a stroke from the day. Shivering, they assembled the comforts of food, warmth and coffee and, still talking, settled in front of the fire. It felt as though they were resuming their conversation on a completely different evening.

But closer, even closer than before, Cass thought with a contentment shot through with the premonition of loss, for perfect as the mood was it was essentially of the moment.

'I don't think I should come down to see you at the barn,' she said, not even knowing she was going to say it, accepting the moment as it came, taking the leap into the new situation between them with cold courage. For one instant of wild regret she wished the words could have been recalled, thinking them too high a price to pay for living here. Then sense prevailed. However technically correct and circumspect, what she had begun to feel for Rick could not have allowed their peaceful times together to continue.

Rick laid down the knife with which he had been carving himself a workmanlike slab of Cass's cooking Cheddar, and raised his head to look at her. For one tense moment Cass thought he was going to protest – protest about missing me, her trampled ego implored – but he only said, 'Yes,' in a toneless voice, as though in that stretched second he had absorbed all she meant, reviewed it and accepted it.

Cass was torn between admiration for the simplicity he brought to everything, and a base despairing longing for him to have fought against the decision.

'You know I want – I'd really like—' she began uncertainly.

'It's all right. I know,' Rick said, reaching to take her hand

and folding it up in his, then returning it to her. It lay on her lap as forlorn and needful as though it had a separate life of its own. 'You live here now,' he said. 'And that's the most important thing. You have your life to get together again, and there must be nothing here to mar it. But it's important that you feel quite free. You must go wherever you want to, at whatever times you feel inclined to. Do you understand what I'm saying?'

Cass nodded mutely. That, she knew, was the only answer. Not to get caught up in doubts and second-guessing, avoiding or calculating or hoping. How much Rick had covered in those brief words. Acceptance of how they both felt; an understanding of the implications now that she had so startlingly moved the goalposts; the facts of his own situation which could not be changed.

It would not be easy to live with him at the bottom of the drive, yet the resolution she was going to need to build a new life alone was inextricably tied up with knowing he was close by, rocklike and dependable.

She went with him down the lane, holding on to the last few moments together that could be shared in this way. The calls of the oystercatchers along the river had a different note in the dusk, hollow and unearthly. Bats soundlessly sliced their swift pattern against the stark grey sky.

'I'm still here,' Rick said, stopping at the foot of the track, turning her to face him with another of those brief touches immediately withdrawn. 'Don't forget that.'

She nodded, unable to speak, and she could feel his reluctance to turn and walk away.

But she did not know that he went swiftly past the lights of the bungalow, paused briefly on the bridge and then with a dissatisfied exclamation as though that was not enough, set out to walk swiftly up the river towards Allt Farr. And she could not guess how anger tore at him, deep churning anger at the hoops that bound him. He had accepted them for years, he could go on accepting them, he told himself. But tonight was different. Tonight he had heard the incredible news that Cass was here for good. He no longer had to torment himself imagining her with that cold-blooded bastard who refused her the warmth and love a woman like that cried out to be given, but instead he had to adjust to the knowledge that she was close by, all the time, not dragged continually away by a complete and separate life. She was here, in the glen. With all the guts in the world she was intending to make a living here, putting behind her the disaster of her marriage.

How much he wanted to help her, and it was the very thing he couldn't do. There were no choices to be made, he knew that. His debating and deciding had long ago been done.

Chapter Twenty-six

Walking into the Perth office and knowing it was now her sole place of work made it feel a very different place. Even picking up her briefcase, shutting the door behind her, driving down the lane, had felt novel and special today. The A9, which according to received glen thinking was busy and dangerous with its notorious accident black spots, seemed to Cass a pussycat road, a holiday road, the beauty of its course down the valley of the Tummel and then of the Tay making more impact on her than it ever had before.

She realised as she approached the office that her uncertainty as to how Lindsay would feel about the new arrangement had deepened to apprehension, and knew she would mind if it caused any problems. It was important to her that this area of her life should be positive and full of goodwill. But she needn't have worried. Lindsay was an employee at heart, and had no territorial resentment that her office, even if it happened to be situated in her own house, was about to become the boss's office too.

'You do know, don't you, that I've no intention of barging in and taking over?' Cass began the moment greetings were over. She meant it, but Lindsay knew her well, and knew this was exactly what would happen. Cass's easy-going, almost casual, air cloaked an energy which Lindsay perfectly understood she could never match and didn't aspire to match. Though she couldn't guess the need behind it at present, the need for the focus and reassurance of a new challenge, she was perfectly resigned to Cass running the show. The main thing that concerned Lindsay was that her job was safe, which it clearly was. Beyond that it would be a bonus to have Cass on the spot instead of trying to contact her here, there and everywhere as she flitted round half England. She also looked forward to having company; Phil soon reached saturation point on the subject of domestic dramas.

'I don't want you to feel your house is being taken over,' Cass was saying, anxious to have everything up-front between them. 'I intend to work from home as much as I can but I will be in and out of here quite a lot, and you may feel I've assumed more than our deal was ever intended to cover. If you prefer, we could look for separate office premises altogether—'

'So that I'd have to go out to work every morning? Oh, please,' Lindsay broke in, amused at Cass's unusual lack of cool. 'Here, have your coffee and relax.'

'Thanks. Am I making too big a thing of it? But I do want to be sure working together will suit you, suit both of us, long-term.' She allowed herself the indulgence of the word.

'I can't think of anything I'd like better. But – I don't want to butt in or anything – does this mean things aren't too good for you otherwise? Don't tell me anything you don't want to,' Lindsay hurried on, awkward and embarrassed but full of genuine sympathy, 'but if that's the case then I just wanted to say I'm truly sorry.'

'Thanks, Lindsay.' Cass hadn't thought in terms of such support or concern for what was happening in her personal life. Her mind had been focused on the job and Lindsay's reaction to her presence on an everyday footing. She wasn't ready to discuss Guy or her marriage; they were not close enough for that. But she recognised a good, solid loyalty that she hadn't fully taken into account, and she knew it was something she was going to value. With fresh enthusiasm she got down to work, and when lunchtime came they made it a celebration, summoning Phil to join them and doing very little of any value after it.

Just as the office felt a different place, and the Corrie itself, there seemed to Cass a new quality in all her contacts at Bridge of Riach in these emotionally aware days. She kept the feeling to herself, smiling peacefully at sly but kindly teasing from people like Ed Cullane and Nancy – 'So you're to be a real glenner now?' – fobbing off with bland courtesy less acceptable questioning from people she didn't know so well, who saw her in the Kirkton shop or stopped on the glen road to speak to her.

Joanna asked no questions at all. She passed via the lane one day, in a hurry because she was taking one of the setters to the vet and was late for surgery, and stuck her head in to say, 'We hear you're up for good now and we're all so pleased at the news. Do look in whenever you like. I mean it. Make it soon. I'll give you a ring if you don't appear.'

Kate Munro phoned to say the new nannie, Hannah, had arrived. 'I'm so grateful to you for finding her. She's not a bit terrifying.'

'Of course she's not.' Cass had gone to a lot of trouble in her selection for this particular post. Hannah was a divorcée who although she had custody of her twelve-year-old daughter, had had the generosity to let her ex-husband take her to live with him in Montreal when his firm sent him there for a year.

'Won't you come and see Hannah? Don't you do settling-in calls to make sure she doesn't think we're all appalling?' Kate asked. 'Come and have lunch tomorrow. In any case, we need to entertain her; there's nothing whatsoever for her to do at present.'

Cass laughed. She knew that was as far as Kate would go to make an overt protest. The family had been united in thinking Hannah should arrive in plenty of time. Kate had had an earlier miscarriage and Max wanted no tragedies this time. But Kate, who was feeling extremely well, was beginning to feel a little overprotected.

When Cass ran into people like Penny Forsyth from Alltmore or the Danahers from Grianan, in Muirend or Perth, they all greeted her with the same words. 'So you're up here for good now,' followed by friendly comments like, 'Excellent decision,' and, 'You must come over to see us soon.' Sally Danaher also took the opportunity to corner her about a new staff member for the hotel, saying, 'I can't tell you what a boon it is to have you there on the other side of the hill. I know it can't be that easy, but I feel staff crises are over for good.'

'No, I don't think I can promise that.' But Cass went on her way smiling. There was a welcome in these encounters which was reassuring and seemed to endorse the rightness of what she had done. There were inevitable down-swings, when she would find herself going over and over the debacle with Guy, unable to shed her sense of having failed. How could she have been so blind to his deep-rooted problems? Why hadn't she insisted that they talk much, much earlier? Surely she could have done more to hold on to something once so good? But these sad times gradually became less frequent and painful, the doubts unreal and remote as though she were worrying about someone else's problems.

There was plenty to turn her mind to. There were satisfying sessions in the garden, in particular those which saw the dragging out and removal of the hated fence which blocked the view from the long room. Ed Cullane was happy to do the job in order to acquire the wood, which he bore off (courtesy the Riach tractor and bogie) to patch up the crazy sheds and runs behind the gate lodge which housed one after another the angora rabbits, hamsters, guinea pigs and speckled hens which were to make his fortune – or his beer money.

Cass also took much pleasure in planting ground cover over the wounds of the gouged-out parking space, aided by the vigorous growth of early summer which elsewhere in the garden was softening the suburban look. And there were long drives through a landscape she couldn't see enough of, and which she could at last, however tentatively, begin to feel was hers.

Above all there was the cottage to adapt to her own needs and taste, and this, by a chance she could never have foreseen or dared to dream of, turned out to be the greatest joy of all. The small bedroom had been emptied – in the simple glen way. Cass had been wondering how to get rid of the bed and within the hour word had come that Kate Munro was looking for one for an Allt Farr cottage. Doddie Menzies appeared with the pick-up the following evening and away it went. Then Beverley overheard Cass asking Gina who would be the best joiner to do the conversion into a study, and at once chipped in officiously.

'That would cost a fortune. We don't want you wasting your pennies like that, do we?' (Cass without a husband, Cass with the Corrie as her only home, was the poor relative now.) 'Rick can do it for you.'

Though Cass usually disliked women offering up their husbands as casually as they would lend a ladder or a chain saw, she made no objection this time, hardly daring to believe in the dazzling prospect so negligently waved before her. But it happened, and the hours Rick spent rebuilding a section of the teak desk below the window of the little room, which looked across the burn and up the field towards the Mains, and making a unit for files and stationery, seemed afterwards at once endless and gone in a flash, deeply contented yet unsettling with a happiness eggshell thin and impossible to grasp.

Cass was resolved not to disturb him. She imagined he would want to concentrate, and she despised women who hang about while a man's trying to work. But from the outset Rick made it clear this was a joint undertaking, and the pleasure of being involved in some shared task, finding no conflict in their ideas or approach, chatting companionably or working in silence, gave her a searing glimpse of something precious and unattainable.

Perfect as it was, sometimes later she would be sorry they

had talked so little, knowing such an opportunity was unlikely to come again. For never now could she walk down the lane and through the cool shadows of the stock tunnel to the barn to be with Rick. That could not be. In fact she found it hard to believe she had done so in the past with no flicker of guilt. Because then she had been a transient and it hadn't mattered? Or because Rick, by openly inviting her to come, had accepted responsibility for them both? By letting him do so she had been thinking only of his marriage, yet she too had been 'a married woman'. Perhaps that hadn't entered her mind because Guy had seemed to have nothing to do with this place. Perhaps. But she thought her ease of conscience had more truly lain in the innocence of the friendship. No matter how much Rick attracted her, he had never for an instant permitted a chink in the armour of irreproachable behaviour with which he had protected them.

Occasionally she met him on the hill, almost too thrilled to be with him to be able to talk. He too had little to say, and afterwards Cass saw these meetings as absurd, the two of them perched side by side on a rock, staring mutely at the view. But all the same, Rick knew more of her real feelings, her guilt and sorrow over the past and what her new life here meant to her, than anyone, even Gina.

Indeed Gina at present was looking at little outside her own problems, and Cass was glad to be on hand for her, though not hopeful of being able to help very much. On a superficial level Gina responded to the stimulus of company, managing to shake off some of the depression of the winter months, but she was still a long way from being able to communicate with Nessa, or to evaluate the causes rather than the symptoms of her behaviour.

Cass was actually rather impressed with the way Nessa, who if only Gina could see it was a good deal more level-headed than she pretended to be, was buckling down to her exams. She did briefly try to barter passing for a promise that she could leave school for good afterwards, but Laurie refused to let Gina enter into any such negotiations, and Nessa changed tack, demanding to be allowed to spend the whole summer with her father.

Cass, who had been welcomed as a useful source of lifts, kept off controversial subjects, and was rewarded by friendly chatter and a lot of information about Muirend High School she could have done without. But at home Nessa was still an explosive commodity, putting her mother through an emotional mangle by alternating aggressive criticism with periods of silent contempt.

Cass was worried about leaving Gina on the few occasions when, with huge reluctance, she had to go back to London. She didn't want Diane to feel she had been abandoned, and there were arrangements to be finalised concerning the flat and the complex financial net Guy had woven when they married – which had persuaded him to marry her. In spite of the full and busy intervening weeks that thought could still bite deep, and back in the London scene with all its associations Cass had little defence against it.

She was disconcerted to learn that Guy expected her to come to the flat for their meeting, and even more shaken to find herself, even in anticipation, feeling gauche and vulnerable again. She steeled herself with all the calm she could muster to deal with a hundred memories and to be unsettled by the mere sight of Guy. She had prepared herself for the fact that he would not kiss or embrace her, but afterwards, feeling more desolately alone than ever, she knew the real source of her pain had been his total unawareness of the need for any of these defences. The encounter meant nothing to him in personal terms. Cass had faced alone the painful reminders of a naïve expectation of happiness.

There was one additional element for which she had not been ready, though she could not have said how it was conveyed – the aura of contentment the flat held. George had not even been present; though she was sure, summoning ironic amusement to help her, it wasn't tact on Guy's part which had seen to that, for it was obvious that the idea of Cass finding anything upsetting in returning to these surroundings had not crossed his mind. But from chance comments, from the 'we' that cropped up so easily, the scatter of possessions, even from Guy's relaxed, at-home demeanour, the truth had been obvious. This worked; in George Guy had found a partner for living better suited to him than Cass had been. Or than a wife had been, since that had been the tag which had disturbed the delicate balance between workable sharing and the intense inner privacy without which Guy could not function.

It was a great relief to get back to the Corrie, then have to take off immediately for Skye to see a couple of clients. Cass didn't even mind the persistent silvery rain which blotted out the hills for most of the time. She felt raw and churned up, and needed the long solitary miles to muster positive thoughts again and take the taste of London out of her mouth.

Home again, magic word, she was caught up at once in glen concerns. The Mackenzie twins had recently acquired mountain bikes (they had been offered ponies and had begged off with cries of horror. '*Grooming? Cleaning tack?* Yuk, no thanks, it's bad enough having to smell Laura all the time.') and they believed in the most literal fashion that they would traverse any terrain. They took to using the lane as a speed track and the morning after Cass returned Sasha came staggering in bleeding dramatically down the side of her face and saying she thought something 'rather awful' had happened to Sybilla. A mildly concussed Sybilla was sitting up and shaking her head by the time Cass reached her, but they both needed general patching up, and the episode left little room in Cass's mind for introspection. After this they called often, never staying long, busy about their own affairs, but always lively and entertaining.

Sometimes Laura came with them, or passed on her own riding Persephone, and Cass was the tolerant recipient that summer, since everyone else was sick of the subject, of Laura's anguish at growing out of her beloved Persie, and her conviction that there would never be another pony like her in the world. Cass thought Persephone listened to these outpourings with a remarkably complacent air.

Although she mocked herself for it, Cass knew she was looking for permanence, for belonging, in all kinds of trivial ways, happy to help Nancy stick up notices about a silent auction in the Kirkton hall on what seemed like every telegraph pole in the glen, or to spend hours making a rudimentary alliance between eight mammoth brocade curtains and their linings which Joanna intended to use this chance to get rid of.

'Only I had no idea they were so dilapidated,' she confessed, walking round and over them where they were laid out in the Riach dining-room into which, as far as Cass could tell, the sun never penetrated. 'Perhaps Kate could do something about them. She's handy with a needle and must be bored with hanging about by now.'

A vision of the tiny and heavily pregnant Kate smothered in a ton weight of unyielding folds smelling overpoweringly of age and dirt, made Cass decide to take on the job herself. Gina, co-opted, did one side of one curtain, starting at the bottom with large dashing stitches and ending up with a six-inch pucker at the top which she found puzzling. Beverley said they'd catch something nasty and refused to get involved.

She regularly turned up at the Corrie now, always carefully protected against sudden changes of climate, always ready to put Cass right about domestic matters.

'The sun will mark that table if you put it there. I saw that rug in the silent auction – didn't you notice it's coming away at the end? I suppose you realise if you keep your log basket there all kinds of creatures get into the structure of the house? PVC windows would be your best answer, they do quite cottagey ones nowadays. Remind me to bring up a catalogue ...'

Cass put up with her because she was there, part of the scene, to be accepted along with minor irritations like the Council closing the road every weekday for three weeks as summer traffic reached its peak, not being able to get Channel 4 at all now the work had been done on the transmitter, the washing machine taking hours to fill or some Riach calves spending a night milling round the Volvo, covering the windows with saliva and turning the wing mirrors back to front. Also, though it was far from easy, Cass did her best to accept Beverley because of Rick. However inappropriate the alliance, she honoured his commitment to it.

There were moments, when something reminded her too piercingly of this, when Cass doubted her wisdom in staying. Then she would imagine being somewhere strange, alone, and would draw back from the thought. And perhaps in that other place she would have dreamed unwise dreams. At least here reality faced her, every day.

And here she could, in a small way, make some input. One of her new pleasures was playing golf and at Laurie's invitation she often joined him before he began work. Once or twice, in bald terms which showed not only his distaste for approaching the topic but a telling ineptness at expressing his feelings, he revealed his concern over Gina.

'I sometimes don't think she can be quite well,' he went as far as to say once, then obviously regretting it added briskly, 'I'll give you that,' letting Cass off a two-foot putt she was by no means sure she would have sunk, and rattling in the pin with a dismissive sound. But Cass knew he had come as close as he could without direct encouragement to expressing his real anxiety, and she didn't let the chance slip away.

'She's too much alone, perhaps,' she said cautiously, for Laurie could be prickly at the best of times.

He paused before answering, and Cass saw by the tide of red which rose in his face how great an effort it cost him to do so. 'I don't know what she wants,' he brought out at last. 'She hankered to live somewhere remote, or thought she did. Now she barely goes outside the door, even to walk poor Tiree. She can't be bothered with the garden, which she used to love. The only thing in her head is her music, and she can't seem to share it, only use it as some sort of escape. But from what? What are we asking of her that's too difficult?'

Cass winced at the baffled pain in that question, guessing how many times he had asked it of himself.

'Domestic life?' she suggested. 'The role that comes with a family, no matter what one's bent?'

Laurie heard the diffidence in her voice, her fear of being too frank even though he had asked for answers. He nodded abruptly, staring away from the tee as though calculating his drive. 'Well, who knows?' he said brusquely. 'Our lives may change soon anyway, whether we like it or not.'

'Have you heard anything?' Cass's concern was still tinged with guilt for what Guy had done.

'Nothing definite. We limp along.' Laurie stooped to push in a peg tee. This he didn't want to discuss.

Would they leave the Mains? It had been on the cards since the news came out that Sillerton was in trouble, but what a gap it would make not to have Gina there. It struck Cass that the decline from the laughing, warm, vivid Gina of the early days, with her creative interests and busy life, had been no more swift than Cass's own swoop from honeymoon to pending divorce. Why did men and women try to live together? she wondered as she walked down the fairway after her ball on a line a good deal less true than Laurie's for all his jangled emotions. Perhaps Rick had the right idea; accept what was there and get on with it.

Chapter Twenty-seven

The wounds of uprooting gradually healed in the long days of a warm summer, which never seemed to include the empty times Cass had feared – or the idle times she had rather looked forward to. This promised well for achieving in time a rounded and satisfying life at the Corrie, and she felt secure enough to admit to herself that she had not been truly confident that would be the case. She could also recognise now that it had always been in Guy's sarcastic voice that those doubts had been expressed.

'Hardly the most cerebrally challenging place one could find. Don't you realise you'll be bored out of your brains inside a month . . . ?'

Bored? When had there been a moment to be bored? Just as Cass had hoped, the agency filled a need in Scotland, or more specifically north of the central belt and, by a division of labour which suited them both, she did the leg work, interviewed clients and fulfilled the role of 'ear', while Lindsay stayed mainly in the office as she preferred to do. Cass enjoyed the driving, the more distant the destination the better, and loved getting a peep into amazing houses miles from anywhere, especially those situated in the beautiful Western Isles, and meeting the colourful variety of people who lived in them, from a kilted Arab polishing agates to an ex-steel-worker from Corby farming goats.

There was plenty of eccentricity to be enjoyed nearer

home and Cass particularly relished the acerbic humour and down-to-earth views of old Mrs Munro at Allt Farr. Fortunately she approved of the au pairs Cass had produced for her daughter and daughter-in-law.

'How I dreaded a return to the dark days of nannydom,' she would say, with that little gleam in her eye which mocked herself. 'And I do believe you have produced two perfectly sensible human beings for us.'

At Riach doors and windows stood open all summer and the family used the house as a vast dusty cupboard where they kept a few clothes. Both houses and the Allt Farr cottages swarmed with friends and guests, and there was much sociable toing and froing in which Cass was generously included.

Beverley couldn't understand it. 'You're quite a newcomer,' she would pout. 'We've been here much longer than you. I suppose it's because they know you'll be able to get them servants.'

'Tut, tut, Beverley. Not a word they'd use,' Cass would reprove her gravely.

'Well, not to you maybe, but among themselves.'

'Ah, I see.'

Perhaps it was this which provoked Beverley to give what she referred to as her garden party.

'Shouldn't we try to stop her calling it that?' Cass asked Gina. Privately they might enjoy the joke of Beverley, but this *folie de grandeur* roused a kinder instinct to protect her from herself.

'Well, it will be a party and it will be in the garden,' Gina pointed out. 'I'm not sure how we could get the point across to her.'

Rick too did his best to deter her but failed.

'Will you come to the party?' Cass asked him, though she did not pretend the question wasn't prompted more from her own interest than concern about Beverley making a fool of herself.

They had met at the wooden bridge below the barn. Cass,

overjoyed to see Rick, thought it was by a lucky chance, for she had made herself accept so scrupulously the circumstances of his life that she went out of her way to avoid even the appearance of engineering such meetings. Rick did not.

'I think this time I'd better appear,' Rick said, his face unusually grim. The fiction that he wasn't fully recovered from an illness swathed by Beverley in mystery had been allowed to fade away, but the separate life patterns it had established remained convenient for both. Kept Rick sane, Cass would guess. No one would have been at all surprised if he had absented himself from such a performance. However, even more strongly than Gina and Cass, he felt he must try to save Beverley from her worst excesses, and if that proved impossible, then at least be there in support.

Beverley booked what she called 'my outside caterers' which turned out be be one sullen, unclean and patronising youth in a van, and hired plastic mock-wrought-iron tables and chairs. Cass wondered, as she often did, quite where the money came from. Though as Rick said, there seemed enough derelict furniture in the big houses of Glen Maraich and Glen Ellig alone to keep him busy for a lifetime, Cass didn't think he exactly made a fortune with his efforts, which he was always ready to abandon for a new book or a fine day. Beverley must be eating her way through their capital at a great rate.

However the affair was subsidised, a hot day in July saw gathered obediently in the wire-enclosed compound of Sycamore Lodge several kind or conscientious people, or people who liked Rick, who had groaned and cursed mightily at having to clean up and change on a glorious afternoon when they had been perfectly happy doing something else. They dotted themselves about the shadeless and almost grassless lawn, seeing no point in moving since the entire enclosure could be seen from where they stood, and talked to the people they saw most often, courteously consuming soft vols au vent with their lids balanced on humps of pallid scrambled egg mixed with salad cream, minute triangles of sandwiches with a trace of pink in the middle, and tartlets with fruit welded by some sticky substance into a lump which refused to be bitten into and, once disengaged from the teeth, had to be swallowed whole. Tiree would have loved it all.

There were envious mutterings about Joanna, who was known to have called in person to refuse her invitation with great warmth and goodwill, saying, 'It's so kind of you to invite us, but I'm afraid we never go to proper parties . . .'

People didn't stay long and there was a tendency for thanks to be overdone. Rick did his best for Beverley, welcoming and at ease, keeping a sharp eye nevertheless on the shifty-looking supplier of all the nasty food, who had a tendency to drift housewards, and calmly making the rounds to talk to everyone. Cass observed with interest that he seemed to know them all.

He didn't entirely keep out of trouble. Ed Cullane, drawn by the unwonted activity from a peaceful session under a van he'd just acquired, came to stand for a while in the middle of the Riach drive entrance, watching what was going on with unembarrassed absorption. One or two people shouted, 'Hi, Ed,' across the road, which made Beverley pinch her lips. When Rick suggested he should be invited to join them she could hardly contain her fury, and people either gazed up at the Bealach as though they'd never seen it before, or talked fervently among themselves about whether the fine spell would hold up for the hay. When Beverley overheard Rick accepting a commission to cover two chairs for Pauly Napier from Drumveyn, *discussing work,* the party was over.

The sad part was that she believed – apart from being let down by Rick – the whole thing to have been a huge success, and was all set to throw a drinks party every Sunday lunchtime for the rest of the summer.

'Everyone would know it as my special at-home time, and appreciate having somewhere nice to meet . . .'

How Rick dissuaded her was never disclosed, but the plan did not come to fruition. Beverley received a few invitations to what Mrs Munro referred to sardonically as 'catch-alls', like the traditional Alltmore barbecue on the first Sunday after the Twelfth, and a Garden Open Day at Dalquhat near Kirkton, where Beverley was incensed to discover the public was let in too. Apart from these highlights she had to make do with the inferior entertainment offered by the Corrie or the Mains.

Cass saw little of Rick after the 'garden party'. First Diane appeared for a long weekend, then other friends spent two nights en route to Ullapool, then Roey came for a couple of weeks, most luckily shedding her boyfriend the day before she was due. There was an almost forgotten pleasure to rediscover in being on their own, with no outside demands of any sort. Roey loved everything about the Corrie, and entered into whatever was going on with a readiness Cass much appreciated. She was there for the final WRI meeting before the summer break, and could hardly contain her joy when she discovered that the topic of the evening, organised through the offices of Beverley, was to be 'facial makeovers'.

Cass, to Laurie's gratitude, had persuaded Gina to come with them. The three of them sat in a rigid row, their very chairs quivering, jaw muscles clamped, as up on a screen flashed terrifying slides of the composition of the skin, tubes, growths, bulbous roots and gaily coloured veins, and an audience of mainly elderly farmers' and shepherds' wives, with untouched leathery outdoor skins and grey wind-torn perms, surveyed them in unmoving silence. They returned to animation with obvious relief when a member arriving late burst in with uninhibited English fluting, 'I'm fearfully sorry, but my little treasure got himself locked in the woodshed and I couldn't just leave him there, could I?'

Roey's eyes met Cass's in fearful speculation.

'Her dog, not her husband,' Gina hissed, and their chairs creaked in unison.

Roey was nearly undone when the secretary, giving a preview of 'pencilled in' plans for the autumn, reported, 'We tried the Samaritans but they didn't answer.'

The lecture over, everyone tramped forward with dour faces and grim wariness to see if any of the beauty products were going cheap.

'Aye, well, that'll just do me,' announced one hatchet-jawed seventy-year-old with whiskers sprouting on her chin and eyebrows like eaves, buying a pot of cream the size of a 10p piece. 'Ye maun creep afore ye gang.'

Roey was called to order by the shock of being, as the visitor, asked to judge the crochet competition.

'People still crochet?' she asked Cass blankly.

'Shut up, get on the platform and do it. This is serious.'

Serious it was, and Roey conscientiously applied herself, finally deciding that though a sort of tabard in gold lurex (which looked likely to stretch as dangerously as a thirties' swimming costume) almost blinded her to every other entry, it was after all only one stitch endlessly repeated, so for first prize she settled on a tiny offering labelled 'baby's matinée jacket'.

Sensation. Offence. Like mercury the sisterhood coalesced into two camps.

'I don't think we'd better stay for the eats,' Roey suggested nervously.

'Are you out of your mind? You're the judge, you sit at the top table with the bone-china cups and the lump sugar and the fairy cakes. Get on with it.'

'They'll tear me apart,' Roey moaned.

'Very probably.'

Going up the lane she said, 'I did my best. Look, I bought about twenty of these neat little mats. Fourth prize, or since there were four entries, bottom, depending on how you look at it.'

'Expensive piece of crawling,' Gina commented.

'Worth it. I'm going to stitch them together to make a top. Look.' Roey stuck out her breasts and draped an ecru web over each.

'That's Nancy's best work,' Cass warned her. 'For pity's sake don't ever let her catch you wearing it.'

Roey was there for a joint party at Riach for Laura's birthday and the twins', though it turned out to be more an estate ball. James Mackenzie had revived the custom two years ago and had so much enjoyed it that he had decided to make it an annual affair. Everyone in the glen seemed to be there but Rick, Cass concluded sadly, having raked the crowded room from end to end, then taken a turn through the other rooms. These Joanna had opened up for the party in the most literal way; she had opened the doors. Few other preparations had been attempted. No one cared.

Rick stayed away because, the practice of Beverley socialising without him having been established, he very much wanted to maintain it. And he found it hard to deal with meeting Cass in public.

Beverley had come to the ball *en grande tenue*, and was startled to find Doddie Menzies inviting her to dance. She refused, of course, but rallied sufficiently to say to Cass, 'How good of them to let the workers in. How they must appreciate it.'

'It's good of them to let us in,' Cass retorted, but Beverley didn't hear, trotting off with a radiant smile to head off a loose admiral who would shortly regret straying from his party.

Roey had a wonderful time. She made a hit with Ed Cullane and danced with him as long as he could stand up, depositing him tenderly in a corner when he finally sank into a coma, and turning her attentions to the saturnine Max Munro, though with markedly less success. He had only looked in for a short time and his mind was not on dancing. Kate had had her baby at the end of June, after being in labour for thirty-eight hours. She had only just survived and she and her tiny son had not been allowed home till two days ago.

'Isn't it amazing how the traditional feeling of a place like this still persists?' Roey said reflectively, as she and Cass walked down the caterans' track the next day after a visit to Allt Farr to see the new arrival. 'Even with all the changes and the empty houses and the different population.'

'I'm interested that you feel that,' Cass said. 'Guy used to tell me I just saw it because I wanted to.'

'Oh, well, you did go a bit over the top on all the Scottishness.' They had got their discussions about Guy out of the way by this time, and what a relief and release they had been to Cass. 'I suppose I was too young to care when we left Dalry, one place was as good as another to me. I used to think you were quite potty with all the photos and pictures and posters and maps stuck round your room. But our roots are in this world, even I can feel it, and I can see why you want to live here.'

'Roey, do you? Honestly?'

It meant so much to Cass. An endorsement which she had subconsciously needed. But the pleasure of sharing the glen with Roey was two-edged. It reassured her that she could make a satisfactory life here, but it showed her how much was added by having someone so compatible with whom to enjoy it. It could be like this with Rick. The thought was never far away. Perhaps it's time I found a new man, Cass told herself. That's what Roey would do. But the thought seemed a million miles from her own reality.

There was one thing Roey was unexpectedly outspoken about. She didn't approve of Gina.

'She should get off her backside,' she said flatly. 'That house is a tip. And what does she have to complain about? Most women would give their eye-teeth for a life like that. No wonder her daughter did a bunk.'

Nessa had found a job in a caravan park at Bolton-le-Sands, was cadging free bed and board from Clifford and Ruth, and was adamant that she wasn't coming back to Glen Maraich or to school.

'I think you should sort Gina out,' Roey said. 'Does she really believe Nessa's gone because she's cut off from her mates living here? Can't she see it's because no girl likes to watch her mother letting herself go like that?'

'I know. Nessa really minds all the hassle and mess. She does her best to keep her own life organised, but Gina always defeats her in the end. And I think Nessa, who's such a neat, slim little thing, hates the way Gina's getting so fat.'

'Of course she does. And Laurie must hate it too. Can't he do anything about it?'

'I think he's got his own problems at present. He's not exactly what you'd call a communicator either.'

'Well, you are. And you're her friend. Get talking.'

Cass knew she was right.

Roey couldn't get enough of Beverley and was down at Sycamore Lodge as often as she could manufacture an excuse to be there.

'She's a prize, a bonus, the icing on the cake of Glen Maraich. She's sparing some of her valuable time this afternoon to show me how to do my lips as I didn't seem to pick up the technique properly at the makeover lecture. Define, dust and blot. How lucky I am that never again shall I face the world with a blurred outline.'

'I must book in with you at three-monthly intervals,' she told Cass when she came back. 'My image requires it, apparently. Also nothing less will do to monitor the hedge. It's beginning to ramp away now, and by this time next year no common people will be able to see over it. Perhaps Beverley will train it to turn in at the top like the wire on a prison wall, or even meet in the middle so that she never has to worry about bird droppings or low flying jets or skin cancer.'

This was a threat Beverley took seriously, never allowing the sun to do more than briefly touch her patted and nourished neck and throat, though she did 'like to enjoy her garden', an undertaking which involved half an hour's work assembling the appropriate essential oil to repel insects, aerosol for jetting at passing flies, Mexican peon's hat, tanning milk for use in or out of the sun, sunglasses, fat novel preferably with a rich and successful woman on the cover, and the weakest possible Pimms clashing with ice and clogged with fruit.

Roey had left and it was Cass and Gina who were there one afternoon, wiping their upper lips after trying to nudge past the junk and get to the alcohol, while Beverley, disposed on her petunia-patterned hammock with valance and white-fringed shade, occupied herself by smiling in six stages to firm up the flesh on her cheekbones.

'You should put on some of this in case of bites,' she interrupted the exercise to order Cass, tendering a brown bottle. When Cass had obeyed for the sake of peace she saw that the small print warned, 'Not to be used prior to exposure to strong sunlight.'

She was about to say what she thought on the subject when a taxi appeared at the gate, bearing its totally unexpected passenger into their lives.

Chapter Twenty-eight

'So this is where you've been hiding yourself, my girl.'

The stumpy figure had struggled grumbling out of the taxi, impeded by a fistful of bulging carrier bags in either hand, taking two heaves to slide its bottom off the seat, and was now standing with feet, in the sort of white rubber-soled shoes an American psychiatric nurse might wear, planted well apart on the gravel. A woman perhaps in her sixties, with a frizz of grey-white hair, in a cheap blue-and-pink floral dress bagging in front and hooked up on her broad rump behind, a V-neck baring a triangle of mottled red flesh. She had a pointed chin like Beverley's thrust aggressively up and out, and little round eyes which were at once contemptuous and derisive.

'You'd best be giving him something, then,' she said in a smoke-abraded voice, her sardonic look deepening at the sight of their startled faces, jerking her head at the taxi driver who was lifting out a lop-sided expanding suitcase with cardboard scuffs at its corners. The sight of it seemed to electrify Beverley who had come to her feet with the others, and then had stood, jaw open, as though refusing to accept what she saw.

Now she leapt from petrified shock into heedless rage. 'What the hell do you think you're doing here?' she screamed, and even in the drama of the moment Cass noted that the careful vowels had suffered a dreadful flattening. 'You can't come walking in here like this.'

'Can't I? Well, I have, like it or lump it, so give the bloke his fare and let's be getting the kettle on.' The new arrival sounded grimly unfazed at her reception, and gave Gina and Cass a nod which was next to a wink. ''Ow much then, love?' she asked the driver, who stood at her shoulder unconsciously presenting the appearance of a heavy there to make threats stick.

Beverley let out a thin wail of helplessness and denial. 'No! You're not staying here.'

'Don't talk daft.' The tone was comfortable, dismissively familiar. Indeed, some sort of relationship was unmistakable, Cass decided, though she had understood Beverley had no family at all.

Beverley made an inarticulate sound somewhere between a moan and a whimper. It appeared to gratify her relative, of whatever degree.

'Can one of you—?' Beverley asked faintly, turning to Gina and Cass and gesturing at the waiting driver as though in this extremity they would naturally be there for her.

'We don't have bags with us,' Cass said, turning her empty hands wide, while Gina shook her head with the same message, lifting her shoulders in apology. Nice try, though, Beverley, Cass thought, as she added, 'I'm sorry we can't help,' to the newcomer, who nodded back with an amused grunt, as though more pleased than surprised to find someone else had Beverley's measure.

'Twelve pounds,' the man put in, thinking he might move matters forward a little. Though by the sound of it he might be in luck and get a fare straight back to the station. That blonde one was fit to be tied. He wouldn't mind; the old bird had been a laugh. 'Hot enough for you?' he asked Gina politely, to fill in the interval. He had taken her lads up and down the glen a few times.

'But you can't just—' Beverley was hissing at her unwelcome guest, darting a furious look over her shoulder which

Cass knew meant that she and Gina should fade tactfully away.

'Says who?' Amusement was gone. The narrow chin jutted fiercely, the round eyes were hard little beads. 'Just you watch me. Put your hand in your pocket for once, our Bev, and take that look off your face while you're at it.'

'It's not convenient for you to stay. We'll arrange something—'

'Get the cash.' The little woman began gathering up the collapsing carrier bags. 'I'm stopping.'

'Let me help you. I'm Cass, by the way, and this is Gina.' As Cass took a couple of the bags, which seemed to be stuffed with the sort of clothing normally destined for relief parcels, she saw that Beverley's face was contorted with rage. Worse than the smiling exercises. This uninvited guest was a brave woman.

The taxi was turning. Beverley, with an oath one would not have expected from her genteel lips, stamped into the house. Her visitor turned to the forlorn suitcase, but Gina was before her.

'Oh ta, love. Fetch it in for me, would you?' She set off after Beverley with a waddling gait and a look of iron determination mixed with relish.

Beverley, returning with her crocodile skin wallet, snarled wordlessly to find Gina dumping the suitcase on her willow green carpet, while Cass propped the creased and splitting plastic bags against the copper pot of the *ficus benjamina* in the hall.

'So what do you think of my girl?' The woman, looking weary now, dropped with a gasp of relief onto the sofa and wiped her hot face with a mottled forearm from which a flaccid pouch of flesh swung.

'Your girl?' Cass and Gina spoke together.

'Hah.' It sounded like satisfaction but there was an undertone of wry pain which Cass caught if Gina didn't. 'My daughter. Didn't tell you she had an old mum hidden away, did she? No, I thought not. Win Hogg, that's me.' Her face twisted briefly into a bleak expression which made Cass look hastily away, even as questions and implications whirled in her brain.

'But why on earth did Beverley pretend she was an orphan?' Gina demanded in bewilderment as they started up the lane. 'All that tough childhood rigmarole.'

They had not been offered tea. Beverley had flounced in after thrusting some money through the taxi window – Cass somehow didn't think it would have included a tip – and had disappeared to her bedroom, slamming the door.

'Little madam,' her mother had said, perking up as though the sound promised a level of warfare she was going to enjoy.

'Look, would you like us to stay?' Cass had asked. Or fetch Rick, she had longed to suggest.

'Don't take me wrong, love, but best to have the decks cleared for this one. Live nearby though, do you? Who knows, I may come knocking on your door yet.'

Cass couldn't bring herself to enter into Gina's joyful conjectures as to what might be going on in the rarefied purlieus of Sycamore Lodge. She urgently needed to be alone to try and think out what this development meant in relation to Rick. Had he known about Beverley's mother? Of course he must have done. Then he must have gone along with the pretence on the subject. The lie, Cass corrected herself obdurately. But why? What purpose had it served? And if he had been part of this deception, what else had been false? Had all the odd business about his illness been invented? There had always been a sense of something he wasn't telling her about that. She had a frightening feeling of being adrift, as though her life here suddenly had no foundation.

'Win Hogg! Oh dear,' Gina was saying, not unkindly. 'What a tough little trooper, though. Beverley's going to have some explaining to do. Our Bev.'

Ordinarily Cass would have loved the joke but she found it hard even to respond.

'Come to us for supper,' Gina begged. 'There's nothing

much to eat but Laurie's been more than averagely tetchy of late, and he's always in a better mood when you're there. Andy's out and I can't face one of those husband-and-wife evenings.'

'Gina, I'm sorry, I've got things I simply must do.' It was true. Cass had a lot of work to clear before going to London to cover for Diane while she was on holiday, which for this first year she had agreed to do. Never had she felt more reluctant to be dragged away.

She got rid of Gina at last and almost regretted it as time at once slowed to a crawl and the unhappy minutes ticked by filled with doubts and distrust. She found herself unable to concentrate on work, her brain ranging over conversations with Rick, trying to pin down exactly what had been said, reviewing accepted facts in the light of the afternoon's events, and all the while resisting any interpretation which hurt too much.

You just don't want to believe he knew, she told herself angrily. You don't want to believe it because if Rick's been lying, to protect Beverley or for whatever other reason, then the last thing he's going to do is appear to explain.

But he came, and from his held-in, shell-shocked look Cass saw at once that Win's arrival, Win's existence, had come as a shattering blow to him, a blow whose full significance he had scarcely had time to assimilate. Her own immediate instinct, to go to him and wrap her arms round him in comfort, told her that her doubts had vanished in that single glance.

She reached a hand towards him as she came to her feet to greet him, but let it drop. She didn't go to him. She forced herself to focus on the severely practical. Although it had been a hot day the evenings were always cool at this altitude and, thankful that the fire was ready laid, she put a match to it and made coffee.

'She'd always said – all that stuff about foster homes and having such a hard time – it was all – her mother brought her up, was there all the time. She cleaned offices at night, still does. She did all kinds of jobs to look after Beverley. She's always lived in the same house in Birkenhead, is living in it still. She brought Beverley up on her own.'

The fragmented thoughts jerked out, uncoordinated, out of sequence, Rick's tone that of a man who is repeating what patently cannot be true, and Cass said little, glad he had come but knowing he had done so blindly and unthinkingly, and wasn't ready yet for coherent talk.

'She let me believe she'd never been loved or cared for by anyone, that I was the first person to—'

He kept returning to this point, clearly the one that hurt him most, and Cass understood how his mind must be groping to put into this new perspective the years of loyalty and in the end self-sacrifice, though she did not imagine either word would be in his mind.

She listened to him quietly, letting him know her sympathy and support were there, but accepting that she herself did not figure in Rick's awareness at this moment. He didn't look at her as he talked, but gazed unseeingly into the fire, as one by one he dragged painfully out by the roots the preconceptions on which his life had been based. Cass found it hard to witness, especially when he dazedly revealed a different wound.

'She was glad when I was ill.'

'Rick, no, that can't have been true.'

'She just said so, said it gave her the chance she'd always wanted to uproot and leave everything behind, cut herself off from everyone who knew us, and make a fresh start somewhere else, where she could pretend to be whoever she liked.'

'She *said* that?' What violence of anger and ruthless revelation had shattered the pretentious veneer of Sycamore Lodge this evening?

'She said she knew I'd never amount to much socially, and had always held her back when she'd wanted to better herself.'

How did Beverley square that with the ease Rick had found in making contacts at every level here at Bridge of Riach, contrasted with the courteous refusal of intimacy she herself had met with? But it was not the time to leap in with such protests.

'She said she wished I'd really had ME and had gone on being ill.'

'Oh, Rick, no.'

'Oh, yes.' He twisted his head to give her one tight smile, then turned back to the fire as though unable to cope with anything outside this immediate unburdening. 'Then she could have kept me hidden away, couldn't she? Gone on telling people I was washed up, useless, and that she was a heroine to look after me. Didn't you understand that she was ashamed of me?'

Cass, calm, equable Cass, felt the actual taste of rage in her mouth, and forced it down.

'But my God, not even to tell me her mother was alive, never to let us meet, in all these years. Not to go and see her herself even ...' Rick pressed thumb and first finger of a broad hand against his closed eyes, shaking his bowed head.

'But she must have been in touch with her mother?' So much here was unbelievable that Cass hardly knew which question to choose.

'She's never seen her or spoken to her or written a word. And her mother was living just across the river, a ferry ride away.'

'But how did Win find her here?'

He shook his head. He hadn't asked, and if the explanation had emerged in the yelling match he had walked in on with such disbelief, it had not been repeated after his appearance, when Beverely had hysterically redirected her fire against him.

Apart from the question of how Win came to be here, why had she come? Cass longed to ask.

'All that story about Beverley's father, how she adored him, the war hero, all of that,' Rick went on, still sounding dazed. 'Her mother says she never knew who he was, and didn't care. She raised Beverley entirely on her own, and after she left school found the money to let her train as a dietician, only Beverley found that was too much like hard work so she gave it up and stayed at home, living off her mother, for I don't know how long.' Rick rubbed his hands hard back over his skull as though he could drive these distasteful half-digested facts from it. The gesture seemed to recall him to the present. 'God, Cass, I'm sorry to come pouring all this out to you. I'd better clear off.'

'Don't be silly.' She longed to hold and soothe him, hating to see the stunned look of betrayal in his eyes. Nothing, no one, should be allowed to hurt him in this way. 'You know I don't mind.'

'It didn't occur to me to go anywhere else,' he admitted. 'I just had to get out of that house. I still can't . . .' His voice trailed away as the enormity of what he had learned hit him again.

'Of course you had to come here,' Cass said. 'I'm glad you did.' Glad on her own account as well as his. It would have been a hard evening indeed to get through if he had not.

They talked for a long time, but Rick held on even now to a certain reticence. Cass knew he needed time to take in what had happened, and saw that, little as she liked the fact, an ingrained loyalty to Beverley was still in place. Rick could not throw aside in an hour the habit of protectiveness which had been the foundation of his actions and decisions for years.

But when at last he left, the bruised look still in place, tramping grimly down the lane to walk back into the splintered shell of his life, Cass found an inner voice refusing to be suppressed. Sadly it protested to him, 'But you didn't *say* anything.'

What had she wanted him to say, or expected him to say? There had been no room in his mind for her tonight. Her mind went back to the lesson Roey's visit had taught her. Her new existence here could be full, busy and content, but it would not hold the one vital element for which she longed. Now the lesson had been reinforced. Whatever happened to Rick's life it would not include her.

It was not from Rick but from Win that further revelations came.

Chapter Twenty-nine

Win came toiling up the lane two days later, days during which Cass had been unable to keep out of her mind forebodings as to what was going on behind the closed blinds of the bungalow. She had even been briefly tempted to delay her departure to London by twenty-four hours, then had realised that to do so would show how far she was from accepting that whatever was happening it had nothing to do with her.

'I hope you don't mind, love,' Win gasped, accepting Cass's hand to help her up the steps. 'I just had to get out of that place, it's doing me head in.' She was breathless, her face red, her dark upper lip beaded with perspiration. Cass had been sitting on the bench against the wall in the sun, but led Win inside to the shady room in concern, noting that her breathing didn't at once subside even when she had sunk with a sigh of relief into a chair.

'Would you like something cold to drink?' Cass asked, bringing another cushion, for Win's misshapen legs were too short for the deep seat.

'I'd rather a cuppa, if it's not too much trouble,' Win said yearningly, brushing her face with her wrist and leaning back with her eyes closed. 'Cool in here. It was like being in an oven, coming up that road of yours.'

Cass hardly liked to leave her to make the tea, but hoped

it would revive her. It was odd, she reflected, as she filled the kettle and assembled a tray, how much at ease she was with this bellicose old woman, as though some innate honesty in Win instantly communicated itself. No wonder she needed to escape from Syc Lo.

'Oh my, that's good,' Win gasped, after a loud intake of tea by suction, sieving the liquid through her stained teeth as though to savour it to the full. 'Lord, how I needed that.' Her breathing was still not quite even. Toiling up the lane in this heat had clearly been far beyond her normal level of exertion. 'Nice place you've got here,' she observed, brightening up enough to look around her after another thirsty swallow. 'I don't mind the old-fashioned look myself. My Bev's done well for herself, though, when all's said and done.' She offered this with a disparaging huff, yet there was a trace of defiant pride there too, as though she was defending her daughter to some unseen critic. Then to Cass's concern the defiance crumbled, her pursed-up lips mumbled wordlessly, the flesh of her chin puckered. Pushing herself upright she scrabbled at her belt, then plunged a hand down the front of her dress, producing a grubby rag of handkerchief. Cass was glad she hadn't had to continue the search into the leg of her knickers.

'You must wonder why I came,' Win said, after a moment's fierce struggle for control, hitching her left buttock further back into the chair and easing her feelings with a resounding sniff. 'You must think I'm daft, getting myself in this state.'

'I don't at all,' Cass said gently, with something oddly close to affection. 'You just take your time. You can talk to me about anything you like, if it would help.'

'I knew I could. I said to myself the minute I saw you, that girl has her head screwed on all right. I've been going just about dotty down there, what with all the carry-on. What Bev did to me was bad enough, but what she's done to that bloke of hers, decent and all as he is, that's past belief, that is . . .'

She was crying now, roughly and awkwardly, apologising

and angry with herself, worried about what Cass would think of her, but unable to check the tears once they had started.

Cass knelt beside her and laid an arm round the rounded shoulders with the pad of thickened muscle put there by too many years of heavy work, noting the pink skull visible through the thinning hair, the coarse texture of the permed ends, the lank straightness where it was growing out, the blackheads round her nostrils, the cobbled texture of her skin. Was this what Beverley was fighting against, this and all it represented? Cass tried to hold her mind from questions; none of this was her business. All that mattered was to comfort this stricken person, if she could, because the tough resilience was breaking down, and Cass felt that whatever had happened Win didn't deserve this pain.

'She never let me know where she'd gone, you know, not a word. Wanted shut of the lot of us. But dragging that man of hers up here to this godforsaken place when he was ill and didn't know what was happening to him, that takes the biscuit, even for our Bev. That should never have been allowed. But enough's enough, in my book. She's got away with murder, always has, but that's not to say she should go on ruling the roost without nobody never putting their foot down.'

She was getting agitated with the effort of putting this into words, and Cass tried to calm her.

'Don't try to talk till you're ready. Have some more tea. Would you like a biscuit, or some shortbread?'

Win looked at the plate Cass was holding out, and suddenly her whole face wavered and broke in a look of despair, more moving than her anger had been.

'No, love.' She pushed the plate away with the back of her hand. 'Death sticks,' she added, crushing her balled-up handkerchief against her mouth to stifle a sudden sob.

'What do you mean?' A premonition chilled Cass, as though Win's distress had made her perceptions unusually alert.

'That's it, see.' Win's muffled voice held a bleak finality. 'That's why I come. I made our Hayley tell me, she's always known where the money was coming from, trust her for that. No flies on her, never has been. So I just thought to myself, right, that's it, I've had about all I can take. If I want to see my own girl before I go, nobody's going to stop me.'

'Before you go?' What money, and who was Hayley?

'That's it, love, go, keel over, drop off my perch. Though no one will say it in so many words. But I do, no sense messing about. Ticker. Always been the trouble in our family. Connaries. Every one of me dad's family went with connaries before they was seventy. Every one. So where does that leave me? High blood pressure, klestrel sky high, some number or other they told me, I can't remember. Well, life's not worth living if you can't eat what you want, that's what I say. I've had one or two bad dos lately, I can't pretend I haven't, so I just said to myself, "Well, Bev my girl, there's a lot you've got away with in your time, but you're not getting away with this." I wanted to see her before I went and soon as I knew where she was, off I come. Though now that I do see her I reckon I need my head seen to for bothering.'

She wound up her dramatic recital on such a prosaic note it might have been someone else speaking, and Cass smiled in spite of her concern at what she had heard.

'Who is Hayley?' she asked, thinking Win might prefer her to stick to the same matter-of-fact level.

Win stopped grinding her sodden handkerchief into her eyes and pursed her lips in a look of tired contempt. 'Bev's kid. I suppose she's never breathed a word about her neither? My lord, she's a hard one, she is, though search me where she gets it from. She had all any youngster could ask for, growing up. But I'll tell you one thing straight, she'd slit my throat or anybody else's soon as look at you if she thought it'd make life easier for Number One.'

Getting rather shakily to her feet to fetch a box of tissues, Cass tried to take in this startling new information. Had Rick known? But of course he couldn't have. How would the uncovering of such a secret affect him? How would he react to a discovery which shifted the parameters of his life yet again? Would he see this as a new responsibility for him? As she held out the tissues, trying to drag her mind back to immediate demands, she found Win was talking about him.

'Can you believe, I'd always had him down as the same sort she was, hard as they come? Bev said right from the start that he wouldn't have anything to do with us, that he'd leave her if anyone ever found out the kind of place she'd come from. She said if it got out the money she sent for Hayley would stop. I never thought anything of it, it seemed to make sense to me, some well-off bastard that didn't want to touch muck. You could have knocked me down with a feather when I met him, and he never knew a thing. All this time, he never knew a thing. Beats me how she pulled it off, but that's our Bev for you ...'

London was misery. With every atom of her soul Cass resisted having to be away at this time, longing to be back in Glen Maraich, near Rick. What happened in his life might have nothing to do with her, but goodness, how she needed to know what effect Win's disclosures had had.

She stayed in Diane's flat, and though it was convenient and comfortable she decided in the end it had been a bad decision to use it. Somewhere more anonymous might have shielded her from the pain of associations and reminders of the past. She had not been prepared for the memories of Guy that swarmed in, though even more unsettling were the doubts which attacked her all over again – doubts about her share in the failure of their marriage. Had her respect for Guy's independence and privacy been after all a form of laziness, a too easy acquiescence? Had she let a relationship which had much good in it slip away without a struggle, and was she as much to blame as he for a lack of commitment? A truer perspective would have returned had they talked, but Guy was away and they didn't meet, and the questions formed an unhappy background to the busy days, coming with unwelcome persistence between her and thoughts of Rick.

She had planned to see far too many people and fit in far too many things, as though she had already forgotten the toll of time and effort which getting about London exacted. It had sounded fun when planned from Glen Maraich – seeing people in the office, catching up on friends, revisiting old haunts, but she could recapture no pleasure in any of it and could not believe she had taken for granted the noise and movement and polluted air when she lived here. She felt harried and alien in a way she wouldn't have imagined possible after so short an absence.

The original idea had been to stay on in the flat for a couple of nights after Diane returned, to give them a day at the agency together, after which they were to meet friends for drinks, theatre and supper. Nothing was said at the office that couldn't equally well have been communicated by phone or fax, and Diane was still too full of her holiday to be much interested in what had gone on while she was away. She was also full of the new restaurant where they were taking Cass tonight, tossing out tempting details as they were getting ready.

'Gorgeous roof garden ... menus out of this world ... fabulous polenta with porcini mushrooms and white truffles ... vin santo ice cream ...'

It was obvious that Diane was enjoying her new affluence. Suddenly Cass couldn't bear it, couldn't endure one more moment in this place. Diane's cases spilling out a tangle of unwashed holiday clothes, the spew of frivolous presents she had tossed about, the too-musky scent she wore, the prospect of the evening ahead, friendships that had become meaningless with the basis of daily exchanges knocked away, the silly food – it was all vapid, unreal, nothing to do with her.

She swung round from the dressing table. 'Diane, look, I'm sorry, but I've got to go.'

'What are you talking about?'

'Leave. Go. Back to Scotland.'

'But we've booked a table! You can't imagine how difficult it is to get in. People have to wait weeks, we were incredibly lucky ...'

The very level on which they argued had neatly summed up her alienation from the scene, Cass reflected, as she added one more to the chain of dipped headlights pouring up the M1. She would mend fences with Diane; they had always got on well – and they needed each other. But now, at last, she could release her thoughts, letting them leap forward to where they had wanted to be through the clogged and dragging days.

If only she could have talked to Rick before she left. But would he have been ready to talk? Or would his scrupulous sense of loyalty have made it impossible? Or, and Cass knew this was the thought that more than all the rest had troubled her, would he think these new facts changed nothing? How little she knew him; yet no one in her life had ever felt so familiar, so like herself. When she was with him his calm wrapped her round; she looked neither forward nor back. Self-doubt and questions ceased to exist. She was simply herself.

On a drab morning of threatening rain, with mist obscuring the Bealach and shafts of subdued light raying down from bulging clouds, the bungalow, blind-eyed, kept its secrets.

I can only drive by, Cass realised with a gut-twisting wrench of anticlimax. This is what I've come back for, hurtling through the miles, fizzing with anticipation. This is all there can ever be. This is reality. Driving by. Whatever is going on in that house concerns only that family.

But still she longed, with a need that actually hurt in her chest, to leave the car and walk down the slope, under the road, and across the wet grass to the barn. How long since she had been able to do that? There were tears in her eyes as she parked below the steps. Tiredness, she told herself, and indeed she felt weary to the bone, dragged down by a new and hopeless loneliness, as though, frighteningly, she was as separate from everyone here as she had been in London.

'No, this won't do,' she said aloud. This was where she belonged. She could not afford to let loneliness in here. She would sleep for an hour or two, if she could, then go and see Gina. That would provide solacing company, and Gina had probably been missing her too, but also there might be news, specific news she would be unable to duck, and then she could finally put aside the last lingering shreds of hope.

She almost thought it had been a mistake to come and that she wasn't going to be able to bear it, when Gina rushed into the story before Cass was well inside the door. But, Cass had to admit, she would probably have related the news in the same cheerful vein herself, if it had not had such painful private significance for her.

'Win's gone,' Gina announced, picking up a packet of digestive biscuits she had dropped and tossing the broken pieces to Tiree who caught them with loud gollops, swallowing each with his eyes fixed on the next. 'She was rather a dear, wasn't she? I took her down to Kirkton one morning. She'd started walking, sure that a bus would come along sooner or later. Can you imagine Beverley letting her? Luckily I caught up with her before she'd gone too far. She didn't strike me as very fit.'

'I think she has heart problems,' Cass replied, thinking even Gina must notice how odd her voice sounded.

'I should think Beverley's enough to give anyone heart problems,' Gina remarked, looking in the biscuit packet and realising at last that if she gave Tiree all the broken bits there wouldn't be anything left. She tipped the remaining fragments onto a plate and put it on the table, Tiree's nose pursuing it. 'But Mum certainly stirred things up while she was here. Sycamore Lodge is on the market, would you believe?'

'*What?*' Cass stared at her, too shaken by this news to worry about how she looked or sounded, or what Gina might think. 'Are you sure?'

But Gina didn't seem to find her consternation surprising. 'It's a bit of a turn-up, isn't it? This coffee doesn't seem very hot, does it? Perhaps the kettle wasn't boiling after all. How's yours?'

'Fine, thanks.' Cass hadn't tasted it. 'But how do you know they're selling?'

'Beverley said so. Her present line is that she's always hated the glen, it was a mistake to build such a lovely house in a place like this, back of beyond, no proper social life, etc, etc. In other words, the usual garbage, but the truth is she can't bear to stay now that Ma has blown the gaff, as Win would put it. She's amazing, she really got about in the few days she was here, talked to everyone. Beverley was livid of course, too stupid to see that far from her mother lowering her in people's estimation she would improve her image.'

'But does – I mean, what does Rick think about all this? He must have a view.'

'He never says, though, does he? And I suppose he doesn't much mind where he lives, he's so easy-going.'

He does mind. He loves this place. He will hate leaving it. Yet why do I think this; what do I really know of him?

'Perhaps Beverley will change her mind.' Frailest of straws to clutch at, but she had to offer some response.

'Oh, please!' Gina cried in mock horror. 'Actually, I think someone's coming up tomorrow to look it over and write the blurb. They should have asked us, we could have let our pens run riot.'

But for Cass laughing over the horrors of Sycamore Lodge seemed very much a joke of the past.

Chapter Thirty

Rick came to say goodbye. Cass felt further from him than she ever had, miserably aware of the tenuous quality of their friendship. There had been so little to give it substance – chance meetings, occasional conversations which should probably never have been indulged in and which in retrospect appeared trivial and impersonal. Even the opportunity offered by making the new study had been squandered. She had read too much into things which had had no significance, seduced by her own need and her growing unhappiness with Guy into believing there had been some marvellous accord with Rick.

He had clearly never found anything of the sort. His curt words and abstracted air indicated he was holding in check feelings which had nothing to do with her, and his attention seemed concentrated on controlling them.

'You're really selling the house?' Cass asked, searching for something acceptable to talk about, wincing at the aura of pain and disillusionment he carried with him. This man had had the last twenty years of his life smashed to pieces in his hand; did he have the capacity or will to salvage them? Any words of hers could only be intrusive. Even her question had been superfluous. The 'For Sale' sign was up. Everyone knew the Scotts were leaving, and though many would be sorry to see Rick go, and the households whose furniture had been returned to them on a regular basis beautifully and skilfully restored would miss him, no one was greatly surprised. There was a pattern of people selling up in the south at prices three times higher than property fetched here, buying, renovating, selling and departing.

'Where will you go?' Cass tried again.

'Go?' Rick looked at her as though the choice of word was extraordinary. Then he gave a little smile she didn't like at all. 'Oh, Beverley wants to go back to the world she knows. Her foray into Scottish country life can hardly be said to have been a success.'

He got up with a restlessness unusual for him, crossing to the window with a new heaviness in his step, standing in silence to look down the falling miles of the glen, once more visible past the open lawn and at present ribbed with the long shadows of evening. Was he deliberately hiding his face from her? Cass thought so, and she ached for him. What about his roots? Had the chance gone for ever for him to create the sort of life he wanted in a place he loved? Liverpool again. What would he do there? Start up the sort of business he'd had before? But his capital must be pretty well gone by now, she imagined. And how long would it be before the bungalow found a buyer?

But she couldn't ask about any of it. Rick's life was his own, or rather, his and Beverley's, as it had always been. Cass knew she had built up out of all proportion the pleasure and peace she found in being with him, and she was only thankful she had never let him or anyone else know what it had meant to her. Then a more generous impulse swept her. There had been happiness between them. She couldn't have imagined it. It would be strange and cold to let him go without offering some sympathy.

'Rick, I'm so sorry about – all this. Sorry you've had such discoveries to cope with – and that you'll have to leave the glen.' But seeing how her last words could be misinterpreted she checked in embarrassment.

To her relief Rick turned, his shoulders sagging in a release of tension, saying wearily, 'Oh, Cass, that's nice of you.' Shaking his head as though trying to clear it of thoughts he could still hardly assimilate and was tired of thinking, he came to join her by the fire.

'A daughter.' He dropped into his chair as though he had no energy left. 'And I never knew, never guessed. Beverley always told me she couldn't have a baby because of the abuse she'd suffered as a child.' He made a brusque movement as though physically rejecting this image. 'She's been sending Win money for her ever since we married. At least thank God she did that much.'

But why stay with her? She's lied and cheated and taken. Haven't you done enough for her? What hold can she have on someone like you? To keep herself from voicing these questions, which she knew would come out as the wild appeals she mustn't make, Cass focused her mind on what Rick had said. The juxtaposition of the two sentences summed him up so well. Another man might have found the financial support he had unwittingly given something to be angry about. Rick would have been appalled if it had not been provided.

As Cass sat helplessly silent he went on as though he scarcely knew he was speaking, haphazard thoughts jerking out. 'I thought she needed help, needed looking after. She made me believe she'd had such a hard time. She'd never been in a foster home at all. I just wanted to make everything all right for her.'

A hopeless envy filled Cass, such as she would never have guessed herself capable of. To have that sort of care lavished on one – yet Beverley was as indifferent to it as she was to the dramatic beauty of this place she was so ready to abandon. The words had not been directed at Cass and still she said nothing. Yet this was all the time they had left. She could feel it running like cool ribbon through her fingers, and her helplessness to check it, to alter anything, filled her with a dreadful sadness.

'I'd better go.' Before she was prepared for it, before she

thought the moment even close, Rick was on his feet, his bulk towering over her – and that too was something she would miss unbearably.

'Yes, of course.' She scrambled up so quickly in her determination not to seem to cling to the moment that her head swam.

You'll have a lot to do tomorrow. She caught back the platitude. A lot to do on moving day indeed. Desolation spread inside her like a stain.

'Goodbye Cass.'

No, *no*, not like this.

Then Rick took one step towards her, and she had time to see his face twisted in mingled anger and helplessness before he wrapped his arms around her, folding her in, clamping her against him with a fierce need which answered the appeal she had suppressed. The hard, silent embrace was deeply satisfying, treacherously unmanning. Without defences, Cass clung to him blindly, drawing all she could of comfort from that longed-for contact, against the emptiness to come. She felt his cheek against her hair; that felt so good. His body was strong and warm, solid yet accepting the contours of her own.

This is almost beyond bearing, she thought helplessly.

His arms were loosening. She felt his lips soft for an instant against her cheek as he drew gently away, and even as she realised with piercing dismay that this was all there was to be, some deep honesty agreed that this was all there could be.

Rick took a single step again, this time away from her. They stood for one taut moment of such awareness of themselves and of each other that every detail of where they were, and the objects around them, was obliterated. Then Rick turned away, going quietly to the door. Cass didn't stir, just flinched as his shape darkened the small window as he passed, and listened with head on one side for any sound as he went down the steps. There was none; he had gone.

* * *

It was ironic, she thought as the days passed, trying to dredge up humour to help her, that tenanted or untenanted Sycamore Lodge looked much the same, the only visible sign that it had been abandoned the flaunting red-and-white 'For Sale' sign, which caught her eye every time she passed with a shock that never lessened. Then gradually a raggedness appeared in the trim garden, a couple of Fanta cans were lobbed over the fence, the tattered shreds of a binbag lodged against the gate – and upwards raced the *leylandii* with silent menace, Cass would add, trying to blunt the images of desertion and decay.

But mockery didn't help. There was nothing to laugh about in thoughts of Beverley now. Cass felt arbitrarily bereft of something that had mattered to her, and as she had done after the separation with Guy, wondered if she had been too passive, too much at the mercy of other people's decisions. But what could she have done? She must just settle for what she had here. She felt she had been repeating that dreary lesson for months and still it hadn't sunk in.

The struggle for self-discipline now met with a devastating setback. Gina was leaving. Not immediately, not till the end of the season, but the enterprise at Sillerton was folding, its future uncertain, and Laurie had lost his job. The Frasers would be going from the comfortable, shabby farmhouse which Gina had first made so beautiful then allowed to slide into such unappealing squalor.

'But what will you do?' Cass asked. She had cried a lot in private since Gina had broken the news the previous evening, but thought she was sufficiently in control today to show interest and support, especially as Laurie was present, which would keep the tone practical.

'My brother's opening a leisure centre in Stirling,' he told her. 'Well, it will be a leisure centre eventually, he assures me. It's more like a gym at present. But there's room for expansion, and we're thinking of going in together.'

'Laurie's always so cautious. It was all agreed last night,' Gina put in. 'Though as his brother's nearly as keen on his own way as Laurie is I can't see it working out too well.' She had her back to them as she spoke and missed the quick colour which rose in Laurie's face and the way he compressed his lips.

Cass however did not. 'I'm so glad you'll have something to go to at once,' she said to him quietly. 'That must be a huge worry off your mind. It must have been a nightmare, never knowing from one week to the next whether your job was safe. But, though it's horribly selfish of me, I hate the thought of losing you all.'

'And I hate the thought of losing my lovely house and garden,' Gina declared with some of her old vigour. 'You'll have to come and see us often, Cass, I shan't know a soul.'

Cass gathered that she was to do the travelling.

'Of course I will. You know I will.'

It was Laurie who, unexpectedly, came to put a comforting arm round her shoulders.

'Don't worry, Cass, you'll never be short of friends, wherever you are. You've fitted in to life in the glen so easily, you'll hardly notice we've gone.'

He meant it kindly, but he got a little too close to home. His words echoed with a hollow sound Cass's feeling of having to make the best of what was left. Gina's departure would leave a huge hole in her life.

Gina hardly seemed to realise it. She was more preoccupied with drawbacks to the plan.

'I just hope we find somewhere reasonable to live. Not in Stirling itself, of course, I should loathe that after being here, and what would poor Tiree do cooped up in a town? He needs so much space, he'd never—'

With a harsh exclamation Laurie drove back his chair and walked out.

'What on earth have I said now?' Gina demanded aggrievedly. 'He seems to be in such a bad mood all the time these days.'

Cass took a careful breath to make sure she could strike a reasonable tone. 'Gina, the poor man's been worrying about his job for months. And now he has to face a new beginning that doesn't sound too—'

'Then why do it?' Gina interrupted crossly. 'He and his brother fight all the time, he knows that perfectly well. It's madness to think of it.'

'He's doing it, at a guess, because he has to support you and the family.' Cass could feel an unfamiliar slow anger gathering somewhere deep inside her.

'He wants to get back to a town. He always said it was impractical to live here,' Gina said, not listening, harking back to old resentments.

The swell of anger in Cass rose and burst. Piece by piece, it seemed, what she wanted and enjoyed was being chipped away. She had no alternative but to absorb the shocks and claw back to a positive attitude again. Yet here was Gina, with everything offered to her on a plate, a family, a husband who was prepared to settle for a job which clearly would not be ideal in order to keep them all going, and she remained oblivious to what he was doing for them, and indifferent to any benefits Nessa and the two boys might find in such a move. And, though when she first told Cass the news Gina had done a lot of wailing about how much she would miss her, Cass didn't feel entirely convinced that she would. Well, why should she? Gina was not alone, just as no one else Cass knew seemed, in the pain of that moment, to be alone.

Cass looked round her at the attractive objects with which Gina had filled the room, most half-obscured by the unsightly silt of everyday living, none cleaned – objects which though most had a function were not performing it, heedlessly bought by Gina because she liked and wanted them. She had gone on indulging in this extravagance even when she knew Laurie's job was in jeopardy. And Cass thought of the food she had seen wasted in this kitchen, filched by Tiree, or tossed out because

Gina hadn't got round to using it before it rotted. The anger swept her away.

'Gina, how can you be so selfish? Don't you ever think of anyone but yourself?' She registered with surprise that she was shouting and didn't care. 'What about poor Laurie, tossed out of a job he'd started with such high hopes? What about Andy and Steve and Nessa? A move to Stirling might suit them very well. And what do you care about this house or the garden? Look at them! When I first came here they were lovely, but you've let them go to rack and ruin. What does living in a town matter to you? You never go out of the door. Tiree could be no more cooped up in the middle of London than he is here, the way you're living nowadays—'

She broke off, suddenly appalled at the rage which had seized her, so rare for her that it felt as though some outside force had taken her over. And as it ebbed, she knew its cause lay in something much deeper than frustration about what Gina was doing to her life. Gina was gaping at her, thunderstuck, her raised hands in the filthy glove ends of an oven cloth looking absurdly as though they were manacled. But in spite of Gina's expression and the awfulness of quarrelling, Cass was glad these things had been said at last, and knew she wouldn't have recalled one of them.

'Gina, I'm sorry I yelled like that,' she said, getting up to slip a hand through Gina's arm. 'But I think it's time some of these things were said. Come and sit down, and let's talk. Will you talk?'

Still too startled to object, Gina let the oven gloves drop off her hands and allowed Cass to draw her to the table. 'I don't see why everyone's so cross, though,' she protested unsteadily, her yellow eyes brimming with tears.

'I know, I'm sorry. But look, Gina, this could be a new chance for you, and I don't want you to throw it away before you even begin.'

'I do think of Nessa and the boys, you know. I think of

them all the time. And I suppose Nessa might be happier in a place like Stirling where there's lots going on. Or will she blame me all over again for separating her from her chums in Muirend? I just feel sometimes that whatever I do I can't please her.'

Cass recognised the moment and grasped it. 'She's cut off from her friends in Lancaster, and she chose to be there. No, Gina, that's only part of what it's about, just as her complaints that you do more for the boys than for her are only part of it.'

'What do you mean?' Where Nessa was concerned Gina could switch to full alert in an instant.

'This may hurt you, and that's the last thing I want to do, you know that, but have you ever thought that perhaps Nessa minds most about you? For you?'

Gina stared at her, slack in her chair, her heavy shoulders slumped in defeat. Her eyelids and nostrils were red; there were tears on her cheeks. 'Go on,' she said.

'Oh, Gina.' Cass reached to take her hand, and felt its resistless weight in hers with compunction and anxiety. Could she really help this unhappy woman?

'Gina, don't you see, your own life is so empty and unsatisfactory that the people who love you hate to see it happening to you. Not only Nessa. You know this isn't just about her. But Laurie too. And me. You've got into this downward spiral and none of us can help you. Nessa can only deal with it by fighting you, and appearing to despise you. Laurie has a go about the little things, the domestic shortcomings. I just try to cheer you up, but that's only camouflaging the symptoms. Are you hating this? Shall I shut up?'

Gina was sitting with bowed head, the shielding curtain of hair in place, and Cass waited almost without breathing, terribly afraid she had said too much.

Then flinging back her hair, Gina straightened up and faced Cass with jaw squared. 'Why stop there? I've let everything get beyond me. This—' a sweep of her arm encompassed the messy room '—and this.' She took a brutal handful of the folded flesh below her ribs. 'That's what it's all about, isn't it? I'm a mess, I've let myself go and I can't do anything about it. I begin every day with a hundred good intentions, but I never make them stick.'

'And you turn to the piano as a refuge?'

'And waste several more hours. Yes. It's the only time I feel safe and truly myself. Yet in an awful way, though it helps at the time, afterwards I feel even lonelier, as though music and what it gives me have carried me even further from the people I care about.'

'Look Gina, I'm no psychologist, and I realise there are no easy answers, but it seems to me you're going against the grain all the time, and no one can be happy like that. Wouldn't it be possible to go with the music, let it work for you?'

'Oh, that's all in the past,' Gina cut in swiftly. 'I can hardly play at all now. You don't understand.'

'I know I don't,' Cass agreed humbly. She minded the fact that music was a closed world to her more than she ever admitted. 'But you could play again, couldn't you? If you wanted to. I know living here you probably didn't have much incentive to do anything about it, but if you were in a town, couldn't you take it up seriously again, or perhaps teach as you used to?'

'I don't have time, there's always so much to do,' Gina objected flatly, but Cass was heartened that she had chosen a practical excuse.

'What is there to do, seriously? Moving and settling in will be busy, of course, but after that? The housework only seems a huge chore because you hate it so much. So get someone else to do it. Do your own thing for once – and get paid for it. That would give you new contacts, as well as satisfaction, or fulfilment, or whatever you like to call it without getting too pompous. And if you were happy you know how that would rub off on the family.'

'I'm so out of practice. You've no idea how much work it would need to play even half decently again.'

Cass waited. She had caught a new note. Gina was arguing with herself now.

'There must be hundreds of redundant teachers of piano up and down the country. No one wants to learn these days.'

The seed was planted. Whether Gina would let it grow or not was in her own hands, and Cass would not be there to help. 'Why am I bullying you into all this positive thinking?' she wondered aloud. 'You won't do a thing about it if I'm not there to prod you.'

Gina laughed, a straightforward cheerful laugh. 'Very subtle. Goodness, I'm exhausted with all this emotion. But that's what I needed, a good kick. I've been on the very brink of getting a grip so often, now I really feel I can do it. Let's celebrate.'

Just like that, Cass thought, shaking her head as Gina went to find a bottle. Soaring from hopelessness to certainty in minutes. How long it would last it was impossible to guess, but at least the moment of decision had been there, and might make the vital difference between action and inaction the next time Gina sank into depression.

'God, I'm going to miss you,' Cass said, producing the corkscrew from the pencil jar as Gina began a noisy hunt for it through various unlikely drawers.

'Oh, Cass, I know, it's awful to be going just when you're here all the time. Odd that Beverley's gone too, though I suppose you can live with that.'

Three incomers, Cass thought. But I shan't follow that pattern of brief sojourning, of failing to find a toehold. Rick wouldn't have followed it either, if he had had a choice. But didn't he have a choice?

Cass raised her glass to Gina, throat tight. 'You've been part of this place since the very first moment.'

'The rain and the mud and those cross men, and you stalking in here like something out of *The Man from Snowy River* . . .'

Gina, woman of easy emotions, was laughing again.

A picture of the Corrie as it had been on that day rose before

Cass's eyes – its simple beauty, its air of undisturbed peace. Rick had gone, Gina was going, but she was in the place where she wanted to be, she had the means to survive, there were other friendships to build on. But as she went down the field alone, it struck her as ironic that of the three marriages the two which seemed so incongruous would survive, while hers, so rational, so suitable, had simply faded away.

Chapter Thirty-one

The laden van made nothing of the steep gradients leaving Muirend, Rick was relieved to find. It might not be the ideal vehicle for Glen Maraich in a bad winter but in other respects it would suit his purpose well. It had been his only major outlay on his own behalf, once the sale of the bungalow was completed and Beverley had been set up in the Bromborough beauty salon she had wanted. She had even seemed moderately pleased with it. At least she was on the same side of the river as Win – and Hayley – and perhaps would see something of them.

Rick's jaw set grimly. She certainly had a capacity, unrivalled in his experience, for dismissing from her mind with effortless thoroughness anyone unimportant to her. He himself had become redundant as soon as he had provided all she wanted, the solid thirties' house with the bay windows up and down, the salon equipment, the creosoted privacy fencing between her and her neighbours, the rockery . . .

He shook his head in exasperation. If only he had her ability to wipe unwanted thoughts from his mind. But he knew in a way he needed them, needed to cling to details of the past few weeks which had seemed to go on forever, dogged by chore after tedious chore. But nothing must be left undone; that had been his overriding compulsion. This time there must be no mistakes, no loose ties of responsibility or obligation to drag him back. Beverley could have everything they owned. He didn't want it, didn't need it, longed only for the freedom of starting again, aided this time by nothing but his own hands and his own skills.

Win had given him several drubbings on the subject. His expression lightened involuntarily as he remembered them, then returned to grimness as he recalled how the energy expended had drained her, how her small work-distorted hands had gone to her breastbone and her eyes had closed and mouth had pursed in angry pain. He was glad to have got to know her for this short time. The thought of how for all those years he had had no idea of her existence, or of Hayley's, filled him again with a rage he knew it was going to be hard to put behind him.

The thoughts were a screen. He was very close now. The road was beginning its long climb up the glen. Behind him lay the counting down of the miles as the signboards came up with dreadful slowness, as motorways and traffic and towns held him snarled in that other life.

Now at last he could let his thoughts range ahead. The barn was waiting. Behind him in the van was enough basic equipment to make him comfortable there till something better could be found. Max Munro had been more than helpful, in his laconic way, and had made no objection to a long-term rental agreement and the addition of extra plumbing. In fact, Rick knew, the 'something better' did not attract him at present. The prospect of bothying in the barn did. The simplicity of fending for himself, tucked away in that quiet curve beside the river, with plenty of work to hand, was all he needed for the present. Later he would move on to the rest of the plan. It would be no good to him to be indoors all day. He would return to what he knew about – fencing, but this time it would be fencing and dyking as his grandfather had fenced and dyked in the wide moorland above Lochindorb, out in the weather, out on the hill, solitary and undisturbed. There would always be a demand, perhaps not enough to support him, but a welcome supplement to the work on the furniture.

He was nearly at Kirkon, and none of these thoughts, bad or good, could any longer keep at bay the real reason for his being here, for having longed every moment of every day since he left to be here again. He thought of Cass's face when they had parted; thought as he had a thousand times of those aware, slowed-down moments as he held her close; the swarming, clamouring feelings which had so nearly got the better of him. He had known he would come back, but those moments had lighted a torch in his mind, changed the equilibrium of his life for ever.

In the weeks between he had said nothing, done nothing. He had felt unable to make contact in any form, the trapped feeling of the years of his marriage swelling to a huge stifling constraint from which he had been incapable of breaking free. It was as though he could only go ahead, inch by inch, task by task, unhooking the links in the chain, making sure there were no hidden snags and claws which could drag him back again, and then, when he was sure he was really free, turn his mind to Cass.

What must she have thought? What, truly, did she think and feel about him? He had barely dared to let himself ask these questions. Now they rushed upon him, shaking him with doubt, as the hills at the top of the glen crowded up, the evening shadows swiftly climbing their flanks as the sun slid behind the western ridge.

He would see her tomorrow. Then practical difficulties, which his mind had refused to consider in the one overwhelming image of seeing her again, presented themselves unnervingly, as though with every yard he drove reality overtook the dream. She might be away, working, have friends or family staying.

Though he had been trying to ignore the fact, he knew if there was a light at the Corrie he would have seen it by now. Nothing. The fear he had been doing his best to push out of his mind refused to be ignored any longer. Cass might have decided not to stay in the glen. Why should she stay? She and her husband had bought the cottage together, and had since divorced. It would be more convenient for her work to move nearer Perth. Rick found his palms sweating and cursed himself in terms he rarely used as he tried to whip up some reassurance. Of course she would still be here. She loved the Corrie and the glen. But would she be there for him? And why was there no light?

His shoulders ached and he found his arms were rigid. She could be out walking, as she so often was, before the last of the light died. How often in the past had it been the only way he could be sure of seeing her? There would be plenty of time to meet now, he told himself, trying to quench his anxiety. Time and freedom.

The road swung close to the river, the new section curving away wide and pale to the left. Rick took the old road with a relief and delight which fought unsettlingly with the apprehension building inside him. The lane winding up to his right gave away no secrets. No light, no light. What did it mean?

For the first time the van went through the underpass and lurched across the grass to the silent shape of the barn. Home. Whatever else happened, here he would make some kind of life for himself. And tomorrow he would go to find Cass.

He pulled up in front of the big doors and jumped down stiffly, aware of the tension that had held him during the hours of driving. The sweet air of a cool autumn evening filled his nostrils and bathed his face and he said aloud, 'Thank God to be here,' in a voice whose huskiness he was not ashamed of. The sound of the river filled his ears, bats flitted through the dusk.

Then, without conscious decision, he turned and walked back the way he had come, to take the familiar track up the hill. He had to know.

As he turned the corner below the cottage he saw that the car was there.